# WINDFALL

Other Works by Colin Dodds:

## NOVELS
*Fun and Its Monsters*
*What Smiled at Him*
*Another Broken Wizard*
*The Last Bad Job*
*WATERSHED*

## POETRY
*Last Man on the Moon*
*The Blue Blueprint*
*Heaven Unbuilt*

## SCREENPLAYS
*Refreshment*
*But Let's Not Talk About Work*

# WINDFALL

Colin Dodds

thecolindodds.com

Cover art by Adam Lewin
Interior formatting by Aubrey Hansen

# PART ONE

---

*The Greek god Apollo, for instance, seems to have begun as the Demon of a Mouse-fraternity in pre-Aryan totemistic Europe: he gradually rose in divine rank by force of arms, blackmail and fraud until he became the patron of Music, Poetry and the Arts and finally, in some regions at least, ousted his 'father' Zeus from the Sovereignty of the Universe...*
> -Robert Graves
> **The White Goddess**

*Shine out, fair sun, till I have bought a glass,*
*That I may see my shadow as I pass.*
> -William Shakespeare
> **Richard III**

It wasn't the booze or the drugs, not the failed marriage. It wasn't the years of training to be a lawyer that left him nonetheless employed as a killer. It wasn't the seizures and fugue states, the hormones in the meat, or the carcinogenic sunlight. It was the waiting, Seth would say, that made him feel evil. It coiled his innards and froze his face. It shut him down, made him swallow the impulse to start up the rented Hyundai and drive off into the sparse evening traffic, and run.

From the car, he watched the lit vestibule of the apartment building on Twenty-Fifth Street. A new building, nice, condo probably. Not much foot traffic in DC at that time of night, once you left the main avenues.

"What's this guy driving again?" William said.

"Green Smart Car."

Seth watched the vestibule in his rearview to keep from looking at William, who was jumpy and all too eager to talk. But talking didn't calm Seth down at times like this, it distracted.

"Smart Car. That's the one that looks like half a hatchback, right?"

Seth half nodded. William laughed to himself to keep talking.

"Smart Car. I guess we better watch our step. Dangerous character. Big balls on this guy."

Seth took a breath and glanced up through the windshield at the orange light that made the street, even on the target's condo-lined block, look like the inside of an underfunded prison.

"How do you end up in one of those things? Did he get bullied by a hippie when he was a kid? Big balls. Smart Car. Big Balls," William repeated, only half embarrassed that Seth hadn't laughed.

They waited in silence until the green Smart Car pulled up. The target, a thin man in a tan sports jacket named Eric Eggleston, parallel parked it cautiously, back and forth nearly a dozen times in a big space until the nub of a car was flush with

3

the curb. At the building vestibule, he fumbled with his keys enough for Seth to read a few drinks into the guy's evening.

"Wait here. I'll call if I need you," he told William.

"I thought we were going to do the old good cop, bad cop."

"Just wait. Play the fucking radio if you want," Seth said. "Tell you what—call my phone in fifteen minutes."

William started to say something, but Seth was already out of the car. The suit was tight on him. He'd gotten it back when he was interning in law school, when he was broke and had yet to put on the weight of his early thirties. The ill-fitting suit was part of his act. William had gotten him the badge and gun. Seth wore a red, stained tie at proper cop length, its tip well below his belt buckle. The only thing that spoke against Seth's disguise was a $200 haircut. He bent his face down from the security camera and used the phony badge on the intercom camera to get buzzed up.

The hard part done. Getting started was always the hard part. Seth could feel the resistance in his body. He didn't want to do this, though he didn't know exactly what it was yet. He played it out in the pale-wood interior of the elevator. He thought of the money. He had enough money, until he thought about it. He played out the job: make a threat, make an offer, and make a judgment call.

Seth flashed the badge again when Eric opened the door and introduced himself as a city detective.

Eric had a wispy blonde beard and rectangular glasses with fine, gray metal frames. Seth picked up the intelligence and the submissiveness in his eyes. That and the size difference made Seth stoop and offer a soft hand. Eric's apartment smelled new, like drywall, fresh paint, and wood finish. It was big enough that Seth couldn't make out its full extent on the way to Eric's living room, which sprawled out to a glass wall.

The room was meticulous, pictures framed, furniture precisely arranged, no clutter, none of the detritus ordinarily strewn about by a bachelor. Eric offered Seth a drink, tea or juice. Seth demurred, took a seat, and gestured to Eric to do the same. Leaning forward awkwardly from one of Eric's big beige Bauhaus chairs, with his tie adangle between his knees, Seth began.

"You seem nervous, Eric. Is something wrong?"

"No, it's just… I just wasn't expecting any visitors," Eric said, his eyes darting toward the hall and back down to the floor.

Seth fought back a smile, knowing he already had Eric on his heels. No need for a bad cop. He asked where Eric had been for the last thirty-six hours, pressing him, asking when he was there, what he was doing there, who could vouch for him and so on. The story fit the kid, in that it was harmless enough. He worked, drank micro-brews with friends in DuPont Circle, and slept. Seth had his nervous, obsequious target write down contact information for corroborating witnesses. He hammered away at the meaningless details of Eric's day. It went on for a while, Eric getting more and more agitated at the innocent questions. Finally, the small man slapped down his pencil halfway through a coworker's email address. Eric looked into Seth's eyes for a long moment, his body tensing up like he was ready to be smacked. Eric Eggleston had found his courage.

"I'm not going to write anything else down until you tell me what this is about. I have rights. I mean, should I have a lawyer present?"

Rights. The problem was that Eric did have them. Rights always made for trouble for the fake-cop bit.

"Fair enough. You deserve to know what all this is about. It's about Sandra Lynch. She's gone missing."

"Sandra's missing? But I just talked to her yesterday, or I guess the day before, the afternoon, I mean. We have plans this weekend."

"You do? What's your relationship with Ms. Lynch?"

"We're friends. We travel in some of the same circles."

"How long have you known her?"

"Two, three years, I guess. Two years and six, maybe seven months."

"How close are you?"

"Pretty close. I guess I'm one of her best friends here in DC. We talk a few times a, probably, a week."

"And the relationship—pardon me for asking, but is it a romantic one?"

Eric blushed, cocked his head, started to shrug and cocked his head at another angle. His face reddened some more as he began to speak, then stopped himself and reconsidered his answer.

"Are you and Sandra Lynch sleeping together?" Seth pressed.

"No. We're just, um, just friends."

"Was that your idea or her idea?"

"What do you mean?" Eric said, rubbing his beard.

"Being just friends," Seth asked. "Did you want it to be more than that?"

Eric shifted in his seat, the color draining and nervous embarrassment flashing in his eyes while he decided whether to come off indignant or confess to an unrequited crush.

"It was both of us. We decided… together. I don't know. It just turned out that way. When did she, uh, disappear?"

"We're not sure. It was called in this morning."

In fact, Sandra Lynch's body was in a vacuum sealed laundry bag in the back of William's rented Hyundai—one more thing Seth had to ignore to do his job right.

Seth nodded silently, solemnly. He let a silence hang before speaking. He was warming to the job. He always did.

"What do you do for a living, Eric?"

"I'm an organizer at GreenPac. It's a political action group committed to sustainable farming—organic, local food, barter systems for farmers, and advocacy programs to get healthy…."

"It must pay well," Seth said, cutting Eric off, looking around.

"I wish. I mean, I work very hard. And the work we do is important. Seriously, it's only a matter of time before the mega-farms start failing. The days of plentiful, genetically

6

altered food are numbered. But, to answer your other question, yes, I did get some money when my grandmother died. That's not illegal, is it?"

"Not at all. If you'll finish writing down those contacts, I'll be out of your hair," Seth said breezily.

Eric nodded and resumed writing. Seth began silently estimating the sticker price on the condo, and the money you'd need to have in the bank to blow so much on high-end furniture. He leaned back in the deceptively hard Bauhaus chair, imagining how a pair might look in his place in New York, and deciding that the young man bent before him was too rich to be bought off.

Seth scanned the cream-colored walls, the framed art prints, stopping on an oversized, framed black-and-white photo. In the photo, Eric was in a young and agitated crowd, yelling into a bullhorn. The banner in the upper-right-hand corner of the photo was cut off so that all Seth could read was *NO*. In the lower right-hand corner of the picture, a woman in a bandana, pretty except for a wisp of mustache at the corner of her mouth, gazing soulfully up at Eric. The photo was signed and numbered below the girl's chin.

It made Seth's guts sink and his mouth water all at once. Shit, he thought. He looked for a frivolous counterpoint among the room's sober décor. His eyes fixed on a mahogany-framed, poster-sized photo of Gandhi, with his glasses and walking stick. It held a prominent position on the wall that divided the living room from the kitchen.

Eric was running out of names to write down, making it nearly judgment-call time. The size and lush furnishings of the condo spoke against a payoff, or a threat to the kid's employment. The bullhorn picture spoke against intimidation. And now the goddamned Gandhi picture spoke against a beating. The next-to-last approach left seemed to be bullshit, to which Seth deemed Eric all too susceptible. He knocked his knuckles on the wooden coffee table between them.

"This is nice. Where did you get it?" Seth asked.

"The table. I picked it up in Vermont. There's a craftsman there who makes furniture out of reclaimed wood."

"Reclaimed, huh? Like stolen?" Seth said, playing the dumb cop.

"No, it means that the wood was part of something else before. It's like recycling, but more artistic. This table used to be part of the axle of a colonial-era flour mill."

"Huh. That's nice."

Eric Eggleston seemed to be calming down. He'd fought the power, and now he'd educated the underprivileged. Seth had him where he needed him. He leaned in.

"Now listen carefully, Eric. I don't want you to worry about Sandra. I'm sure she'll turn up. As far as we can tell, she's only been missing thirty-six hours, at most. We normally don't even get involved until forty-eight hours, except we got a call from her boss, who's always been a friend to the department."

"Janine called you?"

"No, her other boss, the senator. We're taking these extra steps, and doing it off the clock, as a favor to his office. Like I said, Sandra probably took a trip and forgot to check in. But if no one hears from her in the next twelve hours or so, the department could open a more by-the-books type of missing-persons case. So if any other officers come question you, I'd personally appreciate it if you could leave my visit out of it."

"Leave you out of it? Why?"

"Like I said, I'm off the clock. I don't normally do these cases."

"So what do you normally investigate?"

"Sex crimes," Seth said, blurting what came to mind.

"That's appropriate," Eric said, again trying to look Seth in the eye.

"Yeah? Why's that?"

"That senator, her boss, the friend to the department, Chet Mankins. She was having an affair with him. And he was a, I don't know how to put it exactly, but he was rough with her. A few weeks ago we were out, and all of a sudden, she started crying. I guess he did something. She said that she didn't think she could have babies because of him. I mean, if she's missing… if she's really missing, then he's really, probably the one you should be looking at. I hope you throw the fucking book at that asshole."

"Did anyone else know about the two of them, anyone in the office?"

"No, I don't think so. Sandra was very private, very much *in* herself. She only told me about her thing with Mankins that once. I tried to bring it up with her another time and she told me not to talk about it. Not to her or to anyone."

Seth and William had just left Mankins, who was calm when he walked the two men to Sandra's body. There was blood all over her legs, and all over her face. Mankins was a former All-American quarterback, then congressman, a onetime presidential hopeful and presently a senator. He sat in an armchair turned away from the corpse while the two men worked and sipped serenely at a glass of something. The only thing Mankins offered was that Sandra wasn't in there and that he was trying to find her, but couldn't. The killer spoke quietly, his expression sad if it was anything at all. The dead girl lay below a wall of trophies and plaques. Neither Seth nor William asked the tall, hollow-eyed senator anything except where the back door was.

Seth and William were one part of the operation. After they left, others would arrive to get Mankins sober, clean his house, and get his story straight.

"We already spoke to Senator Mankins, and his timeline checks out. So whatever's going on, I doubt he's involved. That's the other thing I wanted to ask you. If other officers come by later tomorrow, could you leave Sandra's affair with him out of any statements you make? Like I said, we already checked out that angle and there's no way he could have been involved."

"If he's innocent, then why should I leave it out? Because he's a senator? Because he's buddies with someone in the police department?"

"Because he called it in. Because he put himself, and me, on the line to help. And because he's not involved in whatever has happened to Sandra."

"Even if he didn't do anything now, that doesn't mean he should get away with what he did to her before. People should know. He deserves that. He shouldn't be able to go on being senator."

"I don't believe Sandra ever filed any charges. Did she?"

"No. But she should have."

"Listen, Eric, in my job I've seen a lot of strange behavior, consensual behavior, over the years. And you learn to withhold judgment. And it seems like it should be up to Sandra to decide what people know or don't know about her private life."

"Well, what I'm saying is that if something did happen to her, then Senator Mankins probably had something…" Eric began. "You know, sometimes you have to stand up for people who won't stand up for themselves. I'm sorry, but if more cops come by, I'm going to tell them the exact same thing I just told you."

Eric jutted his chin and dared nearly a full second of eye contact. And there it was—the righteousness of a young man who isn't getting laid. And that decided it. Seth relaxed his face into a gentle smile.

"Hey, you have to do what you have to do. My boss just asked that I ask. But you probably have a point. You should do what you feel is right."

Eric nodded, magnanimously, Gandhi congratulating him from the wall. Seth's phone rang. It was William.

"How's it going with Smartcar Bigballs up there?"

"Yeah, I'm over there now, getting his timeline. I'll call you when I'm done."

"Smartcar Bigballs Smartcar Bigballs Smartcar Bigballs," William sang petulantly into his ear.

Seth hung up. For someone with his gift for subtle and clandestine work, William had a real obnoxious streak.

"Sorry about that. Looks like it's going to be a long night for me. Is that all?" Seth said, gesturing to the sheet of notebook paper Eric had populated with names, phone numbers, and email addresses.

"I think so."

"Do you know if Sandra had any other close friends we could talk to?"

"Not so much here in DC. I think she still talked to an ex-boyfriend from college. But I don't have his info."

"Write his name at the bottom."

While Eric wrote the name, Seth took out his phone and texted William *be ready*. Seth picked up the paper, folded it into an inside pocket of his jacket, and shook Eric's hand.

"Thanks so much for your help. If we have any other questions, we'll give you a call. Oh, before I go, can I use your bathroom?"

"Sure, it's down the hall, second door on the right," Eric said, relieved to be out of Seth's crosshairs.

Outside the bathroom, Seth felt on the wall for the switch, found it, but didn't flip it. He focused on slowing his breath and relaxing his face, on giving off no signals.

"Hey, Eric, do I have the right switch? The light's not going on."

"Let me see," Eric said, coming down the hall. "It's probably the fixtures. I had the ones in the bedroom replaced when I moved in. You'd think with a new building…"

Griping about the wiring, Eric brushed past Seth into the bathroom and flipped the switch. The bathroom lit up just as Seth slipped behind the smaller man and pulled the inside of his elbow shut against Eric's Adam's apple. With his bicep pulling upward below Eric's whiskered jaw, and his forearm pressed tight to the throat, Seth gently but surely increased the pressure, wary of bruising and wary of breaking Eric's Hyoid bone.

Seth had about five inches of height and at least forty pounds of muscle on his victim, so the struggle was limited to a pathetic slapping and grasping. Seth clenched his eyes against

11

Eric's fluttering hands and focused on the small things. Maintaining a steady pressure and pushing his forehead into the back of Eric's head to protect his face from flailing hands. If he did the little things, Seth knew the big things, in this case Eric's life, would pass without incident. In those moments of struggle, there was no thought, no talk, just complete focus. Those moments transformed a life's petty frustrations into something definite and real. They almost made the stress and the waiting worth it.

Eric flailed another moment, threw an ineffectual elbow into Seth's suit jacket, reached and gained no purchase on Seth's face. It seemed endless until it ended. Eric weakened, then stopped. Seth held on for a half-minute past that. He lowered the awkward bag of meat gently into the bathtub and checked it for a pulse, which was dim, but still there. He pulled on some rubber gloves from his suit pocket, walked into the kitchen, and removed the biggest knife from the dark wood butcher block. Then Seth reconsidered, and swapped it out for a smaller one, guessing that Eric wouldn't want something as vulgar as a butcher knife in his suicide tableau.

He undressed Eric down to his underwear. That was enough. There was nothing so sad as a dead man's dick. And it seemed the kind of propriety that Eric would observe in his moment of self-annihilation.

Picking up the knife, Seth paused. *Right or left, right or left, right or left,* he wondered for a frantic moment, trying to recover the image of Eric bent and writing on the coffee table. Left was it. Mimicking it with his own hand across his own throat, Seth nodded to himself and bent over Eric and drew the knife right-to-left across his neck. The small, wood-handled knife was sharper than it looked, Seth thought, making a note of the brand. It pierced the carotid easily, which gushed more than sprayed, quickly covering half of Eric's shallow chest.

Eric woke only long enough to burble in surprise, to stare past Seth, to convulse and to die. His eyes looked confused and his lips curled into the awful shape that the mouths of babies take just before they begin to wail. His last sight was of

Seth talking into a phone he held in his one bloodless, gloved hand.

"Smartcar Bigballs, is that you?" William answered.

"Cut the shit. Get up here, keep your face down from the doorway camera, and wear gloves."

Seth started the water in the tub. Warm but not hot. He buzzed William up. He was wiping his prints from around the apartment when William knocked softly.

"Where's Smartcar Bigballs?"

"Bathtub. Killed himself, looks like. He couldn't live with what he did to that poor girl," Seth said, eager to stop thinking of the dying man's last confused look of unfocused rage.

"Why would anyone *do* such a thing," William whined, doing his ugly impersonation of a regular person.

"Who knows? Probably because he couldn't get laid."

"He leave a note?"

"A note. Shit. I'll handle that. You go through his stuff, check his computer, start setting the scene."

"Candles?"

"Not too many, three or four."

William handled the printing of the knife with Eric's hand, and its placement. Seth sat down at Eric's chrome Mac Powerbook and tapped out a note.

*To my brothers and sisters,*

*I can't fight the good fight any longer, not after what I've done. Your struggle must go on without me.*

*Love and Peace,*

*Eric*

Short and vague seemed the safest bet.

Seth and William argued a bit before settling on Tracy Chapman's *Fast Car* as the song for Eric to have offed himself to. It had the social injustice and hopelessness that would resonate with someone like Eric in his hour of despair, Seth argued.

"I guess so. But he's like what? Twenty-six? He'd go more modern, I think," William said.

"But it's on his computer. And his iTunes says that he's already listened to it about forty times. He clearly likes it, *and* it fits the mood we want to get across."

"Jesus. Are we covering up a murder or throwing this jackoff a party?"

They laughed. Exhausted and nervous, they kept laughing until they heard footsteps in the hallway, passing by.

Seth put *Fast Car* on repeat, and left the apartment. From the car, Seth called Hurley's man in Frederick and said he'd be by, with a single parcel. The guy said he'd be waiting for them, in the model home attached to the sales office.

William drove. He lived in DC and knew where he was going. He kept it within five miles per hour of the speed limit the whole way. Seth sat back and enjoyed the silence. William shut up and focused on driving.

No talking, no radio, they passed under a golden Mormon angel blowing his trumpet over the highway. Still high from the killing, Seth smirked at the illuminated creature. His body was tired. But something inside of him whispered lullabies in his ear, saying he was exempt from the laws of man, that he was a lion in a world of lambs and that his own death was not yet a certainty. It sang to Seth that there are poor saps buried in the shallow foundations of every McMansion they passed. It always purred like that on the other side of the blare of sensation that accompanied taking a life.

Frederick, Maryland, was asleep when they arrived. The retail lights of its shopping plazas glowed in vain. After several miles on dead quiet suburban streets alive only with the smell of lush September lawns, they came to Oak Pines—a subdivision half-built on old farmland.

Hurley's man—they didn't exchange any names except Hurley's—was waiting in back of the tan model home, which loomed large on its small plot. Smoking a big cigar, he had three shovels ready. It would be a late night. But Seth wouldn't have been able to sleep anyway.

---

14

The thing that whispered to Seth on the interstate out to Frederick that night always whispered. And Seth almost always listened. That night, after the plastic-encased body of young Sandra Lynch had been covered over with dirt, in advance of the next day's cement-pour, it applauded Seth.

The thing in him knew how easily murder-giddiness could topple into bitter remorse. So it sat in the base of Seth's stomach, like a ball of electricity, maintaining the thrill. It knew murder well from its millennia-long career as a ghost, a demon, a wilderness spirit, and as a god. It had passed for a world-creator and for a half-dozen forces of nature. But those names were old homes, now abandoned, windswept and useless. And it had learned the hard way not to hold on to a given name for too long.

But before its divine career, it had been a man, back in the days before men knew what they were. And it was still there, alive in its limited way, still carrying a mouthful of painful, broken teeth.

---

Orange juice, coffee, two eggs, bacon, and toast, overpriced by the hotel, paid for with someone else's money, and carried up to his room on a cart and a tablecloth, woke Seth. He hurried a last bite of egg and toast while knotting a yellow silk tie up to his Adam's apple.

Seth left the hotel with enough time to walk to Hurley's office. He needed the air to be sharp after three hours of shallow sleep. He had to face his boss, Hurley, which could be harrowing. Crossing Sixteenth Street, he saw the White House, and got a momentary schoolboy thrill. Seth wondered if they still told kids that anyone could become president. He wondered if they still told kids they could be better off than their parents. The night before had gone smoothly, had even been sublime in a way. But things were never the same in the morning.

The office building of sandstone slabs and black glass slats was artificially low like the whole city of Washington. The lobby was dominated by a sculptor's massive art-deco rendering of the caduceus, rising from a pair of muscular legs that joined into a single tree trunk, which branched into a bushy, fruiting branch on the right, and an I-beam with a small skyline on the left. Around the legs coiled a single serpent. The lobby echoed with whispers and murmurs of early-arriving lawyers, lobbyists, and such.

Over the caduceus and the lobby loomed the huge sliver logo for The American Institute for the Preservation of Leisure, a cornucopia whose narrow end was a flowing spigot. Seth gave his ID to the man at the desk, and after the usual, cursory security rigmarole, elevator, and a halfhearted flirt with a receptionist and a secretary, he was in Hurley's top-floor office, whose windows peeked at the Capitol and faced another similarly bland office building. Hurley rose, and smiling a smile that showed more effort than joy, shook Seth's hand and gestured to a chair.

Former Senator Robert Hurley was a fit, compact man, handsome except for a few old acne scars on his cheeks and the flawless orthodontic work that played better on TV than in person. He was, at first blush, interchangeable with two dozen other current and former lawmakers. His charm and paranoia had carried him through the posh life of what most Washington insiders termed, on television, a *Washington Insider*. Since leaving the Senate, Hurley headed up The American Institute for the Preservation of Leisure, a lobbying organization fighting to keep what had happened to tobacco from happening to liquor.

"So? Judgment call, huh?" Hurley said when Seth sat down.

"Judgment call. Absolutely. You had to be there, to meet this guy. There really was no other option."

"If you say so. But why only the one passenger on the ride to Frederick?"

"A suicide made more sense."

"Another judgment call?"

"That's what you pay me for, right?"

"Okay. And it will play out as a suicide? Should I get someone to talk to the coroner?"

"It should look right. But if you think it's worth the effort…"

Hurley shrugged and looked over Seth's head, doing the grim risk-and-suspicion algebra of approaching the coroner in his head.

"A suicide, huh?" he finally said.

"I sized up the situation, the guy, and it fit. This Eric Eggleston, he's a privileged guy, full of high ideals. Young and rich but not getting laid. It made enough sense. I also figured that the suicide would play with the girl being missing. It gives the cops an easy out. Either that or a time-consuming dead end when they can't find her."

"Poor girl," Hurley said, wrinkling his tan brow, then rewrinkling it, as if to remind himself to work on wrinkling it more convincingly. "Okay. So we're on the same page if someone asks, why are you in town again?"

"Oh, right. Here's the amicus brief for the FTC case," Seth said, handing him the black folio he'd brought from New York.

"Have you read it?"

"Yeah, I wrote half of it and I oversaw the committee that wrote the rest. You'll see my initials there at the end."

"Look at you, writing briefs. Good cover."

"I'm still a lawyer."

"Strange, that. Bill the usual hours you bill for these things. And here's for your unbillable hours. There's more than we said. It's for the judgment calls, and for not making a mess."

The envelope was downright bulky.

"Thanks."

Hurley smiled and scrutinized Seth. The older man's suit fit perfectly. His tie was lush yet understated. His features rarely strayed from their preternatural repose. A moment of silence passed while Seth tried to figure out what to say to the man who watched him.

"Yes?" Hurley said.

"I guess I'm curious. Is he an old friend?"

"Mankins?"

"Yeah."

"After an affair like the one last night, it seems distasteful to call someone like that a friend. But he and I have some business in common. And business, even more than politics, can make for strange bedfellows."

"So he's a friend to the distilleries?" Seth asked.

Seth knew he was pushing his luck. But something in him twitched around Hurley—a kinship. Maybe just one predator recognizing another. It reminded Seth of the revelatory thrill that came with a stolen pleasure or a stolen life. Hurley swiveled his chair to look at the Capitol Dome.

"How would you feel about leaving New York for a while? You'd still be employed by Ritaloo Fastuch, and we'd still be the client they bill. But the Institute would be your only client. You could bill us out one-and-a-half times, two times your usual rate, and bill us for fifty or sixty hours a week. Plus bonuses," Hurley said, nodding to the envelope in Seth's hands. "I'm going to need someone I trust out west."

"What would I be doing?"

"You asked me if Mankins was a friend to the distilleries. But if that made sense, you never would have asked. So let me ask you, what do you think is going on? And please, Seth, be blunt with me."

"To be honest, I can't figure it out. If this kid Eggleston shoots his mouth off to the cops about Sandra and Mankins, so what? First off, the cops have no body. It's only this nervous lefty kid, whose radical politics make him suspect anyway. Let's say after a month, the girl's parents are still in front of TV cameras and the cops make Mankins a person of interest. I assume we have him alibied for that night and the nights on either side. So it never goes further than a few slanders in the news. He can probably still hang on as an incumbent when he's up for reelection in a few years. The only way it hurts Mankins is if he has his eye on something bigger, like the governor's chair out in California. But why would you care about that?"

"So here's you, Seth Tatton. You're looking at a, well, surprising sum of money in your pocket, and in your paycheck. You're looking at the blood on your hands, and you're wondering what makes it all worthwhile to me?"

"I can usually connect the dots on these things. The only thing that makes sense is that someone has big plans for Mankins."

"Not bad. And *not bad* is all I'll say for now. So will you go to out west?"

"It depends on what the job is. Will I be on this guy's campaign?"

"No. It's something else. I'm moving around some money and some talent out there. I want them moved quietly and managed well."

"Just like that?"

"Think of all the things you've done, in the last twenty-four hours alone, just like that."

Seth felt the weight of the envelope, thought of the stacks of bank-bound bills, and nodded, unable to disagree.

"Good. I need someone out there who can make judgment calls."

New Jersey whipped by the Acela. Seth thought of Hurley and his cryptic assignment to the West Coast. The thought alone stirred something in him, a feeling like hundreds of years, an image like all the Greco-Roman monumentality of Washington, DC, the hollow laughing faces of terra cotta nymphs, scallop-shell and ailanthus effusions of pediments, arches and pilasters, all in a froth sloshing down a damp gutter. Seth shook his head. Images like that always bubbled up not long before a seizure. He checked his watch and decided that a few beers should buy him enough time to get home safely before it hit.

In the club car, Seth sat at the formica counter with his plastic cup of beer and nodded as a rail-thin half-drunk consultant from Stamford enlisted him in a one-sided discussion. The man was on what passed for a roll on the Acela.

"I'm sorry it's offensive, but no one believes in religion or even in the political process anymore. Popular music is nothing but a series of cynical manipulations, and the visual arts are a con game. So what's left?"

"Business, I guess," Seth said, talking to the drunk because it kept the seizure at bay.

"That's what I thought. I thought 'maybe we sold out everything, but at least we still have the money.' But even that's not true anymore. The government owes more than it can pay. Inflation is gradually pauperizing all of us. And if you lose your job—well, you can expect it to stay lost, my friend. And the worst part is that no one even knows exactly what went wrong."

"What are you going to do?" Seth said, shrugging at the animated, half-drunk man like he might shrug at a television and starting on his second beer.

"I don't know. But you have to do something. I watch the news, and they have those revolutionaries in Montana, Idaho—the bearded crazies who want to secede. But sometimes I wonder if they really are crazy. I mean, what do they want after all? A fresh start. What could be more American? It seems a fair enough thing to ask for..."

The consultant went on for another few beers, into Penn Station. Seth took a cab home and locked himself in his apartment, as if that would help.

———

There were no direct flights to Laughlin. It took Seth two planes and a short drive to get there from New York.

Laughlin, Nevada, sprang up on the more permissive bank of the Colorado River to draw Arizona gamblers, bored desert tourists, RVs, and biker gangs. It was a leisure hub in the middle of the kind of nothing that made people name valleys, gulches, and hills after death itself.

In his hotel room, Seth collapsed in the bigger of the suite's beds, turned on the TV, and fell asleep to the sound of two grown men arguing about what a college football coach should have said. When he woke, his cell phone told him that his meeting had been moved, giving him more than a day to kill in the dusty casino town. Looking out on the river and the wastes beyond the shatterproof plate glass that constituted one wall of his suite, it seemed there was precious little else to do but drink and gamble.

The hotel's TV station cheerily recited the area's dining, entertainment, golf, family activities, and, of course, gambling on a twelve-minute loop while Seth showered and shaved. Drying his hair with a towel, he paused at the mirror. Eyes focused straight ahead below dark eyebrows and a peninsula of dark hair, he grinned his predator's grin. It was reassuring. Next, he let his face go slack and his gaze fall unfocused, to better simulate the vague and dimly confused expression of the victims without number who seemed to dominate the earth.

Another merry vacationer, a sheep there for the fleecing, Seth thought, pulling on a polo shirt and buckling his watch. The watch wasn't modern or antique, neither expensive nor cheap. But it told the world there was nothing to see here, only a nervous middle-class professional, so move along, like cops on TV say after an accident.

The elevator let him out in the casino and he followed the deliberately unclear signs down the corridors of screaming, blinking, ringing slots to the front desk. The short walk was enough to tell him his costume wouldn't work in Laughlin. T-shirts advertising barbecue restaurant logos or emblazoned with cavalier attitudes about tits, jeans with elastic waistbands, jogging pants, and morbid obesity seemed to be the rule. So far from the major metropolises in which he usually moved, Seth looked suspiciously wealthy. At the restaurant downstairs, the blonde waitress lingered and showed him her whole mouthful of confused teeth when she took his order.

Casinos always made Seth nostalgic. He'd grown up in a small town in Connecticut, and the casino was the closest thing to a big deal for a hundred miles in any direction. It gleamed from the drear of New England woods and weather-beaten houses. When Seth was a kid, the casino's restaurants were where his friends' families celebrated special occasions. When he was a teenager, the casino was where a fake ID would buy you a whiff of gaudy adulthood.

That Saturday morning in Laughlin, Seth bet a few hundred bucks on college football. Not knowing the teams, he bet based on vague prejudices, vaguer intuition, and a not-altogether-accurate sense of himself as a lucky guy. He sat down in an armchair with a drink holder, ashtray, betting slips, and pencils in its arms and started drinking complimentary drinks and caring about teams he hadn't thought of in years. The old guy in the chair next to him was better dressed for Laughlin, in a ripped pair of cargo shorts and a T-shirt intended to promote a nearby gentleman's club. His face was full of gin blossoms and his cigarette was nearly at its filter when he turned to Seth.

"Where are you from?" he asked.

"Back east."

"I could tell you're not from around here. Where back east?"

"New York, DC."

"DC, you say? I bet you eat well out there," the weathered man said.

"Excuse me."

"I bet you all do pretty well out there, in DC. It's a good racket you got—federal government. I come in here, I *choose* to take my chances. Hell, you could even say I *choose* to get fleeced. The casino, it takes my money and it puts up some chandeliers, gives out free drinks, and even puts on a floor show. Hell, sometimes I even win. But brother, if I don't get around to paying the federal government, they cut off my paycheck, freeze my bank account, seize my home, and threaten to throw me in jail. Now you tell me. Does that sound like freedom?"

"I don't know about freedom. It sounds like the law though."

"It's a ripoff is what it is. And what do I get for my money? An interstate highway? Hell, I could build my own highway for what I've paid those bastards."

"I'll be sure to pass that on."

As a younger lawyer on the road, Seth had heard the same libertarian spiel in every bar from Houston to Seattle. The weathered man was drunk, possibly from the night before, sneering, and still talking.

"So who do you have for today's games?" Seth asked, interrupting the man's rambling interpretation of the Second Amendment.

"Who do I? Oh, I've got some winners in here. I have, I have Michigan, I have Boise State, I have a few parlays, let me see…"

Football proved to be a common language through which the man's regional anger could be peaceably articulated, more or less. Five hours later, the libertarian had lost big, and was pinning all his hopes on that night's Hawaii game. Seth had broken even and gotten slightly drunk. He wandered lazily past the tables of slumped low rollers to a cocktail lounge, where he ordered a burger and a vodka. A brunette in a shiny red dress sang a mix of jazz standards and pop ballads from the '80s, closing with a slow version of "You Were Always on My Mind."

At first, Seth couldn't figure out if she was too good for the casino or if he was getting drunk. He'd finished his burger when she pulled up next to him at the bar. She bent her neck and lit a cigarette. She smoked it, fidgeted and made small talk with the bartender, who responded to her with the defeatist clichés that casino workers speak the world over. "If wishes were horses, beggars would ride. If frogs had wings…" and so on. She chuckled a little louder than seemed natural. Seth looked like out-of-town, which looked good in a town like Laughlin. He gave her a once over. Long brown hair, gap in her teeth, a jumpiness to her. Prowling in the shadows around thirty, but not bad.

She caught him looking and he said nice show. She said her name was Dolores. She asked where he was from, and he said Chicago, because it wasn't true. She asked what brought him out to Laughlin, he said business. She said what business, he said real estate. She asked how long he was going to be in town, he said at least a few weeks, from the looks of it. She asked if he was going to stay for her next set, he said he would. Seth stayed and bought her a few drinks afterwards. She sat close and looked him straight in the eyes when she spoke.

In his suite, they didn't talk any more. Dolores had a bad past with men, from what Seth could tell. She didn't say as much, but the intimate position of her purse throughout the night told him as much. It nestled against her knee by the couch where she gave him head. It rested below the thick arm of the reading chair where she held her ankles over her ears. It followed them to the bed, where it wedged between the mattress and the night table as she arched her back and pressed her tan haunches against him.

Afterward, flushed and with her makeup smudged and askew, Dolores looked beautiful to him, more than she had on stage.

"How long have you been singing?" Seth asked.

"A long time, since I was little, I guess. But I've only been singing on stage for a few months. I was waitressing before that. The last singer quit and the bar manager knew me and liked me, so he said get up there. They don't pay me any more than I made as a waitress. But I'd rather sing than say what beers we have on tap a hundred times a night."

Seth laughed. Dolores reached into her purse, grabbed a cigarette and lighter.

"You want one?"

"No. No thanks."

"Yeah, you probably don't smoke. I bet you're not allowed to smoke in Chicago anymore, like in restaurants, bars."

"I guess you're not."

"Only poor folks, dumb folks, and folks who live in the middle of nowhere smoke these days, I guess."

"Well, we all have our vices."

"Yeah? And what are yours?"

"Cabaret singers."

She punched his shoulder playfully.

"Yeah, well, I guess mine are cigarettes and well-dressed men."

"You could probably do worse."

"Trust me, I have. So what's your story?"

"I buy land, develop it. I have a few deals that I'm looking into out here at the moment."

"Real estate, huh?"

"Yep. There's a lot of land out here."

She didn't ask for cabfare or anything when she left a few hours later. That made Seth nervous—it often meant he'd have to pay in some other, more complicated way later on. But he liked Dolores, and he had no idea how long he'd be stuck out in Laughlin.

After a moment's good-bye banter, she gave him a peck on the lips, turned quickly, and vanished down the hall. Alone in his disheveled suite, Seth felt strangely calm. He slept well past when the sun began to blast through his window.

---

Roberto Mulholland, originally Roberto Mendes, was a tan and gangly hedge fund manager, who Seth was supposed to meet in the casino sports book. When he got there, a little late, Roberto was arguing with a stolid, plain-looking blonde in a pantsuit. A full foot shorter than Roberto, she nonetheless had the upper hand in the discussion.

"First of all, the funds weren't commingled on Friday at four, and they won't be commingled at seven o'clock tonight. Second, our offering letter explicitly permits these kinds of bets," Mulholland said, eyeing the new eavesdropper in their midst.

"Not the parlays, and not the teases," said the small woman, her face, her whole body compact and motionless, in utter contrast to the man she was talking to.

"The parlays are only three teams. And... Who is that? Is that him? Who are you?" he said to Seth.

"Are you Roberto?"

"I don't know, maybe."

"I'm Seth..."

"Oh. I thought it was you. Didn't I say that? I said 'isn't that him?'"

The small woman nodded and held her hand out to Seth. Thin lips, small nose, narrow eyes, not a pretty woman, though it was hard to pinpoint exactly why she wasn't. Something in her gray eyes flashed when she seized his hand. It made the thing in Seth stir.

"Hello, Seth. I'm Frederica. We're glad you're here. We can finally get down to business."

"Speaking of *business*, we only have twenty minutes before kickoff," Roberto complained.

"Fine. Go get Rick."

Roberto waved toward the cashiers. Bespectacled and weighed down with keys and sewn-on security badges, Rick arrived with a hulking middle-aged mute, whose job was to carry a briefcase. Seth, Frederica, and Roberto followed Rick and the mute past the sports book cage to an office where Roberto proceeded to bet a staggering amount of cash on that day's football games. But Frederica had her way—limiting him to straight bets, no parlays, and no teases. The amount of cash clearly made Rick nervous.

"Don't let the pantsuit fool you, buddy. Frederica is a murderess and an instigator of wars," Roberto quipped, half to Seth and half to no one.

"I'm just a Mormon businesswoman who's trying to keep the lights on and the investors from suing us. Did you bring the paperwork?"

Seth nodded. He'd read through it on the plane. It was a series of offering letters, side letters, certified financial statements and so on—generic boilerplate for a pair of fairly large hedge funds. The paperwork also came with a sealed envelope addressed to Frederica, which he didn't open. Seth handed over the folders and the envelope.

"That's right. She's a Mormon businesswoman who gets paid off of my gambling wins," Roberto said, leading them to a row of armchairs the casino had reserved for them.

Frederica ignored Roberto and read through the paperwork. The mute sat at a few seats remove. Cigarette smoke wafted through the room, along with the grumbling and shuffling of dull-eyed men. The gray noise was broken only by the occasional desperate yell for a simulcast horse or an early score.

Roberto was keyed up and talkative.

"This is for the high-risk fund. Sports gambling is up to ten percent of the portfolio. But the plain truth is that I like to gamble, you know? There's something elemental about it—to watch how things happen or don't happen. Like this game, what is it? Chiefs and Texans—not one we're likely to tell our grandkids about. But this play could change the game. Wait for it, will it be, could it be? No. Three yards and a cloud of synthetic dust—ground up tires is what they use on the new fields. But still, here we are, right on the edge of the present, not remembering or guessing, but watching the plays unfold, watching novelty, watching occurrence itself, arranged by the game of football into achievement and consequence among approximately equalized forces. It's a crucible for strategy, for tactics, and for chance. And if you can find where it connects, through metaphor, with your situation, you can understand how almost anything happens or doesn't happen."

"Sports betting lost the fund 8 percent for the year to date," Frederica said without looking up from the paperwork.

"You can ignore half of what Roberto says. He never stops. The thing is that some of the things he says actually turn out to be good ideas."

"Thank you, Frederica. Or rather, half-thank you. Sometimes I worry that you've completely lost the art of the compliment."

"He comes up with the ideas, and we find ways to invest in them without going bankrupt or being sent to jail."

The bank of TV screens flashed and glowed in front of them. Roberto gave the impression of being able to watch all of them at once.

"They have the hard job," Roberto said. "Most of the time, I just ask myself 'What would I do?'—in another situation, given the overwhelming onrush of events, given the resources and skewed perspective granted to each of us, given the enormous, uncontrollable forces driving our lives. From there, I look for an opening, a way to get ahead of the unfolding of creation, even if only by an hour," Roberto's head jerked toward a flurry of action on one of the screens. "Tackling! It's called fucking tackling! You lazy, hormonally disfigured bastards! How in the hell did I ever talk myself into betting on the Jets?"

Frederica went back to her paperwork while Seth and Roberto watched football. For seven hours straight, Roberto rambled on about disparate human motivations in different epochs, about revolution and opportunity, punctuating his zealous speculation with lurid curses cast at the teams who were costing his clients so much money. By the end of the four o'clock game, Seth was worn out. Roberto invited him out to his ranch for the eight o'clock game, but Frederica intervened.

"I need to talk to Seth tonight. Legal stuff," she said, as if dangling garlic before a vampire.

"Hey, Seth, it was great to meet you. You seem to be everything we've heard. Welcome aboard."

Aboard what? Seth wondered, shaking the man's sweaty hand.

———————

The thing in Seth liked the sports book VIP section, liked Roberto's constant talk, liked the big TVs. It devoured what it could of those diversions from its remove.

When it was properly alive as a man, the years were quiet. The ground seemed like it was almost always damp and cold. But what it remembered most was all the time it had. Seth would never know such oceans of time. Even if you only lived to be twenty-five, there was still so much time that there was almost no such thing as time.

The thing in Seth wasn't a boy anymore when he lost his teeth, but he wasn't fully grown, either. The man who slammed his face into the ground had been a friend of his mother's. The man's name was a deep grunt and a gesture like throwing a clump of dirt into the air. Grunt-Gesture attacked the young man on a much-trammeled patch of earth between tents. He grabbed the younger man's hair and drove his face into the ground. Then he slammed it down one or two more times for good measure.

The heel-hardened patch of earth loosened the teenager's teeth. In that disorienting moment, it became obvious to him and everyone around that Grunt-Gesture felt he had a claim on a young woman the teenager had been spending time with.

The older man's cursory show of dominance was supposed to be the beginning and the end of it. But the teenager rose quickly to confront the older, larger man, shouting, mocking his name. He took the blood dribbling from his nose and split lip and rubbed it over his face, as a display of fearlessness, and spat at the man's feet. The older man glared and took a quick step toward him. But the teenager didn't step back. He spat again and shouted a curse.

The older man smiled. He approached slowly, arms wide. After catching a few sloppily thrown fists, Grunt-Gesture smacked the teenager with an open hand and grabbed his throat. When the teenager turned to get away, the older man drove him to the ground. This time he didn't stop slamming the fearless young man's bloody face into the earth until all that was left of him was a bleeding disgrace, whimpering into the uncomfortable silence now heavy on all who had come out to watch the fight. No one dared approach the young man until Grunt-Gesture had left.

When it was over, the young man's teeth, five on the top and seven on the bottom, were broken or gone for good. One incisor hung in the hole it had cut through his upper lip. The young man never again closed his mouth right, never clenched his jaw without pain encircling half his skull. The raw nerves in his gums made eating and drinking even soft foods a trial. And beyond that, his teeth and lopsided face marked him as a failure. People called him Broken Tooth, first out of fun and later as a kind of resigned shorthand. It became his name.

He lost weight and lost patience. That year, as a skinny, ugly teenager, Broken Tooth started a lot of fights and lost every one.

---

Walking with Frederica through the Sunday-night slot crowd, it occurred to Seth that he hadn't left the hotel-casino in thirty-six hours. She led him to what the hotel boasted was "the only high-end Laughlin Italian restaurant." Frederica ordered breadsticks and a double scotch.

"Uh, vodka martini up with a twist," Seth said.

"A twist?" the waiter said.

"Of lemon."

"Olives?"

"No olives."

The waiter repeated the order in a questioning voice, Seth repeated it in a confident voice, the waiter nodded and left.

"We're not in Las Vegas," Frederica said.

"That's for sure," Seth said.

Seth's martini arrived. He sipped it, and it was bad. The vermouth had soured and they'd put a whole lemon wedge into it. He winced and she grinned.

"So tell me, what am I doing here?" he asked.

"For now, this is a get-to-know-you meeting. Roberto liked you, and that's a good sign. He's usually a sensitive instrument on these matters."

"And you?"

"I don't know yet. Hurley told me about you. But I have some questions. For starters, how do you see this playing out for you?"

"This? I'm not sure I know what all of this is. But here's how I see it working out. I trust the right people and they trust me. I do some work and I make some money. I bring in my billable hours, they bump me up the ladder and I move on. We all get where we're going."

"Hurley said you wanted to know what was going on, after the Mankins, uh, episode. Why did you want to know?"

"I don't need to know everything involved in what I do. But I don't like it when things don't make sense. Having some idea helps me do my job better, and it helps me sleep at night."

"Do you think Hurley owed you an explanation?"

"No. But he didn't tell me very much either."

"All right. Well, Hurley mentioned some unbillable hours you'll be paid for. We're prepared to make you an offer…"

What came next were a series of numbers generous enough for Seth to choke down his martini. The food came, and he agreed to a few generous months of employment. Outside, pleasure boats plied the dark river. That settled, Frederica gave Seth his first job.

"For starters, we'll need you out at Camp Pendleton on Tuesday. You're going to meet a colonel, Tom Wozniak. He's been selling information to parties that have been unknown to him, until now. We'll drop the details by your room tonight. You're going to confront him with some photos, some recordings. Let him know we don't necessarily want to hurt him with it. We may need some things from him in the near future. And we need him to remember where his allegiances lie if certain events occur."

"Certain events?"

"That's all you need to say for now. But be sure to tell him that he won't be asked to do anything on his own."

The echoes of the amounts she'd spoken blotted any further questions Seth had. He smiled and they toasted. He eyed Frederica's drink.

"The Mormon thing. You and Roberto both," she said. "I guess I'm a Mormon like you're a lawyer. We all need a disguise."

Her gray eyes flashed enough that he wondered exactly what she knew about him. The thing in him flinched for a moment, with the sense that she knew more than even Seth did.

"Hey, I graduated top of my class at Cardozo."

"Yeah, and I drive out to the temple in Needles every weekend," she said, draining the last of her scotch.

———————

The drive was Seth's. His white Cadillac hummed through the desert, toward San Diego. Scarce towns and no traffic for three solid hours. A lot of time to think. The thing that worried Seth was the money. They were offering too much, it seemed. He raced through the sparse traffic of the Inland Empire, through the suburbs of Orange County. When he checked the speedometer, he was going 110 miles an hour. He took a breath and slowed down.

He stayed the night in Carlsbad. The room was clean and modern, lit by the orange rays of the sinking sun. He nursed room service beers and pondered what the common payoff could be in keeping Mankins's name unblemished and in blackmailing some marine colonel. The thing inside of him was alive with a sense of expectancy it hadn't felt in centuries. He had a hard time getting to sleep. The silent hotel room was vivid, the light under the thick wood door, the waves outside the window.

The next day, Colonel Tom Wozniak required a lot of pushing from the jump.

"How'd you get this number?"

"I got it from the people you've been doing business with."

"Then they should have told you that was a one-time deal. Get lost."

Seth held the phone loosely to his ear. He sat up on the edge of the bed and watched the ocean as each wave overturned the remnants of the last.

"Tom… Tom… you hang up and it all goes bye-bye, your career, your freedom, maybe even your life. Yes, a threat is exactly what this is. The people you're dealing with don't think of it as a one-time deal. And they took precautions—they filmed you at the dead drops, recorded you negotiating your price for the tactical outlines. Hang up and you'll live out your days a traitor in a cell."

There was a long pause on the other end.

"Okay, there's a state park…" Wozniak began.

"Tom, I don't like nature. Let's meet in a restaurant, or better yet, a bar. You sound like you could use a drink."

They settled on a gimmicky fish restaurant by a marina in Oceanside. Seth was early but Wozniak was earlier, already started on an oversized glass of tequila. He was a tan, fit man in his early fifties, his hair cut close and precisely, his golf shirt tucked tightly into his shorts, and his forearms conspicuously muscular for a man in middle age. He sneered when Seth sat down across from him.

"I'm sitting here and I'm thinking I should just kill you," the colonel said, downing an impressive gulp of tequila.

"I wish I could say that killing me would change things for you. But I'm not that high up. You saw what they paid you. They have plenty of others who would fill my shoes. Probably plenty who would fill yours, too."

"So who the fuck are you?"

"I'm the same guy that you became when you decided that there wasn't enough in it for you to stay the good soldier."

Wozniak started to speak and paused. He stared at Seth as though staring might dissolve him. After a small eternity, he blinked and shook his head.

"I had circumstances, a house out in the country my wife and I saved for our whole lives. A forest fire…"

"Colonel, Colonel, can I call you Tom? You're going down the wrong road with this. Look at yourself. You're not a victim. The two of us, we're both grown men in the middle of a complicated world."

The colonel drank and waved to the waitress for another drink. Seth continued, the thing inside of him speaking.

"So you did wrong. Now you're out on a limb and you're scared. Good. Scared means you're alive. You broke through the shell and you've stepped into a broader existence. Now more things are possible than you'd previously allowed yourself to believe. You say you ought to kill me. I say you ought to buy me a drink and listen to what I have to say."

"You expect me to believe that bullshit?"

"I believe it. And I'm the same guy as you."

"And who are you? You're not military."

"No. I'm a lawyer."

"I should've guessed."

The waiter came by with the colonel's tequila.

"What are you having?" he asked Seth, the sneer fading from his face.

"Wild Turkey, ice, thanks."

The colonel was a lot more adaptable after the second drink. He brightened to learn that nothing specific or nefarious was immediately required of him. He brightened at the thought that nothing much might ever be asked of him. And the assurance that he wouldn't be asked to do anything on his own visibly relieved him

"But your people have to know I took an oath. I mean, that isn't for sale. I mean, that's my life. That's not something I can just walk away from."

"Tom, this is going to take some getting used to. But you're a different man in a different world today. The thing you pledged your loyalty to will use that oath to have you disgraced, imprisoned, and hanged if you're uncovered. Hanged. You need to recognize that."

"So the tapes, the video and the audio, will I ever get those back?"

"I doubt it. But if you're useful to us, there will never be a reason for anyone to see them."

"Well since they're holding my life by a string, can I ask who these people are? I thought I was dealing with Israelis."

"You can ask. But I don't know. I just work here."

Wozniak took a small sip, thought better of it, and downed the rest of his glass. It seemed to sicken him. But once safely swallowed, the drink brought a calmer expression to his taut, middle-aged face.

"I grew up not far from here, in Riverside. My father was a Marine. He was good with his hands. He was always fixing up the house, his truck. It's funny, but I haven't voted in more than ten years. And still I work for, and have even promised to die for, some spineless, privileged Ivy-League puke from Michigan. Not to speak ill of the Commander in Chief, but please explain to me how me and that man live in the same country."

"You sound like you need another drink."

"Sure. It's funny. It's a fucking joke is what it is."

Seth stood up, and so did the colonel. They shook hands. The restaurant was filling up with an early dinner rush of noisy families.

———————

Far from freeways, tequila drinks, and ocean-side restaurants, separated by a distance of thousands of miles and thousands of years, the broken-toothed young man entered adulthood as an unbalanced disgrace. He avoided his old friends. The girls avoided him. His mother didn't know what to do. Some of her less-charitable friends suggested that she ask Grunt-Gesture to finish him off. She considered it.

Broken Tooth's mother only had one other idea. One night she visited the oldest man in the group, whose name was a long, calm growl, like a deep sigh of relief. She paid for his attention with the thing she knew he couldn't ignore.

The Sigh was a strange man. He was old, getting on forty. But what really set him apart was that he was fat. He moved slowly, when he moved. Mostly, people came to him with their problems and with gifts. He wasn't exactly gregarious, living a short distance from the main cluster of tents. But he was well provided for, given a wide berth by even the most aggressive men, and left graciously unmentioned in the gossipy circles of women.

The next morning, she brought her damaged, shambling son to The Sigh, and left him there. The young man with his broken mouth and sideways nose was intractable at first. The Sigh gave him a bowl of bitter, hot broth, and a long reed to drink with. It was the beginning of a long apprenticeship.

———————

In his hotel room in Carlsbad, Seth opened a manila envelope. Inside, he found his itinerary. It had him in Farmington, New Mexico, in two days. The following pages gave photos and brief dossiers on three men. One was a small, rat-faced Russian named Michael. The next man was a huge, bearded, hippie type in military fatigues, who'd named himself Jefferson. Seth knew Jefferson from the news, as some kind of domestic terrorist. He was the head of a militia that lived off the grid, lately on a mesa outside Taos, New Mexico, according to the dossier. The last one was an ex-con Native American activist who ran a school in Farmington. He went by Halian, Hal for short.

It took Seth some shuffling and rereading to figure out the larger story: The Russian was bringing in two shipping containers of something to the revolutionary. The Indian schoolteacher was involved in the transaction as the recipient of record for two containers, supposedly of textbooks printed in Guangzhou. Hal's part in the scheme was important enough that the two other men would be meeting him outside Farmington to close the deal. Seth was there to make sure the three strangers got along.

As Seth read, the ocean outside his window seemed to grow louder until he was startled by the sound of it. He sensed a tsunami building, towering above the hotel and the town, waiting for him to take notice. But the water wasn't water. It was something more like previously pent-up unformed potential of time and reality about to release the world from the forms it had taken. A seizure was coming. Seth hurriedly took the papers, piled them neatly, slipped them into the envelope, and put the envelope in the hotel room's closet safe.

Then came the sensation, like his whole life had been a narrow corridor that is finally opening onto a vast space. It's always a relief at first, until Seth realizes that the vast space is impenetrably dark, and that he's not alone in the darkness. The other inhabitant is very familiar. And in the first moment of recognition, Seth remembers all the times he's willed himself to forget both the recognition and the thing he recognizes. The time to remember is infinitesimal before the presence is upon him, its countenance strange but unsurprising. It comes upon Seth wearing the skin of Eggleston, Eric The Victim, using the gash in Eric's throat as its organ of speech.

It says a word that Seth doesn't want to hear. And so the other inhabitant excuses Seth from what is, by all other standards and definitions, his life.

At dawn, Seth came to. Before him, he found a strange scene, but not the strangest he'd ever found after a seizure. He was soaking wet, naked, with fish scales in his teeth, sitting inside a teepee made from the room's two mattresses leaned against each other. A whole sea bass, half chewed on, sat before him.

In his seizure, he'd found his way into the safe. The papers sat before him, below the dead fish, splayed across the floor. Seth took a deep breath, ready to clean up. He reexamined the papers and saw they were arranged by some design. He climbed out of the teepee and looked at them from the other side. The papers had been arranged to spell out the word WAR.

————————

At the Oceanside airport, a tiny, four-seat plane waited to fly Seth to the Four Corners Regional Airport in New Mexico. The pilot was a fat old black man who whistled through his teeth when Seth buckled his seatbelt.

"Don't you know there's forest fires? You know what the jets of air coming off the fires do to a little plane like this? You better buckle up tighter than *that*."

Seth took the old man's advice and was glad he did. The fires below were visible only as dirty orange flecks behind great gray beards. And they tossed the plane around mercilessly for minutes at a stretch.

"You can fly over the fires, but they take it out of your ass," the pilot said, in one of the few statements that rose above the man's perpetual mutter.

The Four Corners Regional Airport was smaller than even the one in Oceanside, and very quiet. The little airplane taxied straight over to an empty hangar, where Hal was waiting. Tall and gracefully balding, he wore a puffy red coat over a denim shirt and jeans. He had classic Indian features, a big nose and big ears adorning a long, stolid face. He introduced himself to Seth and they climbed into his beat-up yellow pickup.

The land around them was beautiful and desolate, with the majestic splinter of Shiprock rising up from what seemed an impossible distance. They drove through the town of Farmington, which seemed ragged and strangely empty.

"Right now, everyone's out in the gas fields. But on weekends it fills up. We get a regular crowd downtown on Saturday nights," Hal offered.

Seth nodded. Hal kept talking.

"I'm glad they sent someone. This Jefferson has a reputation. I heard that he beat a man blind out in

Albuquerque. But the cops don't want to go up on his mesa…"

They passed out of the downtown, past an overgrown churchyard and a pawn shop, past weather-beaten men in ragged clothes.

"Let's go out to the place where we're meeting."

"But that's not for hours."

"I know. But I'd like to have a look."

They looped away from the town, which wasn't too hard to do, and were soon out among the canyons and standing rocks. A thin dust of snow clung here and there. The scenery stirred the thing in Seth, speaking of a wilder and more ancient dispensation.

"Mind if we stop by the school on the way? It's on the way," Hal said.

"That's fine."

The school consisted of six trailers arranged in a horseshoe around a dirt lot, flanked by a pair of basketball hoops and a pair of soccer goals held together with duct tape. Although they weren't new, the trailers had been freshly painted and the basketball hoops had new nets. The trailer windows were adorned with construction-paper art projects, hawks and bears and deer. It seemed like a busy place. Hal ran in and ran back out.

"Sorry. I forgot my cell phone. What do you think of the school?"

"It's nice."

"That's what this is all for. I don't know what they told you about me. But I wasted a lot of years as shadow, as an Indian cliché. I was drunk, high, begging, stealing, and bullshitting. I took a lot from my people in those years. Now I want to give back. I've been sober five years, been at the school for four of those. What about you? You look like you might be Native."

"My father was a Pequot."

"Your mother?"

"A mix. Irish and Lebanese, a hippie."

"Did you grow up on a reservation?"

"Near one. It's different back east. Nobody really cared much about being a Pequot until they built the casino."

Hal wanted to hear more. But Seth didn't like talking about his childhood. Thinking about it made the truck's cab feel tight. Hal broke the silence.

"A lot of families, especially Zuni families, they don't want to send their kids to the public schools. The education's no good. There's drugs. Did you know that the Zuni people have been on this land for more than 1,300 years. We're unique. Did you know that the Zuni language is unique. It isn't related to any other known tongue…"

"You realize that this could be dangerous, right?" Seth interrupted.

"I do. Sorry, I can talk a lot. Which is it, anyway? Drugs or guns?"

"I'm pretty sure it's guns."

"Guns, drugs, whatever. Hey, if the white men want to destroy each other, I don't see why we shouldn't benefit from it."

Seth spurned Hal's attempt at solidarity and said nothing. He stared out at Shiprock in the distance. Hal made him nervous. Sober or not, schoolmaster or not, there was something desperate about the man. They passed a few minutes in silence.

"So why are you doing this?" Hal asked.

"Like you said, I don't see why I shouldn't benefit."

Hal laughed a little too much as they pulled into an abandoned slate finishing plant outside of town. They parked in back, by the old tractor-trailer loading docks, where some enterprising teenager had spray-painted a red, four-by-twenty-foot penis firing bullets on the water-stained cinderblock wall.

Through a broken window, Seth could see that most of the building's roof had fallen in, which made for one less angle for a potential ambush. He walked around the building once in the wind, checking the doors and windows and blowing into his hands every few steps.

"That overcoat looks nice, but it won't do much good out here," Hal said, his hands in his thick, quilted coat.

Seth shoved his hands into his coat pockets and circled the building. It checked out. The land around it was level and the inside of the factory was inaccessible enough. They drove back into town for lunch. Hal carried on about his Zuni pride, about the need to teach the Zuni children so they wouldn't be victims of a poisonous, cannibalistic American culture. Seth knew that Hal was talking more for Hal than him, and tuned Hal out while he ate.

The meeting was set for dusk. Seth was tired and needed a shower, but something told him to keep alert. There were, after all, three possibly volatile men with significantly differing motivations in an arms transaction in the middle of nowhere.

When they returned to the slate finishing plant, Jefferson was waiting for them, with two tractor trailer cabs. Seth and Hal pulled into the parking lot and flashed the pickup's lights twice. One of the trailers turned on its high beams and a burly, bearded man jumped out of a passenger door. It was Jefferson. He was big, almost professional-athlete big. The chrome from the pistol in his belt flashed in the headlights when his army jacket flapped open.

Seth got out of the truck and Hal followed.

"You Seth?" he yelled, walking slowly.

"Yeah. You Jefferson?"

"Seth, I'm glad they sent a damn American. I never thought I'd be dealing with the damn Ruskies. First the Ruskies and now the Indians. Makes you realize how bad the federal government has gotten when those are our allies."

"Well, here we are," Seth said.

"Enemy of my enemy and all that. Who's this?"

"This is Hal. He's the name on the papers."

"Well, how there, Hal," Jefferson said.

"Hello," Hal said, ignoring Jefferson's hand.

"Why's he got to be here?' Jefferson asked Seth.

41

"I run a school. There are textbooks in those trailers for my students," Hal said, turning on the laconic Indian chief dignity.

"Hiding guns in with schoolbooks. Sometimes I swear that smugglers have the most twisted sense of humor I ever saw," Jefferson said to Seth.

Seth nodded. And after a few minutes of uncomfortable silence in the cold, Seth said they would wait for the Russian back in their truck.

"I hope that man gets what he's looking for," Hal said the moment the truck doors slammed shut.

"Hal, I need you to take it easy. No one's here to make friends. It's business. Let's get it done."

"I know, be professional. But a man like that, he won't be happy until he's destroyed everything around him," Hal said, taking a deep breath to elaborate on his thesis.

"Hal, listen, don't take this the wrong way. But when the other guys get here, I want you to wait here in the truck."

"Why? That doesn't make any sense. I have to make sure I'm getting the right textbooks. There should be books for my people in those trucks. And I'm not going to let myself be cheated by a criminal, or by a fanatic," Hal said, his voice high and nasal, all of the chiefly laconic dignity gone.

"Listen to yourself—you're getting emotional. And that's fine, it's great. I'm sure that emotion is what makes you an effective leader in your community. But out here, it puts all of us in danger."

Hal stared angrily for a moment, then nodded and sulked. It was a long sulk. The Russians were late. Out of the darkness, two tractor trailers and a Maserati pulled up. Michael, the Russian, climbed out of the Maserati. Jefferson's tractor trailers turned on their lights, which crossed those of Michael's trucks. In that field of light, Seth met Jefferson and Michael, and made the introductions.

"Good news. We have a new way through customs," Michael said. He was wearing an iridescent black windbreaker with a gold horse stitched across the back. He didn't seem to be troubled by the cold. "We were able to double the shipment."

"But I only see two trucks," Seth said.

"With the new way, we didn't need the cover. Both trucks are full of what you wanted. Go. Look inside."

"That's great. But we don't have the money for both shipments right now," Jefferson said.

"It's been taken care of. You have generous friends," Michael said, shaking his head as he walked away, gesturing for them to follow him to their trucks.

A man climbed out of one of the cabs and opened the containers. Jefferson and one of his drivers disappeared behind the trucks. Michael lit a cigarette and blew smoke into Seth's face.

"So who are you?"

"I'm a lawyer."

Michael looked him up and down, smiled to himself and turned on his heel, toward the trucks. After a few minutes, Jefferson and his driver came out.

"It looks good. And we're all set—I mean, with the money?" Jefferson said, a little embarrassed.

"It's been paid for. Talk to your lawyer," Michael said, with the same smirk when he said the word *lawyer*.

Behind Jefferson, Michael's drivers had begun the process of unhitching the trailers, flashlights moving among the hookups, hitches, switches, and wires. Jefferson nodded, trying not to act surprised or impressed. It was going well, Seth thought, looking around. That's when he saw Hal, outside the truck, walking up to the patch of light between the trucks. Seth headed to intercept him, meeting him on the edge of the lights.

"Hal, we have good news and bad news. The bad news is something happened to the books on the way. The good news is that I'm going to pay for them, tonight, in cash. Just tell me how much."

Hal sputtered about the price of getting a shipment rushed to the school in time for the next semester. He spoke a number that seemed high for textbooks, but ultimately low for the risk he'd taken on.

"Fine. You'll have the money in your hand as soon as we leave here."

Hal nodded, but still tried to walk around Seth toward Michael. Jefferson walked over from his trucks to see what was going on. Seth stepped back in front of Hal, and put his hands on the man's shoulders. Seth's size and quickness made Hal pause and revert to words.

"I suppose you think that's *nice* of you," he barked at Seth. "Probably think you're generous. You're more of a white man than I thought. You lie to me, you cheat me, *use* me and then offer up your so-called charity, and I'm supposed to thank you?"

Hal tried to walk around Seth again. But Seth grabbed him and kept him from getting any closer to the two men and spoke in an urgent whisper about the flimsiness of life. Behind Seth, Jefferson and Michael seemed amused by the angry Indian. And when it seemed that Seth had talked some serenity and reasonable fear into Hal, Jefferson tittered.

Without warning, Hal lunged in Jefferson's direction. But Seth got back in front of him and kept him at a safe, still-humorous distance. After a few failed attempts to get past him, Hal stopped trying. Now the other men were openly laughing.

"Who are you to laugh? You're the joke," he said to Jefferson. "You play soldier when no one asked you to. What happened? They wouldn't let you in the real army? No one needs your war. And even you won't like it when you see it. Do you think that what you have to offer with your guns is better than raising and teaching children? Do you really think that?"

Jefferson muttered something about a drunk Indian. Illuminated by the headlights, Michael smiled in amusement at all of them.

"And you—you're nothing but a thief with a plane ticket. Have you ever built anything? Have you ever helped anyone in your entire life?"

Michael looked on amused, secure and superior in knowing that he hadn't helped anyone in his life. Hal shook his head and walked back to the truck.

"You shouldn't have brought him," Jefferson said.

Michael's Maserati and the two trailer cabs drove off. Jefferson's men finished attaching the trailers. Seth walked back to the truck. Hal had relegated himself to the passenger seat and was resting his head on the dashboard.

"You shouldn't have done that," Seth said.

Hal rolled his forehead on the plastic surface to face him, as if to say no to some question that wasn't asked.

They sat in silence until Jefferson's trucks rolled into the thick winter darkness. Seth opened his bag. Counting the money with his hands in the darkness of the truck, he removed the amount he'd promised Hal. Hal needed two hands to hold it, and more than a few awkward seconds to get it all stowed in the many pockets of his jacket.

"You can buy the books you need with this. See? It all worked out, despite your bullshit."

Hal didn't say anything or move from the passenger seat. Seth started the truck and started driving to town.

"I'm going to find a hotel. You okay to drive?"

"Get a drink with me."

"Hal, I'm not your friend. I don't owe you a damn pep talk and I don't have to sit still for any more of your bullshit."

"One drink. You owe me that much."

Seth didn't agree, but didn't feel like arguing. Hal guided him to a downtown bar full of weather-worn white men and toothless Indians. Seth ordered a bourbon and Hal did the same. Hal raised his and threw it back in an exaggerated motion, spilling a portion of his double onto the change the bartender brought with their drink, the whiskey and money mixing and nearly ruining each other. Hal ordered another and gestured to Seth.

"Bobby, this is the devil. The devil's buying."

The bartender nodded at Seth. He was in his East-Coast-lawyer clothes, and could have passed for the devil in that bar.

Hal put one of the big bills Seth had given him on the bar. After another drink, Seth wandered out into the cold, down Main Street and the lit side streets until he found a hotel.

---

It was chilly, not the night for exploring, when the young man with the broken mouth started down the path that would lead him across continents and centuries. A year after he moved into The Sigh's tent, the old man took him to a distant treeless hill. The trek itself was a portentous event. The Sigh wasn't one for long hikes.

They reached the hilltop around dusk. Once there, The Sigh gestured for the young man to sit and to close his eyes. The Sigh told him a story in their simple lost language: The creators of the world had run off, chasing other pleasures out past the farthest star and leaving their work ragged, like an unfinished basket with loose strands. He told the damaged young man to look into the darkness of his own closed eyes to find the loose strand in the weave. He told the disfigured young man that from that loose strand, he could work his way out.

He told his thin companion not to be afraid.

The escape came easily for the lop-jawed young man. There were fewer words, fewer twists in the labyrinth back then. He closed his eyes and found the break in the seal before the night was out. The shift out of his body was gentle but definite, opening all of time and space to him. He traveled across the face of the earth up to the moon, moving instantaneously, like a thought through a mind the size of the world. He visited his birth and his mother's birth and her mother's birth. He burrowed back to spy his own conception to learn who his own father was, to his chagrin.

That night, swimming in infinity, chasing lights and whims, he flew into the future and a strange, walled city. There he found a perfumed woman on a pile of blankets. There, his hands and feet coalesced into familiar flesh from the idea that

46

he had traveled as. His body hardened from something like nonexistence into what it was earlier that night on the treeless hill. The change reminded him of getting a hard-on, which was also happening.

Suddenly present in the girl's room, he approached her. All the lightness and simultaneity that carried him to her bed left with a thud as his knee banged the bed frame. She was frightened by his apparition and his uneven face. He wrestled her until she didn't resist, and accepted his body, reverently repeating a strange name that he liked better than his own.

That night, passing effortlessly through time and space, he alighted on a pack of wolves, scattering them. Exhilarated and amazed, he perched by an owl, which saw him, blinked, and looked away. He swam back to the low hill, where the older man had lit a fire.

It was the first night of the life that would carry the broken-toothed spirit to Seth, in America, in the third millennium of its misfortune.

———————————

A cab returned Seth to the tiny airport outside of Farmington. The sun was newly risen and the air was freezing. The old black pilot waited for Seth at the airport. Like Seth, he was wearing the same clothes as the day before. Seth asked the pilot how he was.

"I'm okay, you know. Hungover, maybe still even a little drunk, if I'm being honest. But don't worry. I've flown farther drunker. This one crazy Indian kept buying me drinks and chewing my ear about how he'd met the devil and sold his soul. You meet some characters in these cowboy towns."

"What happened to the Indian?"

"Beats me. He kicked the jukebox, broke the glass. Ran off."

The plane took off. The rattling, whistling, rumbling plane carried the two men above the same forest fires

"These fires—you can get used to anything," the pilot said above his ongoing mutter.

Back in Oceanside, Seth was oddly relieved to get back into his rental car. He was so many steps, so many twists, so many seizures, mysteries and small betrayals from anything resembling a home that it would have to do. At the hotel, the front desk blonde gave Seth a FedEx envelope with instructions. Once the door was locked, Seth tore open the envelope as if his identity and his destiny were within.

Instead, the envelope contained a sheet of paper with the name, rank, and phone number of the colonel in charge of Vandenberg Air Force Base. It was a strange name that rang bells in Seth's head—Fieldspurhoff. Otherwise, the envelope was full to bursting with bank-bound stacks of bills. On the back of the sheet of paper was a handwritten note: "deliver the money and take the man's temperature — Fred."

Seth drove up the coast toward the Vandenberg base, trying to remember where the hell he knew that name from. Fieldspurhoff. Fieldspurhoff. He could almost place it. Past LA, the drive was a dream, cliffs on one side and breaking waves on the other.

He gave up on the name and pondered how Jefferson fit in. Big and loud, Jefferson was famous for publicly claiming to have burnt down a post office outside Boise. He took the opportunity to send out a manifesto. It was big news during a slow news month the previous winter. His Boise Manifesto was the usual militia diatribe against the federal government's infringement on individual rights, the collusion of business and political leaders to sell out the American working class, the dehumanizing and disenfranchising effects of new technology, all leading to a call to arms against an illegitimate and spiritually gangrenous political system. In the manifesto, Jefferson referred to the post office fire as the first shot in a new revolutionary war.

A month later, an arson investigator ruled that the fire was caused by a stack of catalogues that fell behind a radiator. But by then, Jefferson was a national figure, the popular face on the varied and long-standing resentments of everyone from survivalist libertarians to hippie anarchists to small farmers to radical Mormons, who all agreed that the federal government was a raw deal. Jefferson drew fellow patriots from all over the West, and New Hampshire.

Seth understood bribes and cover-ups as the cost of doing business in Washington. So arming a yahoo like Jefferson was something new. At one of the better hotels in Santa Barbara, Seth took a room and sent his clothes to the front desk to be laundered. He shaved, showered, and looked out at the Pacific for long enough to convince himself he'd smelled the roses. Then he dialed the number.

"Great. You him?" the colonel said with a commanding impatience.

"Who?"

"The man with the plan. The man bearing gifts."

"Yeah, that's me."

"Good. How about the pier at Gaviota State Park? Three hours?"

"Sure."

Seth looked it up and hopped into his Cadillac. It seemed as though a year's inattention would see the highway crowded out by flowers. The air was sweet. The hills and trees gave way to reveal the sun lowering into the Pacific. And despite the job, despite the lives he destroyed or derailed wherever he went, Seth felt truly lucky to be alive at that particular place and time.

In the early dark of autumn, finding the pier in Gaviota State Park took a while. Seth slowed to a crawl and listened for the ocean above the sound of his tires and engine. Between the sound and the signs, he finally found the pier and parked in the mostly empty lot. He followed the pedestrian walkway under a train trestle and found himself vaulted, with all the grandiosity of the 20th century, above the bluffs, the beach, and the sea. He passed a cluster of teenagers snickering at the darkness in the light of their cell phones, and continued to the end of the pier. A figure, tall and angular, dressed in a bulky sweater against the marine-layer chill, waited there, leaning on the wooden railing. A half-moon lit the scene inadequately, and Seth was grateful for that much light.

"Hey," he said to the figure.

"You him?"

"Who?"

"The man with the plan?"

"Maybe. Who are you?"

"You know who."

"It's a big gift. I want to make sure I'm giving it to the right guy. So say it."

"Jesus. It's me, Colonel James Fieldspurhoff."

"Okay," Seth said, letting the envelope slip from his hands to the colonel, who stashed it in the waistband of his pants, under his sweater.

They stared out at the horizon together for a moment, the stars mixing with the ships out on the water. Seth's eyes adjusted to the darkness. He looked at the man next to him and thought of the other officer, back in Oceanside. Fieldspurhoff seemed more relaxed, resigned even.

"How are you doing?" Seth asked.

Fieldspurhoff didn't say anything for a long time, but gave Seth a long look. His eyes seemed bright with a peculiar torment in the moonlight.

"Your people—do they know what they're doing?"

"I don't know. I don't even know who they are."

Fieldspurhoff coughed out a loud laugh that died fast.

"If you say so. For all I know, I'm talking to the boss right now."

"The way things are, even I wouldn't be surprised."

"Well, you better hope they pull out or pull this off. Anything in between and we're all going to hang, even a shadowy mother-scratcher like you."

"Okay. But when the time comes, you're ready, right?" Seth asked, not sure exactly what he was asking.

"Well, I don't have any choice, do I?"

Seth made to leave the man alone with his misgivings and his cash. But he paused before he pushed away from the rail.

"Can I ask you something?"

"Sure."

"It's been bugging me all day. Your name rings a bell, but I can't place it. Where…"

"I was an astronaut, kid."

Seth studied his face, tried to imagine it in one of those crew photos the papers ran. Fieldspurhoff stared back at him, silently, the dull, confused fury of his eyes saying: *Fuck the details. You know the story here, kid. Now move along.*

———————

With no further assignments, Seth passed the next week in Santa Barbara, among the palm trees and Christmas decorations. He jogged the beach, drank in the bars, even bedded a tattooed girl from UCSB, who tried to drunkenly explain to him how the towns and cities in California could be replaced by independent communal villages that paid no taxes.

He kicked her out in the morning, which she didn't seem too bothered by. He caught up on his emails, which painted a picture of him being gradually and graciously dropped from the many legitimate projects on which he was working at Ritaloo Fastuch. Cases were reassigned, working groups rearranged. But no one complained. He was bringing in as many billable hours as anyone there. If he could swing an entire year like this, they'd have to give some serious consideration to making him partner.

It was a nice week, but when Frederica's assistant called and asked him to get to Laughlin the day after next, he started packing his rolling suitcase as soon as he hung up. The sun dropped behind him as he tore through the miles of verdant farmland. The highway was so dark that the Cadillac might as well have been a spaceship. By the time he crossed into Nevada, he was almost dizzy. He let the bellhop take his bag up to his suite and went straight to the lounge, head down, to grab a drink and to feel the earth, however carpeted, under his feet. Her voice fooled him into thinking he was somewhere better. The voice was singing "Time After Time," jazzy but still maudlin. The voice was a fragment of a home that never was. It belonged to Dolores.

Seth drank another bourbon to wake up. It made his exhaustion feel like a symptom of an unstoppable momentum. The third bourbon made that unstoppable motion feel like historical inevitability. She noticed him in the crowd and he raised his drink. Her eyebrows jumped involuntarily.

Dolores looked good, in a dark blue satin dress, under which her body seemed to move unimpeded. Only an oversized blue ribbon on one shoulder marked it as a Laughlin dress. She sang louder and with passion, the gap in her teeth flashing, her brown-red hair playing tricks with the light. By the end of her set, she seemed to sing to no one but Seth. Truth was, the lounge had emptied out. It was late on a Sunday night and it was getting hard to pretend that Dolores' act was anything more than an ornament installed by management to con the suckers into thinking there was some glamour to the way they'd pissed away their money. At the end of her set, Dolores sidled up next to Seth at the bar, and defiantly ignored him.

He ordered her a drink, which she stirred and drank fast, ignoring him some more. He ordered her another drink.

"Well, hello there," he volunteered.

"Hello yourself."

"That was a nice set."

"Thanks."

"So, how…"

"Save it for someone else, okay? I know all about you. The night after we were together, you were at the Vineyard Ristorante with your wife," she said, pronouncing it like that. *Rist-oe-ran-tay*. "I just want you to know that I think that's gross."

"I guess this is a small town, except with roulette."

"It's a small town period."

"Well, you should have checked with the front desk. You would have seen that's not my wife. Even here, it's the 21st century. Women work in real estate too."

"I'm sure you have an answer for everything."

"Listen, I don't know how to convince you. You either believe me or you don't."

She drank her drink and he gruffly ordered her another one. Somewhere in that drink, she made up her mind. Seth sensed it. Having harrowed him, she'd won the right to stay the night, which she did. And even though he could feel the cost accumulating, Seth was glad to see her there when he woke.

He begged out of breakfast, saying he had work to do. Dolores left and he called Frederica to move their late-afternoon meeting out of his hotel, to avoid prying eyes. She suggested a casino down the street built to look like a riverboat, where Roberto kept a suite.

Roberto let Seth into the suite and resumed working on his laptop, while half-watching a half-dozen flat-screen TVs, each showing a rerun of a different football game. Roberto was wearing navy blue dress pants and a stained undershirt, like a banker after a bender.

"I firmly believe that it is a sickness to try to figure out why you lose," he said, gesturing at the TV screens. "But here I am. Beer?"

"Coffee?"

"I'll have them send it up," Roberto said, typing on his laptop. "There. So I hear all's well on the carrot-and-stick circuit."

Seth thought of Hal spilling whiskey on his money and scowled.

"Some up, some down. But so far, so good. At least as far as I can tell."

"Good. It'll get easier for you. Momentum's a building. We're the pit crew of an avalanche. And we're putting the last wheel on. You'll see. By the way, how do you like Laughlin?"

The suite overlooked the casino's RV parking, an In-N-Out Burger, and a strip mall.

53

"Honestly?"

"I know. It's not even a proper town. It's an ugly place, the bland face of human parasitism."

"So why operate out of here at all?"

"There are reasons. From here, it's easy to keep addresses in three states. We get the states to compete, legislation-wise and tax-wise, to domicile different funds in them. Also, I like to gamble. That's a perk to keep me around. But what I found, and what I like, what I really like, is all the open land. My great grandfather, William Mulholland…"

Roberto was leaning forward in his seat, almost rocking back and forth as he spoke. It gave his bursts of speech the feeling of a tire bouncing down a hill.

"Really? I read that you changed your name from Mendes."

"Okay, well, you ever read anything about William Mulholland?"

"He was a dam-builder in LA. Killed a bunch of people with a bad dam."

The coffee came. Roberto opened the door and brought the tray in himself, placing it on the coffee table in front of Seth.

"One bad dam. Sure. Everyone remembers the bad dam. But the other dams, the reservoirs and the water deals, they made Los Angeles. Before that, no one would have ever considered it as a site of a big town, never mind a world city."

"Maybe it would be better if no one had."

"That's right, I forgot that you're from New York. My point is that Mulholland, he saw it. And he opened the way. From Khufu to Robert Moses, men like that have always been necessary to make the world into, well, the world. You know I never wanted to be a billionaire?"

"Well, if that's your problem…" Seth said, squinting as he sipped his coffee.

"Good. You're funny. But it's true, I never wanted to be a billionaire. I wanted to be an artist, but on a big scale. No blurry oil paintings or bullshit clay sculptures. I'm talking about

54

something big—a city, or something more than a city—I'm talking about reshaping reality."

"Is that what this is about?"

"Absolutely. Before Freddy came to me with this plan, I was going to cash out and buy a bunch of old offshore drilling platforms, out in international waters, and try to start a bunch of new nation states, flags, currencies, different judicial and political systems. But this, this is an opportunity beyond any of that."

"What opportunity?"

"You're kidding, right? I mean, for Hurley and Mankins this is about winning a spot in history, names in the school books and faces on the money. And Frederica loves running things. But reshaping reality itself—that's the thing, that's what gets me going. It's as natural as anything. You have a little success and you want a shot at the top job," Roberto said, getting lost in a third-and-long on one of the TVs.

"Top job? You already run your own business."

"Oh that. CEO—as if. No, I'm talking about the really big job. God. To my mind, it's the only job worth the kind of risk, chicanery, and knuckle-scraping that we're involved with. Me, Mankins, Hurley, you, we're all after the top job. God the creator. God the boss."

"Even me, huh?"

"Absolutely. You have a degree or two. You have a resume. You won't starve. You don't need the complications, difficulties, potential jail time or untimely death that your position exposes you to. If I had to guess, I'd say that being the wrath of God is your kick. It excuses you from the compromises of being a man. You bend the unwilling and destroy the recalcitrant. By the way, what's it like? Killing someone, I mean?"

"I don't know what you're talking about."

Roberto smiled fast and big. He had one of those faces whose age would always be indeterminate. "Come on. You can talk. I own this room. And Frederica makes sure it's swept on a regular basis."

"I don't know what you're talking about."

"Fine. You earned that knowledge. So why share? That's your personal sanctum sanctorum."

"For a hedge fund manager, you talk like a religious man."

"Yeah, that. It's my dirty secret. It's the dirty secret of everyone more than two years past worrying about money who still puts on pants in the morning. Okay. I can see you're not convinced. You're probably an atheist."

Seth refilled his coffee. Outside, the sun was going down and the town was putting on its lights. If he hadn't met Roberto before, Seth would think he was high on something other than his own wild rambling.

"Seth, it may sound strange, but I think atheists are the most religious people in the world. They say they want to do away with God, make a more rational world with science. But that's only another way of saying they want to build a better God—one based on repeatable tests—an inescapable God named Reality. It's the same unseemly monotheistic impulse to tighten the net that's driven the wheel of murder for the last two thousand or so years. Deviate from the Trinity and you're a heretic and you get burned at the stake. But fail to bow and scrape before Reality and, oh shit, you're a lunatic. They can send you away on your next-door neighbor's say-so. And I may be in the minority here, but I'd rather be burned at the stake spouting blasphemies than medicated and reeducated for three or four decades. Let me ask you, have you ever been sent, not on your own accord, not to sort out a few nagging anxieties, but *sent* to a psychiatrist?"

"Once, when I was a teenager."

"Then you know it's not the mercy it seems."

"At the time, I preferred dealing with the cops."

"I bet. Now this thing, this world I want to build, I want it to breathe. I want it to be the gaping hole in the tightening net, to be open and free, open to God and free from God."

"How do you plan to do that?"

Roberto took a breath to answer and was interrupted by a knock at the door. Frederica had a key and let herself in, wearing a pale suit that accentuated her gray eyes and made the colorful world outside seem like an embarrassing trifle.

"You boys having fun?" she said.

With some effort, she dragged a red and lavender armchair around to face Seth. Roberto relegated himself to the study of the football games in front of him.

"Seth, I want to say that we're all impressed with how you did out there. We were nervous about Wozniak. But you handled him well."

"But I never checked in."

"We followed up, and we don't think he'll be a problem. We heard about the complications with the school teacher. Nice work on that. We're going to need more of that kind of thing in the next few weeks—adapting on the fly. Hurley was right about you."

"Thanks."

"Save your thanks. Right now, we have a real problem. What we're doing can require that we show more of our hand than we'd like sometimes. Well, we showed it and now a potential asset, a Steve Burleson…."

"The software billionaire?"

"Yes, that one. He responded badly. And he called the Secret Service. We intercepted the call, but we need to deal with him, and now. We have documentation and a badge for you. There's also a plane to fly you out. We need you there tomorrow night."

"You say 'deal with?' I mean, he has money. He can protect himself. And he's scared. He'll see this coming."

"You can do whatever you need to. And we'll cover you on the ground—pay for anyone you want to hire for the job. But we need him silenced. Money isn't an object. We have you all the way, legally. Money for life for your family if you get caught. You name it."

He saw his life as a free man flash before his eyes.

"So we're talking about killing a well-known billionaire on thirty-six hours' notice. Jesus. I don't think that I can pull it off. I don't know if anyone could. This may be where we have to                            part                            ways."

"Seth, that's not really an option for you."

"Of course it is. What do you mean?"

"You know what I mean," she said.

Seth looked over to Roberto. But he was lost in his games, and of absolutely no help. Tiny Frederica was staring at Seth, making him wonder if he could recall ever seeing her blink.

"Okay. But I want you to say it."

"I hate to do this. But there are other motivations we could bring into play. You haven't always been the most fastidious killer. There is evidence floating around, dots that only need be connected. The question is: Do we need to go down this road?" Frederica said, her menace all the more convincing for being so bloodless.

"Okay. Fine. Can we go back a step, to the money-is-no-object line of persuasion?"

"Let's."

Seth threw out what he thought was a wild pitch of a price. And Frederica nodded, volunteering half up front.

"Okay, so tell me, what does this guy have on you, on us?"

"I met with him last night out in Palo Alto. I let him know the deal—work with us now or pay later. He said he'd think about it, left the restaurant and called the Secret Service from his car."

Seth suddenly understood why Frederica was behaving so rashly. It was her ass in the fire.

"Does he any have recordings, any documents?"

"No."

"Did you use your real name?"

"Yes. I had to, to get the meeting."

"Okay. Can you get an alibi that says you weren't there?"

"I think... yes, that shouldn't be a problem."

"Okay," Seth said, rubbing his forehead, as if to massage a more palatable plan into existence. "Then I think there's another way. We don't have to kill him. We just have to discredit him."

---

When he was more conventionally alive, the Broken Tooth wasn't so glib about death. His first real experience of grief broke him and effectively chased him, all too young, from his life.

In the few years he lived out with The Sigh, the old man taught his moody, impatient student all he could. And that year, when the weather turned cold, The Sigh knew his time was up. The old, fat man ate less of the food people brought, deflating by the day. Talking seemed to tire him some days. Other days, all he did was cough.

One day, his student woke to find The Sigh gone. He searched the tents and the local swamps where The Sigh would go for roots and stalks. Finally, Broken Tooth made the day's hike through a chilly mist, back to the treeless hill. He found The Sigh there, sitting on the ground, but slumped. Birds had eaten his eyes and a wolf was tugging at the exposed flesh around the old man's knee.

The thing that would one day inhabit Seth knew that The Sigh was not gone, not really. But even with his certainty that The Sigh lived on, he grieved. Broken Tooth stayed on the hilltop, but The Sigh didn't visit. He buried the old, fat man who'd granted all of his wishes and given him a world wider and more wondrous than he'd previously thought to wish for.

With the burial done, Broken Tooth couldn't imagine what to do with himself. Everything he'd seen made him despise the small, dirty place that awaited him back by the tents. From the hilltop, he searched, not eating or drinking. After several days, late one night, The Sigh visited his apprentice and told him to return to the tents, to take the position that he'd occupied there among the people. The Sigh said that only by living with his people in the long cold days, by the tents, would the young man learn what he needed to know.

But the young man refused to leave the treeless hill, guarding the grave. He closed his eyes and toured time and space, seduced nervous virgins and wizened mothers, he misled fathers, frightened sheep, and rerouted armies. When he returned to the hilltop, he was hungry, starving even. His mouth was sealed shut with dried spittle and his lips cracked when he yawned. He left for the future, the past, distant lands and walled cities.

On the night of the first frost, Broken Tooth lost the feeling in his toes forever. Not long after, gangrene set in.

------------

Even at that point of Seth's career, there weren't many people he could call at midnight to show up the next day on the other end of the continent with enough liquid LSD to turn the College of Cardinals into a game of duck-duck-goose. But William picked up on the first ring. Seth offered him an amount of money that obviated negotiation and created a worried pause on the other end of the phone before William agreed to be there the next day.

Seth put down the phone and flopped in bed, talking to himself, diagramming his play, and trying to outflank the sense that he was missing something vital that could derail the biggest operation of his career, and worse. There was a knock on the door. Dolores smiled through the peephole. He unlocked, unlatched, and opened up. She kissed him and walked straight in, talking.

"You missed the show tonight. It was okay, except for these assholes. The Monday Night game went to overtime and I guess Green Bay scored a touchdown off the kickoff and the spread was four, and so these assholes thought it was…"

"Dolores, how would you like to come with me to California tomorrow?" Seth said, before he could think, because he was scared, and because she might be useful.

"Tomorrow? I have a show."

"Cancel it. Take a sick day. You'd be helping me a lot with business. And I'd pay for the privilege of your company."

"Oh, I thought you meant…"

"I'm sorry. And I want to take you somewhere, like a vacation, later, when things quiet down. But for now, I could use your help."

"I'd have to move things around, and I'd…"

Seth said a number and that was his mistake. He liked Dolores, and he wanted to get the money part of their conversation over with as quickly as he could. But he'd forgotten where he was, and what her expectations were. The number he said had the wrong effect. It frightened her.

"But how can you afford…"

"What can I say? Real estate is a lucrative business."

Dolores looked at him, pursed her pretty, thick lips and nodded a nod that ended with her gaze on the carpet.

The next morning, Dolores tried and failed to conceal how much she liked the private jet. There was a fridge with drinks and snacks. Foie gras and shrimp cocktail, and whatever else Frederica's carte blanche might buy. She was amazed at having the entire cabin to share with only him. Once they were airborne, she joked about the mile-high club. Why the hell not, Seth thought. Given the job, it could be his last chance for anything. The flight wasn't long and she was on top of him, moving lugubriously and sweet at first, then desperate and fast as the plane nosed downwards, as if they were screwing to outrace a crash.

William met them at the small private airport in a rented red Buick. They drove to the parking lot of a Stater Brothers Supermarket. The drear of a rainy morning was gradually growing brighter. Seth dialed a number on the phone Frederica had given him.

"Steve Burleson?" Seth said at the moment the ring was interrupted.

"Yes. Who's this?"

"Steven Stanson of the Secret Service. I'm sorry to call so early, but we have to talk. I understand you called us early this week with a tip. That call was referred to me."

"I'm glad you called back. I really didn't know where else to go with this. And the person I spoke to said not to call anyone else. Like I said, I thought I was being set up with an investor. Everything checked out. But she was talking about, well, it was treason. And…"

"Sir, I'm afraid I have to advise you to limit what you say on the phone. I've personally been told to leave this matter alone. But it fits with something else that I've been working on."

"Really, what?"

"Sir. The phone."

"Sorry. What should we do?"

"Meet me at the Santa Clara Marriott. There's a restaurant there, called Parcel 104. I'll have a table waiting under the name Jefferson. Please, sir, don't tell anyone you're coming. And, please, come alone. We're both out on a limb with this."

"A limb?"

"We really don't know who's involved. So please, keep our meeting to yourself."

"Will do," the billionaire said.

As soon as Seth hung up the phone, William began laughing like an asshole.

"Man, as crazy as it is working for you sometimes, I have to admit that there's a reason that you're the boss," William said.

"What are we doing here?" Dolores said.

"Don't worry. I'll explain it all in a minute. Let's go to the hotel and get straightened up."

Dolores was silent the rest of the ride to the Super 8. William was laughing, excited. It wasn't his ass on the line.

---

Steve Burleson was called "The Third Steve," after Steve Jobs and Steve Ballmer. He'd made his fortune cracking and then reinventing online security. His company's software, in one form or another, protected military and other government systems from intruders great and small. He owned a swath of the Pacific coast and boasted assets that would shame many small nations. He sat at a table for two in the middle of the upscale Marriott restaurant with a beat-up company baseball hat on. His knee was jumping under the table. His security was obvious at the bar, nursing a Coke and trying to play word find while Dolores tossed her hair and shot him glances one stool away.

Seth, dressed in a dark blue suit and dark red tie, thanked his lucky stars for William, who'd cased the restaurant better than Burleson's people. Seth sat down across from Burleson and looked around. He didn't need to feign his nervousness.

"We could have met at my house. It's secure. There's around-the-clock security. And they sweep for bugs—the shareholders asked for that a few years back."

"Sir, may I be frank?"

"Please, do be."

"With all due respect, don't be stupid. You think you can trust those private-security jackasses? You pay them. Who else do you think can pay them? And I thought I said to meet me alone," Seth said, nodding his head back in the direction of Steve's bodyguard.

"It's just Jan. I just thought of what my lawyer would say and what the board would say and I…"

"Fine, we'll assume that *Jan* is okay. But I don't like it. And for God's sake, order a drink. It arouses attention—you sitting here without a drink."

"I don't drink."

Seth puffed up to browbeat the frightened, confused billionaire a little bit more, when a waiter approached.

"Welcome, gentlemen, tonight we have several…."

"Drinks only for now."

"We have several drink specials designed…"

"Turkey rocks for me and a cranberry soda for him."

"Would you like to hear…"

"No."

Having established an atmosphere of fear, Seth warmed to his theme, pinching the bridge of his nose and taking a breath before he began.

"I need you to tell me what happened. The whole thing."

"It was this woman, Frederica Thenuxberg. A Mormon who controls a lot of money, and a lot of our stock through a group of pension funds and hedge funds based in Utah, Nevada, and Arizona. She had a few questions and she wanted to meet with me. So we met for dinner. I'd never met her before one on one. She's an unnerving woman. She tells me over dinner she didn't call the meeting to talk about threats to our consumer business. She says she wants to talk about the future," Burleson said.

The waiter returned with their drinks. Burleson stopped talking until the waiter had moved a few feet away.

"This woman, Frederica, she said that the country is about to change, to split. She said there's going to be a war, and that some people are going to be on the right side of the new situation. But the others are going to have problems, have their property confiscated. They could even face prosecution as traitors to the new country."

Burleson paused, putting his lips around the straw and looking to Seth for answers. And after weeks of fruitless puzzling, the pieces started to fit together.

"And what did she want from you?"

"She wanted a back door into law enforcement and military databases, and she wanted us to build in kill-switches for our secure communications networks," Burleson said.

Seth made a concerted effort to keep his cow-like victim face on, cheeks and brow slack, his eyes half-focused.

"This is what I was afraid of. Sir, I need you to listen to me. I want you to go to the bathroom. I'll watch the room to see if anyone changes their behavior. We need to be sure that no one followed either of us here."

"Just like, go to the bathroom?"

"Go in there and go through your normal routine. But be precise, be thorough, and don't give anyone reason to think anything's wrong," Seth said, struggling to keep a straight face as he told the billionaire how to pee.

Burleson left for the bathroom and his bodyguard followed, as nonchalantly as such a big man can. And Seth removed a capsule from his jacket and surreptitiously poured enough liquid LSD to make an elephant forget it wasn't a zebra into the billionaire's cranberry-and-soda.

When Burleson returned, Seth kept him talking. He had Burleson repeat his story, especially Frederica's offers and her threats. Being nervous made Burleson drink. Before long, Burleson's straw was burbling at the bottom of his drink, and Burleson was becoming fascinated by the sound of that burble. Seth waved off the waiter and excused himself, to hit the head, he said.

In the men's room, he told William the plan was on. William returned to Dolores, who kept her flirtation with Jan on a low simmer.

Back at the table, the massive dose of LSD had taken quick effect. Burleson traced the wood grain of the table with a trembling finger, as if reading a holy text. His pupils dominated his wide and questioning eyes when he looked up, surprised to see Seth.

"I don't feel so… usual… man. Secret service. Secretservicesecretservicesecretservice. What's the secret, anyway?"

"It's a secret."

"How do you service a secret?"

"That's a secret too."

"I'll bet. But I'm helping you guys out. We should be, like, the same. Listen, all this fork, knife, napkin, cloak and dagger business is no good. We should go outside, and then get a ride outside that, but ride on the outside, I mean way outside. Can we do that?"

Seth waved to the waiter and nodded to Dolores, who plainly propositioned the bodyguard, which spurred William into his faux-jealous frenzy. The much-bigger bodyguard played innocent and tried to calm William with a gentle but authoritative shove. William kicked the big man in the balls, punched him in the throat and smashed a pint glass in his face with a terrifying quickness. The big man hit the floor before he knew which vital to cover.

"Shit. We have to get out of here."

"Is it THEM?" Burleson yell-whispered.

"Come with me. We're getting out of here. But be quiet about it."

The bodyguard rose halfway and tried to charge William, who beat on the back of his neck until he went down. William was still stomping on the man's bull neck when hotel security arrived. Seth ushered Burleson out of the restaurant, dropping a pair of twenties on the table. Dolores followed them.

"We have to get out of here now," he told the tripping billionaire by the blood-red Buick.

"Who's that?"

"She's like us. She's in danger too," Seth said.

"Do they want to kill her? Do they want to kill me?"

"They want to do worse things than just kill you."

Seth opened the trunk. Doing so, he felt a twinge of gratitude to the soon-to-be-imprisoned William for cutting the escape tag from the inside of the trunk lid.

"Worse than death. What's worse than death?" Burleson asked, wide eyed as a child.

"You know what's worse than death. Now get in there. It's the only way."

Burleson climbed willingly into the trunk. Seth slammed it and they drove off. The Buick was big and quiet. It drifted down the roads like a cloud. Dolores stared out the window and said nothing on the ride to the Super 8, and said nothing when Seth dropped her there. Stopped at lights, Seth could hear Steve Burleson kick and flail in short fits, or laugh and sing for stretches as they drove up to San Jose.

They pulled over in a dark patch between patches of streetlight by a shuttered warehouse in San Jose. Seth pulled Burleson out of the trunk by his shirt, seams popping. The middle-aged man squirmed at strange angles, as if he was part liquid by that point. But Seth stood him up. He slapped Burleson in the face with an impact that, to Burleson, sounded like the new universe's crack of dawn fourteen billion years ago. Burleson stared at him with a helplessness so pitiful it evoked what slender sense of common humanity Seth might still entertain. Seth hit him again.

"Get ready. Because when we get you out of the car next time, you're going to be in deep shit."

"Deep shit worse than death?"

"Worse than death. That's right. And you have to kill them or fuck them, or...

"Or it's deep worse than shit death."

"That's right. So you have to…"

"Kill them or fuck them."

Seth retrieved a pint of cheap scotch and doused Burleson with it. He slapped him one more time, unbuckled and pulled down the billionaire's pants and threw him back in the trunk of the car. He drove him another few blocks and stopped outside a well-kept Victorian house in the middle of a dodgy neighborhood. The house was William's particular stroke of twisted genius. Seth stopped the Buick in the shade below a fragrant fruit tree and pulled Burleson out of the trunk.

Burleson gurgled a murky mix of vowels and consonants from the darkness of the trunk. Seth slapped him a few more times. It made Burleson's red face redder, and stripped the dumb smile from the billionaire's face.

"Worse than death. Kill them or fuck them," Burleson said, as if remembering his own name.

"That's right."

"Worse than kill them or fuck death."

"Yes. Our enemies are in there, but only you can face them. Your honesty and your fists are all you need. You, sir, are a hero," Seth said, pointing to the lit front porch of the Victorian house.

"Kill or worse than death or fuck them."

"Now go in there. You've made me proud to know you."

At 11:44 p.m., on a Tuesday between Thanksgiving and Christmas, Steven Burleson walked up to the door of the Victorian house and knocked. A heavyset and worried-looking Spanish woman opened the door. He punched her in the stomach. Seth quietly pulled away from the curb and drove a few desolate blocks. There, he pulled over and dialed 911.

"I want to report a break-in and assault at the St. Theresa's women's shelter on the corner of Drake and Fuller."

Then Seth called the *San Jose Mercury* with a tip that the celebrated CEO and technology billionaire was being arrested for assault at a battered women's shelter on the corner of Drake and Fuller. He wiped the cell phone down, stomped it to pieces and kicked the pieces into a storm drain.

"Let's get back to Laughlin," he said to Dolores.

After a week's psychiatric observation, Steven Burleson would be released from psychiatric care. He hadn't killed anyone, could compensate those he'd injured, and he had good lawyers. He would cancel his outstanding speaking engagements, and take a leave of absence as CEO.

On the plane back to Laughlin, later that night, Dolores didn't say much. She wasn't exactly angry and she wasn't exactly shocked. She had sensed something wasn't altogether above the board with Seth since she met him. It might have been the first thing she sensed.

"What did we just do?" she asked him.

"We took a very rich and powerful man and subjected him to a moment of profound disgrace. Don't worry about him. He has the money and power he needs to recover from it."

"Why did we do that?"

"Because someone even more powerful wanted it that way."

He took her hand and she let him. After a few seconds, she squeezed it. She was frightened of him now, and Seth couldn't tell yet if that made her like him more or less. He was surprised to catch himself caring which.

They landed in the chill of midnight. He paid her in cash back at the hotel. Her eyes didn't sparkle the same way they did when he told her the figure. The reality of the money was somehow worse than the idea of it. She sang that night, poorly.

———————

No one came to look for him on the hilltop. It was quiet there, except for the vultures and coyotes, who'd seemed to smell his decision. Despite the ache and the stink climbing his leg, despite the advice of The Sigh, Broken Tooth thought he was making a good decision.

His life had left him with little except the quiet scorn of the women and men by the tents, utter isolation with The Sigh gone, and a shameful name, Broken Tooth. The young man saw death as the shedding of that one last, bleak hindrance— his life.

*Glad to be through with the stink* was the broken-toothed man's first thought when he died.

But death was not like his earlier sojourns. It jarred and it wrenched. All his experiences to that point didn't prepare him adequately for it. He could still go anywhere and do anything. But he had no home to return to. Strangely, his first impulse was to return to the tents, to materialize there. But when he appeared among the tents, he was unrecognizable, and chased out as any distrusted stranger was.

And so the broken-toothed spirit returned to the treeless hill. He scratched under his chin, but noticed that he did not itch. He realized he would never itch again. And that made him sadder than anything.

The Sigh visited him there. Death made the old man's face clearer, freed it of wrinkles and spots, lent it a faint glow.

But in death, the younger man's face was still crooked and toothless.

"You should have stayed by the tents. They needed you. And you needed them. They were your chance to grow up," The Sigh said.

"I couldn't go back to them. They had nothing to offer me except beatings and insults."

"If that's all they had to offer, that's what you needed. You won't learn anything that you need to know, not like this."

The Sigh disappeared. And even though everything was now possible for the slender suicide with the lopsided face, he would never really shed the trauma of his life and his death.

---

From Laughlin, Seth arranged for a lawyer and for Hurley to do some string-pulling in Santa Clara for William, who'd been arrested for assault, but under a different name. Frederica called to set up a meeting. But Seth begged off until the next day and slept until late that evening. He woke to a phone call from William, saying his charges had gone from attempted murder to drunk-and-disorderly.

He caught Dolores' set downstairs. Afterwards, he said he was tired and she seemed relieved. They said good night in the awkward fashion of people who feel strongly for each other, don't know if they'll ever see each other again, and don't know if they want to.

The next day, he was early to Roberto's suite. Roberto was there with a small Chinese man wearing an enormous watch. Roberto was talking derivatives and swaps, government bailout credits and toxic securities. The man with the big watch was repeating it into a satellite phone in Cantonese. Seth sat down on a couch and watched the news. After a bit about the unemployment rate, the TV showed Burleson's mug shot. Seth wondered who gave him the black eye—a cop or one of the women at the shelter.

Roberto finished up with the Chinese guy, who left without acknowledging Seth.

"There he is! Congratulations on a job well done. Everyone is impressed. Absolutely everyone. Champagne, whiskey, women—you name it."

"Cup of coffee would be fine."

"You got it. Cup of coffee and a bag of cash," Roberto said and gestured to the tray waiting on the table in front of him, and to the backpack next to the table.

Seth poured himself a cup from the burnished aluminum pitcher.

"Thanks, I'm still a little beat."

"Understandable. You did the impossible and put out a major fire for us. When Freddy first told me about Burleson calling the Secret Service, I really thought we were dead in the water. I even got out my box of passports. But the wheel of fortune has turned. I shorted the shit out of SumTech stock yesterday morning. And it's a good day to be one of my shareholders."

"Here's to that. Where is Frederica, anyway?"

"Conference call ran long. She just messaged me. But again, great job. Burleson'll be too scared and confused to say much. And if he does, who will believe him? And the best part is that there's no blowback, no investigation. When Freddy told me about what you were supposed to do—well, I was worried we were going to lose you… well, never mind. Fuck the shareholders, here's to more successful campaigns together," Roberto said, raising his tall glass of cloudy maroon liquid.

As they toasted, a key card slid in the door handle and Frederica swung open the door.

"Hey, Freddy…"

"Roberto, I'll say it again: please use my proper name or don't call me anything at all," she sang as she approached Seth. He stood up and she shook his hand firmly. "Well done."

"We were toasting, to continued successes in the field," Roberto said.

"Seth, I only have a minute. But I wanted to stop in and say good work. Roberto probably told you this already. But you exceeded our expectations on this one."

"Glad to help," Seth said to the woman who'd blackmailed him with prison a few days before. His sarcasm either didn't show or didn't matter.

"Hopefully we'll be able to work together again soon."

She gave Seth another firm, long handshake. And with that, Frederica left.

"What does she mean?" he asked Roberto.

"Right. I talked to Hurley yesterday. He says he needs you back in Washington by the end of the week. You'll be missed here. We have an Air Force guy, a general, who needs another carrot-and-stick type meeting. And you seem to be good at that. Frederica can come on a bit too strong sometimes."

"Yeah, what's with all the military guys?"

"Well, we're going to need as many high-level guys as possible in our region. I worry that we might be going after too many of them. No matter how much homework we do, each one we reach out to is a risk. And we can't have too many of those guys feeling like George Washington when we get this off the ground."

"What do you mean?"

"I mean in this new, liberated United States of the West. The governors will have control of the National Guard units. So that leaves the regular military."

"We have all the governors?"

"All the ones that matter, except one. I bet you can guess which one."

"California? Mankins?"

"Give the man a cigar. Once we get him in office, we're ready to go. California's the lynchpin. Like I was saying, the governors will control the National Guard units. But we need to control a few of the biggest bases, especially Air Force bases, at the moment that we declare independence."

"How does that work?"

"The declaration?"

"Yeah. It seems like we're a long way from 1776."

"Good question. How we do it is important. It has to work, and it has to look right. It starts with lawsuits. The states involved will simultaneously file suits against the federal government, announcing their secession and demanding repayment of damages. We have some serious constitutional scholars working on the suits. They're valid enough to buy us the time we need to consolidate our power and to implement the new government. But, if we control a third of the nation's military capability, that will *guarantee* us the time we need."

"So the lawyers are the tip of the spear?"

"At least in theory. We're still working out the exact details. They say Napoleon could figure out, within minutes of the end of a battle, how many new shoelaces his army would need before the next one."

"No kidding."

"No kidding. With something like this, you can never have too many details figured out ahead of time. So I'd say that hopefully, you'd be back out here soon. But hopefully, we won't need you so soon."

They shook hands. Seth drove back to his hotel, packed up and drove away from Laughlin. He needed to think, and so drove up to Las Vegas, a long drive on empty desert highways. The sun was high and merciless when he left and directly into his eyes by the time he got to the airport.

From the window seat, Seth watched the long shadows of the Rocky Mountains stretch until all was dark. In the darkness below, the great spans of land were so blank they might as well have been water. From that darkness emerged a spark, an orange line of lights that spread into a town, or a blue-and-orange cluster of iridescence around a river or lake, spreading into suburbs, dying into a string of highway lights before efflorescing into a town once more.

The thing inside of Seth narrated the scene below as an infection. The small TV screen on the seatback in front of him flashed a commercial for a new recycled or recyclable thing, the screen said that recycling was one of the most important things a person could do. The thing inside of Seth chuckled at the idea of recycling. It said writing was on the wall. The great infection had peaked and every day brings fewer and fewer seats at the table. It laughed at the absurdity of recycling, of the human infection itself, as if the Black Plague had decided to become milder and more sustainable, like the common cold.

Seth caught his smiling predator's face reflected in the darkened window and chuckled at the idea of himself as a particularly virulent strain of the disease.

The plane landed. The cold in DC snapped everything into place. The darkness locked the lights and shapes into place. Out west, it had been as though the world floated. That wasn't the case here. Seth kicked the gum-stained pavement of the airport sidewalk on the way back to his car.

---

The next day, the secretary waved Seth right in. And Hurley rose and walked around his massive desk to shake his hand.

"Well, counselor, I want to say that you have won yourself a client for life. Roberto told me all about it. And though I guess it was necessary, I don't like how they were using you out there. You were altogether too exposed on that last job. But you came through with flying colors. And we want to keep you happy. Let me ask you, what can we do for you?"

"I was thinking about that on the plane. And what I want is to be a partner at Ritaloo Fastuch."

"How about more money? If you need, we can set up an LLC for you and funnel some of the cash there, as consulting fees, or something like that, if having too much cash is a problem. You know the drill."

"I'm okay for money right now. What I'd really like is to be made partner. Some stability, some status. My mother would like it. I think it's the only thing she knows about being a lawyer. She always asks if I've made partner yet."

"That's sweet. I'll talk to Earl Ritaloo about it. But to be honest, I think that might be a harder sell than you realize."

"Why's that? With the billable hours I'll be bringing in this year, it would only be right."

"I agree. But it wouldn't *look* right. You're not from the right school. You don't have any big cases under your belt. Your big account is me, and we don't need the attention. And frankly, Earl Ritaloo has a vague idea about what you do for us. He's been around long enough to know that you're doing more than drafting contracts and writing briefs."

"Who cares what he knows, especially if he's the only one at the firm who knows it?"

"No one else knows because no one else wants to know. But if you're a partner, people there will ask. Envy and resentment are powerful motivators. So they will dig. And that's where we don't want to be. Let's not give anyone a reason to be curious."

"You asked me what I wanted. And that's the thing. The numbers are there. Anyone can see the money I'm bringing into the firm."

Hurley regarded Seth closely. He gave up on the half-smile he kept perpetually at work, and seemed both younger and more honest for it. He seemed to be calling on a hidden reserve, something that made the thing in Seth stir.

"Seth, listen. This isn't easy to say. And I hope that you don't take it the wrong way. But it's peacetime right now. And in peacetime, assassins don't get promoted. They don't get promoted for the same reasons that high-end escorts don't marry. First of all, it's a pay cut. Second, people in peacetime, people who haven't been tested, have trouble trusting assassins and escorts. That's because assassins and escorts have both shown that they can dispose glibly of what most people hold most dear, or at least claim to. This is a long way of saying that you're not on a management track. Not at the moment, anyway."

"I see."

"I'm not saying never. I'm saying not now. Peacetime doesn't last forever. And when it ends, a man like you can go very far, farther than you've probably imagined."

The thing in Seth was alive with a sense of recognition. Seth nodded, confused by how quickly his sense of dejection turned to enthusiasm. Hurley nodded back.

"There are big changes coming. I think you're starting to get some idea of exactly how big. But for now, be patient. In a few years you'll laugh that you ever set your sights as low as partner at Ritaloo Fastuch."

"So why am I back here?"

"The good news is that it'll be easier than your last job. The bad news is that it's Mankins. We got lucky with his last mistress. Too lucky. She was a clam, hardly any friends, no real confidants, not close with her family. Well, he's got a new girl in his life. Frankly, I'm sick of the guy, but we're too far down this road to change up now."

"So what do you want me to do?"

"I want you to follow her, check her out. I want us to be ready to intervene before this gets out of hand, or to clean up right if it does. It's low-profile work and you can hire help if you want. It's not as exciting as your last assignment, but we need to save you for when we need you. And the pay is still considerable."

Hurley's offer was enough to convince Seth that his new job as babysitter was a promotion. But he left the K Street offices of The American Institute for the Preservation of Leisure feeling so outfoxed that his head spun. Walking past the Capitol, the thing in him purred.

---

With a couple of days off before he began his mistress-watching in earnest, Seth left DC. He struggled up the New Jersey Turnpike in a rainy rush hour, and made a few hard phone calls. His divorce lawyer said that his ex-wife told her lawyer to tell his lawyer to tell him that he could see his daughter, but only the next day, and only if he picked her up from school exactly when it let out. It was the classic brush-off for a busy ex-husband. But Seth was ready for it, and agreed.

In Manhattan, Seth's apartment reeked of lemon and bleach. He'd forgotten to call off the cleaning lady, who'd cleaned repeatedly in his absence. He didn't bother turning on the lights. He dropped his bags by the door and turned on the TV. He caught a familiar face on the news, Jefferson, from the gun buy in Farmington. The screen showed some old VHS footage and a mug shot. The newswoman said Jefferson had killed an undercover ATF agent. A manhunt was underway.

He stayed up late watching TV. Even its horrors were a lullaby compared to what silence brought. He pondered what Frederica had told Burleson of a civil war—a parcel of truth, or another cover story? He remembered the ex-astronaut's talk of the gallows.

The thing inside him warmed to the prospect, eager to walk on the shores of death. It may have ruined what some people would call Seth's life, but it also made him unafraid. TV gave way to a bad night's sleep, full of dreams. Forests of trees full of coiled snakes, old cars that ran on human blood, ten-story-high wheels made of white clenched fists rolling across vast plains of innocent faces.

The next morning, he drove out to Garden City on Long Island. He'd only been to the new house once or twice before. It was a white split-level in a neighborhood with enough trees left standing to conceal the desolation of the shopping centers and the highway beyond it. His ex's new husband answered the door, with his receding hairline, weak chin, and bland disdain for Seth that was tempered only by his concern for his stepdaughter. Seth had only hit his ex that once, and wondered how often she brought it up.

At the door, his little Elizabeth came running out to him, past her stepdad's knees. Bethie, he and his ex had called her. She was taller and leaner than when he'd seen her last, more of a proper little girl now. He reached down picked her up. She squirmed from the kiss he planted on her cheek.

She said good-bye to her stepfather. On the rounded curb of the suburban lane, he struggled to get her into the car seat he kept in the trunk, which she'd outgrown. He cursed under his breath at the reminder of the kind of father he was.

"Bethie."

"No one calls me that anymore. I'm Elizabeth," she said, annunciating each syllable.

"Okay, E-Liz-A-Beth, you're a big girl now. How would you like to sit up front with me?"

"Mom says I need to be in a car seat."

"Okay. But let's not tell her, this time, okay? We'll just drive very carefully. Can you help me do that?"

"You're silly, old Daddy."

"Old Daddy, huh?"

"Yeah. You're old Daddy and there's new Daddy."

He buckled her into the front seat and they drove. The trees were bare and gray. He took her to McDonald's. They ate their sweet and salty mush and she played with the Happy Meal's movie-tie-in toy. They talked in the car on the way to the mall about her pre-school, about why he couldn't be at Christmas. He didn't ask about his ex or about new Daddy. It had been more than three years since he left for good, and his visits had grown increasingly infrequent. He knew he wasn't going to mend his ways or redeem the damage anytime soon. And he couldn't shake the feeling that Elizabeth was a little recorder for his sins. So he did what any delinquent first-husband type would do, and bribed her.

The toy store was crowded with holiday shoppers, older women with strained expressions, carefully examining the brightly colored toy packages. The thing in Seth wanted to chain the doors shut and burn the whole place to the ground. But it knew better than to speak up when he was with his daughter. The thing in Seth still hid in a flawless *nobody-here-but-us-normal-and-abnormal-psychological-processes* cover story. And that meant it couldn't say anything about Elizabeth or the relative sanctity of her childhood.

"Pick anything, anything at all," he told her.

They walked the aisles and Elizabeth explained in effusive bursts what each toy was and how it fit with other toys, followed by a moment of pleading on her part and some playful resistance on his, before he agreed. That went on for two hours. They left with a shopping cart.

His ex was home when he dropped off Elizabeth with the toys. Elizabeth said thank you, said Merry Christmas, and said she loved him. He picked her up and kissed her on the cheek. She hugged his neck and asked him to stay for dinner. His ex took Elizabeth and told her that Seth couldn't stay, told her to go inside and get cleaned up.

Then she started in. She was irate about the toys, irate about his not having a $60 car seat in his $60,000 car. But Seth had nothing to defend and nothing to win anymore. He was the first husband, the old Daddy, the overcompensating asshole. And he would always be that guy on Long Island.

"Do what you want with the toys. Oh, and tell whatsisname that the check will be on time this month," Seth said, turning and leaving.

From the house's front steps, his ex started yelling something true about his many failures of character. Seth felt the urge to turn around and show her some new and improved failures of character. But he was frozen by the awful futility of his life as that angry cliché.

---

The gray brush swamps, low houses, and glass corporate campuses rushed past Seth on the LIE. Long Island was a failed home. They'd lived there when his ex was pregnant and during Elizabeth's first two years. He was a regular lawyer and Hurley a new client. The former senator was a cautious man, talking in circles for a billable day or two before Seth got to his point for him: He needed someone bribed at the FCC. Seth set something up, a shell company whose founding documents could incriminate the commissioner while concealing the entity making the bribes. Hurley was pleased.

Elizabeth was born with health problems, and needed a few surgeries when she was an infant. After that, she cried a lot for her first year. Between the constant worrying and the sleepless nights, it was a trial for Seth and his ex. But the problems in their marriage didn't start until Elizabeth was done with the surgeries and sleeping most nights. That's when the thing in Seth sensed an opportunity, and Seth began to that feel his freely chosen and honestly earned middle-class life was actually the worst sort of prison. And the seizures, which had been intermittent since he was a teenager, intensified. He'd come back to his senses two towns away, shoeless in the winter. Sometimes he would wake up with strange women, his pockets unaccountably full of money. He saw doctors, neurologists, psychiatrists, he took tests and took pills, all to no avail.

His then-wife was understanding. But the thing in Seth made him despise her concern. It was careful and subtle in its management. Dwelling on the bills instead of the people that greeted him at home, and it gradually tilted his perception of every detail of his life.

Since the divorce, Seth lived in a big one-bedroom apartment on Columbus Avenue. To put a positive spin on his failure as a husband and father, he'd put a great deal of time and money into decorating the place. The dark wood dining room table, the distressed leather couch, the modern armchair, wooden venetian blinds, art prints from the Guggenheim and the Whitney. It was something between a fantasy and a costume, a talisman and a consolation. When Seth got back to the apartment on Columbus Avenue that night, his face was sore from smiling at his daughter.

He started in the living room with the framed pictures of Elizabeth, of his brother and sister, his wedding, his mother and father. He pulled the pictures out of their frames and put them into a garbage bag. If someone came looking for him, or a way to hurt him, he didn't want to do them any favors. He went through his papers, keeping very few and tossing most into the bag. He ranged about the apartment, stripping it of anything that might say something about its occupant. He carried three full bags of personal garbage down to the street, and thinking twice, put them in the trunk of his car. His apartment stripped, Seth went to sleep with two suitcases by his bed.

He slept a few hours, then drove up through the woods of Westchester and Fairfield County. A few exits past the Heroes Tunnel on the Merritt Parkway was the nursing home where Seth's mother lived. He didn't visit there often either. He got turned around on the bucolic streets of Hamden, but found a big pharmacy where he picked up a bouquet of flowers and some chocolates.

The home, or retirement community, was a red-brick complex where his mother and others like her could spend their waning years. It was an expensive cloud of flower-scented disinfectant and rosy euphemism. The thing in Seth snarled and reminded Seth of the monthly cost, and every painful moment he'd spent in his childhood home with his mother. The trip to Long Island was already more tenderness and human contact than the thing in Seth was comfortable allowing him. It had Seth gnashing his teeth with impatience and old grievances by the time the automatic doors of the retirement home whooshed shut behind him.

The facility's crew-cut carpet and indirect fluorescent light had the intended effect, whispering that the place was clean, but not a hospital. The Jamaican woman at reception questioned Seth. She said she knew his brother and sister, but not him. He snapped that she should check who pays the bills. She did some tapping at her computer and told him that his mother, Ruth, would probably be in her room.

The hallways were lined with paintings of picnics and sailboats and flowers, brightly colored nothings meant to help the dying ignore the unfair and uneven collapse of their most prized faculties, the thing inside of Seth sneered. *Call it a kindness, but it's a jail where they keep the inmates trapped in their lives, paid for by slightly younger prisoners like you, who are scared and eager to justify your own captivity.* The thing in Seth went on and on like that. Hospitals, churches, and especially the nursing home always seemed to inspire its wild blasphemy.

The Jamaican woman finally left Seth at his mother's private room—part of the Platinum Package. She was talking on an oversized cell phone when he knocked on the door. "...that's probably not appendicitis then. Oh my God, Artemis, it's your brother... no... Seth... I'll call you back."

Her eyes widened as she clapped the oversized phone shut, struggled up from her armchair and embraced Seth. Her words ran together, saying all at once how she never knew when she was going to see him and how had he gotten so thin, the latter part of which wasn't true. He squeezed back, gently. She took his pharmacy-bought gifts, saying she'd be the envy of her friends.

"It's nothing. I'm sorry I haven't been in a while. I was out west for work."

"Well, they must have needed you out there. Did you have a good time?"

"It was all right, a lot of work. It's different out west; the people are different out there."

"I lived in California, this place in Ojai, for a year before you were born," his mother said, a sigh breaking her smile. "I probably won't ever go back there."

Seth hated his mother's morbidity. She sensed his discomfort and changed the subject.

"It sounds like they're keeping you busy. So when are they going to make you a partner?" she asked.

"We'll see. They have a freeze on new partners for now. But I may have another opportunity coming up."

"I always knew you would end up in business, or law, or politics. Even when you were young, you had all this seriousness about you. And I always knew, even then, that you would wind up taking all of it too seriously. You should travel, and not just for work. You should try to enjoy life more."

This was a common line of discussion in his conversations with his mother, one of many that Seth disliked.

"I do enjoy life. I enjoy my work. And I'll make partner soon, either that or something even better."

"I'm sure it will all work out for the best."

Seth had been the end of too many lives. And he had seen firsthand how often it did not work out for the best. If the years had cost him anything, it had been precisely those vague reassurances. He nodded and squeezed on a smile.

His mother was especially sharp that day. And Seth wasn't sure whether or not to be happy about that. She gave him the news about his siblings. His brother, Justus, had made major in the Army. Enlisting was his rebellion against his hippie upbringing. Artemis was a childless midwife, who, unlike her brothers, lived nearby and visited their mother frequently. His mother told him a great deal about each, enough to let him know that nothing much had changed with either. He nodded, bored. But his mother took his boredom for something else and paused, gathering his attention.

"You should call them. We're all your family. I know you think they blame you for your father leaving. Maybe you think I do too. But that's not true. What he did was his own choice."

"Mom, don't."

"Well, they're your brother and your sister. You should call them once in a while. You could even come by for the holidays one of these years. They know that what happened with you wasn't your fault. It was nothing more than bad luck, very bad luck. They dropped the charges, after all."

"Okay. I get it. I'll call them. Can we not talk about it? It was a long time ago."

He stayed a couple hours, scrupulously avoiding old wounds like his father's abandonment and his ugly teenage legal troubles. The past was a half-exploded bomb. There was nothing to be done, but avoid it. To fill the time, Seth lied, inventing details about his daughter, details of what he imagined a normal social life for a man his age would sound like. If his mother knew he was lying, she at least took his lies as a courtesy.

Before he left the nursing home, he met with the director of the place, a sleepy, almost emaciated middle-aged man in a flawless dark blue suit. Once the director's office door was closed, Seth paid for the next decade in cash.

The bills filled a double-paper shopping bag from a men's store. The massive amount of raw cash seemed to offend the director's finely honed sense of euphemism. He kept swallowing, either from fear or because he was salivating. He made a few protests. "It would be better for our record keeping, if uh…" But Seth insisted. The man kept swallowing, trying to make up his mind with his brow until Seth asked for a handwritten receipt.

"You have to realize that I can't be held responsible if, uh…" But the thin, dry-skinned man finally took the money, wrote a hasty receipt and signed it.

Even at their best, Seth's visits to Connecticut and Long Island felt like vestigial strings connected to a tenderness that had died in him. He tried to justify his long-term vanishing act with money. But that's how his disappearance had begun, using his job to hide from his family. The thing in him knew the secret paths and the natural camouflage of society. It taught Seth quietly, and taught him still.

Suitcases in his trunk, Seth didn't stop back at the apartment. With the Manhattan skyline drifting by to his left, he said good-bye to the last place he could still call home. It would be hotels from then on out. He'd tracked enough men to know it was safer to have no fixed address and few fixed routines. He dropped the bags of personal garbage, the tax receipts, medical records, old letters, Elizabeth's drawings, prescriptions, and old family photos, in a dumpster behind a travel plaza in southern New Jersey. He felt like he could breathe freely after that.

Drifting high above the land and water on the Delaware Memorial Bridge, Seth thought of the last few days. Between child support and the home, Seth's few human bonds were expensive. But not as expensive as being there. It struck him that he may have said his good-byes forever. The thing inside him smiled.

"You made me weep. You made me moan. You made me leave my happy home," the voice on the radio sang.

It was Seth's thirty-eighth birthday. No one called. The Washington obelisk and Capitol Dome emerged from a curve in the highway. The thing inside him smiled.

# PART TWO

*Every exorcist learns during Pretense that he is dealing with some force or power that is at times extremely cunning, sometimes supremely intelligent, and at other times capable of crass stupidity… it is both highly dangerous and terribly vulnerable.*

    -Malachi Martin

    **Hostage to the Devil: The Possession and Exorcism of Five Contemporary Americans**

*…it is certain that temples were deeply involved in issuing early coins, many of which bore the images of sacred animals and deities. This practice continues today with bills and coins bearing the likenesses of deified presidents.*

    -Charles Eisenstein

    **Sacred Economics**

Seth hired William for the new job. Compared with Santa Clara, tailing the mistress was a joke assignment, so it was good to have William there to laugh with. The two of them passed a week in stakeout cars drinking and eating, William telling stories about his days as a half-crooked vice cop in Tampa.

They were watching a woman named Sarah Loire, Mankins' new girlfriend. And she was a neat little package, in her skin-tight yoga pants and leather jacket, a compact brunette with brown eyes, a fast walker.

"Gotta hand it to the old creep. It must be good to be a senator," William said, watching Sarah Loire cross the street next to Seth.

"One of the rewards of a career in public service."

"I would like to service that. Her ass is like two softballs wrestling."

Seth looked at the DMV photo in his lap. A Mediterranean brunette. In the picture, she looked haunted and pale, more yellow than tan. In person, all her features made more sense. Her mouth was big, though her lips thin, her nose aquiline and her eyes jumpy and alert enough to keep the two men wary of getting very close. Even from their safe distance, she seemed preternaturally awake. Her expression always shifting like light on the water when the clouds move fast after a storm.

When she walked near the stakeout car, Seth had to fight the urge not to stare.

"Twice in one day to the same health food store. Man, this bitch may be crazy, but does she have to be boring-crazy?" William said, drinking Irish coffee from a thermos.

"You know, you drink a lot for an Asian guy."

"I'm a proud Hawaiian-Irish-German-Chinese-African American, you prick. You talk *and* drink a lot for an injun."

"I only talk so you'll stop for a goddamn second."

They laughed and William passed the thermos.

"Second time today. Boring-crazy is right. Maybe her acupuncturist told her to get something," Seth said. "I wonder what she says to him."

"I wonder if she's fucking him."

"Only one way to find out," Seth said. "You're going in for acupuncture next time she does."

That was three days in. William was bored and drunk enough not to argue. After a morning yoga class, Sarah stopped into the acupuncturist. William followed a few minutes after. A quick internet search showed the acupuncturist was a middle-aged Korean guy, who offered his treatments a few hours a day, along with seminars on meditation and herbal remedies. About an hour later, William came out, smiling and shaking his head.

"Well, there's no way the acupuncturist is fucking her."

"No way?"

"Nah, the place is wide open. And there's like five or six people in there at a time. Plus, the guy's a fag."

"Really?"

"He has to be. An acupuncturist? Come on. Plus, he kept touching my ass."

"Your ass?"

"He asked what was bothering me and I said my back because it was from sitting in these damn cars all week. But he was rubbing way south."

"What about the needles?"

"What do you think? They're fucking *needles*. They fucking hurt. Not a lot. But not something I'd pay for, either. Here's the receipt, by the way."

"How's your back?"

"It's the goddamned same. That acupuncture shit's for women. It's like astrology or Tarot cards. You ever hear a man say, 'boy, I was all kinds of confused—didn't know up from down, didn't know what to do or how to do it. But then I had this Tarot card reading that really straightened everything out for me'? No, you never have. It's all a bunch of placebo voodoo for soft-headed women."

"What about her, was she talking to the guy?"

"I was on the table next to her. And yeah, she talked, but it was all vague stuff. She said that she thinks she's falling for the wrong type of guy again. But then she started in on how she thinks she's getting a cold from the steam heat in her apartment. Then she rattled on some more about how she thinks her anxiety is getting better, except sometimes when it's a lot worse. Also, she thinks her left side is tenser than her right. She thinks that may be where her cold is coming from."

"And the guy, the acupuncturist, did he seem interested?"

"He was kind of yessing her to death. He seems like he gets yakked at all day. He has to at least act like he's focused on sticking in the pins. He seemed pretty tuned into the fact that she was a pay-what-you-want client."

"Huh."

"Man, you should have heard it. The bullshit in that place is neck-deep. I was on the edge of busting out laughing the whole time. And I've sat through voodoo rituals with crack-bombed Florida assholes with a straight face. I don't think I'm your undercover man for this Patchouli nonsense."

So they went back to following Sarah Loire for the rest of the week, from the yoga classes she taught to the ones she took, from her Adams Morgan apartment to her waitressing job at a hotel bar, to Mankins's Georgetown townhouse, from the health food store to the acupuncturist.

Seth figured he wouldn't know what he was looking for until it was almost too late, so they stayed on her. On the eighth night of their stakeout, she broke from her routine. They followed her, in a cab, to a fairly obvious drug corner in Southeast DC.

"Finally, something. Here we go," William said.

She bought a few items surreptitiously and cabbed to a Northwest apartment by the train station, where, jumpy and wobbly, she leaned on the buzzer of an apartment building until a young, shirtless man came down and asked her to please fuck off. The traffic obscured what else he had to say to her.

From there, Sarah walked a long ways, which was hard to follow in the car, to a bar in DuPont Circle. After a half hour, she left with someone, one of those clean-cut white college grads who seemed vastly overrepresented in Washington's Northwestern quarter. A half-pudgy post-grad, he had on the usual blue shirt, yellow tie, with blonde hair cut close.

Sarah Loire walked a few blocks with the young man, William and Seth circling to keep moving and to stay inconspicuous.

"Deja fucking view," William offered.

The loving couple had stopped to kiss and grope in front of a newly built luxury condominium across the street from the newly built luxury condominium once occupied by the late Eric Eggleston. Seth shivered. They parked illegally but inconspicuously diagonal from the action.

And there, between an SUV and a Smartcar, Sarah Loire dropped swiftly into an athletic crouch and unzipped the blonde guy's fly. His penis was imperceptible from their distance. The tip of his yellow tie played in her brown hair. Blondie blushed and glanced around nervously to see if anyone was watching, but didn't see them. She worked on her new friend for a minute or two, and abruptly stood up. They heard some sibilants from her, some low-pitched noises from him in response. She shoved him and called him a faggot for the whole empty street to hear. He reached for her and she reached for his face. He smacked her arms away and then hit her, open-handed, in the face.

Already wobbly, Sarah Loire went down in a heap.

Between the cars, blondie zipped up and started away, into the building, then thought better of it and pulled her narrow body from between the cars. She was writhing more than struggling as he dragged her onto the sidewalk and up the two stairs to the door of his building. He reached into his pockets and fumbled with his keys.

"Wait here," Seth said to William.

Seth jumped from the car and started across the street. The blonde fratboy saw him coming, and positioned himself in anticipation of the angry-posturing-and-possibly-shoving variety of confrontation common to his kind. Blondie held his arms out and said, "What? What do you want..." as Seth speechlessly drove his fist into his nose. Blondie fell back against the beige brick front of the building and Seth landed another fist in the younger man's mouth. Struggling to breathe through the blood and writhing beside Sarah, Seth stomped the guy in the ribs a few times, feeling something satisfyingly give under his heel.

He threw tiny Sarah Loire over his shoulder and she promptly puked down his back. He carried her to the car and laid her in the backseat.

"Oh man, what if she pukes in the car?" William said, ready to pull out.

"That's what you're for. Go."

They took off fast and had gone a dozen blocks away before Sarah woozily asked where they were going.

"We're taking you home," Seth said.

"You're going to kill me?" she asked, her eyes unfocused and her lip bleeding.

"No."

"No?"

"No. We're taking you to your apartment."

"Cab could've taken me. Why'd you come get me if you're only taking me to my apartment?"

William looked at him and mouthed the word *CRAZY* silently, over and over.

"At least she's not boring," Seth said to him.

"What? Hey, how do you guys even know where I live?"

"We're cops, sweetie," William said.

"I thought you were a cab."

"We're both. We're cab cops," William said in his best Dragnet voice, cracking a smile.

"Liar. You're not taking me home. You're just taking me to my apartment."

They drove the babbling wreck named Sarah Loire back to her apartment. Seth fireman-carried her up the two flights of stairs and through her door. He put her down on the couch and looked for a TV to turn on. But after a quick search, he discovered that Sarah Loire possessed no television.

"Hey, don't go," she said as he was going. "You're the guy, right?"

"What?"

"Are you him?"

"Who?"

"You, cutie. Is that you? You look familiar. Is that you? You my killer?"

"No. I'm only a cabbie. Go to sleep."

---

Madness seemed like a possibility, in the early days after Broken Tooth had died as a man. Given access to the whole of earth, vast swaths of time and even some of the distant planets, the broken-toothed spirit was terrified that he would simply dissolve into the infinite. So he stuck close to his home in the tents, by the bend in the river. And for the most part, time carried him along.

He lost interest in what had been his own life after his last recognizable niece died. After that, he spent time in the nearby walled cities, doing a long stint as god-king before losing interest and retiring to a kind of itinerant godhood. He did favors for those he liked, basking in praise, waxing fat on daily sacrifices, sometimes withdrawing completely and holding out for utter supplication, for some extravagant gesture of cattle or human blood. He was a regional spirit, a daemon in the parlance of the times. He wasn't ambitious, smart, or persistent enough to be mistaken for much more than a minor Olympian.

The funny thing about death, and even moreso about immortality, was how little it changed Broken Tooth. He'd died a teenager and remained primarily mostly interested in sex and mischief, in the sacrifices of mystified mortals and in petty conflicts with his fellow spirits.

Centuries passed. It was all a languorous feast of granted wishes. Each of his whims was made real, carved in stone, or made vivid in desperate human suffering.

The broken-toothed spirit wasn't alone among the more or less omnipotent. At that time, there were as many kinds of spirits as there were men and women who'd ever managed to get out of their human situations. The most famous of them were generally the worst of them, as only the worst of the living or the deathless ever seem to care for fame. They thundered, demanded sacrifices and murdered when they didn't get them. Insecure and maniacally priapic, they were the lousiest company of all the immortals.

The truth was that very few of the gods were right in the head. Nearly all of them were at a loss, having been wrenched from their human condition. Most needed the touch and recognition of living people just to stay half sane. The kindest of them were the spirits whose curiosity hadn't concluded when they escaped their bodies, like The Sigh. He had gone on doing what he did best, teaching. But the pot-bellied deity had learned better than to ever again teach the secret he'd taught his broken-faced pupil.

Seducing women by the rivers, singing in the valleys, promising glory to a seditious general, or ordering a king onward in some mad scheme, the broken-toothed spirit played with the centuries like a child. He knew no consequence, nor did any of them. Their wars were fought by men who'd never understand the deep capriciousness that placed them at the end of a spear.

It was an idyll. And the broken-toothed spirit had no reason to think that it wouldn't last forever.

---

The winter sun was a pale disk in the heavy clouds, the streets wet with winter rain. Half of DC had the day off in case the rain turned to snow. The bars in Adams Morgan were full of people enjoying their snow day.

"Okay, I'll say it. What the fuck was that last night?"

"Which part?" Seth said. He hadn't finished his coffee and hadn't slept well.

"Breaking our cover to go save our blitzed maiden in distress. You remember that part?"

"We still don't know this girl. So say the guy takes her upstairs and she gets raped. So say she goes to the police and she drops her boyfriend's name to get the cops to step lively. So her boyfriend's name goes in a file somewhere. And when something happens to the girl, some cop who was made to step lively says 'hey, this missing bimbo's name rings a bell. Think I'll look it up.' And there's Mankins, in the file. And we have all kinds of work ahead of us."

William paused, thinking it over with his lips moving, and turned to Seth.

"That's why they pay you the big bucks. So tell me, what do you think is up with this bitch?"

"Something's not right. She's got four hours of yoga a day, acupuncture, health food, enemas."

"Enemas?"

"Remember that place with the sign that said 'a private and gentle cleanse'?"

"I thought it was like, a pedicure place or a spa or something."

"So she's got all of her *body-is-a-temple* business six days a week, then the cocaine and whatever the hell else that was last night. Not to mention the health risks that come with her boyfriend. The good news is that she doesn't seem to have too many friends, from the look of it. Thanks for getting those phone records, by the way."

"No problem. What do these health-food types do when they hang out, anyway?"

"Beats me. Compare their shits probably."

"When do you think she's going to get up after last night?"

"I checked the yoga place's website. She's supposed to be teaching a class in a half hour."

As Seth said the words, Sarah Loire left her apartment, head down, hurrying. She wore big sunglasses, along with a purple-and-gold scarf, to cover her blackened eye. She looked like a gypsy bent on revenge as she crossed the street to the juice bar.

"Well, she's a trooper. You have to give her that. So tell me this, boss, what do we do next?"

"Like you said, these people, what the fuck do they talk about? What is she saying to the people in the yoga studio? What's she going tell them about her black eye? I think you should start taking her yoga class."

"No way. I'm up for almost anything, but not that. And I wouldn't last a second in there. I almost died laughing when in the acupuncture place. Hire someone else to take yoga."

Not long after, they saw the silhouettes of hands rising and falling on the ceiling of the second-story yoga studio where Sarah worked. That night, they followed Sarah to Mankins's house in Georgetown. Seth watched as light after light in the townhouse turned on, but not turned off, for a few hours. Flecks of shouting made it to the street.

"Uh oh, trouble in paradise," William said.

"Probably fighting about the black eye."

Before too long, the yelling quieted and the lights in the brownstone flicked off one window at a time. Seth and William took turns napping in the car. A taxi came for Sarah a little after dawn. Wearing a different scarf on her head, she lingered over a long kiss with Mankins, who was at least a foot taller than her. She limped down the stone stairs.

Not long after the car was gone, Mankins came out of the brownstone, dressed in a red-white-and-blue nylon track suit. William didn't wake as Seth started the car. As Seth pulled quietly from the curb, the older man trotted across the street, in front of the car. He and Mankins made eye contact for a moment of freighted pedestrian-and-car courtesy. And Seth could swear that Mankins winked at him.

He drove back to his hotel and left William with the car, giving him the next few days off for Christmas. The holiday wasn't his only reason. Seth could feel a vibration climbing his spine, and knew he was due for a seizure.

His hotel room was high up, the biggest suite they had left. He poured himself a onesy of scotch and leaned his head against the plate glass. He wondered if the hotel windows were thicker in DC or Las Vegas, wondered where in America hotels had the thinnest glass, and if those were the places where the human predicament had found its happiest resolution.

Those were desperate thoughts, meant to evade how the park below, with its intersecting web of paved and improvised walkways, billowed slightly like a spider web in the breeze. The park's homeless victims and petty criminals loitered below, barnacles on the gleaming hull of the ship of state. The trees reached their leafless arthritic fingers in an ugly approximation of cooperation, scraping each other in the cold wind.

The window allowed the sound of a bell being rung persistently and arrhythmically by a man in a Salvation Army apron below. Seth watched the sun set beside the bit of the Capitol Dome his room offered. Finally Seth fell onto the bed and absented himself from what came next.

When it was over, Seth was back in his room, which was the only good thing he could say about the seizure. His hand was bloody from a shallow cut across the palm, and his eye blackened. At first, he thought he was paralyzed, but eventually stirred with some difficulty. He'd done something unfortunate to his lower back and his mouth tasted like he'd been sucking on a battery. Wiping the taste from his tongue with his hand, he found a coin in his mouth. It was a sloppy, very old coin, bulging at its edges. The face on it was pudgy, pointy nosed and pointy chinned, like the caricature of a drunken letch.

Seth tossed the coin down on the hotel carpet, where it bounced without a sound. He turned on the TV. It was Christmas Day. There was a parade for it somewhere or other. Everything moved slowly, tentatively, on the TV, as if its brash populace had grown uncertain of itself overnight.

---

Christmas began the week and New Years ended it. Everything seemed both slowed by the holidays and yet rushed by them. The city was empty. William was in Florida. Sarah Loire was in New Jersey. Mankins was back with his family in California. Seth went to the hotel gym, pedaled in place, lifted weights, working around the pain in his back. Aside from a strained phone call with his distracted daughter, there wasn't much to make it a holiday.

He spent Christmas night in the hotel bar, getting stiff with other willful or rueful exiles from the family. The bar was decorated like a classy website, panels of dark polished wood and colored lights. TVs on every wall poured down cable news from around the globe, informing the denizens of a bar in what was, for the moment, the seat of world power.

Clues emerged from the TV's dull blanket. The manhunt for Jefferson was heating up. The TV showed the big bearded man reading into a camera, with a Betsy-Ross type flag in the background. Stars in a circle. His militia had ambushed a team of bounty hunters and an ATF agent outside of Maybell, Colorado, killing three. The TVs cut to a police officer in uniform being taken into custody by men in suits—who the TVs said tipped Jefferson about the raid.

Seth kept his phone close, hoping that Hurley or Roberto or Frederica would call with something for him to do. But no one did. The cabal was officially on vacation.

He stared at the cable news in the hotel bar, its faces deciphered in the closed captioning, with scrolling news below. And still, it wasn't enough. Seth finished his drink, and ordered another, as if that might somehow make the news move toward its conclusion faster.

The man next to Seth caught him staring at the TV, which ran a short bit about Mankins exploring the possibility of a recall election for governor of California. The closed captioning explained that Mankins had come under fire for suggesting that the state legalize gambling and decriminalize prostitution, along with a handful of other recreational drugs.

The man next to Seth was burly and silver haired. He'd been drinking, but didn't seem drunk. He shook his head at the news.

"Great. California wants to reinvent the wheel again," he said.

"Looks like it," Seth said, downing his bourbon.

"So they're going to legalize everything, pay their bills by selling off the cornerstones of Western civilization and the final ballasts of human desire."

"It might sound crazy if our bills weren't so high."

"Desperate times and desperate measures, I suppose," the big man said, raising his vodka. Seth toasted him and went up to his room, to drink alone.

---

Between the godlike freedom and power that the broken-toothed spirit enjoyed for centuries and its current position surreptitiously manipulating an East Coast lawyer with a bad back, there was a fall.

The thing in Seth first conceived of such a fall one quiet day on the bank of a favorite river. There he saw a spirit that looked like himself, but forlorn and ragged, struggling mightily to stand on the river's opposite shore.

Later that day, the broken-toothed spirit was soaking up the incense and blood fumes he'd earned by doing nothing to disrupt the wedding of a farmer to the daughter of a sailor. One of the wiser spirits wandered past. She was haughty, with strong features, and that same dull glow that The Sigh possessed. She was walking beside a man, generously invisible, speaking softly to him. The man gestured as if explaining something to himself. He stepped in a pile of pig shit and kept on walking and gesturing.

The broken-toothed spirit stopped her and explained what he'd seen on the river bank. She nodded, and told him to travel ahead in time, but do so methodically, in short increments. He'd see what lay ahead. She gave him a dismissive look, and left to go find her pupil, who'd since shaken his head and wandered off to go get drunk and play dice.

Her suggestion seemed ludicrous to the broken-toothed sprit, who'd had centuries to explore all of time and space. And even if he hadn't made the most of the opportunity, he assumed that there couldn't really be any very big secrets that he hadn't uncovered. But when he swam ahead of the current, going slowly, ten years at a time, he soon found a time where he was unwelcome.

He stopped there, and tried to visit the glade by his favorite river. It looked the same, but the air seemed harder to breathe. The ground seemed to sting his feet. The place filled him with the inexplicable feeling of being hunted. Soon, he found an old woman, with an oversized wooden pail full of dirty clothes. The broken-toothed spirit approached, meaning to demand an explanation from her. But she couldn't see him.

When he spoke, she paused, and looked around as if she heard something, but couldn't be sure. Without putting down her pail, she stopped, kissed her hand and made a gesture. The simple act of the old, superstitious woman hit him in the gut with a nausea so intense that it blinded him. When his sight returned, he was back at the time and place where he'd begun his travels.

Being forcibly removed from his river by the simple gesture of a washerwoman filled the broken-toothed spirit with dread. He kept on as he had—here as Anubis, there as a wild idea that must be acted upon, here as Mercury, there as a toothless stranger who visits in the night and leaves a fortune behind, here as Dis, there as a sensation in the quiet light of afternoon that makes men stop and back away, here as Hermes, there as an inexplicable pregnancy.

It still had centuries. The women helped somewhat, the wars helped somewhat, the building and destruction of temples helped somewhat. Its life had become a mere balm.

---

After a few days drifting between the hotel bar and the hotel gym, Seth was eager to get back to work, no matter what that work was. It was New Year's Eve. He drove to Adams Morgan, to the yoga studio where Sarah Loire taught. Its website said Sarah was due to teach that day's lone class. It was only five when he got to the studio, but the sun was down. Seth rang the buzzer and climbed the stairs.

He felt a wave of nauseous anticipation over whether Sarah would recognize him, and a general anxiety about interacting with anyone after the week of isolation. The place was dimly lit and reeked of sweat, sage, and lavender. The receptionist was a lanky blonde with a precise haircut and an accent Seth couldn't quite place. On the wall behind her, a Buddha sat on a floating lotus. She seemed to say "You shouldn't mess with us, of course," smiling in a vague way.

"Excuse me."

"Have you practiced with us before?"

"Oh, no."

She gave him a clipboard with a form that he filled with lies. As he wrote, Sarah Loire arrived, shed her parka and stood before him, bending in purple pants to talk to the blonde. She wore a headscarf to distract from the yellow and purple that still ringed her bloodshot eye. Seth finished the form and paid the blonde, sliding past Sarah Loire.

"How was your holiday?" the blonde asked.

"It was, uh, a challenge. But a good challenge," Sarah responded. "You know?"

"I totally do."

Beyond them, Seth saw that a paunchy Asian woman in shiny leggings was already in the classroom, doing slow preparatory calisthenics. Sarah turned to Seth and introduced herself. He took off his coat.

"Is this your first time here?" she asked Seth, looking into his eyes without any sign of recognition.

"Yeah. It's actually the first time I've done yoga."

"Oh, a yoga virgin. That's exciting," she said, smiling faintly, as though obligated, at her own joke.

"If you say so."

"So do you have any injuries I should know about?"

"My lower back is hurting. I wrenched the hell out of it the other day."

"Oh, how did you do that?"

Probably breaking into a museum, retail store, or private residence to steal an ancient coin while in an inexplicable fugue state.

"I was helping a friend move.

"And how did you get that?" she asked, gesturing inadvertently to the faded sepia sunset of bruising above her darting brown eye.

"Hit it with a cabinet. You?" Seth said.

"Same," she said, giving him a conspiratorial smile.

And flashing in him as it had the night when he'd carried her home was an unexpected familiarity, accompanied by a yet-stranger sense that the two of them had embarked upon a fixed series of events.

Seth shed his shoes, socks, and jacket and followed her into the classroom, where the paunchy Asian lady was on her back, breathing irregularly.

"Are you going to practice in that?" Sarah asked, gesturing to Seth's khakis and polo shirt.

"Oh, is that all right?"

"It might be a little constricting. Um, hang on one second."

She returned with an oversized pair of PENN STATE sweatpants and a T-shirt someone had made for a wedding four years ago.

"They're from the lost and found. But they should be all right."

In strange, unwashed clothes and very far from his element, he followed Sarah as she drifted on the balls of her feet across the hardwood floor to the front of the classroom.

"Well, the class is small tonight. New Years. But that's a good thing. It's an opportunity for us to really tune in on our intention. That might be a person who needs our help, or a goal we want to achieve. So let's fix that in our minds and focus on our breathing."

Immediately, the thing in Seth responded violently, agitating against every passing sensation.

*What the fuck?* Seth couldn't help but think, the blasphemy reflex of the thing inside of him lighting up. *Am I supposed to focus on my goal, or a friend, or my breathing? That's the thing about focus is that it can only really go one place at a time. It's actually what* focus *means. What a dumb hippie joke of a waste of time.*

They sat and breathed a moment before she had them say a few Oms, which Seth resented. The broken-toothed spirit saw to it that the whole thing rubbed him the wrong way. Seth wanted to get up and leave, but he'd already attracted enough attention by showing up, dressed wrong, to an empty class. Sarah Loire guided him up into a triangle, with his hands and feet on the ground. He was in that position until his shoulders started to burn.

"Breathe in," she said, and paused for what seemed like an unnatural span of time. "Now breathe out."

*Don't tell me to breathe. You fucking breathe. I've been breathing my whole life just fine without your goddamn help.* The thing in him, so quiet on a jog or when lifting weights, cursed every mild discomfort that the she had to suggest. Seth's only consolation was in stealing glances at her ass here and there.

Sarah patiently guided him into other, more precarious and demanding positions, her hands on his shoulders, pulling them away from his ears, her knee in his back, pushing him forward. Seth had been a basketball player—had gotten a scholarship for it, and starred in rec leagues until not long ago. He was an athlete, and was shocked at how difficult the simple stretches were. He had to stop cursing Sarah and stop looking at her body, and really focus on not falling over with his hands locked behind his back and his head below his knee. Sarah and the Asian lady made him look like a badly built Frankenstein as he groped for his toes, drenched in sweat.

But over the next hour, in the dim light, something changed. His blasphemy reflex diminished and his breathing slowed.

At the end of the class, lying in the darkness, Sarah came to him and rubbed a few drops of oil on his head. The thing inside him withered, and almost seemed to vanish for a moment. In that moment, Seth felt at ease in the confines of his body and his situation. Afterward, changing out of the used and discarded workout wear, he felt disoriented from everything that had brought him there that night.

Sarah and the Asian lady drank tea in their yoga wear, chatting with the receptionist when he emerged.

"My dietician, who's Ayurvedic, says that in the winter you should eat a lot of walnuts, because they're good for your lungs. And nature's way of telling us that is that they even *look* like lungs," the Asian lady with the shiny legs said.

"That's like how you're supposed to eat eggplant during your period, because it looks like a uterus," the receptionist offered.

So this is where the term wives' tales comes from, Seth thought.

"Sorry, I didn't mean to interrupt. I'm going to head out and I wanted to give you back these clothes and to thank you."

"Did you like it?" Sarah Loire asked.

"I did. My back feels better. Do you teach here often?"

"I teach here a few days a week. But I also do private lessons."

She handed him a class schedule and a business card that she'd had in her hand. She smiled at him, but so did everyone else in that place. Seth got the sense that to be unhappy or unfriendly was to let on that you weren't enlightened. And that was a no-no in yoga land. So he smiled back.

———————

The broken-toothed spirit squandered his last decades of relative omnipotence soaking up the blood, the praise, and the many excesses of a particularly good civil war in Italy.

The cold morning, he'd always remember it as. He drifted through the dawn light to the bed of a young woman, the daughter of a Centurion. He'd seen her in the street and planned to visit that morning for the usual sensual pleasures. In her room, he tried to emerge from the airy latency by which he flitted to and fro. He reached for her, but could not touch. To put it bluntly, he couldn't get it up. He remained intangible and frustrated, as she woke and went into the next room for breakfast.

That day, the broken-toothed spirit went to town and lingered by one of his crossroad shrines. But his senses had faded nearly as much as he'd faded to the world. He could barely taste the smoke or the blood offered there. He couldn't menace the men or grope the women. That day, the broken-toothed spirit saw his peers in the streets, displaced and wandering from temple to temple, pulling at their hair and gnashing their teeth. The kinder ones were more dignified, but no less devastated.

The wise immortal woman who'd warned him years ago staggered past, following after her student. The student started a gesture and stopped, muttered a half sentence and gave up. She yelled, pled for his attention, repeating some secret phrase they'd shared at the top of her lungs. And for a moment, the student seemed to hear something, but shrugged it off.

He exchanged a look with the once-sparkling tutelary deity. She'd lost her radiance and looked strangely dirty, with tear-tracks in the dust on her face. She nodded blankly at him and kept on after her student.

What was worse was that on that cold morning most men and women didn't even miss the gods. There was no hue and cry that day. People simply went on with their lives. And before long, they assumed that the gods had always been so invisible, so mute, that the shrines had always been either a harmless waste or a quaint custom.

Back in the hotel that night, Seth stretched out on the hotel bed and turned on the TV. The class had strenuously disoriented him, and had left him with the sense of being cared for in a small way. The thing in him settled into a campaign of shame about how ridiculous he'd looked, trying to contort himself in his lost-and-found clothes, and how bad at the poses he'd been.

Seth picked at his room service cheeseburger and iceberg wedge. He looked up the next class Sarah would teach. Outside, the city was gearing up for a new year, yelling and honking horns. Sealed behind thick glass, fifteen stories above it, the celebration sounded like an extension of the TV, which spoke of more dead in Wyoming and Colorado at the hands of Jefferson's militia. FBI and bystanders. The TV quoted sources who said that authorities were considering an airstrike against the militia's suspected stronghold in Wyoming. The Wyoming governor condemned the notion, and the FBI quickly disavowed its own leak.

A chant drifted up from the street, along with indecipherable lyrics to a TV theme song sung by a chorus of amateur-hour drinkers. Seth wondered how he got so old, drifting off before the fireworks. The next day the TV said that one of the explosions that scratched the surface of his sleep was no firework. It was a bomb outside the IRS building on the National Mall. A group of Idahoans, representing "The Free States of America," took credit.

The next day passed slowly with more TV. It told Seth that Mankins had driven from Los Angeles to Las Vegas with a quarter pound of reefer, which he handed over, in a well-publicized ceremony, to the governor of Nevada. He publicly dared the DEA or any other federal agency to do anything about it. The feds condemned but otherwise ignored the stunt. It caused a stir, especially among the news channel's professional shit-stirrers.

On TV, Mankins was a different man from the one Seth had met. His face was alive with a dozen different types of smile. His eyes sparkled. The crowd at his Las Vegas speech seemed spellbound and energized by the tall, loud man.

And there Seth was, stuck in DC, bored out of his mind on mistress-babysitting duty, far from the action.

He parked two blocks away from the yoga studio, an hour early, and wandered through the cold. The town had the day off, and mostly spent it hungover. He remembered being young and going to a city and wanting to climb in through every lit window to taste the lives he imagined in each one, to climb into a million and one private debaucheries. But the windows he walked by all seemed lit by the flickering blue light of Bowl Games.

When he passed through the bead curtain of the yoga studio, Sarah Loire seemed both annoyed and relieved. She was drinking tea and chatting with the blonde receptionist.

"So, anyway, that's why I know I was a cat in my last life," the receptionist said, scowling at Seth and drinking her tea.

"Hey, someone made it," Sarah said in a voice that seemed almost like a taunt.

"I thought we'd get to go home early," the receptionist said, smiling through her disappointment, as if she was too enlightened to really ever be disappointed.

"And you remembered your clothes," Sarah said, in what seemed like that same taunting tone.

Seth was aroused, the thing inside of him was enraged. It spoke to Seth in a voice that barely passed for his own. *That's right, you remembered your fucking sweatpants. You have argued the law and ended men's lives with impunity. So yes, you are capable of remembering your god-fucking sweatpants,* the millennia-old spirit raged to Seth.

"Yeah, I did. Is there still class—even if it's only me?" he said.

"That's the rule. So it looks like you'll get a private class after all."

The receptionist raised her eyebrows and effectively vanished into the internet. In the warm, dark classroom, Seth sat on the floor. Sarah closed the door behind him.

"So what brings you to yoga?"

"Like I said, my back, mostly."

"Right, your back. How is it?"

"It's a little better."

"And how's your eye?" she asked.

"It's fine. Yours?"

"Better."

In her black leggings and orange tank top, she padded out before him. Leaning over to light a candle with a match, he saw the tattoo on her lower back—*Born Homesick*—in a large, calligraphic strand. She smiled the bland, safe smile that was the only expression he seemed to see in the yoga place.

"Now close your eyes," she said.

He thought about fucking her. He thought about the limp-dicked jackass she'd tried sucking off between the parked cars. He thought of the destruction Mankins wrought on his last girlfriend, about what the senator probably did to her on a regular basis. The lewd dudgeon of the thing inside him had its way with his idle thoughts, summoning animals—snakes and anteaters—to fuck her. He imagined her face splitting open lengthwise in a perverse and supernatural orgasmic groan.

He peeked from his meditation and it all stopped. Sarah Loire, he noticed only then, looked a lot like the girl Mankins had killed. And Seth was filled with pity and fear for her, as well as shame at the state of his own mind.

"Focus on your breathing. If there's someone you want to send your intention to tonight, to help with your practice, think of them."

The broken-toothed spirit raged. *You should help yourself, lady. Your boyfriend is going to play with you until you break and I'm going to have to drive your body off to be buried in the shallow foundation of a cheap McMansion in some godforsaken bedroom community.*

Surprised and repulsed by his own mind, Seth thought *I should help her.* The idea seemed at odds with his job, but was it? He began to ponder the many impossible angles of it.

"Now try to be present to what's happening right now, in your body, in your breathing. Just let your thoughts go."

She was behind him now, working her fingers in the space behind his ears, down the sides of his neck, pressing down and forward on the folds of muscle between his neck and shoulders. At her touch, his shoulders seemed to drop by an inch or two. On his hands and feet, legs straight, and Sarah pulled on the creases of his hips. He lowered his head to raise his ass higher and felt his neck crack like a fist full of dice had gone limp. From there, she took him through a series of positions, coaxing him through inflexibility and soreness, guiding his body with her hands. His blasphemous reflex waned whenever the pain or the relief was at its most intense.

Lying on the floor in the "corpse" pose, he felt an upwelling of wild, hateful thoughts, for Sarah Loire and for the whole world. The thing inside of Seth conjured images of mountains exploding like swollen pustules. It showed a tableau of Hurley, Frederica, William, Dolores, himself, and his daughter all hung disemboweled from the same gallows, while Mankins jerked off in benediction and the world burned. The thing inside him conjured a vision of Seth coasting above a world made into hell itself, riding on an oversized credit card like a magic carpet.

Sarah squatted above him and the thoughts quieted, as though in fear they might be heard. He didn't dare open his eyes. The broken-toothed spirit raced for further curses, blasphemies, but was drowned out by her touch as she pushed his shoulders down. He could smell her stale sweat and some faint, deeper smell of her as well, like urine and rust. She press oil on his head, pressing it up from the space between his eyebrows and then across. His barbaric fantasies blinked out completely, and for a moment he became content with his seat at the table of the living.

They sat and chanted a few Oms. She said a few foreign words and they bowed. He thanked her and changed back into his street clothes. Torn between wanting to make an impression and wanting to remain unnoticed, he waved and left.

"Hey, wait a second. You don't live around here, do you?" she called to him.

"No, I'm downtown."

"Can I get a ride? I'm going over that way," Sarah Loire said, smiling a little.

"Yeah. Sure."

Seth waited downstairs, in the light of the craft shop, where a group of homely young women knitted and drank tea.

"Hey, John. John?"

Seth turned, having forgotten the name he gave upstairs.

"Yeah. Yeah."

"I'm ready. Let's go."

They walked through the damp cold of the swamp capitol, its streets wide and its buildings equally bland in their charm or in their seriousness.

"We don't see a lot of guys like you at the studio, not more than once," Sarah Loire said, slowing her pace.

"Oh? What kind of guys are those?"

"I don't know. You're a big guy, straight, you don't say much about yourself. You're, well, a guy."

"Huh."

"See, that's what I mean. Most men I know would take that as an opportunity to talk about themselves, a little controlled boasting. They would try to *charm* a lady a little. So why did you come to the class?"

They locked eyes in the cold streetlight by his car. Seth tried to choose the most advantageous lie, calculate the consequences of the flirtation. But he couldn't. The fact was that Sarah excited him, and that made it hard to think. Despite his better judgment, and despite the shrill voice of the thing inside of him that screamed for him to stop, he was entranced.

111

That she could quiet the voice inside of him was no small part of the excitement.

"Like I said, I hurt my back. And I'd heard good things about yoga. Here's the car."

"Oh, right, your back. And why are you giving me a ride then?"

"You asked me to."

"Unbelievable," she said and turned from the car. Angry, her too-awake expression became severe, and even more beautiful. Seth knew her anger was a ploy. But that didn't stop it from working.

"Hey, what do you want? Come on. I'll buy you a drink. We can talk. We can talk about anything, even why I'm giving you a ride," Seth said, disarmed.

"No. You have things to do. I have things to do. I'm sure we're both really busy," she said, pronouncing the word *busy* like it was a curse in a foreign language.

"Enough, okay? Get in the car. We can figure out the things that we each have to do once we're out of the cold."

She rolled her eyes and dug her hands into her parka pockets. Seth walked around the car, opened her door and gestured for her to climb in. That made her smile. She got in and he closed the door after her. They drove toward downtown, the peak of the Washington Monument peeping out at intersections among the row houses and storefronts.

"So, can I buy you a drink?" Seth said, breaking the silence.

"Yes, you can. Where do you live?"

"Right now, I'm at the Sheraton."

Seth valeted the car and they went inside. Sarah seemed perfectly comfortable in her black tights, loose parka and headscarf. But Seth was profoundly aware of his middle-class anonymity cracking, first by his own black eye, and now by her. He smiled easily at Sarah and decided to change hotels the next day. In the bar where he'd passed Christmas, the TVs burped that the daughter of an Air Force colonel in Nevada had been kidnapped. Sarah ordered a vodka martini with no vermouth. Seth ordered a bourbon.

"So what are we going to talk about?" she said, but playfully now.

"It's either the weather or your life story. You pick."

And so it began. It wasn't a monologue—Seth interrupted enough to move the story along and steer her towards the interesting parts. Sarah Loire—middle, upper-middle class, Central New Jersey. Private school, UCLA and drugs, back to Jersey for a year before going to upstate New York to finish college. Followed boyfriend down to DC. Found a job at a non-profit, was disheartened to learn how little money went to the supposed beneficiaries, got depressed, cheated on her then-fiancé with his best friend, moved out, quit her job, started taking pills. A second rehab and back to DC to try to work things out with the ex, but no dice, waited tables and got certified as a yoga instructor.

Seth kept asking questions. It kept him from having to answer any. Lies were hard to remember. It helped that he liked listening to her, really liked watching her speak. Something was happening, something surprising, unsanctioned and possibly dangerous. Hurley had been right about that much: Sarah Loire was a wild card.

"So, here I am, teaching, and I'm helping people, I think. And it is. It's a good thing. It makes people healthy. It makes them calm. It's so hard to be calm. Everyone I know, even most of the yoga people, they have panic attacks, like all the time. I don't calm down very easily. I don't think anyone does anymore. It's like, even with all the shit with the stock market dive bombing every other day and the endless wars in the Middle East, everyone is still waiting for the other shoe to drop, like everyone knows the boat is leaking…"

Her eyes departed from Seth, drifted past his ear and upwards. He wondered what she was looking at, until he saw it, above her shoulder, on a flat-screen TV mounted there. Seth turned to look at the screen she was watching, and it was the same thing. It was Mankins. The closed captioning below his face misspelled his announced intention to try to win the governor's seat in a special election in the spring. "CALIPH ORNERY YAH SIMPLE YE CANT WAIT," the letters imperfectly translated below his earnest, slightly puffy face.

"Do you know him?" he asked.

"No. Well, I met him once, when I was waitressing."

"Nice guy?"

"Not really. Well, it's hard to tell. Anyway, so how about you?" she asked.

Seth told a bowdlerized version of his life—divorced lawyer in town indefinitely for a big client. It was easier to remember.

"I thought you were a spy?"

"That's good. I'm glad I can still pass for dashing, even in sweatpants from the lost and found."

She smiled, her eyes flaring.

"You can. You seem like a secret agent. Anyway, next time, I pick the place. I mean, this bar is terrible. All these TVs, these lights. It's not even really a place. It's like a bar for the twenty-first century idea of people, you know?"

"I'm not sure I do."

"It used to be that people were real, like trees and furniture. They were there. Now it's like we're all particles—protons, electrons, signals spinning and shooting across the earth, going too fast to do much except continue in the direction we were pushed. It makes me tired to think about. I think I need to lie down."

"Okay. I can take you home."

"No. I don't think I need to go home. You said you were staying here, right?"

Oddly, Seth found himself more excited about the fact that she wanted to spend more time with him than about the prospect of unwrapping her body. Something was happening. As the elevator doors opened, dumbstruck Seth cursed his damning, easily discovered first lie. The thing inside him said to take her, fuck her, and double down with another lie if she found out about the first. But its voice didn't have its usual traction that night. He paused at the door, between kisses, the room's key card in his hand.

"Listen, before you come in, I have to tell you something. My name's not John."

"It sounds weird, but I kind of didn't think it was. What is it?"

The broken-toothed spirit spouted a dozen prophylactic pseudonyms for him to use. It begged him to please take one.

"Seth."

"You don't seem like a Seth."

"I know. I haven't seemed like a Seth since I was fourteen."

"That's sweet, you telling me," she said, and touched his face.

"Are you sure you want to come in?"

"Is there anything else you want to tell me?"

"I don't know. Not right now. Will you come in?"

"Yes I will, Seth."

For the first time in years, he wanted to tell someone everything. He slid the key card into the slot and opened the hotel room door. Sex seemed a foregone conclusion, one that could wait. They stretched out on the bed and kissed, climbing over each other for better purchase. Clothing came off as a matter of course. Her body was a wonder of clean lines, ribs rising parallel to taut breasts, her back a smooth wonder of interlocking muscles, shadows in the tattooed clefts above her ass. And when they finally began the act in earnest, she was a live wire, bending in places Seth had forgotten could bend. But through the caresses and bites, the democratic quid-pro-quo of their carrying on, her eyes didn't truly light up, her breath didn't ignite with voice, and she didn't come until she'd placed his hands on her throat and pressed them there. That was when she really bucked and thrashed, flailed and ululated in a strangled gargle until Seth began to fear he might accidentally kill her.

At the end, she breathed heavily and blinked into space. And he was gently disoriented, wondering how badly he'd screwed up his assignment, and having a hard time caring. Something was happening. He didn't feel like himself, in a good way.

"That was nice," he offered.

"You're nice. It's a surprise."

"A surprise, huh?"

"Yeah, a surprise. You didn't seem nice."

"I didn't seem like a Seth, either."

"I guess you still don't. So what happened when you were fourteen?" Sarah Loire asked.

"What?"

"When you were fourteen? You said you hadn't seemed like a Seth since you were fourteen."

"Yeah. Seth was my mother's idea. She was a hippie, protester and all that. Seth was the name of one of her protester friends who died young. I don't know if he was a boyfriend or what. The guy wrote poetry, played guitar, organized demonstrations and so on. I guess he took a bad beating at a rally and died of peritonitis a few days after. Anyway, I wasn't like him."

"What were you?"

"I was anything but that. I was a straight arrow, an honor student and a varsity athlete. We lived near an Indian reservation in Connecticut because of my dad. But I went to a Catholic high school over in Westerly, in Rhode Island. It was a better school if you wanted to get noticed for a scholarship and so on. When I was fourteen, I guess I was a sophomore. It was early December and a friend of mine, an older guy from the football team, says he'll give me a ride home. Well, on the way, we stop and meet some of his friends at a McDonald's parking lot. Westerly's that kind of place, with nowhere really to go. I knew some of these guys from school, or from football or basketball. And some of them—my friend, another guy I know and a guy I don't know—are going to the train tracks by the mall to help out another guy, a guy I hardly knew, who was going to fight some guys from another school. I was as big as them, but I was the youngest in the group and I wanted to fit in, I guess. So we get to the train tracks, and we can see the guys we're supposed to fight down under a highway overpass, smoking cigarettes and pacing. The guy I don't know takes out a kitchen knife. He's crazy, jumping up and down, screaming that he's going to stab someone on the face. So four of these guys come out of the shadow of the underpass, towards us. And the crazy guy charges at them. We follow, and by the time we get there, the crazy guy's been knocked flat by this other guy with a baseball bat. So I'm in there, throwing punches when someone hits me from behind. Next thing I know I'm on the ground, and I see the knife, and I grab it. Then the guy who hit me comes crashing down on me. I remember him pushing my face into the rocks in the railroad bed, and I had the knife in my hand. I was squeezing the plastic handle. I reached around and stabbed this guy in the ear, and he rolled off of me. He was holding his ear, not paying attention to much else at that moment. I climbed on top of him stabbed him in the neck, and one more time, I think. Someone yelled that the cops were coming, and I threw the knife away and we all ran off. I found out later that the guy was dead."

"Oh my God. Did you get caught?"

"Yeah, sort of. They brought me in and most of the other guys. They questioned us for hours. My buddy from the team fingered me to the police. And I learned not to say anything. My parents got me a lawyer, a good one. They gave their savings to that guy. They mortgaged the house. Not they, really, it was more my mother. Eventually, they dropped the charges. The crazy guy who brought the kitchen knife wound up taking the rap. But by then, my dad was gone, mom lost the house, and I had to change schools. But I got my scholarship."

"Wow. You tell all the girls this?"

"No. Not even my ex-wife. Not the whole thing, now that I think of it."

"So why are you telling me?" Sarah asked, running an index finger along his ribs.

"You know, I don't know."

117

*Exactly. What the fucking hell are you doing?* the broken-toothed spirit screeched as Sarah Loire bent to kiss him. She spread her palm over his chest. Seth felt relieved for a reason he couldn't identify.

---

At the few crossroad shrines that still stood, the broken-toothed spirit whispered unheard to the young women. It was a fine, warm afternoon that he couldn't enjoy. He held his breath as a procession of priests passed. Mankind's indifference had become an obsession with repudiating the old gods. And his life had degraded into insult after injury after insult. Once the procession had passed, the broken-toothed spirit saw, to his surprise, The Sigh. Though still fat and upright, he also looked tired and dirty. His eyes seemed to wobble in his head.

"I thought I'd find you here. But I hoped I wouldn't. You have to leave town," The Sigh said. His face was streaked, as if from tears, and his face slack. He clearly wasn't accustomed to life in the cities.

"But this is my home. Where can I go?"

"Your home has become something between a closed store and a penitentiary. You have to leave. You can still go anywhere, even out past the Earth. I hear that there are other planets untouched by the Catastrophe."

"Is that where you're going?"

"I've been on the earth too long to leave. I'm going east, over the mountains. I'm exhausted. And this new world is intolerable. I think if I can get away from the crosses for a minute and think... I just need a minute to think."

"What's different in the east?"

"There are no crosses there. Not yet. These things... they make me so disheartened, so nauseous. And beyond the mountains, there won't be so many reminders of how life used to be. It could be the people there handled the change differently, and they can still listen. I just need a minute to think."

"Do you really think that's possible?"

"I don't know. I just need a minute to think," The Sigh said, shaking its head. "No. No. I don't know what good going east will do me. But would you like to come?"

"East, west, it won't matter. Can you teach me a way back? I can still go there, but only for a little while. And it keeps getting harder."

"I wish I could help you. But I can't go back more than a few years at a time. I'm losing the old time altogether."

"I'm going to stay here," the broken-toothed spirit said.

"You never were made for teaching. But you had that rare talent. Sometimes I wonder if you hate me for teaching you."

The broken-toothed spirit said nothing. The Sigh too tired and sat beside him. A woman sacrificed a sick-looking chicken with one foot at the shrine. They made what passed as small talk for a pair of dispossessed gods. The Sigh said maybe the creators had returned and repaired the weave of their creation, so no one could get in or out again.

Every impotent immortal who wasn't too dispirited to speak had its own theory, all plausible enough.

Most of the former deities turned religious before long, glomming onto the mystery cults that flourished after the cold morning. There they found the last places that men and women would still listen hard enough to hear their faded voices. The most aggressive of those cults centered on a man who'd lived around the time of the change. And in the Jesus cult, the spirits found employment performing what small feats of suggestion or airy apparition they could still manage in the name of one of the young religion's new strongmen or saints. It was a way to win back some morsel of attention, to continue to exist. Other spirits went farther, believing they deserved their baleful situation after abusing their power so long. As the new faith suggested, they atoned and served.

But among the spirits, the backlash to the new faith was more common. Coincidence or not, they blamed their disenfranchisement on Christ and his cult. They swore to undo the new religion and destroy its practitioners. And in their hatred, they became more devout than the believers.

The broken-toothed spirit was too cowed to take a side. The cross, the right angles, the singularity of it all, spoke to him not of Jesus, but of a single predominant world, a grid extending forever, closing over him and every aberration like him. The Jesus story never made much sense to the broken-toothed spirit. But the anti-Christian spirits seemed to do themselves more harm than they did to anything else. Both sides seemed to miss the point, which was that the good times were gone, probably forever.

The broken-toothed spirit malingered at the spots where its few shrines stood, chased off by crosses and sneaking back like a stray dog.

---

Seth's cell phone woke him, with its annoying, looping scale of a ringtone.

"I'm at my office. And you need to get here now," Hurley said, enunciating each crisp, hard syllable.

"Sure, uh, twenty minutes."

"No. Now. And Seth, bring the fucking coin."

Hurley hung up. Seth pulled the curtain. Sarah stirred, murmuring in the bed. It was very early. The sun was too low to do much but hint at daytime in the overcast sky.

"Sarah, get up. It's time to go."

"Let me sleep. It's a hotel."

"I'm sorry, but I can't do that. We both have to go."

He washed quickly and hurried into a suit. Sarah went into the bathroom. Seth was about to hurry her along with a knock when he remembered the coin. Still too bleary to properly wonder how Hurley knew about it, he began rummaging through his bags, and behind furniture, finally finding it under the bed. He said a bleary good-bye and gave

Sarah a hasty kiss outside the elevators, breaking away to run for a cab.

The heat in the cab was too high and the NPR too loud. The nasal, painfully conscientious voice said "Mankins," and "the value and viability of Federalism." But Seth couldn't be bothered. It was early and he was scared. He called on the thing inside of him, which he could count on to see around corners and which had steered him from trouble since he was fourteen. He silently asked if he should skip this meeting, then skip town. Hurley's organization controlled the building. Anything could happen, and that wasn't good news.

The thing inside him said to go to the meeting,

Seth made his way through the newly formidable security procedures in the lobby and past the hulking modern caduceus statue, with its branches and skyline. It was too early for anyone but Hurley and his secretary to be in the office. Nonetheless, she made him wait five minutes. In that time, he puzzled at his situation, at the ancient coin in his sweaty hand. His seizures, while they'd left him in many strange places, had never interfered with his professional life.

The secretary, answering no phone and responding to no visible signal, finally told Seth to go in. Hurley was standing by the window, the one with the view of the Capitol, which was brightening with the sun's winter-dim orange light.

"The coin, first off," Hurley said.

Seth handed it over. Hurley nodded his head toward a chair that faced his desk. Seth sat. Hurley examined the coin.

"Well?"

"You want to know how I got the coin?"

"The cameras got most of that. The rest I'll attribute to your skill as a thief. That's one part of your resume I didn't know about. But I guess I'm more interested in why you broke into my home."

"First off, I'm sorry. This is embarrassing. It's not something I bring up, not something I usually have to, but I have seizures. And sometimes they're more than that. They're more like a fugue state. I do things that I don't remember, things that don't make sense. Like this, with the coin. I don't think I even know where you live here in town, at least consciously."

"I don't think we've ever had you over. But you didn't take the coin from my house in Woodley Creek. You took it from my summer house in Annapolis. And that house isn't even in my name."

"Huh. That's what I mean. These things can be strange."

Hurley took a deep breath.

"Does this happen often?"

"It comes and goes. I'll have two seizures in a month, and then I won't have any for a year. There's no real pattern."

"Hmm. Do you ever find that you know things that you shouldn't—even couldn't—know?"

"Like intuition?"

"No, not like intuition. More than that. Actually knowing *specific* information that you have no way of knowing, or even deducing. Like how to find the house in Annapolis."

"Sometimes."

"I guess you wouldn't have survived your many escapades without some guidance. Seth, I understand."

With those words, the thing in Seth *saw* the understanding. Hurley stood below a spirit much like itself, dressed in a dirty radiance. Finally revealing itself, the spirit nodded to the thing inside of Seth.

It all made sense, clearly to the broken-toothed spirit, though only dimly to Seth. His connection to Hurley had always been about more than the money, or the opportunity. The thing in Seth had been drawn to Hurley for another reason, a kinship that its gambit with the coin had finally confirmed. It had been centuries since the broken-toothed spirit had seen that familiar face. Its name was Petronius.

"I understand," Hurley repeated to Seth.

Seth stared down at his folded hands. But Hurley kept on.

"How long have you been having the seizures for?" Hurley asked Seth.

"Since I was in high school, fourteen, fifteen."

"You go to a doctor about them?"

"In college. I got X-Rays, MRIs, EEGs, the whole program. They gave me some drugs. But the drugs didn't seem to help, and I didn't like the side effects."

"People are funny creatures. They know things they shouldn't, while being blind to what's right in front of them," Hurley said, leaning back in his leather desk chair.

"I'm not sure I follow."

"I'm sure it must have struck you as strange that I asked as much of my lawyer as I have of you."

"It did at first."

"Well, I have my own way of knowing things I shouldn't. For instance, I knew you could do the things that you've done. And I knew that you would do them. You haven't blinked once, throughout this whole adventure."

"I was only doing my job."

"It's a hell of a job. Killing takes a lot. Most people can't. They get sick when the time comes. They'll do anything to get out of doing it. Or they break down once they actually pull it off. The ones who can do it and live with it—most of them can't pass muster at Ritaloo Fastuch, or anywhere else. Killing undermines their values, destroys the *sense* they make of the world. Most people will confess the first chance they get. They'll spend their lives in a cage to get some of that sense back."

"So what's your point?"

"I get it. You think I dug up your juvenile record—the one you paid so much to have expunged. Well I did. But that's not how I knew you could do this job."

Seth's stomach sank. The thing inside of him retreated and did its best to scatter Seth's attention, to keep him from listening to what came next. But it was no use.

"I think you can do this job so well because you're not alone in there," Hurley said. The words filled Seth filled with a dizzying unease. He became keenly aware of how closely Hurley watched his response. He forced an offhand grin to his lips.

"I don't know about all of that," Seth said. "I like the action, though."

"Well, think about it. Try to look at it as a gift, I think you'll find that it's an advantage you could probably get more out of."

"I guess so. I never thought about it in those terms. I always saw it as a disability, a health problem."

"And you're not completely wrong. These things inside of us. Sometimes I think they don't care if we live or die. But they are useful. They've been around a long time and they can see things we can't. You have to manage them. For you, I think it's a matter of opening up a dialogue. Do that, and I think your seizures will stop. Next time you're about to have a seizure, try talking to it. Ask it what it wants."

"Okay."

"Okay?"

"Okay. Thanks. I mean, I'll think about it. But as long as we're speaking freely, I might as well ask. Where does this business end up, for you, me, Mankins, the colonels?"

"I'm sure you have most of the picture from Frederica and the rest of them out west. In short, this business of ours ends with nothing less than a fresh start, a place of our own, a new country with room to think—the kind that we haven't had in a very long time. What we're after is nothing less than a break with history, an escape into a new period in which everything is possible again."

Hurley locked eyes with Seth, and everything that had occurred since he was fourteen began to make a kind of sense. Seth looked down and wiggled his toes inside of his shiny leather shoes.

"So we're starting a civil war?"

"Not necessarily. Not if we do it right. That's why we're setting the stage as carefully as we are. We want a peaceful break, and a prosperous one, too."

"By having a dozen or so nearly bankrupt states break away from the nearly bankrupt federal government? How can that work?"

Hurley paused, an easy smile on his lips. He swiveled his big chair and looked out the window.

"All I can say for now is that we have that covered. But let's get back to the business at hand. How are things looking with Chet Mankins's new girlfriend?"

"She's an interesting one. She'll spend a week in and out of health food stores and yoga studios, but then go out on a binge and prowl for strange men. I honestly don't know if you need me on this one. She seems to have a good sense of how to keep her mouth shut."

"Could William handle this on his own?"

"I think so. Definitely. And it's not a good idea to have me on regular surveillance. At this point, she'd recognize me. I went to a class of hers, a few of them, actually."

"Yoga classes?"

"Yeah. And we had some drinks last night. And she spent the night," Seth said, reluctantly.

"Is this something we need to worry about?"

"I don't think so. When's Mankins due back?"

"Not until late next week, I think. So you may as well keep at it. Have some fun. See what she says or doesn't say. But don't go soft doing all that yoga. And don't worry, we'll have some action for you soon enough."

———————————

The domes and colonnades of Washington, DC always reminded the thing inside of Seth of the time not long after the idyll ended, when the former deities were choosing sides, or fleeing altogether.

The broken-toothed spirit didn't sign on to work miracles for the bishops or actively rebel. But he was friendlier with the rebellious spirits. One of them boldly went by his human name of Petronius. He'd been a courtier and an administrator in the most recent empire. And he held the unhappy distinction of being the only person to escape his mortal condition after the terrible change had made beggars of the gods.

125

Petronius had learned the secret from a priest in the east whom he'd imported for the emperor's amusement. But the emperor had settled on a different idea of divinity that week, and never got around to meeting the sage. Nonetheless, the guru fascinated Petronius, who entertained, inebriated, bribed, and blithely threatened the inscrutable man for his secrets. Eventually, he prevailed. And the priest taught the clever courtier how to leave his body, his time, and his place.

At the time, it seemed fortuitous. Not long after learning the trick, Petronius fell out of favor with the emperor, a mortal demotion. So Petronius opened the veins in his forearms, bound the wounds and bled out over several days, drinking with friends, telling the emperor's secrets, and giving away exorbitant gifts. Then he unbandaged his arms in a bath, and skipped the hangover.

As the newest of the ousted divinities, Petronius made friends fast and appropriated their outrage even faster. He first met the broken-toothed spirit lingering by a butcher shop, vainly inhaling blood fumes meant for no one in particular, trying to get up his strength for another swim against the current of time.

In the century since Petronius had died, his features had contorted into a permanent, sly leer. Like the broken-toothed spirit, he was more talented than wise.

"What are you doing here? That blood wasn't spilled for you. That's disgusting," Petronius said to the ancient spirit.

"Well, I have to live, don't I?"

"I've seen you before. And I imagine that you've been around too long to call this living," Petronius said.

"Do you have a better idea?" he said, turning his crooked face up from the rancid puddle.

"I do. I say we fight."

"Fight what? There's nothing to fight."

"We fight the crosses. We fight the people who wield them and paint them everywhere, the pious fools who act as if they'd won something other than a short lifetime of drudgery. Let's spill some blood."

"How do you plan to spill blood?"

"With most of them, it doesn't take much. Even the best of them are on the verge of murder half the time. It doesn't take more than a few well-placed insinuations. Tell the holy ones that killing the impious is holy. Tell the others that the priests are running a scam."

"I don't think so."

"Come on. Let's show these people that if they want to live without us, they'll live in a nightmare."

"Why do you want to fight a war that we've already lost?"

"It beats living like a beggar and a thief. You should be the angry one. You *saw* what it was like. You had the fattest calf, the ripest girl, and the tearful pleas of the powerful. At least show some dignity."

"Look in the mirror. None of it, not even the dignity, is coming back," the broken-toothed spirit said, having lost his appetite.

———

After the meeting with Hurley, Seth needed some air. He walked through the morning rush hour foot traffic, down in the direction of the White House.

He pondered Hurley's Words. *Not alone in there.* The thought had never occurred to him. But he had the creeping sensation that it wasn't supposed to occur to him.

The notion rattled him in a way he hadn't been since he was a teenager in the Westerly police station, with his hands cuffed and the sight of his scab-crusted knuckles, red and white, exaggerated and almost two-dimensional in the harsh fluorescent light. It was there, terrified, that he offered a desperate prayer to whatever might get him out of there.

It all came back to Seth. The first detective was a thin man with reddish tissue-paper skin and a French last name. He must have been in his mid-forties. With a nearly inhuman stolidity, he silently held up a dirty kitchen knife in an evidence bag, and calmly informed Seth that his life was effectively over if he didn't start talking. Seth couldn't decide whether to apologize or to lie. But something, not more than a twitch in his stomach, told him to keep his mouth shut. The second detective was an effeminate and feminine Italian guy. He said that they didn't think Seth did it, but the dead kid's parents were out of their minds with grief and they needed his help with the case. If Seth would say who did it, they could send him home in the next hour. They even said they'd give him a ride home.

Seth wanted to lie, wanted to tell the truth, wanted to talk, badly. But he only said one word, to each cop, one word to his former friend from the football team in what he can only guess was a staged encounter in between interrogations. The word, which some new instinct he'd discovered told him to cling to, was *Lawyer*.

The instinct was right. And it guided him through the threats from the police, through the final gambit the assistant district attorney tried before he finally dropped the charges. And in the years to come, the uncanny presence in Seth's stomach helped him maneuver the malicious whispers that followed him to his new high school. On the basketball court or the football field, it told him who was behind him, and whether to await a snap or a whistle on his heels or toes. It told him how to approach women, with kindness or coldness. And later, when he was doing real wrong, it told him when to hang back and when to charge ahead, who to trust and who to lie to.

Seth walked past the White House, past the camera-strapped gawkers who braved the bitter cold, past the old administrative palace, trying to figure out how literally to take what Hurley had told him about himself and their endeavor.

*Room to think.* It seemed more like a plea than a utopian vision. But some part of him wanted precisely that and wanted it more than anything, a break in time and space—a war and a border—that would separate him from the sins and failures of his own past. He dodged joggers and crossed the Mall, pausing to look at the Capitol building, which seemed for a moment to mean something other than it did. His head swam. The

Washington Monument seemed to be the only fastener nailing the whole city of abstractions to the earth. A flock of pigeons launched upward and circled, and Seth felt the beginning of a seizure coming on.

"Room to think. Room to think," Seth repeated aloud to whatever it was inside of him. After a minute, the seizure abated. The cold gripped his face. The ground hit back at his heels. Crossing the tidal pool, the cold grew colder. On the bridge to the Jefferson Memorial, Seth tried to listen, as Hurley had suggested.

*What do you want to say to me?* he asked in a low voice.

Seth couldn't tell if he was hearing or daydreaming what came to him next. It was a moment in the future, when he would be living through a bloody war of independence, a violent rending of West from East. The thing inside him whispered that it would only be a skirmish, documents drawn up, hands shaken, and a détente, in the shadow of weapons too terrible to use.

The broken-toothed spirit whispered to Seth of an escape from the slowly bankrupting Atlantic capitols of failed speculators, exhausted ideologues and baffled bureaucrats. The new West would rise with no debts to the old, and a new understanding would take hold. They would redream the old dreams with new endings, free from the gloom of the cross and the king, it whispered to Seth. *They're reading the entrails of goats on the coast*, it said.

The last bit didn't make sense, but Seth trusted it would. He looked up to Thomas Jefferson in his coat and pantaloons, feet firm but splayed, his balls open to what would come next.

---

Back at the hotel, Seth called William and told him to follow Sarah that day. While all of DC hustled out for lunch below his window, he took a nap. Waking in the late afternoon, he went out to the movies.

Seth chose a western, about a Bowery boy accused of murdering a Park Avenue plutocrat. The Bowery boy flees to Montana. There, he herds cattle and befriends a band of Comanches. When the plutocrat's family finds the Bowery boy and sends the Pinkertons after him, he and the Comanches fight and slaughter the lot of them. The Bowery boy takes a Comanche wife as the music swells and the credits scroll.

The movie was predictable enough. But the shots of the west, with its forever prairies, standing rocks and colossal mountains, really made it worth the trip to the theater.

Back at the hotel, he found the card Sarah had given him. On the phone, she sounded distracted, like she had someone with her. He asked her to dinner. She said she had plans that night, but that she had two tickets to see a famous yogi speak the next night. He said sure and agreed to meet her at the theater. He hung up and dialed William.

"Where's our girl right now?"

"She's with Mankins. At his place."

"I thought he wasn't due back until next week."

"Go figure."

The next day, Seth gave William the night off, and met Sarah at a small auditorium in Adams Morgan. Inside they joined the kind of crowd where the person introducing the main act has to encourage everyone to move up to the front. The main act was a yogi with a name that took up three lines on the poster and a beard that grazed his ankles when he sat on the big orange cushion in the middle of the stage. The old man spoke cheerfully about meditation and reincarnation in his little accented voice, before leading the group in an interminable ten minutes of silent meditation.

The yogi didn't seem like much to Seth, at least not until the question-and-answer. A young, shorthaired woman in a pantsuit asked how the yogic lifestyle extrapolated out to politics, particularly the upcoming elections. The yogi batted it right back, saying that yoga didn't extrapolate to anything, that extrapolation itself was the opposite of what yoga was about. Next up, an agitated blonde man in a blue suit asked if meditation wasn't just the thin end of the wedge to get people to worship Hindu deities instead of Jesus Christ. The man had a hard edge in his voice. But the yogi didn't hesitate. He said that, in fact, it was the deities who were the thin edge of the wedge to get people to meditate, much like how the Christian promises of heaven were only valuable as an inducement to get people to pray. A middle-aged woman with a braid down to her waist and a skirt whose bells jingled when she stood asked the yogi what his years of meditation, especially in India, had taught him about the environment, especially about living sustainably through recycling, buying locally and taking part in social action. A few similarly dressed ladies actually clapped for her question.

"Recycling has nothing to do with meditation. Your religion, your opinions, your political affiliation all have nothing to do with meditation. They belong to a world of opposition, a world of ghosts. Imagine a horror movie about a haunted house. There are all these ghosts that come out at night, and they are very frightening. In the horror movie, these ghosts are the empty husks of once-living beings, and they chase you all over the house. These ghosts are the once-living ideas you have about yourself, the things you've been told you are—you're a Democrat or a Christian, or that you're good because you recycle or because you tolerate your mother-in-law. In the horror movie, the dawn chases the ghosts away. And the sun is the direct attention of meditation. It simply becomes too bright for the ghosts to be seen."

The guru's beard shook as he spoke and the beatific patience of his vocation gave way to a kind of bright rage as he finished his answer. After an uncomfortable pause, the black man in a cardigan asked if reincarnation, as a philosophy, would tend to make people procrastinators.

"It may. In India, where many people consider reincarnation to be a reality, things certainly don't tend to happen on time. But that could also be the heat," the yogi joked. "Still, you shouldn't redesign the universe just to make the plumber show up on time."

Afterwards, Seth and Sarah Loire went to a bistro down the street. Under her coat, Sarah wore a shiny black dress that made a show of her cleavage.

"Sorry for kicking you out the other day. I had to meet with a client. And I didn't have time to get where I had to go, and to put all my documents away in the safe."

"*Documents in the safe.* Listen to you. You sure you're not a spy?"

"Pretty sure. But sometimes even I wonder."

He smiled. She laughed, and the laugh made her wince. She put her wine glass down so she could bring her hand to her stomach.

"You okay?"

"Yeah. It's nothing. I just pulled a muscle."

"You sure?"

"Yeah. It's nothing. What did you get up to yesterday?"

"Meetings, some work. I went to sleep early."

"So, how did you like Ramachandra?"

"It was, uh, not my usual evening. I'll say that. But he was good. I liked him once he got his blood up and started shooting down the idiots."

"I'm glad I didn't ask a question."

"Did you have one?"

"I have a lot of them. But what about you? What did you think of what he had to say?"

"What, like reincarnation?"

"Yeah."

"Sure. I guess so. I don't think I know any more on that front than anyone else."

"What about karma?"

"That's the thing where if I kill someone in this life, I'll be killed in my next life?"

"Something like that."

"I don't know. It sounds too fair to fit the facts on the ground. People get away with murder every day. And I'm no criminal lawyer, but karma seems like it would be a hard law to enforce."

"It's not a rule. It's like how everything you do or say or think opens the way for the next thing that happens, but also leads you back to where you started. One guru I heard said karma was like a mobius strip, where you come back to the same place. I don't know."

"I don't know how you'd prove something like that."

"It's more like a sense that I have. It's hard to explain. Sometimes it's a sense of familiarity, like you know someone that you've never met. It's like you. You never said anything. But I felt like I knew you, like we'd met before somehow."

Seth understood what she was talking about but was reluctant to agree. So he said huh.

"And there's this other part of it. This force pushing for correction. It's like I can feel the universe trying to make itself right through me. Like there's something I have to do, or something that needs to happen to me. And until it does, nothing can be right. I guess that's also like with you. Like a lot of the guys I've been with, you have this kind of violent side. Am I freaking you out?"

"It's strange, but you're not."

Sarah lowered her face over the table's tea-candle and spoke softly.

"I guess you'd know better than me. Maybe I'm wrong. But there's something about you, something dangerous. I mean, don't get me wrong, it's sexy. I can tell that you try to hide it. And I think it's sweet that you try to hide it."

"So if I'm a violent guy, and I'm not saying that I am, then what does that mean for me? According to karma, am I going to be beaten up or shot or something?"

"It's not always one to one. Like, if you were a violent person, then karma would mean that your punishment is never being close to anyone, because you always have to hide. Or it could mean that people close to you would be hurt or killed. I don't know. I mostly know what it means for me."

"And what does it mean to you?"

"It's like this debt. I mean, I think I'm doing okay. I volunteer, I give to charity, and I try to help others in my classes and wherever else I can. But I get the sense that's still nowhere near enough. I feel like this life is one big repentance for me. Whenever I try to ignore that feeling, it only gets worse. It's like a life of repenting won't be enough. I think something will have to happen to me."

"Like what?"

"Okay, you probably think I'm crazy now. But I think something terrible is going to happen. And I'm okay with that. I think I almost want it. Sometimes I feel like I'm going to lose my mind waiting for it."

"I don't think you're crazy. But I don't think that's karma, either. It's human nature—like the dopes asking questions tonight. Everyone feels guilty, either because they're alive and someone else is dead, or they're eating while someone else starves. Some people call it original sin, some people call it social injustice, some people call it karma and some people call it global warming."

"What do you call it?" Sarah Loire asked, her dark eyes wide and entrancing.

"I don't call it anything. I don't look back. And I don't look down."

"Like a shark, huh? Always moving?"

"Something like that. There's nothing for anyone in the past."

"But the past is inescapable. Whatever you do, practice yoga or practice law, the past is why you do it. Isn't it?"

She'd stopped him flat with that. Seth wanted to say the reasons don't matter, as long as he had something to do. But that sounded desperate, and he supposed it was. The only option left was to reconsider his life, which was too much to ask so late in the game. She had confused and aroused him in one fell swoop.

"How old are you, anyway?" Seth asked.

"What does it matter?"

"I'm not trying to argue. I just realized that I didn't know."

"Twenty-five. Why?"

"You're smart. That's all."

She smiled at him. They finished dinner and he drove her home. In the car outside her house, they kissed. It was a long kiss, held like a note to keep silence at bay while she fumbled with his belt and pants.

"Whoa. Let's take this inside."

"My place is a mess, I don't want you to see it."

"I don't care."

"No, I…"

"Come on. I'm sure I've seen worse."

"Okay. But listen, we can't do it tonight. I, uh, I have an issue down there right now."

"Are you all right?"

"I think so… No… It's nothing. It's my period."

Seth's mind flashed back to Eric Eggleston, the easy victim, and what he'd said about Mankins' mistress before Sarah: *She couldn't have babies because of him.*

"Is that all?"

"Yes. It's just, just a bad one," she said and smiled a brave smile. She reached into his pants and leaned over the walnut console of his luxury car. He caught her on the way down.

"It's okay. Let's go inside. Let me make up for not taking you out for breakfast the other day."

And so it went. They stayed up late talking in bed and went out for breakfast at noon. Hurley called as their food arrived, and told Seth to get out to Laughlin by the day after next. Seth was excited to get back in the action.

———————

The next night, she came by his hotel room. Sarah still couldn't make love, but it hardly mattered. She was a dangerous woman with more than a few tricks up her sleeve.

"Why do you have to go to Las Vegas?" she asked as he packed his things.

"It's a client, a land deal out there."

135

"A client in Las Vegas? Is this a mob thing you're involved in? You can tell me. I won't tell anyone."

"You won't tell anyone, huh? So why do you want to know so badly?"

"I just do. I don't know. I'm going to worry about you if you don't tell me. I mean, you come here and then you just leave, and that's it?"

"I'll be back."

"When?"

"A week, two at most," Seth said.

"You're going to have a lot of fun out there, I bet."

"If working twelve-hour days counts as fun, it'll be a real blast."

"Oh, so it's work."

"Yeah, it is. That's right. It's my job. It's what I do to make a living."

"And what is that? What is it exactly that you do?"

"Real estate," Seth said, more sheepishly than he should have.

"Right. Real estate."

"Yes. Real estate," Seth said more forcefully, but it was too late. She had him on the run.

"You know, I should have known this was coming."

Seth let that hang in the air for a moment before succumbing to the fight's gathering momentum.

"You should have known what was coming?"

"That you'd be like every other man—another sociopath who hides behind his work. As if that makes it magically okay to come and go as you please. You look at the woman you're supposedly making love to, or I guess I'm nothing more to you than some *chick* you're fucking, and you leave and say, 'It's just work.' Then you go off and rob and kill, or whatever *real estate* actually means and you say, 'It's just work.'"

"It is just work. It's how I make a living."

"A living. I know you. You'd neglect and degrade your own children and say, 'It's just work.'"

By Seth's standards, he'd opened himself up to this woman in unprecedented ways, for reasons he couldn't understand, and been as vulnerable as he'd allowed himself to be in decades. So her accusations stung. He clenched his jaw, but not his fist, and took it.

"Nothing to say? Of course not. Because under all that strong-and-silent…"

From there, Sarah Loire had a good go at him. It was a lengthy, no-holds-barred provocation. Some of it was true about him, true enough to sting. He supposed some of it was true about her father, and some of it was true about another guy, maybe Mankins. It didn't matter. He was taking the rap, and it pissed him off. It seemed she wanted him to hit her, to mark her, to show that he cared enough to claim her with an inexcusable swipe of his fist. He'd met women like this before, and thought he'd gotten better at avoiding them.

It went on and got worse. Sarah cracked the room's flatscreen television with a coffee mug and fled, after a failed assault with her fingernails, into the locked bathroom. Through the door, he threatened hotel security. Between sobs, she threatened to press rape charges. That was when it dawned on Seth that she was looking for something more than a punch in the mouth. She wanted him to deliver her penitence.

Ultimately, it was his job that allowed his hands to stay at his sides.

"I'M NOT HIM," he yell-whispered through the door. She whimpered something back.

"I'm not happy that I have to go," he continued. "And I get that you're upset. But I'm not him. I'm not going to hit you."

She cried. And cried. Finally, he heard the door lock click open. But she didn't open the door. He left it alone until he'd packed his two bags. He brought her out, onto the bed and kissed her until he began to feel her relax.

"Listen. It's not all real estate, what I do. There are other things. And some of them are bad things. But if I tell you about them, I'll be putting us both in danger."

"That's bullshit."

"I wish it was. I didn't think this would happen. You and me, like this. I really didn't. And I don't want it to stop. But I can't think of... well, why don't you get out of town for a few weeks? Go to New York or New Orleans or something. I'll cover everything, airfare, hotel, car, you name it. You should try out a new city. If you like it, you can, I mean, we can start a new life there."

"Seth, that's very sweet, in a crazy-creepy sort of way. But I have a life here. I have responsibilities."

"Well, please consider it. I'm serious. We could do it together. But let's get out of here. If it doesn't work, you can always come back."

"Be safe," was all she said.

He swept her up in an embrace that solved nothing. She wept, but she'd been weeping on and off for more than an hour at that point. Seth's eyes filled too. Something was happening. And though it may have been a mistake, it was a strong enough mistake that, despite everything, he submitted.

---

It was around 250 AD, give or take, when the broken-toothed spirit made a big, decisive mistake.

The disaster was predictable enough. He'd seen other spirits make the same mistake, and seen the profoundly diminished wrecks that they'd become for it. But he had, after a few centuries of attenuated existence, begun to feel himself vanishing. His memories, even his personality, seemed dimmer. Having faded to the world around him, he was fading to himself.

It was a busty baker's daughter who did him in. She resembled the long-ago woman over whom he had his mortal teeth bashed out. It was something about the shape of her eyes and the spray of freckles on her neck. But that wasn't all. She was keener than most of the girls in her small town. She sensed him, even seemed to see him. Unlike the others, she refrained from crossing herself when he drew near. It seemed that she even enjoyed his lascivious presence, his whispering in her ear. In her silent way, she welcomed him.

One day, between the well and her house, he penetrated her. Incorporeal and impotent, it didn't live up to what he'd imagined. Instead, he found himself inside of that strong and playful girl, completely in control.

Falling to the dirt path, he dug her fingers into her crotch and diddled her until she came, and until she was raw. When her family found her, he had her lash out, run away. Once cornered, he had her strip her clothes off, sing lewd army songs from foreign nations, scream dirges from centuries past.

The broken-toothed spirit exulted in the absolute power he had over her. And no power is truly absolute unless it can be exercised arbitrarily. So he was as arbitrary as he'd been as a god, but with a much smaller arena to operate in. But now he was cruel. He'd become a connoisseur of cruelty, because causing pain was the only sure proof left he had that he still existed. He had her spout secrets, and then about anyone who happened past.

After a day and a night of befuddlement, the girl's family overpowered her and tied her down. He had her bite at their hands, spit in their faces. But she was only a girl.

Once restrained, it dawned on him that he had no plan. Reduced to verbal assaults, he did his best on everyone who came near the house. When they wept, he would demand tributes to the names he'd held in previous centuries, and to all manner of unfashionable divinity.

Eventually, the family had a priest come, a young man. Washed and oiled, he was the cleanest human being for miles around. He tormented the broken-toothed spirit with his ornate cross. The former god forced the girl to rattle off well-practiced blasphemies, and to announce to all those present the priest's deep fondness for an illustrated codex of Genesis that he kept in his room.

He rubbed the girl's wrists and ankles raw and bloody against the twine restraints. But the priest kept on with his wounding words. Behind the clean man, the broken-toothed spirit could see another spirit, with whom he'd shared an honor after an athletic contest in another time. The traitor spirit reassured the clean young man.

The exorcism was the closest that the broken-toothed spirit ever came to faith in the new religion. The name of Jesus wracked and injured him terribly at the time. And the mind of humankind had changed, become so like the unwelcoming world, that its unkind attention was enough to send him running down the street.

It was a long, painful day that the priest won. Demanding, repeatedly, the broken-toothed spirit's proper name, the priest broke the spirit down. And learning its name, the priest forced the spirit into a goat, which the family slaughtered.

Afterwards, the broken-toothed spirit wasn't properly dead, but was far worse off. He could no longer move any faster than a man walking. His words were far fainter. Profoundly weakened, he was able to wade against the newly insurmountable force of time just once more, to the riverbank he'd loved most during the idyll.

Unaware of his own filthy, ragged appearance, he struggled to linger in that distant, lovely time and place. There he saw a young, untroubled god. The other god looked up to see him, stared a moment, wrinkled his brow and looked away.

---

An icy drizzle stranded the plane on the runway in DC for three hours. The misery of the other fliers, their entreaties, diatribes and moans reached Seth only when he removed his headphones to ask for a fresh scotch. The delay made the plane ride a very long time to think, and Seth needed it. Sarah Loire and Hurley's competing news about his soul had tangled his thoughts hopelessly.

The little seat-back TV in front of him was tuned absentmindedly to one of the supposedly highbrow channels, where they were panning slowly across old lithographs and talking about Beethoven. "...deaf, with no patrons and no audience, he was, quite simply, a man possessed," the old man's voiceover intoned. *Possessed.* The word made Seth sit up straight. Isn't that what, at the bottom of it all, Hurley had said he was—possessed? It seemed impossible, some relic of pre-psychiatric religiosity.

The plane finally taxied and Seth chugged his scotch to stay the seizure that seemed near. He pressed his head back against the blue leather headrest and tried desperately to listen to the thing inside of him, to inquire what it would have of him. And the seizure's grip lessened, and he could almost hear it, not exactly audible, but somehow comprehensible. The plane lifted. And it said what it had been saying for years—that he lived in a world far broader than that of other men, that he was someone for whom few rules applied and for whom more things were possible. An exception. It said he would bring about the future, that he would inaugurate a land without monuments, without centers—a nation of individuals, contented sexually and chemically, joined by networks of twilight language that floated invisibly in the air.

Like a faint star, the thing in him vanished from direct attention. Peripherally, though, it became clearer. And Seth could make out that his companion was a man, of sorts. Preoccupied, Seth asked it if such a thing was even possible. It shrugged, as if disappointed he would ask such a question. Seth asked, like a teenager preoccupied with his sweetheart's favorite band, about reincarnation. The broken-toothed spirit said, in the first words that Seth could properly hear: "I don't know much more about death than you. We're both hitching a ride here."

Then it was over, and Seth was left to his scotch, his seat-back TV and to the rectangular and circular farms below. The circular farms gave way to the nothing but highways and mountains of desert wilderness.

*How?* The deathly scarcity below asked Seth. How will the new country make a go of it? The larger nation, lush as it was,

141

seemed to be sliding unavoidably toward an incredible bankruptcy.

---

In Las Vegas, Seth skipped his connecting flight and rented a car. The thing in him advised that he act spontaneously, break his patterns, take active steps to elude the easy traps and easy surveillance.

The two-hour drive down the utter desolation of highway 93 convinced Seth that no one was following. He pulled past the four-story illustration of a tidal wave bearing his hotel's name, parked, and checked in. He cleaned up and drove two hotels down the road to see Roberto. At Roberto's suite, Frederica was alone and the main room was dark, except for the glow from a laptop and a light on in the kitchenette.

"Sorry. I'm still doing most of my regular day job, while keeping all of this," she said, waving her hands up by her ears and sighing. "going. How was your trip?"

Seth followed her around the suite as she turned on all of the lights.

"Fine? Where's Roberto?"

"Beijing. He won't be around for this one. Hurley and I are heading out of the country for a few days as well. But everything's fine."

"Okay. Why's everyone leaving the country?"

"It's a surveillance issue. There's a strong chance that at least one of us is being watched."

"Should I even be here?"

"Your cover is fine. Anyway, it's not the police or the FBI. And I doubt they're watching you. The upshot, however, is that all of us will have to keep a few thousand miles away from our big demonstration. We'll be eavesdropping as best we can. That's why we need you to be our eyes and ears there."

"At what?"

"It's a geological demonstration, a few hundred miles north of here. It's for some of our colonels, generals, and captains of industry. We need everyone who's on board to stay on board. And the demonstration is a morale builder, of sorts. We want someone there to look and listen, give us a better idea of whose morale needs watching."

"Sure. I guess I can do that. But who's watching you? The Secret Service? If someone's already onto us, shouldn't we…"

"We don't have to worry about the authorities. We have friends in every agency that would be interested. It's the Chinese who'd be watching."

"Why would the Chinese be watching?"

"Hm. Hurley must have told you less than I thought. But if you're going to the demonstration, you may as well know. This endeavor of ours started with the Chinese. A classic foreign policy gambit on their part: Subvert and divide your rival by funding and arming domestic insurgents. It goes back to the Bronze Age. It's something we've done for years. China wanted civil unrest in the US, and they had an ocean of cash. So they contacted Hurley, back when he was in the senate. And Hurley passed the Chinese money, on a one-for-you-two-for-me basis, to a bunch of separatist and militia groups in Montana and thereabouts."

"Jefferson?"

"Him and a few others. The separatist movements mostly spent the money on satellite TV dishes and new trucks. But they did use some of the money to buy guns and put out better pamphlets. And when Hurley had too much cash on his hands, he came to me. I'd helped him with something similar in the past, spreading out the appearance of campaign donations. But the amounts of money he was talking about were another story. And I knew that Roberto needed money to cover some unreported trades. So we took Roberto's toes out of the fire, and he helped us clean Hurley's money."

Her candor scared Seth. It meant he really was in too deep to ever get out. Frederica seemed to sense his trepidation.

"I thought you wanted to know what you were dealing with," she said, her gray eyes like granite.

"I do. Sorry. Please. Go on," Seth said.

"And so it went. Hurley and the militias did what separatists and revolutionaries have done with the under-the-table cash of empires for ages: They hoarded it, squandered it, and handed back excuses and minor capers to their patrons in exchange for more cash. This went on for a few years. Hurley, Roberto, and my pension funds all waxed fat on it. So did the belligerent hillbillies up north. But one day, back when Hurley was still a senator, someone tried to bribe him in a way that was so careful and so ingenious that Hurley knew something unusual was up. As a connoisseur of bribes, he was impressed. The person sent to contact him had no idea of the massive personal wealth Hurley had already squirreled away. Out of curiosity, Hurley played his contact, goaded the man, and finally recorded him making a more bald-faced offer. That's when he threatened to call the FBI. The man rolled over."

Seth blinked. The faux-opulent suite was sort of drab with the all lights on.

"So what was the bribe about?" he asked.

"Oil shale. Apparently, the guys who hired Hurley's contact had found a very cheap way to extract the one point five *trillion* barrels of oil trapped in the oil shale of Wyoming, Utah and Northern Nevada. One point five trillion barrels is five times the projected reserves in Saudi Arabia. But these guys had a problem. Three quarters of the oil-shale land is owned by the federal government, part of the Strategic Petroleum Reserve. On the record, Hurley told the man to work the land he could buy, and to let the people of the United States benefit from the rest."

"But the oil man didn't take his advice?"

"Not exactly. It chose to sit on the new extraction method and to work on buying, or at least leasing, the Strategic Petroleum land from the government. And Hurley put two and two together. Between the money coming in from China and the new extraction technology, there was an opportunity so big that it was nearly inconceivable at first. So he talked it over with Roberto and me. And where Hurley smelled an opportunity, Roberto saw it in color."

"So now where are we?"

"The shale technology will calm a lot of our jumpy allies. It changes the risk-reward equation. Profoundly. But we don't want the Chinese to know we're laying the groundwork for a new superpower in the Pacific theater. And that's what this technology means. We still need too much from the Chinese to complete the secession. That's why the secrecy about the shale."

"Okay."

"The demonstration is up in Wyoming. Locally, we have this covered as a secret demonstration by a black-budget military contractor. And there are enough of those in Nevada, Utah and Wyoming for this to pass without notice."

"When is it?" Seth asked.

"Two days from now. You fly up tomorrow."

*Reading the entrails of the earth out west*, the thing inside of Seth said, almost chuckling.

---

"I heard that they're reading goat entrails in the north," Petronius said to the broken-toothed spirit. "They're whispering to the trees. I think we can win a following."

The broken-toothed spirit was glad to see a familiar face after the devastation of his exorcism. Ragged and lost, barely strong enough to make a superstitious soldier spit in the dirt. He nodded at his old friend, Petronius.

Over the last century, Petronius had kept busy, outrunning the missionaries and playing hit-and-run for a few dozen local deities around the edges of the empire. But as the edges of the empire grew ragged, the churches consolidated. And Petronius was running out of holy fools, or anyone, who would listen.

"From what I hear, there are almost no crosses in the north. It's open country. The people are out in the fields, interpreting the birds, listening for whispers. I think it would be a good change for us. You look like you could use a trip out of town," Petronius said, staring into the broken-toothed spirit's hollow eyes.

So they traveled north together, Petronius moving slowly on account of the wounded, older spirit.

---

Seth walked past the lounge and saw Dolores singing. She sounded good from a distance. But he kept walking, exhausted. He stripped down and slept on the big king bed, next to his packed suitcase. When the room's phone rang the next morning, the sun was so bright it blinded him in his first wakeful blinks.

"THIS IS RUSTY. I'M SUPPOSED TO TAKE YOU UP NORTH," the voice on the phone roared above the dull ringing of bells and pealing of slot sirens in the casino lobby.

Seth yelled back that he'd be down in ten. He skipped the shower, put on yesterday's suit and grabbed his carry-on.

Downstairs, Rusty fit his name. Red hair, cheeks full of freckles on bad sunburn. In his twenties, he had too many wrinkles for his age. He drove Seth to the Laughlin Bullhead International Airport, where Seth retrieved his other suitcase. Rusty's car smelled of cigarettes, sweat and whatever it is that unmitigated sunlight does to plastic.

At the hangar, they climbed into Rusty's two-seater, which smelled the same. Rusty gave Seth a headset. There was no runway traffic to speak of, and they were in the air in five minutes. Once they were in the air, Rusty turned to him.

"NOT MANY FLIGHTS TO NATRONA LATELY. I MEAN, MORE THAN USUAL. BUT STILL, NOT MANY."

"Natrona?"

"NATRONA COUNTY AIRPORT."

"Where is that?"

"WYOMING."

"Oh, right."

"YEAH. YOU SAID YOU'RE PAYING CASH, RIGHT?"

"Yeah."

"AWESOME. FUCK UNCLE SAM. THAT'S WHAT I SAY."

Seth nodded and didn't say anything to Rusty for the rest of the trip. That seemed to be fine by Rusty. Seth paid him and walked off to meet whoever he was supposed to meet at the tiny airport where he'd been left. Rusty waved from the fueling truck, wrinkled and deaf and not even thirty, smiling with the goodwill of someone who feels they've gotten a good deal.

Seth turned around and a tan SUV pulled up. It was big all over, conspicuously muscular, with big tires. Out of it stepped a pretty black woman in a tailored pantsuit that showed off her amazonian curves without giving you the wrong idea. She took a few steps from the SUV, looked around and waved to Seth. The inside of the SUV was warm and smelled new.

"Seth, right?" she said, too preoccupied with driving to offer her hand. Her hair was tied down to her scalp in braids.

"Yes. And you?"

"Rachelle Winfield, account executive at Norridge Solutions."

Norridge sounded familiar, but it took a second for Seth to recall it from some of the documents he'd brought to Roberto on his first trip to Laughlin.

"Oh. Pleased to meet you. Where are we going?"

"The test site. It's about three hours."

They drove through the snow-crowded scrub, the low trees and sudden mountains upon which the sky seemed to be stretched. In the late afternoon, the sun fell to one side of the highway and the moon rose big and orange on the other. The moon was the only light on the road when they passed a ski mountain with lonely snow groomers rising and falling on its face. The pale moonlight flashed on the spinning blades of the few working pinwheels of a run-down wind farm, followed by a long stretch of nothing, where the wind blew the plowed snow across the road.

"Long drive."

"I've been doing it two times a day lately. In the other months, we can usually land the planes out there. I think that most of the people are coming in on the helicopter tomorrow."

"No kidding."

"Twelve hours a day driving. And to think, I got a masters degree for this," Rachelle laughed.

They pulled onto a well-plowed dirt road whose signs warned in English and Spanish that the land beyond promised the use of lawful, deadly force. The landscape was flat, broken by a pond here and a stand of bare trees there. At the top of a low hill, they hit the checkpoint.

"Button up, it's cold. And we have to get out of the truck here," Rachelle said.

Two men searched them, two men searched the car and two men checked out Seth's ID. That left at least another six men inside the double-wide trailer by the side of the road, from what he could tell. Rachelle underwent the examination with resigned calm. When it was done, one of the men held up Seth's cell phone.

"Sorry, but we have to hold this until you leave. But we can forward any voice or text messages to a proxy phone that you can use while you're here."

Seth agreed, and after a few minutes, the man gave him another cell phone. Rachelle drove him through a valley in which the wind blew billows of fog around in the bright moonlight, affording glimpses of the vast valley floor, dotted with small mesas of snow that rose and sank to brown, wet prairie grass. At the center of each patch of brown grass a concrete opening coughed up steam. Seth could also make out small sheds at the end of straight paths carved into the snow. Beside them stood massive tanks, like the bodies of huge limbless deer.

"Strange out here."

"Spooky's more like it. But they're doing great work. Try to imagine a battlefield where you knew where every enemy combatant was at every moment. It's the future of…"

Rachelle went into her account-executive routine. It was her way of being something other than a high-priced chauffeur. She recited, with gusto and considerable polish, the cover story Frederica had explained to him—a subterranean sonar system to locate enemy troops and armor. It was, Frederica had told him, the easiest way to explain the secrecy and all the holes in the ground.

"…canopy jungle and other in environments where satellite coverage is unavailable or impractical. Well, here we are."

She took him to an aluminum trailer. The snow drifts on either side made it look like a small hill. But inside, it was done up like any other high-end hotel room.

"If you're hungry, just dial zero. I think the kitchen is open for another hour. Is there anything else you need?" Rachelle asked, her features severe but gorgeous in the subdued light of the trailer.

"I feel like I should give you a tip."

Rachelle's eyebrows shot up and she gave him a smirk that said he would be an asshole for saying it if it weren't true. He closed the door.

After the last few days of planes and cars and looking over his shoulder and complying with searches, of passing from the half-hostile embrace of Sarah Loire, past Dolores and Frederica and into this odd hotel-like abyss, Seth could not sit still. He paced the room, opened the trailer door, was rebuked by the frigid wind, and paced some more. He stripped to his underwear, sat cross-legged on the floor, and focused on his breathing.

An hour later, he was kneeling, with one foot in front of him and one up the wallpapered wall. His quadriceps screamed and his stomach ached as he reached his arms up and his shoulders against the wall. The pain was such that he had no thoughts. Something gave way. It started in his hips, where they joined his back, but spread so that it felt as if his guts were spilling out. He reached and breathed one more time before collapsing to the floor in a bizarre state of joy and relief.

149

He had broken some knot on his stomach that had held all the shit in. And that carried him back to where the knot had first been tied, the Westerly police station. And he wept. There were reasons—his abandonment of his wife and child, his complicity in the likely murder of Sarah Loire—and there were reasons beyond the known reasons. He wept until he was too empty to do anything but sleep.

The next day, he woke to a banging on the door, and to the angry voice of the thing inside of him. *Next time just jerk off, you fucking freak,* the broken-toothed spirit rebuked him. At the door, Rachelle banged and repeated his name. He climbed from the floor, the static impression of the thick wool carpet fresh and pink on his face.

"They said you weren't answering the phone, so I thought I'd come by to wake you. Mr. Mulholland says you have a call with him in an hour."

Rachelle's eyes drifted over to the still-made king-size bed.

"Is there anything I can get you?"

"Yeah, uh. Coffee, and breakfast. Eggs, bacon, sausage, toast. Everything you have."

Rachelle smiled the same smile as in the car. The cold air woke him. The sun was dull in the fog behind her.

"What? No tip?" she joked.

---

The call with Roberto was short, mostly because what Seth was supposed to be looking for was of the know-it-when-you-see-it variety. That day, the test site filled of security people, politely patting down and confiscating cell phones from the VIPs. They arrived throughout the morning, shuttle helicopters sinking and rising at the checkpoint, or in vans. Once double-checked and checked in, they all wound up in a big steel building done up to look the part of a hunting lodge.

It was an uneasy group. The CEOs felt naked without their cell phones, the corporate security felt naked without their earpieces. The military officers, identifiable by their haircuts, felt naked without their uniforms. It was only the politicos who seemed at ease in the atmosphere of conspiracy. Seth wandered among them. The assignment reminded him of playing free safety in high school, prowling around before the snap, trying to sniff out the play. He'd been at gatherings of the powerful a few times in his career. And this get-together was unique in Seth's experience in that everyone was American.

A common strain bound the guests. Each of them noted in each other a potential snitch who could undo them, as well as a bargaining chip they could play should the conspiracy unravel. For the hour or so before the demonstration, as guests filed in, the two dozen guests dissembled carefully and calculated. From the general reticence of the crowd, Seth could see why the demonstration was necessary. Still, it was a ballsy move by Frederica, he thought.

"So they got to you too?" said a voice from behind Seth.

It was Burleson, who had quietly returned from a short sabbatical to his CEO's chair at SumTech.

"Oh, excuse me?" Seth said, buying time to see which way his former victim would jump.

"I know," Burleson said, looking Seth in the eye. "I'm in the same boat. I don't know whether to act like I don't know what's going on, or to pretend that I'm not really here. Anyway, I saw you across the room, and I wanted to say thank you for trying."

"Trying?"

"Trying to help me. But I guess that if they could get to you, then even the Secret Service must be in on it."

Seth blinked, and tried to comprehend the interpretation Burleson had applied to that night in Santa Clara.

"Well, it's one of those things. If you can't beat 'em…"

"Sometimes that's the only thing to do. I remember after we met. I was in the limo between the press conference and the mental hospital, I mean, wellness retreat. And I looked at the fresh leather of the limo seats, at the grim determination of the other drivers caught in traffic with me, and I realized something. I mean, the psychotic break was understandable. I was under a lot of stress, trying to be a CEO and being forced to decide whether to be a traitor or a patriot. It was too much. But I realized that I was on a ride I couldn't stop—and I don't mean this revolution, I mean the ride that I've been on since I was born."

It's funny, Seth thought, he thinks he's absolving me.

"It's like after the last click on the roller coaster. There are no more choices. It's that simple. So you shouldn't feel bad," Burleson said, putting a hand on Seth's shoulder.

Burleson was one of a handful to make use of the open bar. Given that it was ten in the morning, the ratio was still high. He was the only one talking so freely. People had gathered around, as inconspicuously as possible, to hear what he was saying.

"You always have a choice," Seth said, surprised at his own words.

"I mean, well, of course, but… What do you mean?"

"Even something like this. You count your options, look at the outcomes, and make a choice. You go in with your eyes open and try to make it work. But you're a still free man, like me and everyone else here."

"I agree. That's why I brought one of the geologists. From MIT. We flew him in late last night, blindfolded," Burleson said. "Very cloak and dagger stuff."

"Hell of a way to travel."

"Well… he's being paid well. Anyway, if this proves out, we may all go into the history books."

Once everyone had arrived, and they all did, a caravan of SUVs arrived to take them through the eerie fog and snow piles of the test site. Seth rode with Burleson, an Air Force general, the governor of Nevada, and Burleson's geologist. The general drove. Burleson explained that there would also be two independent chemists and another independent geologist looking at random spots on the site to make sure that all the claims checked out.

"So all this is steam, is that right?" Burleson asked the geologist, a thin Spanish man whose thick black beard made him look even thinner.

"If they're using geothermal heat to liquefy the shale, like they say, then it makes sense. The snow, and the earth around the holes, looks undisturbed. And the steam looks like it's coming from the ground. I'd like to see what's in one of the sheds. Can we pull over and take a look?" the geologist said.

The general pulled over at one of the sheds, and the other SUVs followed suit. Pretty soon everyone was crowded around one of the sheds.

"Spooky out here," Burleson said. "The fog and all."

"Sasquatch country, I bet," said a black-haired older man with a thick New York accent.

In the shed, the chemist inspected the machinery inside like it was a crime scene. He took his time, looking at things that didn't seem to warrant inspection, checking the dust on an engine casing, rubbing it in his fingers and smelling it.

"Well," the old, thin man with pale tissue-paper skin said in his dry New England accent. "It's a pump."

The crowd crowded and followed as the old man traced a pipe through the wall of the oversized shed to a small nozzle, from which he extracted a minute amount of pale brown liquid into a beaker, which he tested interminably in the cold wind that penetrated the walls of the overcrowded shed with equipment he'd brought in an old leather suitcase. He spent several tense minutes mixing, pouring, examining, adding liquids, paper strips, even using a pop-up centrifuge from his bag.

"It is," he said, pausing and reexamining the sample in front of him, "definitely kerogen."

"Oil," Burleson said quietly. "Motherfucker. Welcome to the new Unites States of the West."

"So it works?" the general asked the scientist.

"The process, as it has been described to me, appears to work. The geothermal heat is liquefying the oil in the shale, which the pumps extract," the scientist said.

"Good-bye, Dubai," the general said and whistled.

The thing in Seth said *I told you so*.

After that, a second geologist and chemist pair examined a similar site on the edge of the property. The crowd had grown gregarious, with the formerly shy officers, executives and politicos milling about and introducing themselves. Those second pair of scientists found the same as the first had: The geothermal heat from the deep holes had cooked the shale to where it would release the oil in a liquid, easily refinable form. The second geologist, eager to upstage the first, went a step further, saying that the steam from the deep holes could be used to power the pumps used to extract the oil.

From the edge of the hill where the billionaires and powerful breathed their wary sighs of relief, Seth looked out, transfixed on a rock formation that lurched out of an otherwise gentle hillside in the distance. It looked like a deformed penis with a horse's face. Seth stared out at it, while the second geologist put on a show of his knowledge of the earth's layers.

"What the hell is that?" Seth asked no one in particular.

"If I'm not mistaken," Burleson's geologist said, "that's the Teapot Dome Formation."

From the hill, Seth could see miles and miles into the distance. Huge clouds, dark and flashing, dropped their gray tendrils of snow and sleet onto the snow-covered distance.

Back at the lodge, the two dozen VIPs postponed their helicopter trips, drank drinks of relief, downplayed their misgivings and networked some more. At the end of it, Rachelle drove Seth and Colonel Tom Wozniak from Fort Pendleton back to the Natrona County Airport.

"Listen, I've been wanting to talk to you. And you seem to be the man to talk to. I think I know some other guys like me in Nevada, Montana, Colorado, who may want to get in on this thing," Wozniak said to Seth once the SUV was on its way.

"Tom, this isn't something you talk about. Not with anyone," Seth said.

"I know. And I haven't, except in a vague way."

154

"Write their names down and give them to me. I'll run them up the flagpole. But go no further with this on your own."

"And write them down for me too," Rachelle said, raising and passing her business card into the backseat.

"Hey, Rachelle, why don't you give the colonel here a fuller picture of what he saw out there," Seth said.

And so Rachelle ate up the next hour and a half, giving her spiel about the bogus battlefield sonar project. Seth watched the colonel's expression pass from embarrassment to boredom as she did.

"Like I said, be careful who you talk to about this," Seth said.

At the Natrona County Airport, the colonel climbed aboard a nice chartered jet, and Seth found Rusty, eating chicken in his two-seater. Rusty yelled something about dodging the storm, something about a long day and something about getting good and high like the lord would want once he was back in Laughlin.

From there to the Laughlin Bullhead International Airport in the bouncy two-seater and back to the hotel in the duct tape and reek of Rusty's old car, through the resigned cursing and slot machine sirens of the lobby, Seth's thoughts remained fixed on the test site. The steam coming out of the ground excited the thing inside of him. It spoke of a tremendous latency and made Seth powerfully desire the revolution.

It gave Seth a vision of the continental United States as a kind of massive beast, with a small dinosaur brain in Maine, with Texas and Florida as its legs. The thing inside showed Seth a vision of the beast wounded between its ribs and rear haunch. From the wound, it showed tremendous wealth, power, sex, all the desirable things pouring out.

In his room, exhausted, Seth breathed and kept his eyes fixed on a spot on the ceiling. He listened to the thing inside of him, and battened back another seizure.

For the first time, the broken-toothed spirit wondered if Seth might be smart enough or willful enough to throw it out. It knew that the aftereffects of such an expulsion could be as devastating as they had been after the exorcism. The thing in Seth wondered at the possibility, but let its thoughts drift back to the promising mist billowing softly from the depths of Wyoming.

---

Seth woke from turbulent dreams still tired, threw on a polo shirt and shorts—his best Laughlin disguise—and drove down the road to see Roberto, who was ruminating over one of last week's playoff games. He had coffee waiting, which Seth went straight for. Roberto paused the game.

"Everything. I want to know everything. What was the mood like?" he asked.

"Not great at first. People were nervous. But the mood was definitely lighter after the tests. Are you sure it was a good idea getting everyone together like that?"

"We had to do it, and we had to do it fast. In affairs like this, people can lose their nerve. And nothing makes people feel safer than being part of a crowd, especially a wealthy crowd. Did you notice any trouble spots?"

"Not really. Colonel Wozniak, out of Camp Pendleton, seemed a little too chatty, but that's all."

"Chatty with who?"

"With me, but also with some of his peers. Here," Seth said, digging a scrap of paper out of his pocket. "He gave me some names of generals, colonels, who he thinks would be interested."

Roberto scanned the paper, nodded at some names, squinted at others.

"Thanks. We have to be careful with military types. We need them to make it happen. But bring on too many of them, and I'm worried that they'll have us in a constant state of crisis, just to stay in charge."

"I just thought I'd pass it along."

"Okay. We'll drop him a line about that. From what we're hearing, he's okay. But there's someone who isn't okay. His name is Jaime Bergman—ring a bell?"

"Bergman… Movie guy?"

"Yeah, a movie producer and an obnoxious, overgrown trust-fund punk. He found out early what was afoot from his drinking buddy, the honorable Senator Chet Mankins. And to be fair, he made himself useful for a while. Did you see *Bowery on the Colorado*?"

"Yeah. Was that his?"

"Well, he produced it. But we paid for it, cast it and even rewrote the script."

"I didn't know you were in the movie business."

"Well, that was my idea. It's a way of priming the pump. We've done a few movies, a few TV shows. You put the pollen in the air, get the right themes in front of the public, so that people don't react badly to the big change. *Bowery on the Colorado* is a really pretty way to put out the whole Dying-East-Coast-reaches-its-bony-hand-out-to-strangle-the-nearly-infinite-promise-of-the-West theme."

"A little pre-revolt propaganda?"

"You know, *propaganda* is exactly the word for it. Did you know that propaganda was the original name for what later became known as marketing? Sigmund Freud's nephew came up with the idea. And after the world wars, some finer propaganda mind decided to rename propaganda."

"I had no idea."

"Well, anyway, my point… my point, my point. My point is that we want our revolution to make emotional sense to the American public, who by-and-large live in an infantilized fantasy world of movies and TV. Even for the easterners, we want the change to *feel* not merely acceptable, but inevitable, in a bittersweet way, like a child leaving home to go to college. That's another movie we have coming out next month, a real tear-jerker. Blonde math genius with hopelessly alcoholic parents."

"So it sounds like this guy, Bergman, has been useful."

"Yes, to a point. But mostly, he's been useful to himself. His latest gaffe is that he's called his investors, offering to horse-trade information about the Wyoming test for up-front cash in his next movie. Mankins has warned him about this kind of thing. And he's already had his second chance. So, it's Wednesday now. Let's get him gone by this time next week."

"Gone?"

"Yep. Gone. We're past any kind of judgment call with this guy."

"What do you want it to look like?"

"That's up to you. You won't have Hurley's resources for cleaning up available in Los Angeles. I trust that you'll be creative."

Roberto gave Seth a manila envelope of cash, and promised more. For the first time, Seth noticed how thin Roberto looked. When he handed over the heavy envelope, Seth noticed that the man's fingernails were almost entirely chewed away. From his hotel room, Seth called William.

"I need you out in LA tomorrow. I'll double the Santa Clara pay."

"That's what I love about working with you, Seth: I never have to negotiate."

"When you land, I need you to find me a nondescript car, a used Camry or something."

"You bet."

"Great, I'll see you...hey, uh, wait," Seth said, interrupted by something he couldn't put his finger on. "Actually, one more thing. Get us both some California IDs. Good ones, ones that will check out if we need them to."

"Okay, but you know that's not cheap."

"And you know that's no problem."

"That's another thing I love about working with you: You never question my expenses."

"Oh, and how's Sarah doing?"

"She's been chasing it pretty hard the last few nights, to the drug house in Southeast one night and to Mankins' place the next. She's wearing that headscarf of hers and the big sunglasses again. I'm starting to think the thing they hired us for might happen."

"Really? You don't think this is a blip?"

"Could be. But I knew girls like this back in Tampa—they keep it together long enough so they can throw it all away that much harder. We better hope there are still some unbuilt houses out in the burbs."

"Okay. Thanks."

After so many mundane assignments, the thing inside of Seth was eager for the rush of absolute victory that came with killing. It bubbled with ideas on how to pull it off. But Seth's thoughts kept going back to Sarah Loire. He thought of the flat concrete slabs they built those suburban houses on, of her balled up inside of one of those slabs. He wanted to fly to DC that night and keep it from happening.

But that was impossible, the thing in him said. He had killing to do.

———————

Where Petronius and the broken-toothed spirit ended up wasn't so much a city as a big village. But the people there sensed them immediately and seemed glad to have the spirits there. Even the broken-toothed spirit with his small, crushed voice could speak and be heard on the rutted tracks that passed for streets there. In time, the people gave them the names of gods who'd fled long before, making them spiritual stepfathers of the land. And among the dreamy herders, illiterate farmers and astronomers of that place, Petronius and the broken-toothed spirit regained some of their old dignity.

It was there that Petronius taught the broken-toothed spirit how to properly possess. The trick was to move in gently, gradually, with the consent of the person. Petronius taught the older, still-hobbled spirit to find the outcast, the unsatisfied or the accused, and to offer them something. Even a single word of solace could be enough, at first. Once inside the person, speak softly, manipulate indirectly. As the possessed increasingly relied on it, the spirit gained trust and control, without the person being the wiser.

But, Petronius warned him, choose your host carefully. Because once you're in, you're in until the person died, or found a way to throw you out. In those centuries, Petronius and the broken-toothed spirit took turns all over the cold, rainy land, playing prophet, general, king, heretic, and sacrifice. They set the scenes and played the parts, manipulating the wars and rumors of wars that constituted the human mind. Petronius, though younger, could speak the mind's twilight language masterfully. He could tweak the outcome of a footrace, the appearance of birds in the sky, the colors worn by women to spark that always-combustible mixture into a massacre, a messiah or a war.

Their time in the north wasn't exactly idyllic. The two spirits' entertainments took a lot of work, and didn't always play out right. Occasionally, one or both of them would become trapped in a particularly recalcitrant man or woman whom they could neither control nor leave. But it was still better than they'd had back in the empire.

Trouble arrived with the cross and an army. But Petronius knew what to do. He'd find the poorest and most ragged of the soldiers, who silently cursed through his prayers. Petronius promised the soldier some small deliverance from his damp, dreary obligation of a life. Petronius would enter, sometimes quietly, sometimes in a wild seizure that looked to the rest of his regimen like an attack of the Holy Spirit. Before long, the soldier's toothless, rotten mouth spewed forth wild, uncompromising pieties and promises that led his regimen to mutiny, then to decimate its own ranks for purity, and then slaughter itself over a series of theological disagreements.

Decades later, another cross-bearing regimen came to clean out the wild-eyed, heretical few who remained of the village. From among the new army, Petronius picked out an officer passed over for promotion, and screamed into his ear all about the will of God, the glories that awaited, and the terrible punishments that would befall sinners, so that the man could almost hear. The officer gathered a few followers, and they assassinated their commanding officer. And so on.

But the broken-toothed spirit knew that even Petronius couldn't keep the crosses at bay forever from that cold and rainy place. And after lending his voice to a few more mutinies and a few more heresies, he parted ways with the younger spirit, wandering into the forests, and in search of a quiet moment to think, drifted over the ocean.

---

Seth packed his bags, drove through the night from Laughlin to Santa Monica, checked into a waterfront hotel in the early morning and sent all the clothes he could spare to be cleaned. As the sun came up, he drifted off to sleep, the sounds of the ocean and the traffic hushing the dawn.

After so long in wintry DC and Wyoming or barren Laughlin, the late afternoon in California was like a narcotic dream of sweetness and fecundity. Orange blossom and eucalyptus scents wafted through the sunlit parking lot. The roads were crowded, but wide. Seth drove to the Hollywood bar that William suggested.

Over beers, William handed him a driver's license. The guy on it looked somewhat like Seth, younger, but close enough to pass.

"Don't shave for a day, and maybe throw on a baseball hat, and you're there," William said, pointing at the license.

"Great. Let's get started."

"Now? I haven't even gotten into my California state of mind yet."

"Yeah, well, there's a guy here who has to go. And I want to get back to DC."

"It's twenty degrees there. Why rush it?"

"You're going to start asking *why* now? Is that something I should get used to?"

"Okay. Okay," William said, holding his hands up by his ears.

Seth rented a second car using the fake ID. With Seth in the new rental and William in the beat-up Camry, they began following Jaime Bergman. They tailed his Mercedes from outside his office, to the tail end of his kid's soccer game, watched him exchange some words with his ex-wife before driving off to dinner with a young tan gentleman and two young women the gentleman brought along and left with. After dinner, Bergman drove the 405 to Pasadena, where a young woman welcomed him, and where he spent the balance of the night.

The next two days passed like that. Following, waiting, watching. On the beach in front of Seth's hotel, they drew up assassinations in the sand.

"I agree, the security at Bergman's house and at his office is too much to make either practical. I don't even like the idea running any more surveillance around there," Seth said, looking out at the amusement pier and the beige bluffs over the beach.

"But his home and his office are the only places he goes every day. He seems to go to a different restaurant, or a different bar every night. All that leaves is the girlfriend in Pasadena, who we've seen him visit twice. If we moved fast, we could do a home invasion there," William said.

"Well, we don't know what else we'd be running into at the girlfriend's. She could have roommates, or kids, or a pimp."

"This is California. She could have all three."

"That's my point. We don't have time to follow this guy *and* get to know what goes on at her place. And I don't want to kill more people than we have to."

"So what should we do? Wing it?"

"How about we hit him on the freeway? Set up a fender bender, like an air-headed lane change in the Camry. Bergman gets out to bitch and to exchange insurance. His car's too nice for him not to pull over. We plug him on the side of the road.

162

We put him in the trunk of his own car, swap out the plates and leave him in long-term parking at LAX."

"What about the cars driving by?" William said.

"It'll be late. They'll be going too fast to get a good look. And what's it to them? Nothing, a minor car accident. Have a little faith in human indifference."

They spent the next day driving the 405. The crush traffic gave them a good chance to scope out what they wanted—a quiet stretch with a wide shoulder. They found it near the Mulholland Drive exit.

The next night they watched Bergman and a TV actress whose name neither of them could quite recall. They could watch the pair eating a late dinner from Seth's rental car across the street. The Camry was parked around the corner. It was crummy enough that it would be conspicuous near the restaurant.

"Whatsername—she looks taller than she does on TV," William noted.

"They can't have the leading man look short, I guess. See how short Bergman looks next to her."

"She doesn't make Bergman look short, she makes him look like dogshit."

Truth was, Bergman didn't look too bad for a man of fifty. His hairline had been assiduously reforested and tinted, and what would be his jowls had been pulled tight to his jaw by experienced surgeons. But the effort showed, especially next to the blonde's effortlessness.

Bergman and the blonde finished dinner. Rising from the table, the blonde's small black satin dress showed off her legs, which were supernaturally long and glistened in a way that singled her out as one of the special people. Jaime Bergman held the door for her.

"No way does he get to go home with that," William said. "No fucking way."

"There's no justice to it."

"No damn sense to it."

"Except money. And, well, power."

"Right. That."

The thought of grubby Jaime Bergman climbing all over this vision of television-actress perfection made them both especially keen on the murder. Seth and William watched as the blonde accelerated effortlessly from the glass door that Bergman held. And, walking straight on her long legs, she reached the valet a few steps ahead of the producer, the ticket ready in her hand.

"Oh wait, maybe not."

Bergman caught up to her. But, again, the effort showed. From across the street, they could make out Bergman's brazen invitation, as well as the actress' polite and apologetic retreat, her insincere thanks, and her vague promises of a future meeting, all spoken through a smile whose glamour outshone its falsity. The actress gave Bergman a one-armed embrace, offering not so much her cheek as her chin, turning toward her car as she did.

"Thank God. Now let's see if he decides to open door number two," William said

"Miss Pasadena," Seth said.

They walked around the corner and started up the Camry. The valet was slow with Bergman's Mercedes, leaving them no choice but to double park in the warm night air for a long, tooth-grinding minute. They followed a few cars back as Bergman approached the 405 onramp. Seth's stomach sank as Bergman hit the onramp without signaling. There wasn't much traffic on the highway so late, and the Camry struggled to keep pace with the Mercedes, which hit the left lane and stayed there. Near the crest of the highway pass, William nodded slightly. Seth noticed the nod, like he noticed everything at times like this. He pulled up in the lane next to Bergman, and kept pace slightly ahead of him for a second, then made an abrupt lane change. There was a jolt and the sound of cracking plastic. The Camry skidded slightly, but Seth kept the car on the road. He signaled his way to the shoulder, and Bergman followed. Seth took deep breaths.

At the shoulder, he flipped the safety off the pistol William had given him and tucked it under his UCSD sweatshirt. Shorts, flip–flops and the sweatshirt were Seth's unthreatening-California-dude costume. He slowly pulled himself out of the car and ambled toward Bergman, who had jumped awkwardly from his Mercedes.

"Dude. What *was* that?" Seth said in a mellow and exasperated tone. His heart raced and his stomach lurched, wild to do the deed, and equally wild to falter and flee.

"Why don't you learn how to drive, you moron," Bergman said, apoplectic, his tan face hard to read in the darkness of the highway's shoulder.

"Hey man, I'm not the one who's running into people. You hit me, man, from, like, behind."

"Just go get your insurance."

Seth went back to the car and grabbed a handful of papers the previous owner had left in the Camry's glove box. When he returned, Bergman was leaning against the open driver's side door of his car, his Blackberry and his insurance card out. He handed the card to Seth, who handed him a dirty handful of papers. Seth looked at the card and frowned.

"Yeah man, I'm going to need to see the registration, like, to make sure it goes with the insurance. I've been burned on this kind of thing before."

Bergman widened his eyes, exhaled impatiently, and almost seemed to sympathize with the California dude. And for a moment Seth could not ignore the common humanity under the black suit, plastic surgery and luxury car, the child that had grown old and never understood so many things.

Taking a deep breath and leaning into the Mercedes, Jaime Bergman rested a knee on the driver's side seat. The effort showed. So did the baldness at the crown of his head. The interior of the car was all dark wood and black, softly glowing leather. It was somewhere between a library and the cockpit of a spaceship. Even the dome light gave off gentle, upscale glow. Seth couldn't help but admire it as Bergman unlatched the glove box, which opened slowly, with a grace and gentleness that its owner seemed to lack.

Without hurrying or missing a breath, Seth dropped the crumpled paperwork on the ground and pulled the pistol from under his sweatshirt. He fired a shot into Bergman's back, where his heart was. The shot was loud, the smell of the gunpowder acrid. Bergman grunted, tried to cough, but couldn't. The force of the shot shoved him against the passenger side door. Seth fired a second shot next to the first. And Bergman jumped, and slumped, gravity wedging his shoulder into the leg well. The second shot was louder but the highway was deaf.

Seth swept a bullet casing off the flawless leather upholstery, onto the concrete. He walked around the car, opened the passenger side door and pulled Bergman's body into a proper sitting position in the passenger seat. The bullets hadn't exited Bergman, leaving a fairly neat corpse. Seth reclined the passenger side seat and fastened the older man into place with the seatbelt. He threw the Camry's paperwork into the scrub by the road.

But before he had the Mercedes' doors closed, with the gunpowder smell still fresh in the car, the hillside above them flashed red and blue. Cops were roaring toward them, a lot of them. Seth froze and tried to come up with a halfway plausible story. He started toward William to hash something out in the seconds they had left before they would be separated and interrogated.

With the sirens, however, came another sound, high and guttural. A souped-up Japanese car with a light-kit from the year 2050 and no muffler blasted past them, with three police cars, all lights and sirens, flying after it. They vanished over the hill as fast as they'd come.

Seth shrugged and William started to laugh. They drove off, Seth in the Mercedes and William in the Camry. Bergman seemed to shake his head in a long sloppy *no* whenever Seth took a tight corner. Seth was lost in his admiration for

Bergman's Mercedes. It was everything that Bergman wasn't: Beautiful, sleek, and most of all, effortless.

By the time they'd vacuum-sealed Jaime Bergman in one of William's laundry bags, swapped the plates, parked Bergman and his car at LAX, wiped prints, ditched the Camry and the guns on a quiet corner of the ghetto, and found their way back to Santa Monica, it was three in the morning. They parked Seth's rental car across the street from the hotel, out of habit. They looked at each other and breathed a tired sigh of relief, almost in unison.

"I thought we were fucked," William said.

"I did too. I had a story ready. But it was very thin."

"You going to hit the sack?"

"No. I don't think so. I'm on the first plane back to DC."

"What's that give you, three hours?"

"Two."

William produced a pint of whiskey, and held it up in the light. Seth nodded. They drank it in the car and talked about everything except what they'd just done and why they'd done it. William was partway through a story about the time in his life after he'd been thrown off the Tampa police force, and was living more or less as a pimp. Seth's phone rang. It was Hurley.

"How's California?" Hurley said, his voice tired and cheerless.

"Fine, unless you heard otherwise."

"I didn't hear anything. Will I?

"Not for a few weeks, hopefully. What's up?"

"You almost done over there?"

"Pretty much. Why?"

"Our girl's in the hospital. From what I hear, she's going to be okay. But I need you to go over there and find out where her head is at. When can you go?"

"Tomorrow. Tomorrow night?"

Hurley hung up. Seth's heart sank and his jaw hung loose. A too-late sort of numbness rang through his exhausted, half-drunk skull.

"What was that?" William asked.

"Nothing. Sorry to interrupt your story. Go ahead."

"So in Tampa there's not a lot of Asian people. And I was definitely the only half-Chinese pimp in town. And this girl, the one with the third nipple, she…"

William's story continued, half-hilarious and half-sad. But it was as if he was speaking underwater. Seth leaned back with the bottle and stared out the windshield. The air coming through the windows was cool, but still sweet and moist, salty from the ocean. Past the hotel, the waves crashed. A cop drove by and shone a light into the car. William stopped talking. Seth lowered the bottle between his legs. Once the police car disappeared around the corner, Seth and William broke up laughing.

---

The whiskey gave Seth and William another hour with the camaraderie and exhilaration of the kill. But next came the lull, and with it, the undertow of remorse and paranoia. It struck Seth hard in the hotel, as he packed his bag. Seth knew about that terrible lull and how to contend with it. He avoided mirrors. He focused hard on the million small things that needed doing.

He double-checked the hotel room to make sure he wasn't leaving anything behind. He took refuge in the matter-of-fact. Beyond that, in the realm of emotion and imagination, anything was possible—mostly bad things. That was the thing inside of him speaking. But in the dark lull after a killing, Seth relied on its voice. The exhaustion and moral hangover followed Seth to the airport in the early morning. He nearly gave a security guard at the airport his fake ID, and passed a few awkward moments trying to explain why he would rather give one driver's license rather than another to a disinterested old Mexican woman. Nonetheless, the sloppiness terrified Seth. He slept fitfully on the flight, a massive storm system over the Midwest flashing in the clouds below.

He called Sarah Loire's cell phone twice on the drive from the airport. DC was cold and damp, but snowless, all tan lawn and black, gnarled tree branches. Sarah didn't answer. He considered asking Hurley what hospital Sarah was at, so he could visit, but quickly realized how that wouldn't add up.

He checked into a hotel, one closer to Adams Morgan, and waited for Sarah to call back. It all came back to waiting. The suite was big, with pink-cream walls. The place had a sort of old-world air, with a sprawling, ornate lobby and a pool out back heated and open even in the dead of winter. From his window, Seth could watch the darkness render Rock Creek Park below impenetrable. He dropped onto the bed and fired up the TV. News anchors fought to conceal their exhaustion with the human condition, giving voice to a rumor that the FBI was again considering an air strike on what it believed to be Jefferson's stronghold, now in Montana. The TV showed the faces of the latest dead FBI and ATF agents, before cutting over to Mankins and the governor of Montana giving a joint press conference to denounce the rumor. The governor of Montana, in a bolo tie, blamed the FBI for escalating the situation. Mankins called the FBI's abuse of power in the Western states sickening and treasonous. Eventually, the TV turned its attention to a murder-suicide in Minnesota where the weapon of choice was a snowplow. Seth muted the sound and closed his eyes. He was halfway to sleep when his cell phone vibrated to life against his shirt button. It was a DC number he didn't recognize. The voice was Sarah's. But it was different, tired.

"Hey you," she said.

"Hey. How are you?"

"I've been better. Are you back in town?"

"I just got back."

"Hey, listen, if it's not too much trouble, can I get a ride?"

"Sure. Uh, where?"

"Thanks. Actually, it's a little more than a ride. They say I need someone to check me out of here. I'm in the hospital."

He tried to sound surprised as he asked what for. She just said she was okay, that she'd tell him about it when he got there. She gave the address. At the hospital, Sarah Loire looked pale, fragile and a little absurd. She'd applied some audacious makeup, vivid aqua-blue eyelids and bright red lips. Seth did a double take by the last desk before the hospital's final set of automated doors.

"I guess I look ridiculous. I stole some makeup from this old woman that I shared my room with. Don't laugh. You don't look so hot yourself."

"Long day."

"Tell me about it."

At the front desk, Seth signed her out. The thing inside of him guided his hand into the depths of his wallet to dig out his fake California driver's license for the sign-out. The nurse behind the desk called him by the fake name on it—Mr. Gordon—as he pushed away from the reception station. It took him a second, and the nurse had to call his fake name, Alec Gordon, twice more before he returned to the nurses' station to fill in a section that he'd missed on the form. Sarah raised a bemused eyebrow, but said nothing.

Seth pulled the car around. Sarah rose easily from the hospital-required wheelchair and walked to the car. She climbed in, but winced as she did.

"So, are you all right?"

"Yeah. It was just, just some bleeding," she said. Seth could tell she was dreading a follow-up question, and so left it off.

"Where do you want to go?"

"I just want to go home. Can you come over?"

"Sure."

"Seth, I'm glad you called. I know we didn't leave things so well. And I guess I could have called a few people. But right now, I can't handle their *concern*, you know? That sounds strange, doesn't it?"

"No. I know what you mean."

"I thought you would."

They parked in front of her apartment building, which was a mid-century brick rectangle on a quiet side street north of Adams Morgan. As soon as he had the car in park, she reached for his crotch and began rubbing him through his pants.

"Sarah, you don't have to. Really. It's…"

"Let me. I want to. Let me," she hissed hoarsely.

And Seth did. And she did, bringing him to the finish with a desperate impatience. After she'd zipped him up, she reached for the door handle.

"I hope you're still coming up," she said, her eyes wounded and awake.

Her words shamed him so deeply that all he wanted to do for her was everything. But all he could do was nod. Seth didn't like Sarah's small and spartan apartment, with tapestries tacked over the windows, a mattress on the floor, and no TV to palliate the discomfort of being alone, or the discomfort of being with someone else.

"I need a shower. Will you be all right?" she asked.

Sarah's shower took a long time. Seth picked up a bright-orange paperback by the bed: *The Perfection of Wisdom in 8,000 Lines*. He read a few lines, closed his eyes, and dropped off to sleep. When he woke, Sarah was back on top of him, her hair dancing around where she'd unzipped his trousers. She was topless, in sweatpants. For some reason, her sweatpants set him off.

"Not so sleepy after all," she said.

"I guess not."

"I'm sorry, but I can't, well, do it tonight."

"That's fine. Really. Don't worry about it. You don't have to do anything."

"That's sweet. But I like to. It calms me down. You don't mind, do you?" she said, smiling mischievously.

"Mind? That? No," Seth said, chuckling.

"I didn't think so."

Their laughter died into a pause. Sarah took a few heavy breaths and swallowed. She was getting ready to speak, but couldn't. Finally, she began.

"I shouldn't even tell you. But you probably want to know what's going on with me being in the hospital. And I guess I have to tell someone," Sarah said.

"Go ahead. I mean, you don't have to, but you can."

"It's this other guy I'm seeing. Shit, I shouldn't tell you."

"Go ahead."

"Does that upset you? That I'm seeing another guy?"

"No. Not that part. I mean, I'm not thrilled about it. But we never had that particular discussion, either."

"I know. And maybe we could have that talk. Not tonight. But maybe when I feel better, I mean."

"Yeah. I'd like that. But go ahead, tell me."

"Well, this guy, he's got, I don't know, he's got strange tastes. He wants to do more than most guys. Sometimes he likes to use things on me—candles, remote controls—you know? And sometimes it's okay. Well, the last time we were together, he took out this statue, this like, trophy. And he gets this crazy look to him and he…"

Her voice cracked, but she didn't cry.

"Go ahead."

"And I told him to be careful. Because the trophy is, like, real metal, first of all. And it's big, and kind of jagged."

"Jesus."

"And I guess he was careful at first. And I was actually kind of getting off on it. The trophy is this humanitarian award that he won. It's a bronze thing with a kid on a guy's shoulders. And it's like this kinky thing, like this big sanctimonious trophy being put into me by this guy who's supposed to be a humanitarian, but who's actually a pervert. I really shouldn't be telling you this."

"Go ahead. It's okay."

"So he does this for a while. Then he says that we both know where this is going. And he says that we should get it over with. And that's when he starts, like, pressing it and

172

twisting it. And I tell him to go easy, then I tell him to stop. But he just laughs and does it harder. It really hurt and he wasn't stopping and I was too scared to kick or move because of the pain, and I couldn't get away. Finally, I guess I passed out. When I woke up, he was yelling at me for bleeding all over his carpet. I got dressed and ran out, and took a cab to the hospital."

"So who is this guy, this humanitarian?" Seth asked, clenching his jaw.

"He's this guy I was seeing before I met you. It's not serious, not really a relationship exactly. He's a politician here in town. It really doesn't matter. He's leaving soon. It's over."

"Who is he?"

"I don't want to get into it. I know you're mad, but that's not why I told you. It's my fault. I kind of knew this guy was, well, dangerous. I could tell. That was all part of the thrill. Like with you, *Mister Gordon*."

All Seth could do was shrug at that one.

"I mean, I kind of knew he was an animal, but I didn't count on him being a monster," Sarah said. "Anyway, let me take care of it."

"Take care of it how?"

"I'll get him to cover the hospital bill. Maybe have him buy me a car or something. He's rich enough," Sarah said, yawning.

She climbed up his body and curled up into his armpit, signaling that she didn't want to talk anymore. Seth stayed very still. That night, he slept in his shirtsleeves and slacks, so as not to wake her. When morning came, Seth slipped out and brought back bagels, coffee and juice. She was up when he got back, in sweatpants and a transparent black bra, smoking a cigarette in bed.

"Oh, I thought you'd left."

"No, I ran out to get us some breakfast. I figured you'd be hungry."

"Bring it over here."

They passed an hour, eating bagels in bed, ignoring the crumbs and drinking coffee. Seth rose to go to the bathroom and grimaced with the familiar pain in his back. Sarah saw him struggle to straighten himself and stood with him, grimacing with her own pain. She had him stand straight up, with his feet together, and as she had done in yoga class, she gently guided his hands over his head, pressing his shoulders down and away from his neck. She lit a cigarette, and with it in her hand, she lifted his ribcage and pressed down on the top of his buttocks. She dropped to a crouch, gripped his legs and turned his kneecaps toward each other. And Seth's back loosened palpably and immediately. At the same time, previously bottled sensation flooded into his right leg and the muscles in his abdomen relaxed.

"Oh, I heard that," she said. "Would you like to do more?"

Seth nodded. The anxiety that had been in his gut since he entered her TV-less apartment was gone. She went to a corner and brought back a rubber mat. For the next hour, she put him through the paces, with a mix of maternal care and what, in moments of extremity, could only be considered flirtatious sadism. With Seth bent at odd angles for what felt like hours at a time, the thing in him grew desperate. It reminded Seth that he was by now a millionaire, so what exactly was he doing in this squalid apartment with this crazy, doomed woman, sweating in his undershorts? Why was he doing these painful things? It didn't demand an answer to its questions, but commanded him to leave. Still Seth kept on, the pain muting the insistent diatribe of the broken-toothed spirit.

Hanging upside down in a closet doorframe, from ropes that dug painfully into his hips, full of the basic terror that comes from being upside down and not in control, it reminded him he'd already busted his nut sufficiently and demanded that he name any reason on earth why he was embarrassing himself by doing what he was doing. And in that moment of pain, Seth revealed his own buried intention to the broken-toothed spirit and to himself. *Why? Because I want to be free. That's why.*

In that moment, the thing in him fell completely silent. And Seth was left without all the broken-toothed spirit, without that powerful antibody against empathy and remorse. It all came crashing in: Bergman, Eggleston, the two before that he'd killed for Hurley, and the poor dumb kid back in Westerly. They came to him with their humanity the same as his, their sense of themselves as the warm, important center of the universe the same as his, their yearning to see what happens next the same as his, their desire not to die the same as his. The flash of compassion was staggering. It was the true cost of the freedom he'd dared to desire.

The wind howled through the apartment's loose window panes. Seth fell out of the ropes into a heap on the floor, shuddering. The thing in him was still there, but tenuous. It whispered that, on his own, Seth was a common murderer and a petty opportunist with nothing to redeem his actions. Seth wept, coughing thick gobs of brown phlegm between sobs. Sarah didn't seem surprised. She threw a blanket over him where he lay on the floor. She rubbed his back and hummed while he sobbed and heaved.

His tears drying, a blood-dark mucous on his lips, Seth was comforted by the soft pressure of Sarah's hands on him. For a while, they stayed in a heap on the floor like that. Sarah mentioned the time, and said she needed to get to the pharmacy before it closed. Seth got dressed and drove her there. She went in, asking that Seth stay in the car. While he waited, Hurley called.

"Seth, I was worried. Is everything okay?" Hurley said.

"Sorry, I was with the lady."

"*The* lady?"

"Yeah."

"How's it going?"

"It's okay. I picked her up at the hospital. She's going to be all right."

"That's good. Are *we* going to be okay?"

"Yeah. I don't think we have a problem. She plays it very close, especially with people's names, even with me. I think we're okay here."

"You sure?"

"Sure as I can be."

"Are you okay? You sound, uh, a little off," Hurley said.

"I'm tired. That's all."

"Why don't you come by the office tomorrow afternoon, say two?"

Seth agreed and hung up, breathing a sigh of relief before the paranoia returned. Had Hurley somehow known what had happened to him in Sarah's apartment? He'd called just minutes later. And given the revelations of the last few weeks, anything seemed possible. Sarah returned from the pharmacy with two big shopping bags. Peeking down into one, Seth made out the words *adult diaper* and looked no more. He turned on the car and suggested they pick up a pizza.

"Bagels, pizza. Might as well get fat—with everything else going on," she said, relaxing at Seth's suggestion.

Back at the apartment, she unpacked most of the pharmacy shopping bags into the back of the bathroom closet. She came out with a big orange bottle of pills.

"Percocet?" she said, unscrewing the white plastic top.

"You probably need those more than me."

"It's no fun flying alone."

*Alone* was the word that reverberated. That was another consequence implicit in his moment of freedom.

"Sure."

She poured out a few pills for him and dry-swallowed a small handful herself. She turned on the radio to a Soul music station and they sat down to eat. He was through his second slice when he realized that he was, in fact, very high.

"Ooh, I like this part," Sarah said.

"It's nice," Seth offered, blinking.

"I like it too much. More than is good for a lady. Truth is, I spent a few years not doing much else than this kind of thing. Back then, I used to hate Percocet."

"Why?"

"They cut the oxycodone with acetaminophen so that if you take too much, the acetaminophen destroys your liver. It's like some weird punishment for junkies."

"You were a junkie?"

"I don't think there's another word for what I was. I was always high. I did a lot of things, bad things, to stay that way."

"Like what?"

"Bad things. Bad things. But I guess you showed me yours, killer. Some of yours, anyway. Mine wasn't as bad as all that. I fucked men, for money, for drugs, I fucked men on camera. Sometimes a lot of men, at once, on camera. I don't know. I was a kid, nineteen. And there'd be three, five, twelve guys at a time, sometimes. It could get scary—the crowd. And the guys were big. They'd get rough, start competing, start shoving. And I was ninety pounds, all bones, all wasted from whatever I could get my hands on. It wouldn't have taken much of an accident for one of those guys to really hurt me. As far as my parents knew, I was at UCLA. But a neighbor saw me on the internet and told my father. So my dad came out to LA with my uncle and some intervention guy they hired."

"How long were you clean for?" Seth asked, too high for the news to rattle him.

"A few years. Long enough for people to stop asking. But not so long that they were too surprised when I relapsed."

"But you still drink, and you still take the pills. Isn't that supposed to be a no-no?"

"Yeah, I guess. I did the recovery thing for a while. I had to, to keep everyone off my back. Now, it's more like I'm managing it. Suicide by drugs is as boring as being in the program. I guess if I have to die, I want to build up to it. I want to tease it out, get close and personal with whatever or whoever is going to do it."

"Right. So this is your death wish, your sacrificial-lamb karma thing. We're back to that?" Seth said, hearing the drugs in his disjointed words. "Is that what I'm doing here?"

"I don't even know what I'm doing here, nevermind you. But I knew. Like I knew what you are capable of. I don't know how I know. But I can smell something that I like."

Seth smiled, turned on in a deep way, as he was from the start, by her headstrong vulnerability. He liked how she could see the predator in him and didn't flinch.

"It's like I'm pushing against a tide," Sarah Loire said. "I've tried being clean, really tried the sober, healthy life. But in the end, my highest hopes and my deepest wishes, and also my worst habits and worst grudges, all lead me back to this desire, for, uh, for annihilation, I guess."

"I don't think that's true. There's a lot for you, out... uh, in the world. Look at what you did for me now, what you showed me today. You really helped me."

"Oh, here comes the *concern* part. You're so *worried* about me. Let's not waste a perfectly good high waltzing down that primrose path of bullshit."

"I don't want you to think you have to die."

"We think different things. But that's not because one of us is wrong and one of us is right. We think different things because we are different things. We want different things."

"And what is it you think I want?"

"Oh Seth, you have to know it—you're still digging your hole down into the unfolding of time, rifling through the bottomless bottom of the world for your reward. It's different with me. I'm already down at the bottom of all that. It's all ashes, and I'm trying to climb, or I'm trying to grow wings, to fly out of that same hole called the world. Somehow we met halfway, in the same place. And that's beautiful. I think it's special and rare. But it will always mean different things to us."

"You know, you really talk nice when you're high."

"Maybe. But so what? I'm another little bubble who learned too little too late to do very much except pop. So much struggle and pain for so little progress. For someone like me, death will be a triumph. Death, that will be my windfall."

Seth was out of his depth and too stoned to conjure a response. Sarah reached for his crotch, but there was nothing doing there.

----

The broken-toothed spirit wandered the ocean to the rocky shores of what would become Massachusetts. The new continent wasn't completely unknown to the broken-toothed spirit. Some of his peers had engineered a terrific death cult down in Mexico. Others had found a kind of benevolent retirement out in the plains. The broken-toothed spirit was exhausted from the long empty trek, and settled in the woods by the ocean, in the mist and the damp leaves. It was quiet there. At times, the broken-toothed spirit almost thought he could hear his own breathing. In the winters, he could almost see his own shadow crossing the wind-smoothed snow.

In that silence, the men could hear him. They weren't an inherently devotional bunch, so he started by telling the men where to find deer. He told weeping women which young men to lavish their charms on. And so he became known, by another god's name, but known nonetheless. Those he possessed, he possessed warily. He contented himself with his place among them. It wasn't much, but it was tranquil.

That lasted until the tall ships came, their huge masts like crosses, enraging the broken-toothed spirit. He began possessing some of the more pliant men. He started with an angry teenager, a chief's younger son. Through subtle hints and angry whispers, he spurred the young man into a bloody, doomed war. The young man and most of his followers were killed, and the people the broken-toothed spirit had lived peacefully among were soon as dispossessed as he was.

They abandoned him and moved into the victors' towns, businesses and churches. Soon no one visited his hill of pine trees for insight or for help. So he searched the towns, finding very little but disapproval, bland food and endless prayers. Where he could, the broken-toothed spirit would seize onto

179

the fervent horny prayer of a minister, or the sworn homicidal vow of a daughter against her sister, and inhabit that desperate soul. Through careful machinations, he would destroy a congregation here, a family there, and almost always the individuals themselves.

He granted their prayers, and he was paid in some tearful or bloody affirmation that he still existed. In time, there was nothing he yearned for more. And so he found a new way to live among the constant prayers that ground dull, slow and fine like the millstones the rivers turned. He kicked up human dust, hid in barns, in empty bedrooms and the attics of big clapboard houses. He strolled the lonely graveyards and pine barrens. He accepted his lot as a kind of criminal.

––––––––––––

The next morning was all cost. An ache ran from his balls to his ribcage like a spring had been overstretched to a squiggle of useless wire. Seth was constipated, and struggled to ignore the bloody maxi-pad in the trash bin next to the toilet while he strained. Sarah slept deeply in the next room, while Seth shivered and crept from her apartment. The prosaic morning of grim commuters, modern office blocks and Greco-Roman monuments of the DC streets all whispered a gentle, sexless sanity to him, for which he was grateful.

In his hotel room, Seth turned on the TV. A pretty anchorwoman bewailed the rising price of gas and then men argued about some detail of the coming Super Bowl. Seth was glad to hear them do so. Apparently, candidate Mankins had worked his way into their argument, with one of the men saying that the Super Bowl should be moved from San Diego if Mankins didn't retract his latest statement about the FBI. The other man took the opposing point of view, saying *come on*. A shower took the edge off the nausea and the anxiety that hung in his gut like an electric fetus. He lingered over a big breakfast that he couldn't bring himself to eat. He left the hotel in the early afternoon. Lunchtime in DC was a happy time—a few hours to eat well on someone else's dime.

At Hurley's office, the security was more time-consuming than before, with new, dead-eyed personnel examining his credentials and cell phone before letting him pass. The long line to the X-ray and metal detector made the huge bronze caduceus statue loom even larger over the lobby. Seth sat in the reception area of Hurley's office for a few minutes. When the office door opened, Mankins emerged, in the middle of a farewell handshake with Hurley. Mankins was taller and wider than Hurley, angular and fit for a man in his fifties. Powerfully oblivious to the shock of discomfort he'd roused in Seth, Mankins smiled an easy TV smile, and held out his hand. Being a well-practiced stranger to his own heart, Seth rose quickly, matched the smile and shook the hand.

"Steve, right?"

Mankins stood a few inches taller than Seth. But Seth guessed that the senator hadn't been in a fair fight in decades. Seth was also about fifteen years younger. The thought of Mankins' brittle bones kept Seth's smile lit.

"Close, it's Seth actually. And it's good to see you, Senator. How's the campaign trail?"

"It's long, but it's getting shorter by the day," the senator said in his deep, reassuring voice, smiling at his half-joke. "I'll be happy when I can stop sleeping on planes."

"Well, the way things are going, it looks like you'll be in the big chair in Sacramento in a few months," Seth smiled back.

"Well, we've had a few lucky breaks. And we have a lot of good people on our side," Mankins said, smiling through his collection of clichés as though he really meant them. "And I hear that you've been one of them. Well, listen, Seth, I have to go. But after the election, we should sit down and talk. Hurley says that you're a capable and creative man. We're going to need people like you."

"Thanks, Senator. And good luck"

"Okay, Seth, keep up the good work."

And like that, Mankins was gone, gliding past Seth like he was stepping up in the pocket on second down. Hurley's corner office had two big banks of windows, but with the lights off, it still felt dark. By the time Seth entered, Hurley was leaning back in his leather desk chair, gazing out the window.

"I didn't expect to see him here."

"Well, I've known Chet Mankins since long before we got started on this adventure. It may seem reckless, but it would actually look stranger if we didn't see each other. Nothing is simple in this business, is it? How are you feeling?"

"I'm all right. I've had a few long days, with the hospital and Los Angeles before that. But it's nothing a good night's sleep couldn't cure. How about you?"

"I'm fine, thank you. I heard that someone filed a missing person's report out in Hollywood. It's a tragedy, no?"

"It's definitely a tragedy. I'm sure he'll turn up eventually. But not for a while."

"I suppose that no one can say how long these things will take. But if you were a betting man?"

"At least a month."

"No problems out there?"

"No, everything was smooth. Hotels and cars booked under other names, all of that."

"Good. And the mistress?" Hurley asked, wetting his lips.

"Honestly, she's in rough shape. Our friend…" Seth said, nodding to the closed door behind him, "…he did a number on her."

"And how about you?"

"What do you mean?"

"Did you do a number on her?"

"If I was less than a gentleman, then it was in the line of duty," Seth said, flashing his best predator's grin. Hurley responded, arching an eyebrow.

"I saw the hospital reports. Internal bleeding and they had to put a few stitches in her. I'd like to know how you managed it."

182

"It's the twenty-first century. We've all have to get creative sometimes," Seth said, careful not to rise to the bait. "It's true that she's hurt pretty bad. But even in pillow-talk, she wouldn't give up his name."

"And you, uh, pushed her?"

"I did. And she didn't say a word. But our friend ought to know that she's going to hit him up for some money. Hospital bills and a little extra—nothing much."

"You think he should pay it?" Hurley asked, staring down at the blotter on his desk.

"Definitely. It's the cheapest solution."

"It's not always as cheap as it seems. She could come back for more."

"No, I don't think so. That's not her. But at the same time, we should get her away from him, get her out of town. This seems like it's headed in that bad direction."

"That's not really our place."

"Isn't it? It would save us all some work and, more importantly, some serious risk down the line," Seth said, struggling to keep his breath even and his face flat.

"So, some money and a ticket out of town. That's all?"

"Well, it depends on what you want. It would seem that you already have Mankins by the neck for the last girl. To let this continue toward a similar conclusion, it seems like overkill, no pun intended."

"Is that what you think happened with the first girl? I was tightening my hold on Mankins?" Hurley said, offended or at least acting like it.

"I don't think *that*. You took an inconvenience, and you turned it to your advantage. That's simple problem-solving."

"It's just funny to me, how admittedly-the-call-of-duty you've been on this admittedly boring job. You like this girl, Sarah Loire, don't you?"

"I like her enough to not want to see her dead for the entertainment of Senator Mankins. I also consider burying a body to be a real shit job, a massive risk and a waste of my talents. But I'd like to know what your guess is—does he like killing, or does he just enjoy watching us scramble to clean it up?" Seth said, a sneer finding its way onto his face.

Hurley chuckled.

"Seth, you're full of surprises. And you make a good point. It's not practical for us, or for our man, to play this out to the bitter end. He's only in town another week before he goes out to California pretty much full-time for the campaign. We'll get her a little too much money, a plane ticket to someplace nice and far from here or California, along with a stern warning."

"I can do it."

"First you want to save the girl, and now you want to come clean *and* play the heavy? This operation is messy enough. Jesus. We have to get you back out on a less domestic task before your manners get the best of you. Trust me, we'll take care of it."

"Thank you."

"Anything else I can do for you?" Hurley asked, still smirking.

Seth shook his head, afraid another word would undo what they'd agreed to, and might undo more than just that. Hurley spun in his big leather chair.

"Now, onto the next matter," Hurley said. "We need you to go back out to New Mexico. We're getting complaints about the Indian there, Hal."

"We had problems with that guy on the first run, months ago. Why are we still using him?"

"You know how it goes. He was the original name on the orders, the customs paperwork, all of it. Even though he was a pain in the ass, whoever was in charge there decided it would be more of a pain in the ass to set up a new customer with a new back story and so on. It's funny, but even in something like this, with death and glory on the line, there's still a certain inertia that rules people."

"Laziness in the face of death?"

"It's the story of a lot of people and a lot of nations too. Go out onto the street and look around at the shining scab of

184

bribery and inertia that's grown up here. You're old enough not to be surprised, I hope. Anyway, this Hal is becoming an even bigger pain in the ass than we anticipated. He was arrested for domestic battery last week, and the cops found enough meth at his house to get their attention."

"Oh man," Seth said.

"The good news is that we're on the last of the deliveries before the election in California, and then the big show. The situation in Montana makes it harder and harder to keep up the shipments. So this should be about it. We just need you there to keep Hal out of the way, keep the cops off of the trucks, and to take delivery of Hal's textbooks."

"Textbooks?"

"Yeah. The textbooks are still the cover story. They've been sending this guy thousands of textbooks over for the past few months. Those Navajo kids are going to be set for homework for the next century."

"So, the same as before: Handle the transfer, and get Hal the books?"

"That, and handle Hal. He's still setting up the meetings. Go to him, find out where it's set for, and make sure he stays as far away as possible."

"And after that?"

"After that, we're done with the guy."

"Done?"

"No, not that. Just done working with him. He's seems capable of making a fool or a corpse of himself without our help. Can you get there tomorrow?"

"That soon? I was thinking I'd stay here through the week."

"Don't worry. We'll take care of the situation with your lady friend. But we need you out there tomorrow."

Hurley handed him an envelope with directions, phone numbers, addresses and meeting times, and a bigger catalogue-type envelope with cash.

---

At the airport, Seth felt a reluctance to leave. He took out his phone to call Sarah. He wanted to warn her, to urge her to take the money and run, or to forget the money and run. He felt an urge to confess who he was and his place among the forces that at that moment idly toyed with the notion of destroying her. But the thing inside Seth spoke calmly. To make such a call would go against everything that had kept him free and alive all these years, it said. To make that call would contradict the mission that had taken the place of a home and which ordered his life. Seth put his cell phone away.

He took a big plane to the big airport, and a small plane to the small airport. When he landed in New Mexico, there was a message from Sarah Loire, saying she was busy that night, and asking if he was around the next. Walking across the freezing tarmac to the tiny terminal, Seth turned off his phone. He needed to focus. He pulled up his collar against the cutting wind, remembering Hal's mockery of the dark wool coat he wore.

Seth's rented green sedan stood out in Farmington mostly because it was clean. The town drifted by like a honky-tonk tune with its neon, its proud movie palace, the ragged men and women dressed for the elements, the light and life in the bar windows at night. He checked into a hotel in town, double-checked the info Hurley had given him and hit the road. From town, he drove up a hill into the suburban darkness and found the address. It was a big house, with a wall around it, but the gate had been left open.

He knocked on a solid-wood door ten feet high and half a foot thick and tried the bell. A minute later, the door drifted open on its hinges, pulled with both hands by a small woman whose features and bearing indicated that she had once been pretty. Her cheeks were sunken, her skin raw and picked at. He told her he was there to see Hal. She smirked and disappeared around a corner, her pink panty bottoms showing below her ski parka.

Not explicitly invited or uninvited, Seth entered. The foyer was two stories high and its walls, as well as the walls of the next room were lined, floor to ceiling, with cardboard boxes. Here and there, someone had pulled down a box and ripped it open to reveal big, glossy hardback books with titles like *Voices of Our Land* and *Horizons in Math*. In the middle of the room, boxes had been arranged as two seats and a crude table. There was no other furniture on the first floor. But there was music, which Seth followed down to the basement.

Hal sat on a green leather couch, his shirt off and a big grin on his face. In the intervening months, he'd grown thinner, while his face had bloated. Between that and his stupefied expression, Seth had to look twice to be sure it was him. The woman who'd answered the door was sitting in a big easy chair, looking pissed, with her legs folded so that her bony knees jutted. Coming down the stairs, Seth saw the woman Hal was watching. She was a topless tan girl, young and expressionless, pulling and pawing at her yellow bikini bottoms as she danced. Several big, flat-screen TVs flashed cartoons silently behind her. The big room was cluttered with trading-post tchotchkes, life-size wooden Indians with full headdresses, oversized dream catchers, a fake stuffed buffalo. Seth was down the stairs and around the first wooden chief before Hal even noticed him. Hal's face went white.

"Hey! The devil! I see you waited until I'd made something myself before you bothered to turn up," Hal said, his voice lazily ranging over octaves.

"Hal. How are you?"

"I *was* doing good, until about five or ten seconds ago."

"Yeah, well, I'll keep it short. It's about tomorrow. You're not going out to the meeting. I'll be overseeing the exchange. You'll get your books and your money. All you have to do is take it… take it easy," Seth said, gesturing with his eyes toward the girls, the endtable full of booze and the saran-wrapped ball of powder on the coffee table.

Hal's face dropped. His neck bent. He stared at his silver belt buckle.

"But the meetings, they're my part. They're what *I* do."

"Yeah well, it was never supposed to be what you do. What happened to your school?"

"Those… fucking hypocrites. They threw me out. They said… I… Shit. Do you know anyone who wants to buy some textbooks?"

From there, the conversation went in circles for a while. Hal said he needed more money, said he knew who the guns were *really* for, unleashed an incoherent theory of why he'd been asked to stay away from the school he'd started, said he suspected that some people, like the two girls, were deliberately becoming less real when they went to see him. Seth realized that a conversation was impossible. So he removed a small stack of bills from his jacket pocket and asked where the meeting was set for. Seth gave the shirtless paranoid the money and his most innocent smile, got the information he needed, and said goodbye.

"Hey, you, Pequot lawyer. I have to ask you something. For what we do, is the devil proud of us at least?" Hal yelled as Seth climbed the stairs. "Is he proud?"

Seth doubted that he'd made his point. And the last thing he needed was Hal showing up in anything like his current condition to the next day's meeting. Stopping on the ground floor bathroom for a piss, he spotted a survival knife on the top of the toilet. It was a big, Rambo-style knife with an eight-inch blade. It looked like it had never been used to cut anything except lines. Seth pocketed it. Outside, he picked out the two cars that he judged to be Hal's, a Land Rover and a Jaguar, and slashed their tires. He slashed the tires of the two crappy cars in the driveway, to be on the safe side.

He slept a few hours, waking early. The meet was one town over, on a stretch of concrete behind a car dealership that had gone out of business before it opened, its Tyvek building skin flapping torn in the wind and its windows still X-ed with masking tape, still too innocent to invite wanton teenage vandalism. By noon, everyone was there.

Along with his drivers, Jefferson had sent a black man in his fifties who was dressed like a farmer, and a teenage tomboy with her hair in a short bowl cut. They seemed more comfortable with the Russians than they did with Seth. The tomboy had a blurry blue skeleton tattooed on her neck. It took Seth a moment to figure out that's what it was. She kept asking him who he was.

"I'm someone your friends sent to make sure everyone gets what they want," he said.

"What friends?"

"Don't worry about what friends."

Behind her, the drivers were swapping out boxes of books for crates of grenades with a forklift.

"What happened to Hal? Did these friends of ours do something to Hal?" she asked, squinting at him in the freezing light of morning.

"Katie," the old black man said.

"It's okay," she said. "All I'm doing is asking the man a question. He's a *professional*. I'm sure he can answer it."

"Hal's fine."

"He's anything but fine. He's effing crazy is what he is. That's what they do. They hook you on drugs. Effing feds," the girl said, her wild rage barely contained. She spat on the ground by Seth's feet.

Seth shrugged. The forklift made its short trips, consolidating the textbooks into two trailers and the weapons in the other two. Seth watched them work so he wouldn't have to look at the sneering tomboy. The truckers remarried the trucks to the trailers, swapped ID decals on the containers, and the license plates on the trailers. Seth followed the first truck back to Hal's place as the late afternoon sun set. None of the cars had moved.

Back at the hotel, frustrated and full of dread for reasons he couldn't pin down, Seth set his head to pillow, and fell into a deep, overdue sleep. When he woke, hours later, he'd missed his flight and discovered that he'd missed an alarming number of phone calls.

---

189

The broken-toothed spirit had fought the war Petronius had imagined. And he'd tried to live peacefully and profitably in the quiet, secondary position allowed him in the world of men. But the centuries had finished their work, and made the broken-toothed spirit a criminal.

And small towns are hard places for criminals. The chances of detection are higher and the penalties more thorough. But no one in the cities could hear or would listen. So he stayed in small towns. The dullness made people receptive to the odd voices that echoed and twisted their prayers. And the very smallness of those towns could make unrequited love a cosmic catastrophe to the lovelorn. A personal slight could quickly grow to towering enmity. Personal matters were do-or-die simply because there were so few people.

So many desperate prayers rose from those clapboard houses that he could pick and choose the souls who lacked the introspection to suspect his influence, or the will to resist it. He thrived on the guilty, who'd already built catacombs of forced forgetting and distorted memory in themselves. There he worked best, safe from the suspicion of those he manipulated. The centuries fermented his penchant for mischief into bitterness. Stopping before a shop window one morning on the town's main street, the broken-toothed spirit saw himself, his features warped into a bestial mask, like the skull of a dog with bulging black eyes.

The towns grew and proliferated. And in between the short and grim lives he coauthored, the broken-toothed spirit took to haunting police stations. There he heard the wild, desperate, earnest prayer that he needed to gain purchase. Any prayer, made earnestly enough, is a kind of contract.

In the decades before it found Seth, the former deity had a good run with a red-haired fat man he'd met in a small town police station. Although no dummy, the man had killed his father for reasons that wouldn't impress a judge. But the red-haired man prayed fervently and the broken-toothed spirit came to him, teasingly at first. As the case against the patricide crumbled in unlikely and spectacular fashion—the loss of a claw hammer from evidence, coupled with the testimony of a schizophrenic who half-accurately took the blame. The red-haired man came to trust the spirit, and to afford him space and agency as a corruption that he could afford. The man moved out of the small town and went on to make his fortune in heroin and slot machines on the outskirts of Providence. Through the red-haired man's tumultuous business dealings, the spiteful, broken-toothed spirit got its much-needed dose of blood, sex, and forlorn rebellion against the still-tightening order of the world. But nothing lasts forever. The red-haired patricide was murdered by his nephew one cold night outside Providence. The spirit could have warned him, but knew from experience that old age wasn't something it wanted to stick around for.

When it found Seth, he was weeping in a holding cell. No dignity to it. The boy had been tremendously unmoored by the murder itself, exhausted from the effort of keeping it to himself for the two days after the act, and all but destroyed by the sense of species-wide disapproval that comes with being accused of murder. It was plainly too much for the fifteen-year-old. The cops left him for a few hours, figuring he would soften himself up for an easy confession. When he wasn't weeping, he was replaying the murder in his mind, trying to unwind the events to where none of it had ever happened. Or he was praying, desperately and intently. And the spirit heard him.

*Don't worry,* it said.

Seth couldn't hear it exactly. But he sensed an easing of his hopelessness. He felt less alone without knowing why.

*Calm down. Say nothing. Not yes, not no. Nothing.*

Seth sat up on the bench. He'd never really been in too much trouble in school, and had no real experience of being on the bad side of authority, its questions and its bullying.

*One word will get you through this. Do you want to know what it is?*

*Please,* Seth begged, listening intently to the faint voice.

*Do you remember what you promised?*

Seth's prayers were filled with the many concessions a child makes—to get better grades, to treat his mother better, to help his brother and sister with their homework and chores, to go straight home after school, to never kill anyone ever again, to do whatever was asked of him, no matter what.

*You need to listen though. You can't ever be so stupid. Never again.*
*You need to listen from now on. You need to listen to me.*

"Okay. I will," Seth said aloud, his lips numb. He could almost see the word that the voice was about to say. It was a key, in a hand that reached down from above.

*There's a word to tell the cops. It will make this go away.*
*Tell me. I'll do anything.*
*The word is* Lawyer.

---

Disoriented from the nap, Seth showered and called the airport to learn that there were no planes out of Four Corners Regional Airport until the next day. Wrapped in a towel and sitting on the bed, he listened to a series of short messages and started returning calls, beginning with William.

"Hey man, did Hurley call you?" William asked. From the sound of it, he was driving.

"Yeah, he left me a message. He said to call you. What's going on?"

"I'm in Georgetown. When can you be here?"

"I missed my flight. I'm stuck out here for the night. What's up?" Seth asked.

"You picked a hell of a time to miss your flight."

"Why? What's going on?"

"I don't know. You should call the man, see what he wants you to do."

William was being phone-careful. Seth demanded to know what was going on, and William hung up. He dialed Hurley's cell phone. Hurley picked up in what sounded like a restaurant and said he'd call back, which he did a few minutes later, from an unfamiliar number.

"Where are you?" were Hurley's first words.

"Still in New Mexico."

"Is everything okay there?"

"Yeah. It's done. We got some real crazies out here, but it went smoothly. Listen, I missed my flight. What's going on?"

"Shit. Well, it's nothing. We'll talk about it when you get back. It's something that I thought you could help out on tonight. But…"

Seth's stomach dropped. His phone hand trembled and went numb. The cell phone slipped partway down his cheek.

"Sarah? Is it her?"

"We did what we said. We tried, anyway, or we were about to. But, well, from the sound of it, we didn't get the chance. And, according to our friend, she didn't leave us with too many choices. We can talk about it when you get back."

With a click, Hurley was gone. Seth paced horseshoes around the hotel bed, clenched his fists, shook his head, sat down on the bed and wept.

There were thirteen hours until the next flight out of Farmington.

Seth needed to get back, but not for the reason Hurley or William wanted him there. He needed to get back to Washington for a reason that he didn't even feel safe explaining to himself.

# PART THREE

---

*In this Age of Disenchantment it also became possible to consider that the gods might not exist in any form. Among the intellectual elite, the Epicureans were formulating the first materialistic and atheistic philosophies. What remained was belief in the lowest levels of spirits, the spirits of the dead and demons. If you read the literature of the time, such as the Gospels of the New Testament, you see they record that the world was experiencing an epidemic of demons.*

-Mark Booth
**The Secret History of the World**

*… the unseen is proved by the seen,*
*Till that becomes unseen and receives proof in its turn.*

-Walt Whitman
**Song of Myself**

Eyes blurry, Seth jogged through the cold to the gas station catty-corner from the hotel and bought a six-pack of beer, so he could breathe. He bought a phone card with a Spanish word and a picture of a lobster on it. He drank a few beers in his hotel room, then walked back through the biting cold to the gas station's pay phone. In the wind and the bright brutal bland faces of onrushing cars, he practiced the call twice to get the squeak out of his voice.

"William, it's me. I talked to our man. What's the plan? Are you taking a ride out to the suburbs tonight, like before?"

"Yep. Suburbs. That's the plan," William said.

"Okay. Listen to me. I need you not to do that."

"Why not?"

"It's a bad play. I don't like it. What's the weather like out there?"

"I'm freezing my ass off."

"Good. Hold off until I get back. Should be there by noon or so."

"Hold off? What am I supposed to do?"

"Just sit tight."

"Sit tight? Are you crazy?"

"I'll explain later. But we have to stay out of patterns. Trust me. You'll be glad you did. Okay?"

"Okay. Shit. I really don't like being exposed like this, but… You better know what you're talking about."

Despite the premeditation that went into buying the phone card, practicing of the phone call, the beers, Seth's purpose wasn't yet clear even to himself. He couldn't let it be. The nearest he'd admit was that he wanted to bury Sarah Loire properly. His vagueness had a purpose, because he was not alone in there. Nonetheless, the thing inside of him wasn't happy. It pressed for answers, gnawed at him with a constant anxiety. But Seth found a part of himself that was separate from the thing inside of him and willed that part silent. Back at the hotel, the walls had that unforgiving solidity that mundane objects take on when something terrible has happened.

*Why the hell did you do that?* the thing inside of Seth demanded.

The broken-toothed spirit had so much planned for Seth, for the empire promised by Hurley, and for the tacit possibility that it might ride the newly released energies of war into an existence beyond that of a whispering shadow. And Seth endangered that. So it raged, and tried to seize him on the edge of the unmade bed. The silver can of beer dropped from Seth's hand as he stiffened, billowing foam. But he took control of his breath and addressed the thing, demanding *what do you want.* The seizure softened, faded.

*Why did you tell William to do that?* it demanded.

Seth responded with the image of a quiet burial on a wooded hillside. The thing inside of him had lied and hid for decades, and now Seth would do the same.

*William will have to hold onto a corpse for sixteen hours or more. It's a crazy, unnecessary risk,* the broken-toothed spirit chided him.

Seth pictured William's Lexus serenely parked in a freezing-cold paid garage, with Sarah Loire resting in the car's trunk. *It will be fine,* he responded. The thing in him kept at him, alternately questioning him, cursing Sarah, and promising him the world and all it contained. But Seth remained in the space to which it had no claim. There, Seth knew what he was doing—planning bloody revenge on Mankins, Hurley, Frederica, all of them.

*What you're thinking with the body: Don't you dare,* the broken-toothed spirit said, trying to draw it out of him.

But a determination was building with all the fury of his grief for Sarah. It burned with a disgust at the profound corruption that went into surviving his needlessly violent life. Seth coughed until he vomited up the sweet domestic beers, the bile of his empty stomach, then dark goo, stringy like phlegm, but rank. The thing in him kept at it, screeching between the heaves.

*You will be all alone. They will all turn on you. It will be like the police station, with no one on your side, and everyone right to condemn you.*

*But worse. You're not a kid. You have no excuses. You'll pay for everything you've done, and for things you haven't done, they'll...*

The fears were all rational enough. But during those long late hours in the crummy Farmington hotel room, they mattered less than ever before. And so Seth asked, out loud.

"Who are you?"

It paused for a few seconds, but resumed its particularly gruesome rendering of Seth being gang raped in a psychiatric ward for the criminally insane. But as it ranted, the thing in Seth became more distinct. And as it did, Seth grew calm.

"What is your name?" Seth asked the empty room with a firm, raspy voice.

Seth could feel it recoil with animal suddenness from the question. In pain and shame, the broken-toothed former god hissed and piled curses upon Seth's heritage and lineage. But that only made it more distinct from him. And so Seth asked again.

"Who are you?"

It recoiled again. Seth was emboldened, having found a way to hurt it. But more than that, he really wanted to know. After so many years in a life not entirely his own, he wanted to know precisely who it was that promised murder with impunity, who claimed his family was a prison, who spat on all human gentleness, who wielded a vision encompassing centuries and despised the present day.

"Tell me your name."

It retreated quickly. The feeling was like a deep, dull electric shock. Seth coughed hard and vomited up more black snot, this time in silence. He flopped back down and slept a few hours, more alone than he'd been in his adult life.

———

Seth woke before dawn with tears in his eyes, packed up and drove to the airport. He paid extra money for the first flight to Phoenix. On that trip, there was little solace. Car ads on the monitors around the airport, a song hanging in the background as they boarded the plane, all of it reminded him of Sarah. He did what crying he needed to do in bathrooms. He'd have to hold it together and hold it tight. Even greasing the wheels as best he could, it took forever to get to DC, forever to get his car, and forever to get to the shopping plaza in Fairfax, where William waited in a little rented Toyota.

Seth parked next to him and waved at him to get behind their cars.

"Hell of a time to miss your fucking flight. You're fucking lucky it's the dead of winter," William said. He looked greasy, his eyes sunken, wild with exhaustion and anxiety.

"Don't be such a fucking pussy. All you had to do was park it. I'm saving your ass here. So don't forget to thank me when you can still sleep through the night in your own bed five years from now."

"I'll try."

"Why don't you try getting her into the back of my car? Let's make this quick."

Seth opened the trunk of the Lexus. William removed a blanket and some newspapers and there was Sarah Loire, half-dressed and enclosed in plastic like a frozen dinner. The suction-sealed laundry bag clung to her. She'd bled from her temple and mouth. The blood mixed with her hair and pressed flush to the plastic. Seth knew not to look too long. But what he saw set up camp in his brain. No one had bothered to close her brown eyes and the pupil of one touched the plastic, fluid collecting at the contact point and in the corner of the eye. Maroon blood stains bloomed in the crotch of her tight green army pants. She was curled up, but Seth would never know if that was a last line of defense, or how she'd been fitted into the bag.

The vacuum bags were supposed to be a space-saver for housewives looking to store out-of-season garments. But with a body, it served another purpose. After the first mistress, William explained to Seth how the bag sealed in hairs, fibers, tissue, and blood—all the forensic evidence that you could accidentally put on a body or that could stick to your clothes or car when you moved it. At the same time, the vacuum seal bought you time. As the body released gasses, the vacuum-sealed bag could fill and expand for a few days before it popped and gave off its telltale stench. William first saw the bags on a late-night TV ad.

William helped Seth lift the body—cold and loose in its taut wrapping—into the trunk of his Mercedes. Seth fought a shiver and covered it over with the blanket.

"Hurley pay you?" Seth asked.

"Yeah, but…"

Seth reached into his suitcase and counted out a few dozen bills, folded them and handed the wad to William, who checked the denomination and pocketed the wad.

"I know he likes that guy out in Frederick. But Hurley's never really had to do this kind of shit before," Seth said. "Thanks."

"So you're all set with this?"

"I'm fine. You go by her place. Get her notebooks, diaries, things like that, and her computer. But go easy on the place."

"Is that all?" William asked petulantly.

He nodded and William turned back to his car. He left in a hurry.

---

Seth rolled a shopping cart into the plaza's *Target*. He bought candles, incense, big boxes of mothballs, plug-in air fresheners, aerosol air-fresheners, rubber gloves, duct tape, an air mattress, and some contractor bags. He pushed it back to where his car waited next to the withered hulk of a snow bank.

In DC, Seth passed his familiar haunts, the restaurants and bars, hotels, offices, monuments, and museums. He kept driving until he reached the bulletproof liquor stores, the markets that advertised lotto and beer ahead of food, the fried chicken storefronts and knockoff fast-food chains, the somber Social Security offices, the apartment buildings with front doors swaying in the frigid breeze. The faces were black and the streets were busy with young men in huge winter coats. Seth drove until he found a well-maintained building with a FOR RENT sign. Seth parked and dialed the number on the sign. A few minutes after a short conversation, an old black woman came out. Seth got out of his car and introduced himself. The woman said her name was Tamar. Seth repeated it as a question.

"It's from the Bible. Right in the beginning. You should know that. Everyone should," she said, shaking her head.

After that, she stuck to the facts: The rent; what was and wasn't included; when it was due; what she would put up with and what she wouldn't. As for the place, it worked. Big building, seven apartments to the floor. Concrete walls and clean-swept halls. Working people, Tamar said. The apartment Seth rented had a small back bedroom, with a window, but no fire escape. She didn't try to sell the apartment, or ask much about him. In the first-floor studio apartment that acted as a maintenance closet and office, Seth paid the whole thing in cash, which made Tamar uneasy.

"I'm a meat wholesaler. I have to keep a lot of cash on hand," he said, with a flat expression.

She raised her eyebrows and dug out a rental application.

"There's a police sergeant whose mother lives on your floor. She says he'll be a lieutenant in the spring. He comes by every few days," Tamar sweetly warned.

"That's good to know. Safe building."

He used his fake California ID to fill out the application. She gave him the keys and said she'd see him soon. Seth shook her hand and drove off. At a discount department store a few blocks down, Seth bought a massive, wheeled suitcase, blinds and a few tools. He drove out to a set of train tracks across from a burnt-out warehouse to wrestle Sarah's stiffened body into the suitcase. Back at the apartment building, he grunted as he dragged Sarah Loire up the stairs in the hard-shell suitcase. Tamar was waiting at the top of the first landing.

"That sounds like a heavy bag. What's in it?" she asked, not suspicious anymore so much as curious and lonely.

"Everything I have."

Tamar followed him and Sarah's body into the apartment and poked around while Seth unpacked his shopping bags.

"Why do you have so many mothballs?"

"I have a lot of wool clothes. And I've had moth problems in the past. Listen, I'm going to get settled here."

"Go right ahead. You only have an air mattress?"

"Just for tonight. But I have to…"

"You don't have to drop hints with me. If you want me to go, just say…"

"Tamar, I want you to go."

She bunched up her face with the focus at her chin and nodded. After another few minutes of neighborly offers and assorted niceties, she left.

Alone with Sarah Loire, Seth locked the door and pulled on his rubber gloves, rolled the suitcase into the back bedroom and unboxed the air mattress. It rose three feet above the dusty linoleum as it inflated. The mattress served no purpose except to make Seth feel better. He lifted the suitcase onto it as gently as he could, unzipped it, and slowly dumped her onto it. By now Sarah was stiffer, as if her fetal clutch was intended to keep something from him. Her open eye looked past him. The plastic of the vacuum bag played the part of the distance over which Seth would never be able to reach Sarah Loire ever again. His breath caught in his throat.

He wanted to stop, to weep and to collapse. But he kept to the task at hand. The task was all he had left that carried any weight. Seth got to work. His grief mixed with what he knew of crime-scene forensics to produce a sort of impromptu mummification. He wiped down the smooth plastic of the vacuum-sealed garment bag, caressing away any fingerprints or stray tears. He pulled one trash bag over her legs and one over the top of her, dumped half a box of mothballs in the top bag and the other half in the bottom one and sealed the bags together with duct tape.

With her out of sight, the work went faster. He arranged scented candles around the mattress, and lit them. The apartment didn't have a thermostat, and the radiators kept the room too warm for the body to go unnoticed for long. Seth took a wrench and twisted the valves on all of the apartment's radiators shut, fighting through layers of paint and rust. With the icy wind blowing through the window, the place was frigid by the time he put the shade up in the bedroom's window frame. He cleared the tools and detritus from the room, dumped a second box of mothballs in a horseshoe around the air bed. He locked the bedroom door from the inside and pulled it shut. He was in the process of duct taping the edges of the bedroom door when his phone rang.

"We need to talk," Hurley said, interrupting Seth's hello.

"Sure. Can we do it tomorrow?"

"Get your ass here now."

"I can't."

"Can't? You *work* for me."

"I know. And if you want to stop and think for a moment, that's what I'm doing right now—working for you, overtime."

Hurley sighed. He was a charmer and couldn't play the hardass very long or very well.

"Okay. When can you get here?"

"Say two hours?"

"Meet me at the restaurant around the corner from my office, the steak house. I'll be at a table."

Seth hung up and sealed the rest of the bedroom door with duct tape. He plugged odor-covering devices into the outlets of the front room, gathered all the leftover bags and packaging into the rolling suitcase, wiped down the doors and doorknobs. In the hallway, he locked the doorknob and deadbolt and removed his gloves.

He dumped the suitcase in a dumpster by a condominium construction site a few blocks from Union Station, and slipped his California ID into a storm drain. His Mercedes was clean and responsive as he navigated the well-swept and tasteful streets of Northwest Washington, DC, with its blandly utopian modern office buildings and muscle-bound neoclassical institutions.

---

The restaurant where he met Hurley was decorated in the tradition of wealth at peace with itself, dark wood, brass fixtures and crimson leather. The lighting was low and the ceiling high. It was crowded. Murmurs and cackles echoed through the dining room. Hurley waited with an untouched glass of red wine at a corner table. He shook Seth's hand without rising.

"Here I am. What's the problem?" Seth asked.

"Sit down with me."

Seth sat. A waiter came by immediately. Hurley told the man to bring Seth a scotch. Seth nodded and the waiter was gone.

"So, what do you want to know?"

"I want to know a few things. First, you miss your flight back from New Mexico, then I find out from William that you had him hold onto the package overnight. Then he tells me you wouldn't let him use our space out in Frederick. So you tell me: What is the problem?"

Seth looked over his shoulder then bent toward Hurley.

"My problem is patterns. If we go out to Frederick once, or even twice on unrelated business, that's fine. Anyone looking into it has a million and a half leads and nowhere to start. But if we go there twice on what's essentially the exact same business, they can figure out half the story as soon as they find the second one. Not to mention the possibility that someone will find the first and start looking for more. I don't want to be looking over my shoulder the rest of my life over this business. And I doubt you do either."

Hurley took a sip of his wine and stared over Seth's shoulder.

"I guess that makes sense. So where did she end up going?"

"I have a spot. She won't be found."

Hurley seemed discomfited by Seth's bald-faced reference to the murder. But the room was loud and the other diners too impressed with themselves to pay them any mind. The waiter brought Seth's drink. He gulped it half down.

"I get nervous about things, especially with freelancing," Hurley said.

"I get nervous about things too, especially patterns and even more nervous about prison," Seth said, loud enough to make Hurley uneasy.

"Is everything okay with you?" Hurley asked, grinning a calm, artificial grin.

Seth hated the man and his question. But he knew that losing Hurley's trust would be the end of him. And he knew that to roll over, to placate Hurley would be to admit guilt, so Seth scowled into his drink.

"Yeah, I'm fine. But I want to talk about my compensation."

"Really? Even with inflation, I thought we were paying you good money."

"I don't mean that. You've been fair as far as that goes. But there's more to life than money. And what I'm thinking about is afterwards, when all of this plays out. Have you given it any thought?"

"Actually, I have. I've thought of you in particular. When this is done, there will be a transition period and we're going to need security. Not everyone will be glad to be part of our new nation. There will be, uh, loyalists. And I think you'd be uniquely qualified for that kind of work—like a J. Edgar Hoover type."

"Secret police? I hate that I have to keep reminding you, but I'm still a lawyer. And I was thinking of something more judicial. Not the new Supreme Court necessarily, not right away. But something like that is more interesting to me."

"We'll see. Like you said, probably not at first. We're going to need our courts to appear legitimate very quickly."

"And no one trusts killers and whores. Right?"

Hurley smiled. And if Hurley did sense something had changed about the man across from him, Seth wanted him to think it was nothing more than the spurs of ambition. The older man showed all of his perfect teeth in a wide smile.

"Right, killers and whores. Well, who the hell isn't one or the other?" Hurley chuckled, taking a deep drink of his wine.

They finished the rest of their drinks in what passed for each other's good graces, talking freely in code, Hurley trying to figure out how many empty promises he could get away with, and Seth trying to figure out how he could put the man across from him into the earth.

As Seth rose to leave, Hurley passed him two envelopes bulging with cash and documents to take out to Laughlin. Seth said he'd need a day or two before he left. Hurley nodded and Seth left with a hearty handshake. Hurley placed his left hand atop the clutch, to get his approval across, saying "we'll work all this out," as they shook.

Over the drinks, the broken-toothed spirit spoke with Petronius about the plan for secession, and about their mutual hopes for a long and bloody civil war. But the former god was careful to conceal Seth's betrayal from Petronius. The broken-toothed spirit considered Seth's resistance a hiccup. And it didn't want to lose its place at the table.

When Seth exited through the well-dressed and well-fed crowd, he couldn't help but reflect on how much he'd rather Sarah Loire be walking the earth than anyone in that restaurant, or than anyone he could think of for a hundred miles in any direction.

Outside, he phoned William.

---

William answered with a slurred, irritated hello, the sounds of a bar in the background.

"You get everything?" Seth asked.

"Yeah. It's done. I was trying to relax."

"Relax later. I need the stuff now."

William reluctantly agreed to a meeting in a McDonald's parking lot in Tenleytown. There, the two men rolled down their windows. William grunted and heaved a backpack into Seth's passenger seat.

"You wipe all this stuff down?"

"Of course."

"All right. Go get some sleep. You did good."

William nodded and pulled out hard. Seth waited until William's stuttering, impatient brake lights had vanished from the lot, and he hit the highway.

The traffic was thick and slow out to Frederick. Once there, Seth roamed the suburban streets, past all the lit windows of dinner time in the land of the nuclear family. It took a while of wandering, in search of something that struck a chord of memory. He knew it was a new development, and remembered vaguely that its name didn't exactly make sense. But the town had no shortage of such developments, with signs offering *HOMES FROM THE $350s, TOWNE HOMES FROM THE LOW $300s, LUXURY HOMES FROM THE UPPER $400s*. But none were right.

He knew it as soon as he saw it—*OAK PINES*. That was the place. He followed the billboard directions another exit down the I-270 and found the coil of tightly-spaced beige and gray houses. He stopped inside the complex and ransacked his memory for details. That night, they'd parked at the model home. But the development had almost doubled in size since that night. He remembered how the model home sat on a corner, which had seemed absurd when there were no other houses around. But that once-audacious acute corner now blended in with the other houses around it. He found the corner and puzzled over whether it was two or three lots they walked before coming to the unfinished foundation under which they'd buried the girl. He remembered the crisp autumn air, remembered the two-by-four house framing, and it came to him—they'd walked three lots.

Seth marked the address where they'd dumped that first unfortunate girl and drove back to DC, so tired he was almost dizzy. But he nonetheless pulled off the highway in another bedroom community and drove around its empty streets until he could be fairly sure he wasn't followed.

---

Seth woke early to go to the bathroom and couldn't get back down to sleep. So he put on his leather winter gloves and wrote out a short note on a legal pad in block letters. The note explained that the dead girl in the apartment was the work of Senator Chet Mankins, who'd had help disposing of her and another girl from his friend retired Senator Robert Hurley. The other girl, the note explained, was in the foundation of 9 Bluejay Lane in Frederick, Maryland. Seth tucked the block-lettered note into the pocket of the backpack William had given him.

He dressed and drove off through the monuments, the steel and glass alluvium from which the nation is governed, and into the ghetto, to his quiet shrine. Opening the door of the apartment, the perfume smell from the scented plug-ins was thick, all disinfectant, lavender and acrid rose. The apartment was freezing cold, or the smell might have carried. He set the backpack on the kitchen counter and unpacked it, looking past his desire to keep Sarah Loire's diary. He set his own folded block-letter note on top of it. With one last long look at the duct-taped bedroom door, he turned and left.

Locking the knob and deadlock, the thing in Seth spoke.

*Don't do it. Hurley will crucify you.*

Seth took the key to the apartment's deadbolt off its ring and inserted it back into the lock. He inhaled deeply and took out his wallet.

*It's still not too late. Don't do it,* the thing inside of Seth said, screaming from a great foggy distance.

Seth silently demanded its name, and the thing inside of him relented long enough for him to press the wallet's flat edge to the side of the key that jutted out of the deadbolt lock.

*You're signing your own death warrant.*

"Tell me your name," Seth replied, out loud, so it echoed embarrassingly in the corridor. And the voice went silent.

With one short, abrupt movement, Seth snapped the key off in the lock.

Taking the long way home, he stopped for coffee in Adams Morgan. Despite his sleep lack and ragged emotional state, he had made few mistakes since Farmington. And his luck had been, up to that point, nearly impeccable. But two steps into the café, with its customers watching the internet on Macintoshes, or reading best sellers, he was spotted by the receptionist from Sarah's yoga studio—the blonde with an accent he couldn't quite place. She came up to him, a blonde with a smooth face, pale as milk and wide blue eyes.

"Hey, you."

"Oh, hi. How are you?"

"I'm good. It's funny running into you. I was actually hoping that I'd see you. Have you seen Sarah?"

"No. Not lately."

"Ooh. I'm sorry. Is this awkward?"

"No, why would it be?"

"I guess, I just thought you guys were, I don't know, seeing each other?" she said, wincing at the word *seeing*. "But you haven't heard from her?"

"No, it's… it's not awkward. But I've been travelling a lot lately. I just got back from a trip. That's why I haven't seen her. Why? What's up?"

"Sarah missed her class last night, and the one she was supposed to teach this morning. It's probably nothing. But it's really not like her to miss a class. And I thought that because you two were, uh, friends, she might have said something to you."

"No. Like I said, I haven't heard from her. I was out of town."

An uncomfortable silence passed in which the blonde tried to figure out how she felt about him. Seth wore a freshly pressed suit, which would always make him suspect. In that same quiet moment, Seth tried to remember the name he gave when he signed up at the yoga studio. He drew a blank.

"Okay, well…"

"If I talk to her, I'll tell her you asked."

"What's your name again?" she asked.

"Steve. I'm sorry, but I forgot yours as well."

"Meena."

"Okay. Did you try calling her?"

"A couple of times. It went straight to voice mail, and now it says her voice mail is full."

"That's strange. I'll try calling her later tonight."

The impatient welcome of the barista ended their conversation. Seth nodded as he hurried out the glass door. But Meena had him dead to rights in her window seat as he climbed into his car. He looked, and she was watching. Seth smiled and waved as he climbed in the car, hoping that would be enough to keep her from writing down his plate number.

Back at the hotel, Seth called Frederica to let her know when he'd be getting into Laughlin, then sat back and drifted in and out of sleep in front of the TV. The news reveled in a handful of late-night bombings of FBI offices in Ogden, Spokane and Boise—no deaths, the TV anchor seemed disappointed to announce. In other news, Mankins was campaigning hard for April's recall election. In a speech on Venice Beach, Mankins said the current governor should refuse to allow the Super Bowl to be played in San Diego if the federal government didn't release two dozen of Jefferson's militia members. The FBI had caught them operating outside of Indio, and sent them out to Guantanamo Bay for interrogation.

In a daze, Seth counted the hours since the first class Sarah missed. It was a seven-o'clock class, which meant that she'd be officially missing forty-eight hours later that night. Assuming the worst—that someone filed a missing persons report immediately, and that Meena had taken down his license plate—then, well, Seth was too tired to think it all the way through.

———————

The next day, like too many, was spent in transition. Seth washed, dressed, packed up his clothes and papers, checked out of the hotel and drove to the airport, where he half-unpacked and half-undressed for security. After the bombings out West, it was an orange alert day at the airport, and it seemed like everyone was getting stripped down or felt up.

On the tarmac, the plane to Las Vegas lingered. There was ice on the wings, and a long line for the de-icing truck, the pilot explained. The waitresses brought snacks and drinks to the first-class passengers. With an hour to kill before the five-hour flight commenced, Seth drank coffee and opened the envelope Hurley had given him. Inside were a loose set of documents and a second, sealed envelope. Seth read the loose documents. The first set pertained to Roberto's hedge fund, and to a mining company it owned the majority of. They were SEC documents, one-time event notices, offering-letter amendments, securities-lending agreements, equipment mortgages and so on. The upshot of the disparate and deliberately complex documents was the same—a massive disinvestment in all the assets held, a huge cash withdrawal starting later that week and going on through April—when Mankins would likely win the governorship of California. Seth read through the documents, which were all sound in and of themselves. He barely noticed as the plane took off.

Airborne, Seth did something he hadn't done in all his time working for Hurley: He opened the sealed envelope. Inside were two binder-clipped, bulky documents, heavily highlighted and underlined, with handwritten notes in the margins and on fluorescent yellow and pink Post-it notes. Seth blinked when he saw the heading, and looked around to make sure no one could read over his shoulder.

*The Declaration of Independence of the Western States of America* read the header on the first document.

*The Constitution of the Western States of America* read the second.

Seth blinked when he saw them. His eyes went for the editing marks—underlines culminating in question marks, red parentheses with arrows leading to notations, such as BROADER MARRIAGE LANGUAGE (MORMONS), in the margin. Seth flipped through the documents quickly. The notes were few, and he could only guess that an agreement was close. When Seth turned to the end of the *Declaration*, he saw why. The document was dated for late April, eleven weeks away.

Late April. Mankins would be governor of California, in charge of the state and its National Guard. Jefferson had enough guns to keep up his hit-and-run campaign through Wyoming, Idaho and Montana until then, generating enough carnage to make people pick a side, and possibly become a martyr ahead of the real revolt. The generals and colonels would have their bases ready for a change in command. And Burleson's tech people would be able to throw a monkey wrench into any first response by the government in DC. Frederica, as near as Seth could tell, was cutting deals with the governors of the other states through her pension connections, while Hurley and Roberto dealt with the Chinese.

A voice reminded Seth that it could be the beginning of a great future for him. But all Seth could think of was Sarah Loire, looking out past his reach from a plastic garment bag, her hair mixed with blood, her eye pressed against the plastic. The bag would pop by early April in an ordinary Washingtonian spring, and the smell would be overpowering, Seth guessed.

After a quick gloss, Seth could barely stand to read the damn *Constitution*. Anyway, it read like a more comprehensive, but less eloquent version of the original. He could hear Roberto's voice in the writing—a kind of ecstatic and obsessive libertarianism. The *Constitution* guaranteed new freedoms concerning drugs, sex, even death. The lengthy section on euthanasia was one that Hurley had drastically cut. The document embodied a start from scratch, with new taxes imposed on newly legalized drugs, and on churches. Judging from the red ink, Hurley was especially keen on taxing churches.

The plane crossed a vast body of farmland. Seth ate a chicken wrap. The stewardess liked him, and her batch of questions met his batch of lies. Seth shielded the document from her eyes when she came by to chat every ten minutes or so.

The *Declaration* opened with a series of abuses committed by the federal government against the western states. From there, it opened onto a larger polemic, accusing the government of heresy against its founding impulse of liberty. At the end of the *Declaration* was a list of signatories. Mankins and the governors of twelve other states were there. So was Fieldspurhoff, the Marine colonel, one Supreme Court justice, two generals that Seth never met, a handful of university presidents, as well as Roberto and Hurley, whose name was at the very bottom of the list.

In Las Vegas, Seth again skipped his connecting flight to Laughlin and rented a white Cadillac. He cruised around the blinding winter daylight of residential Las Vegas until he found a mom-and-pop copy shop in a faded and frayed mini-mall north of the city. He bought a few envelopes and settled down at the quarter-a-page copier, making copies of the *Declaration* and the *Constitution*. The young Mexican man behind the counter said it would be quicker and cheaper if he handed the documents over to have them copied at the big machines in back, but Seth demurred with a wave of his hand. An hour and a few rolls of quarters later, Seth walked out with a series of neat manila envelopes.

He drove into the spooky land of nuclear test sites and UFO sightings down to Laughlin. In Laughlin, Seth poured himself a whiskey from the minibar. He couldn't afford to be sloppy, but nerves seemed the greater danger. The setting sun cast the hotel's shadow on the Colorado River and the crumbled hill beyond it. Seth relaxed in front of the TV for an hour, drifting in and out of the national reality coming through the screen. Ads for a new movie about a young, handsome woman trying to break her ties with her alcoholic aristocratic family were in heavy rotation. Poor Bergman, Seth thought.

The news showed days-old footage of burning office buildings along with mugshots and DMV photos of corn-fed country boys, white and black, overall suspenders visible in some of the photos. The earnest jowly face of the governor of Montana was asking, with all possible politeness, that the ATF withdraw entirely from his state and leave the investigation of the Boise bombing to the state police. With a sad shake of his cragged head, he called the ATF's investigation a blatant provocation.

Seth checked his watch and was out the door. The lounge in the casino featured a zaftig blonde with a too-high voice singing pop songs and dancing a little desperately. He drove down the string of hotels to the riverboat-themed casino where Roberto kept his suite. The marquees announced the talent in town, mostly failed TV actors who offered a variety act, or half-known comedians. And under one of the big names—an obese comedian whose stint on a game show had nearly killed him—Seth saw her name: *Dolores Navarro*, in big black plastic letters above the discount lunch buffet on the five-story marquee. She had gotten her name on the sign.

At the riverboat casino, Seth parked and passed through the obligatory wash of lights, sirens, robotic elders and the giddy muttering young, the bad carpets, triple-redundancy-certain slot machines and the constant wash of surveillance, to the elevator. In his suite, Roberto was watching six football games at once, all of them paused.

"Sorry. The steaks will be up in a minute. You like yours medium rare, right?"

Seth nodded. The place was for once a mess, with papers everywhere. Seth nodded and looked around. Roberto, more manic than usual, kept gabbing.

"A mess. I know. Freddie's sending her secretary over tomorrow. If you think Freddie's a tough one, you should meet her secretary. You ever meet a gay Mormon? Fastidious is not the word. We need a new word for this guy. But he knows his business. He'll probably be the head of the new IRS, after everything is said and done, though I'm sure that after all this, they probably won't call it the IRS. How are things with you?"

"Busy. I've been watching out for some people. And that's a job that's never done."

"Especially when you have to watch out for some of the incontinent maniacs we have to do business with. Let me guess—Mankins?"

Seth limited himself to an arched eyebrow.

"No shit," Roberto said, nodding.

The food came and they started eating. The blood and fat on his lips calmed him. Roberto picked, considered his food, and set his fork down.

"It must be hard on you, having to see the bodies. Things that were alive, and now aren't. They call me the visionary. And that means, ironically, that I never have to actually *see* any of the consequences. Funny, that. So unless you're a sociopath, which I don't read you as, you must be getting pretty sour on this business by now."

"It's like you said—business. There's never any benefit in getting emotional about it."

"I get emotional about it," Roberto said.

"Well, you tell me. How do you deal with some of the things we're planning to do?"

"I try to remind myself that there are always necessary evils. And when you start to remake the world, those evils will necessarily increase exponentially. Think of the French Revolution or any of the revolutions of the last few centuries. You ask me, and I say that we're getting off easy with Mankins and Jefferson."

"I guess we'll see."

"Fair enough. How do you deal with it?"

"This business we're in is going to be good for me. Without it, I'm another lawyer, waiting to lose his job to a younger, cheaper and more eager version of myself. So I can tolerate what happens in the meantime."

"The *meantime*. That's the phrase! Among men like us, men with plans and ambition, how many lifetimes have we spent *in the meantime*? You ever see Speer's plans for Berlin?"

"Never did. And I'm sorry to interrupt, but Hurley wanted you to have these," Seth said, handing over the taut envelopes.

"Oh great. I hope he didn't mess around with the tariff structures again. I spent days on them. Did you read it?"

"No. It was sealed. I dozed on the flight."

Roberto flipped through the hedge fund papers quickly.

"Boring, boring, boring, boring," he said, putting the papers on a table. "I'm sure Frederica's man can put these where they need to go. He's a capable one. Good old Mormons. They still take it seriously, after everyone else has fled to psychopharmacology, cynicism and blind greed. Of all the states, Utah drove the hardest bargain."

"Bargained for what?" Seth asked.

"Tax breaks, complete religious freedom, polygamy, Salt Lake City rechartered as a theocratic city-state, you name it. Of the thirteen states coming along with us, they're going to have the most Congressional representatives per capita."

"Thirteen?"

"Yeah, it has a nice historical symmetry. We're even going to use the original flag. Thirteen stars in a circle. It's fitting. I think it might be the first real chance at Democracy in more than a hundred years. We have to get the idea back to a scale that it can work at. You ever read Montesquieu?"

"I think so. But refresh my memory."

"Montesquieu said Democracy couldn't work in too large of a country. And I think he's right. I think that the people have voted for his point of view by not voting much anymore. And it's more than the smaller scale of the new country that's so exciting. We'll be starting with real resources, thanks to the shale. According to the latest estimates, we're looking at more than the trillion and a half barrels that we thought. Almost double, really. Incredible wealth—enough to revive Democracy for real."

"That's great and everything. But what does oil money really have to do with Democracy?"

"Go back in history. Look at the slave states, the feudal states, the more recent European and Asian totalitarianisms. And consider the vast personal freedoms you and I enjoy here and now. Now consider the feeling in the air, the sense that those freedoms have begun to dwindle. The sick, cynical truth is that freedom is not a principle handed down from on high, it's a human behavior based on a number of factors, one of the biggest of which is the availability of resources. Freedom costs and costs..." Roberto said, aware that the point he'd meant to make had since escaped him.

"I agree, it does cost," Seth said.

"But you were going to ask something. What were you going to ask?"

"Which thirteen states are we talking about?"

"The West. Arizona, California, Colorado, Idaho, Montana, Nevada, New Mexico, North Dakota, Oregon, South Dakota, Utah, Washington, Wyoming. All of them unloved territories who've found a new identity. If you look at it on a map, it's a clean break."

"Why that group?"

"Call it geographic and ideological similarity. The West has always had its own unique worldview, its own set of priorities. Truth is that we almost had fifteen states. But the governor of Hawaii gave us a bad feeling. And Texas is going to go independent again when we make our move. It's too bad, really. Texas would have given us a lot of revenue, and a window on the Atlantic. But adding them would also make a fight with the East more likely."

"You really think there won't be a fight?"

"Not based on the elements that we will put into play. But like I said, I'm the visionary. I don't see all of what goes on. I haven't seen Jefferson's bodies. Right now, I'm trying to make one last killing on this Super Bowl, so I haven't had time to keep a close eye on all the guerilla activities up north. I'm eight for ten on my bets in the playoffs."

"Okay, but I don't see how the secession can happen without a fight. Look at the Civil War. The North fought for five bloody years to keep the Union together. What president wouldn't force the issue, even if just to look good next to Abe Lincoln?"

"Lincoln is one word we're trying to keep out of all this. Anyway, the president we have now is no Lincoln. He's weak-minded, maybe given to romantic gestures, but only as long as they don't cost much. Otherwise, he's easily bamboozled by his experts, advisors, and charts. Nothing against this president. Really, only an idiot would want to the job. It's like campaigning to be scapegoat."

"So what's to keep the president from doing something stupid and going to war?"

"First of all, it's not the 1860s. The public has been disabused of its notions of the glory and valor of war for the last fifty or so years. And also, this president has his hired adults. They'll see the sense. We'll send our negotiators, and the Chinese will send theirs. Ours will bring projected casualty figures. The Chinese will offer money—right now the number is fifteen percent. Fifteen percent off of all federal debt owed to China and Chinese companies if the federal government lets the secession happen. It's a nice lump sum of debt forgiveness, when you consider the interest."

"But fifteen percent? That can't be worth it. Can it?"

"According to our figures, it is. The states we're taking are 23 percent of the population, and generate a little less than 20 percent of federal tax revenue. You throw in the Social Security payments to the people here over the next few decades, and that should settle the issue. Washington would essentially be spinning-off a money-losing operation. They're dealing with a debt that is, for all political purposes, impossible to pay down. Then you add in the fact that China has the stick to negotiate with."

"Which is?"

"A gargantuan sell-off of Treasuries, and of the dollar itself. That, when you couple it with an evenly matched civil war fought with modern instruments of destruction, would devastate the United States in a way it very well might never recover from. So I don't see any way that we don't sell a peaceful secession. Don't be surprised if the president says it was his idea."

Roberto smiled and turned his attention back to his steak. He seemed satisfied. But Seth's mind was bristling with betrayal.

"But what if China has something else in mind?" Seth said.

"Like what?" Roberto said, avidly.

"What if China tells Washington that it sees the American West as our Tibet? What if it says Washington needs to get its wayward states in line or it will lose confidence and sell off its t-bills and dollars? What if it plays the carrot and the stick the other way?"

"Why would it do that?"

"What if they want to sit back and watch a long civil war destroy their main rival on the world stage? Sure, they might lose money, but they might also wind up on top of the heap."

The thing in Seth stirred with excitement at the thought. Having lost so much power in so little time, the thought of mass bloodshed aroused it.

"But no one thinks that will happen. Frederica doesn't think it will happen. Hurley doesn't. I mean, we have assurances," Roberto said, his voice shrinking with each word.

"Maybe no one does think it will happen. But there's a reason they keep a visionary like you around. Isn't there?"

Seth took a bite of his steak. Roberto didn't seem eager to talk for the first time that night.

"I think we can trust them," Roberto said halfheartedly, turning his gaze to the paused football games.

Seth kept eating until it was clear that Roberto didn't have any new tasks for him. In the oppressive quiet of Roberto's rumination, Seth said good-bye, and heard the cacophony of six simultaneous football games resume as he opened the door to the suite.

He drove a few blocks down South Casino Drive and wandered through the bells and sirens of a new casino, to its lounge, where Dolores was singing "Just in Time." Under the lights, almost glowing in a red dress, she belted out the song. He found a stool, ordered a drink, and turned around to watch her. The lights were brighter at this lounge, and she couldn't see him in the crowd.

When she finished her set and saw him, she stopped in her tracks and her eyes widened. It was a moment of fear. And her fear could easily have become revulsion. But it became the other thing instead.

———————

"Well, it's nice to see that you're doing all right. At least you're not malingering by a butcher shop," Petronius said to the broken-toothed spirit.

It was a suffocating summer day in New Jersey, during an earlier war for independence. Petronius possessed a Lieutenant Colonel Burr. And the broken-toothed spirit inhabited a lascivious army messenger from Massachusetts named Eatwell. The two spirits spoke while Eatwell and Burr discussed provisions, on the eve of a battle with the English.

"I wondered if I'd ever see you again," the broken-toothed spirit said.

"Oh, you know I couldn't resist coming over here. If I was burned at one more stake, I was going to die of boredom. And look at this—what a war!"

"I've seen better."

Petronius disagreed. The Revolution, as he called it, appealed to Petronius. It smacked of regicide, a regicide of a very abstract and all-encompassing sort. And if one thing persistently dogged Petronius through its centuries of struggle, it was a sense of regret that he hadn't killed the emperor who'd had him condemned so many empires ago. Petronius always equated that betrayal with the one that he'd died into.

"So what do you have in mind for him?" Petronius asked, meaning Eatwell.

"I plan to get him through the war, make him rich, and take it from there. He has some interesting appetites that I can work with."

"That sounds like an idea. But you never were too ambitious. Why not get him into the new government, wreak some real havoc?"

"I would, but this one's not too bright."

"If you say so. He does sweat a lot," Petronius quipped.

"I do what I can. I have to be careful. I've nearly been expelled from men not much smarter than him. I don't know how you manage the smart ones."

"I simply approach them as if it's a business deal. I'm ambitious. They're ambitious. No reason we can't work things out up front."

"You always were a better talker than I."

"You don't need to be much of a talker these days. What a war! If the revolution succeeds, then we can build a new world, free of the superstitions of the past. If the revolution fails, we can have our way with the tattered remnants of a once-hopeful continent."

The next day's battle was a draw. Eatwell died of heatstroke. The broken-toothed spirit drifted back to New England and didn't see Petronius for decades.

―――――――

"Shit," Dolores said from under the tangled blankets.

"Good morning to you too," Seth said, tipping the room-service man and wheeling in the cart.

"What time is it? Fuck."

222

Seth wheeled the food in. Dolores started dressing, wrangling her breasts into her black bra, retracing her steps back to her panties.

"No breakfast?" Seth asked.

"No, I have to go. I'm supposed to spend the day with my kid. I know I didn't tell you about him. But whatever. It's not like we have that kind of thing."

"It's okay. I have a kid too. Who had yours last night?"

"My mother. She's over in Needles. She has him most days. Who has yours?"

"My ex and her husband. What's your kid's name?" Seth asked.

"Keith. He's nine, almost ten. Yours?"

"Beth—Elizabeth."

Dolores took her red dress into the bathroom. Before the mirror, with her purse, she was all serene focus as she worked the hotel body wash onto her tan skin in a circular motion.

"You know, I swore I wouldn't see you again," she said.

"I did not know that."

"Well I did. I *swore* it."

"Why's that?"

"I don't know. Maybe because you used me to kidnap a man in California. That's what us gals like to call a red flag."

"I guess so. But you handled yourself well. I was impressed. I thought the money would smooth over the unpleasantness."

"It did, sort of. What did you tell me that you did for a living?"

"Real estate."

"Right…"

Dolores laughed into the mirror, rinsed her face a few times. In black underwear, her body seemed to rebuke the mundanity of her actions. She patted the water off with a towel and commenced with the yet more serious job of applying makeup. Her focus and confidence increased to meet the task.

"Real estate, huh? I think I'll stick to singing, even if it doesn't pay."

"I saw you made the marquee."

"That's me, the headliner—right below the buffet."

"I may have something for you, if you want to make some money. All you'd have to do is hold on to some documents and mail them where I tell you, when I tell you."

"Mail them, like…"

"Write an address, put the stamps on, and drop them into a mailbox. It's a complicated situation for me. All you'd be doing is holding them and mailing them. I'm going to need to get them somewhere. But it can't be me who mails them."

She looked down and to the left and quietly asked how much money. He held up a few banded piles of cash. She raised an eyebrow, lifted her chin a degree and nodded. He gave her the envelopes that he'd assembled in the Las Vegas copy shop. She put the money in her purse, tucked the envelopes under her arm, kissed Seth hard on the mouth, and went back to the mirror.

Seth ate in front of the TV. The current governor of California, looking old, said he was still considering deploying the National Guard to the Super Bowl. In counterpoint, Mankins urged the people of California, Montana, and all Americans who loved freedom to boycott the game and its advertisers until the Indio twelve were freed and "the so-called law enforcement agencies" ceased their "illegal war" in Montana, Idaho and Wyoming. Mankins looked good, aggressive, righteous and tan. His broad face gleaming in the TV lights. Polls said he was a shoe-in come April.

Frederica's assistant called and told Seth in a steady, clipped voice to meet Frederica in an hour. He repeated an address across the river to Seth twice, chimed that he shouldn't be late, and hung up.

Dolores and Seth parted in the casino lobby and he drove across the river into Bullhead City to a small house at the edge of the city's electrical grid. Seth rang the intercom at the entrance to the driveway. It clicked twice, buzzed, and the gate slid away silently. Behind the wall was a smallish one-story, white stucco house, set on an acre. What it lacked in size and luxury, it made up in security. Cameras gazed over the yard and inward to cover the space under its eaves. Frederica answered the door, in her usual pantsuit, a glass of wine in her hand.

"Seth, it's good to see you. Come in."

"Likewise," Seth said, wandering into the living room of the small house. It was plain inside, with wall-to-wall carpeting, entertainment system, plush burgundy furniture and a glass coffee table. The only thing he noticed was that there were no paintings or photographs on the bare walls. No paint or wallpaper, only plaster with a coat of primer, as if more than that had never occurred to her.

"Nice place. How long have you been here?"

"Three years. What the *hell* did you say to Roberto? I had to spend half the morning talking him off the ledge," she said.

Frederica was a small, hard woman, whose efforts at pleasantry never held up long. She rattled Seth with her questions.

"We were just talking. He told me about the negotiations with China—about the debt reductions they plan to offer to let the western states go their way. And I simply brought up another scenario, where China decides that what it wants is actually to force a civil war. I mean, we're not telling them about the shale. Who knows what they're not telling us?" Seth said.

"Seth, what's your job?"

"My job?"

"Your job?"

"What are you getting at?"

"You kill people. You deliver documents. You clean up messes both complicated and delicate. You're a smart man. You're very good at what you do because you're a smart man. You pick up pieces of the big picture, as you *clean up messes*. But you don't know the big picture. And you certainly don't know enough to start *opining* about the big picture. In fact, your *opining* is a luxury none of us can afford at the present moment."

Like a newscaster, Frederica's face hardly moved as she spoke. Her gray eyes flashed with superhuman fury. Her syllables were hard and definite. The broken-toothed spirit quietly cheered as she tore into him.

"Like I said, I thought we were just talking. You know Roberto. It's always a free-for-all once he gets started," Seth said, hating the high, defensive sound of his own voice.

"For him, it's a free for all. That's who he is. He's the visionary, quote unquote. But most of his ideas are bullshit, and some of them are dangerous. He needs people to hold the reins. What he *doesn't* need is someone frightening him. Now, I hold the reins. That's who I am, that's my job. I do my job. You need to do your job. You have no business *opining* about things that you shouldn't even know about. Are we clear?"

Seth nodded.

Frederica turned and sorted through a pile of envelopes on the glass coffee table, leaving Seth with a metastasizing ball of doubt. Why hadn't she tried to disabuse him of the notion that they might well be steering the country toward a bloody, protracted civil war? A small detail or a reasonable argument could have turned him around. Instead, she chose to browbeat him. And if he was so wrong, why had it taken her hours to disabuse Roberto of the notion? Preoccupied in cowed silence, he waited for Frederica to find the proper envelopes for him to ferry back to Hurley.

"Sorry I had to speak to you like that. But you have to understand the importance of discipline, even when you're talking to someone like me or Hurley, but especially to Roberto. He can be, for lack of a better word, delicate."

Seth nodded and mumbled an apology. Frederica walked him back to the door and put a small, strong hand on his shoulder.

"I know. It's stressful. But we're almost there."

Seth drove back to the hotel, packed up his things and drove a few hours through the dusk-kissed desert to Las Vegas, which burst like a compromised constellation from the dark desert floor. The first two hotels he tried were booked. At the third, a small bribe to a reluctant desk clerk scored Seth an overpriced suite. He was due back in DC Monday, but wanted one more night out under the big skies, in the weird winter weather of the desert. Las Vegas was jammed with gamblers for the Super Bowl. Below his window, the strip was full of cars, the sidewalks full of gawkers and drunks eager for all the controlled madness that the town offered. Seth's hotel was a kitschy version of New York, its hotel towers mimicking famous skyscrapers. He couldn't answer the pseudo-orgiastic call below. He dialed down for dinner, and ate a cheeseburger in the bathtub. He slept in a bathrobe and woke with the dawn. In the casino downstairs, it could have been midnight or noon. The hardcore winners and losers kept at it, spilling their beers and money on a wild career they wouldn't remember, but would lump into a vague reassurance that they had indeed once really *lived*.

He wandered through the milquetoast saturnalia to the sports book. Tomorrow was the big game, the Steelers versus the Packers. In San Diego, the weather for the game was supposed to be warm and clear, with a slight chance of riots. Seth eyed the point spread, over/under and the money line and placed a few bets. The old woman behind the window didn't look up as she handed him his betting slips.

Outside, the night's desert chill was still on the early morning streets. The sun found its way clear of the distant mountains, and it warmed up fast. Seth walked past a summary of the last five thousand years of human civilization as told in family-friendly casinos. Pyramids and riverboats, medieval castles, cowboy saloons and oriental palaces, renaissance palazzos and space-age towers, Roman mansions and the Eiffel Tower, all distorted for the eyes of passing traffic, or to hold five hundred rooms. Seth walked for what felt like miles, until he ran out of spectacles by the space needle and the heat had become impossible to ignore. He took a cab back to his hotel and read through the documents Frederica had given him. Most of them were related to the hedge fund and other filings that he'd brought out. But he also found the states' lawsuits against the federal government. That was where the real work had been done. The *Constitution* and the *Declaration* were for suckers and schoolbooks. The real founding documents were actually the lawsuits asserting the states' claim to the federal land within their borders.

Seth read through them in the air-conditioning. The next set of papers he opened was ominous. They were executive orders, amending the newly signed *Constitution* for the duration of the war, outlining suspensions of civil rights, making immediate claims of eminent domain for strategic sites, imposing martial law on border territories and cities, requisitioning resources, labor and so on.

Reading through the various executive orders, all signed but left undated by Mankins himself, as the *President of the Western States of America*, Seth realized that the simple, easy transfer of sovereignty, greased by insurmountable debt, overseas money, and a powerful aversion to spilling American blood on American soil, was not the certainty that Hurley and Frederica had presented it as.

For the first time, Seth wondered if they might actually *want* a war. He thought of the thing inside himself and felt an electric chill.

---

Lying in the Las Vegas suite, staring at the ceiling, Seth tried to comprehend the executive orders in his hand. Their tone chilled Seth. Very matter-of-fact. A civil war made no sense to him, not at first anyway. Seth thought about war, which he knew only through history classes, movies, the news, and his mother dragging him to sit-ins outside one military contractor or another in Connecticut in the '80s when he was a kid.

No war ever made sense, not at first, she'd told him, referring then to the atomic Armageddon she imagined Reagan would soon trigger. Whenever a war began, she'd said, it began with the promise that it would be short and painless. But once a war begins, the acts of killing and justifying that killing reinforced and intensified each other until there was no way to stop it. Even as a kid, Seth had always took his mother's politics with a grain of salt. But now he could see the same mechanism playing out on a personal scale. Seth thought of the first pay-murder he did for Hurley.

It was only three years ago. He was still a lawyer with a family and the world to lose. He was two mortgages and a half-dozen credit cards behind the eight ball, but so was nearly everyone he knew. Elizabeth's medical bills were one thing. But between inflation, the recession and so forth, leading that normal, middle-class life put his family finances slightly in the red each month. And that added up. On his quiet, tree-lined block in Garden City, he wasn't the only one hanging onto the suburban dream with his fingernails. No one spoke of it, but it started to show. People put off repairing dinged bumpers and doors on their luxury cars. The winter saw few ski-racks on the tops of the family vehicles. In the spring, driveways cracked, crumbled and went unrepaired. Cursing with frustration, Seth mowed his own lawn, weed-wacked the edges and bagged the clippings for the first time since they moved out to the suburbs.

Hurley raised the idea of a murder at the perfect moment. It was a Monday, and that weekend Seth learned that there were cracks in the foundation of his house. The concrete needed to be resealed. Water was getting in, ruining the carpet in the finished basement. The job cost what everything cost in those days: More than it seemed it should. Getting the concrete resealed and replacing the carpet forced Seth to do some serious juggling with his household finances, using three credit cards to pay down a fourth, which he used to pay for the basement.

To Seth, Hurley was an ordinary, corrupt former-lawmaker-cum-lobbyist. True to type, Hurley wouldn't come right out and say he wanted someone killed. The target was a woman, a banker named Brenda. In their attorney-client candor, Hurley explained that Brenda had laundered money for him at one point, but that he'd started moving money through someone else. Brenda didn't like being phased out, and had begun blackmailing him for her usual fee, into perpetuity, or else. Brenda had a taste for cocaine, Hurley said, as if that explained everything. He gave Seth the woman's address, driver's license picture, and asked him to *do what he could* to make her see the light, to offer her rehab, but no money. Any cash offer would be one more thing she could blackmail him with. He offered Seth a lot of cash, off the books, if he could make the *problem go away*. There was no wink, no nod.

But, without understanding why, Seth understood exactly what Hurley meant.

The money was enough to convince Seth to stay in DC for the week. That was back in the days when he didn't like being away from his family for that long. It was back when his wife understood, when she still could.

That week, he followed Brenda, a tall but drooping middle-aged blonde, for a few nights, from her office to her house, sometimes a few drinks in between, sometimes to a big apartment building in Columbia Heights, where she never stayed long. That was the place, the thing in him said, where she scored, and where she was most vulnerable.

Back then, Seth was an ordinary lawyer. He had no idea where to get a clean gun, and only a dim notion of how someone could ever hope to get away with murder. Maybe it was resealing the basement, and maybe it was the thing inside of him. But the prospect of Hurley's money had already transformed from a happy windfall to a dire necessity to something that was owed him. After all, he could be laid off. Unemployment wasn't only for the lazy or the obsolete anymore. Every day, the news, the FOR SALE signs on foreclosed houses on his tree-lined street, the idle, pointless emails of former coworkers reminded him of that much. And there was Elizabeth, so young. Every day he seemed to read something about a child with one of those all-too-numerous disorders whose best case scenario was bankruptcy for the parents. There was a constant shame and fear at finding himself an educated, hard-working professional paying the minimums on his credit cards.

And there was also the thing in him and the still-small home he'd made for it. It played up his money woes, his private shame and anxiety. It kept Seth out drinking with Hurley into the night, when dark contingencies could be spoken. The broken-toothed spirit whispered: *Playing by the rules has gotten you as far as Garden City, but only on a mortgage and wishful thinking. Now the water's rising. And from high above your mess, Hurley's extending you a ladder.*

Seth followed Brenda until Thursday night, when she headed to the apartment in Columbia Heights. He followed. He was new at it, impatient. But he'd thought the job out. He dressed like someone else, in a pair of designer sweatpants and a baggy hooded sweatshirt. He bought a Buck knife from an outdoor store down in suburban Virginia. It was big and sharp enough to shave with. He bought a plastic badge from a toy store and hooked it inside his wallet.

Brenda parked in front of a hydrant, reckless, hungry and not planning to stay long. She had a short walk from there to the apartment building. Seth circled the block before finally settling on an illegal corner spot. He wanted to walk away from the scene of the crime against traffic.

A wild excitement kept him from nausea. The thing inside him kept the fear at bay. This was its night. Seth reached for the door handle of his Acura. He wanted to be outside, in the chilly night air, waiting for Brenda. But the thing inside of him said *no, not yet.* It said to wait until she comes back out, though every fiber in him screamed for the release from the awful tension of what he had to do. He gazed out the windshield, and could make out Brenda's path from the apartment building to her car. His fingers, naively un-gloved, released the interior door handle. It clicked back into place. Seth wondered if there was a sound more opposed to how he felt than plastic tapping against plastic. Car seat buckles, car door handles, modern movie theater seats going up or down, the keyboard on a computer. While he waited, a group of young women walked up to the building from a different direction. They were talking margarita loud, maybe tequila-shots loud. The one who lived there fumbled in her purse for a key. The crowd gathered behind her and grew quiet. Seth timed the thing out in his head. He would have walked into about six or seven eyewitnesses if he hadn't stayed in the car.

Seth tried to take a proper breath. He watched the door of the building. It had a sleek, art-deco aluminum awning, like an apology for the rest of the bland, pale brick building. The homage vice pays to virtue, he thought. He was eager to think of anything else. Brenda was taking her time, it seemed. Teeth grinding, finger tapping, muttering half-sentences to himself, Seth watched hard. Brenda finally issued from beneath the graceful awning. Seth paused, for his wife, his child and all he might lose, and pulled his car door open. He walked swiftly to intercept the woman.

"Ma'am," he barked when he'd closed to within five yards.

Brenda stopped, said something Seth couldn't make out in a low voice.

"Police," he said, the badge upraised in the cloudy dim streetlight.

Brenda froze and raised her hands. She started asking what is this about, when Seth grabbed her uplifted hands and shoved them clumsily behind her back. She half resisted, given the incongruity of his outfit, his story and his actions. He pulled one arm up behind her back, feeling a surprising warmth in the loose skin of her forearm. He shoved her awkwardly against a nearby SUV. That's when she knew something was wrong, and tried to turn. But it was too late. The thing in him knew how little to say and how fast to move. Seth pulled the unsheathed Buck knife out of the abdomen pocket of his hooded sweatshirt immediately. He stabbed her below her ribs before she could get any force behind her free hand. Her manicured claw tickled his shaven jaw in a prickly, failing caress.

The shock of the first thrust disarmed her utterly and she began a slow fall. There was a pitiable pause before she could fathom the pain or the damage done. Seth overruled the thing in him and withdrew the knife, reaching back and thrusting high, driving the blade through the fabric of her dark blazer, her bra strap, skirting past her ribs and into her heart. Her knees gave out and she collapsed into the side of the van and onto the ground. Seth let her fall. For a long moment, she stared into his eyes with an expression of incredible hatred and astonishment.

After his first killing, he could have been called a dumb kid in an unfortunate situation. But that night in Columbia Heights, there could be no doubt. He was a murderer. Seth ditched the clothes and the knife in a sewer a neighborhood away. From there, he drove straight home to Garden City, where he sat up with a bottle for a few hours in the silence of the empty dining room.

The next week Hurley told Seth, with an air of dry surprise, that the problem with Brenda had taken care of itself. The police decided Brenda's death had to do with the dealer in the building. Hurley said nothing more about Brenda when he handed Seth an envelope full of cash. It took Seth a few weeks before he could stomach the idea that he would get away with murder. And it wasn't until two months later—when Ritaloo Fastuch sent out an email saying there would be no bonuses and no new partners that year—that Seth could think calmly about the murder.

*You see,* the thing in Seth said.

It felt stronger and more hopeful than it had in centuries.

———————

To escape his thoughts, Seth pulled on his pants and went down to the sports book to watch the Super Bowl. The sports book crowd was split between the Steelers fans, Packers fans, and the usual ragged crowd watching simulcast horse racing in a corner off in the back. Aside from the simulcast corner, all the TVs and a dim movie screen were devoted to the Super Bowl, whose prolonged pre-game was nearing its end. The producers cut the blimp shot short, but not before Seth could make out the riot squad ringing the stadium and the crowd of protesters milling defiantly a few feet from it.

A man with a big plastic hunk of cheese on his head bumped into Seth and said excuse me and sorry, pausing with menace in his eyes to make sure Seth accepted the apology. Seth forced a small smile onto his mouth and nodded. A waitress dressed like a gangster's moll from the '20s asked Seth what he wanted to drink. He ordered and the game started. The Super Bowl started badly for Pittsburgh, whose kickoff man fumbled. Green Bay had seven before the game was two minutes done. Pittsburgh stalled on the next drive. It was fourteen-nothing Packers as the first quarter drew to a close.

Coming back from commercial, the Packers kicked off and the Pittsburgh return man brought the ball all the way to the forty-yard line. That's when a man in a referee's uniform walked to the fifty-yard line. Having somehow gained access to the referees' PA frequency, the man began preaching the need for a republic to be in a state of continual revolution if it is to remain a true democracy. It was a memorized statement and the false referee was not a stilted public speaker. As black-jacketed SECURITY men neared, he pulled a small pistol from his belt and shot the first of the security guards in the leg. The camera jerked away, unsure of what to do for a moment, before settling back on the false referee.

He pulled his jersey off, revealing a massive tattoo of Jefferson's thirteen-star flag on the front and back of his thin, broad torso. He spoke into the wire-microphone in his free hand and spun with the pistol to keep the dozen or so security staff at bay. The black-shirted security men divided into one group arranging help for their fallen comrade and the rest in a ring around the shirtless shooter. The camera stared at him as he continued to speak, though by now the stadium had switched off his access to its PA system, leaving only the scared and confused murmur of the 70,000 spectators. The

234

speaker, denied his voice and surrounded on all sides, lifted the pistol to the underside of his chin.

The TV network switched over to the stunned maws of the former quarterback and the narrow-faced son of a sports announcer who were supposed to explain the game. They stammered and apologized until the network cut to a commercial. It was a thirty-second, state-of-the-art, computer-animated cat food epic that concluded with a promise that viewers could watch it again, in 3-D, on the cat food company's website. The blandly handsome face of a junior anchorman from the network's nightly news filled the screens. He explained that the Super Bowl had been interrupted by violence, and that he'd pass on more information as it became available.

To the men and women in the sports book, the violence didn't matter. And new reports kept flashing on the screens over the next half hour, far beyond the false-referee's barely off-camera suicide on the fifty-yard line. Riots in and around the stadium, professional-seeming assassinations in two luxury boxes at the game. The people in the sports book watched the TVs with clenched jaws and burning eyes and responded to the news given by the anchor and the confused sports reporters in silence. But it wasn't until the junior anchorman, with his manicured eyebrows and camera-ready jawline, said that the game would be cancelled for the night and rescheduled that they cared.

Deprived of their good time, deprived of the valediction and vindication of their symbolic regional victories, they wanted, at the very least, their money. That's where the problems started. The people who'd bet the Packers wanted to be paid as if they'd won. The people who'd bet the Steelers wanted their bets refunded. The parlay people studied their tickets to try to figure out exactly what they were ready to kill for. Together they formed a shoving throng at the sports book window that the clerks were not remotely prepared for. The cash windows slammed down on grubby, insistent fingers. Those fingers poked into the faces and chests of pit bosses, security guards, and cocktail waitresses, freed by their outrage from any notion of human dignity or decency.

Seth sat back in a nice, high-backed imitation leather chair that had been vacated when the referee fired his first shot, and enjoyed his drink. The real violence started with a pit boss, who was trying to calm the loudest, most wild-eyed of the Pittsburgh fans, a big Italian guy in a novelty construction helmet. The pit boss had waded into the fray after the novelty-helmet guy kicked a bar stool in the direction of the simulcast horse bettors. The pit boss wanted to control the situation, while retaining the helmeted man and his ilk as valued customers.

That was half the problem. In another time, pit bosses were the favored toughs of Kansas City, Cleveland, and Newark. Now they were UNLV graduates waiting to get into the management track at the casino's parent company. And they lacked the menace to keep the weekend-warrior crowd in line. So while security drew up a plan, the guy with the novelty helmet slapped the pit boss in the face and demanded his money back. If he'd punched the pit boss, the other pit bosses and casino staff might have responded more rationally. But a slap isn't a punch, so much as an emasculation of you and all your sort. So, unarmed, the casino workers who weren't hiding rushed at the guy in the novelty construction helmet. And in beating the crap out of him, they enraged the Steelers fans, who outnumbered them, and soon took to beating on the casino workers. That brought out a humanitarian streak in the Packers fans, who tried to intervene, gently at first, in the name of universal brotherhood and sportsmanship, and were by the Steelers fans told to go back to their frozen cheese-eating hellhole and shut up like the cunts they were. The Packers fans took offense at this, and the fracas soon encompassed everyone except of course for the simulcast horse-racing bettors, who didn't seem to notice. The beefy pink fists of Packers fans collided with the black-clad distended stomachs of Pittsburgh fans, and eventually with the faces of the security guards sent too late to restrain them.

Outside the sports book, on the casino's main floor, Seth heard chips tinkle on the carpeted floor by the Pai-Gow tables, followed by shouts of authority and defiance as the losers on the casino floor tried to take advantage of the mayhem to recoup what they could. The TVs above the riot mirrored the action, showing fires and looting in San Diego, Los Angeles, Oakland and Seattle, as if they were another thing to bet on. The brawl on the casino floor was like Las Vegas' pyramid or its Eiffel Tower—a distorted replica of something, lacking the original's inspiration, done only for the money and because it could be gotten away with.

Seth wandered through the riot, too big and too awake to attract bullies or the randomly violent. He ducked careening bodies where he had to, finally joining the aged and the peaceable by the elevator bank. When a fat man in a Packers' jersey tried to incite them to revolt with an appeal to their racial pride in taking back the Jews' stolen casino money, an old man in shorts and a Senor Frog t-shirt mumbled something a bit too loud about the Packers fan being a typical Midwestern moron. Seth noticed that the pockets of the old man's cargo shorts were already bulging with chips. The Packers fan waded into the elevator crowd and reached for the old guy's narrow neck. Seth blindsided the Packers fan, taking two steps and landing a well-wound-up fist in his nose. After that, the Packers fan spoke mostly of his nose, and mostly to the floor.

The elevator finally came. Everyone piled in, but they gave Seth plenty of room.

Safe in his suite, Seth watched the mayhem flare up and die down in little clusters on the streets below. The local news, once it had something to say, said that other casinos had it far worse. The Excalibur, for one, was on fire and wouldn't be extinguished until the next morning. On the cable news, they spoke as if aroused, like they could almost see the world ending. Their eyes bulged and they seemed to pant as they explained that local militias had torched ATF offices in Salt Lake City and Sacramento. Seth turned the TV off. He stretched out in bed and closed his eyes. His cell phone rang. It was a DC number. He answered it.

The man on the other end asked if it was Seth Tatton, and introduced himself as a Detective Carlson, with the Washington DC Police. He asked when Seth could come in to talk. Seth hesitated, shook his head and gathered his senses. He told the detective he could meet for coffee Tuesday or Wednesday. Carlson agreed, and hung up. Seth went back to the window.

Fires, sirens, assaults and even a few murders unfolded below. Despite the sealed windows, he could hear screaming, shouting, gunshots and an oddly lengthy car accident below his hotel window until he fell asleep.

———————

Leaving the hotel was the day's first pain in the ass. In the course of the previous evening's mayhem, a woman had drowned in the pool around the hotel's phony Statue of Liberty. There was police tape everywhere and the valets were too busy gawking and gossiping to get Seth's car. Throughout that long wait, the other hotel guests avoided eye contact.

Civilization might be ending, and no one wanted to be caught doing their job when it did. At the airport, even the usually perfunctory rental car drop-off took a little short of forever, as revelers tried to find loopholes for what they'd done or had been done to their cars. Every function of the airport seemed overcrowded and understaffed. Everyone wanted out of town. The security check-in took three and a half hours, with city police walking up and down the line, checking faces from a hastily stapled-together mug book of men and women who'd been the most egregiously berserk, according to the casinos' thousands of cameras. Seth saw two men arrested out of his line.

Finally, Seth won a seat on an overbooked afternoon flight that was already delayed two hours. Waiting at the packed airport gate, the aluminum-framed TV beamed news and ads down on the weary crowd. The network had cleaned up the footage of the false referee shooting the security guy. Tattoos aside, the shooter was no idiot. He'd been a Los Angeles County sheriff, and had even done a term on the city council. The screen flashed file photos from the man's campaign. In its hurried buildup to commercial, the TV flashed scenes of sober burning office buildings in the twilight-tinted downtowns of Western America. That's when the man next to Seth elbowed him and apologized.

"I never thought I'd see the day," the man said. He was a heavy, older man, with a gray beard and a Steelers baseball hat on.

"Riots happen. We were probably overdue," Seth said.

"Yeah, I guess. I wasn't thinking that. I mean the Super Bowl. So some assholes get out of hand. So what? I don't care if they knock over the Washington freaking Monument. You don't just bend over, spread your cheeks, and cancel the Super Bowl."

"Is it cancelled?"

"Might as well be. I heard they're going to do it in Dallas next Sunday instead. But you don't stop a game, especially the Super Bowl, not after it's already started. Those La-La-Land sons-of-you-know-whats went too far. It's over."

"What's over?" Seth asked.

"America. We can't even hold a Super Bowl," the old guy said, his voice cracking. He fixed his watery eyes on Seth, trying to see which way he'd jump.

"Well. I guess we'll have to see."

And with that parting blandness, Seth wandered to the airport bar. The TVs there told of an investigation into the National Guard's very late and very ineffectual appearance at the riots. The anchors had the problem of having too much to report, to which they were clearly unaccustomed. The sheer volume of footage was astounding. A pair of RPGs hitting an IRS building in Tacoma showed up on about a half dozen cell phone cameras. It exaggerated the one real bombing of the riots until it seemed that all of Tacoma had been reduced to rubble. The man beside Seth in the bar, a Chinese guy from Milwaukee, fretted at painful length that the NFL would start the game in Dallas from the beginning, effectively erasing the Packers' 14-point lead.

The flight back to DC was long, and when Seth got back, he bought a bottle in downtown DC and went back to the old hotel he liked near Adams Morgan. He spent the rest of the night watching TV news and sipping scotch.

He woke early the next day and delivered the documents to Hurley's office. The security there had elevated, with assault-rifle toting guards and even a bomb-sniffing dog. It seemed absurd for an office building full of lobbyists and non-profits. Hurley wasn't in, so Seth left the documents with his secretary. He dumped a quart of Chinese food on his nervous stomach, and drove back to the hotel to meet the detective. In his room, he prepared a story that would slalom the few things the cop might know, while arriving at the conclusion that Seth Tatton knew nothing of importance about the disappearance of Sarah Loire.

In the hotel lobby, Detective Rudy Carlson stood out. Six foot five, dark black with a shaved head, he was well north of three hundred pounds. Though he limped, he moved with an odd grace across the pink and gold carpet of the hotel lobby. Seth recognized the detective right away by his suit, a deeply creased gray-silver three-button job. He approached the detective and extended his hand, which the man engulfed gently with his own, his grip like the toothless mouth of a giant fish. They introduced themselves and found a place to sit in the capacious lobby. They talked through the basics, of who Seth was, how he knew Sarah Loire, what their relationship was, and when Seth had seen her last.

"It was last week, right before I left for a business trip out to New Mexico."

"What business was that?" the detective asked.

"Real estate. I have a client out there who's developing some of the old gas fields near Farmington."

"And you say that you and Sarah dated for about a month?"

"I'd say that it's more like we saw each other than dated. But yeah, it was around a month."

"So you each saw other people?"

"I think so. Most women are pretty darn clear when they want exclusivity."

"And that never came up?"

"Not really. I travel a lot. I assumed she saw other guys."

"Did she ever mention an Alex Gordon?"

"No," Seth said, wanting to swallow in fear, but keeping his eyes steady and his face unperturbed. Gordon was the name on the California fake ID he'd used when he picked up Sarah from the hospital, and the one he'd used to rent the apartment he used as her tomb.

"You ever see this guy around?" the detective said, holding up a DMV photo of Gordon. Blown up beyond the inch square on a license, the differences between Seth and Gordon were reassuringly clear.

"No. Who's that?"

"He looks a lot like you. Don't you think?" the detective asked, watching Seth's response.

Knowing there was no right response, Seth shrugged.

"Who is he?"

"We don't know yet. He lives up in Northern California, or so the license says. Did Sarah ever mention the names of any other boyfriends?"

"Once, she started to. But who wants to hear that?"

"What did she say?"

"She said she was out on a date with some powerful guy, a politician. She got that it annoyed me, and dropped it."

Detective Rudy Carlson nodded. He was inscrutably fat, with the flesh above his eyes closing his eyes into slits. His mouth sat in a half frown, not of disapproval, but from the weight of his jowls.

"Did you want your relationship to be more than it was?"

"Look. I'm divorced. Badly divorced, with alimony, child support, scheduled visits, and a new guy who my kid calls Dad. So I'm not in a hurry to go marching back down that road," Seth said, acting annoyed.

With the thing inside of him quiescent, Seth felt more afraid than usual. Moreover, he felt the criminal's primal urge to just confess, to get right with the power and glory of the workaday world, no matter the cost. But he was also too practiced a liar to screw up an interrogation so preliminary.

"When you were with Sarah, did she ever talk about leaving town, going on a trip?"

That was a trap. A guilty man jumps on it, says yes, that's exactly it, and with the specificity that only lies ever possess. A guilty man gives a handful of far-off, nearly uninvestigatable destinations.

"No. Not really. It didn't seem like she was making that much money. And she seemed to like her job. She talked about getting a new car more than leaving town."

"Would you say that she seemed depressed?"

Trap two. A guilty man might press on the suicide angle.

"Not around me so much. But we'd only been seeing each other for a little while. You know how it is in the early days," Seth said.

"But do you think she might have been depressed?"

"She did yoga like four or five times a week. I doubt that depressed people exercise that much. But who knows? You could also say that people don't exercise that much unless something's bothering them."

The enormous detective nodded as if to agree. He flipped through the few notes he'd taken.

"You know there's a reward for information?"

"Huh."

"I guess her parents are pretty well-off. It's twenty thousand. So if you hear from her or hear anything about her, you should let us know."

The detective stood up and handed Seth his card. And though the man had pressed here and there, it was still a missing-persons case. They hadn't found her body yet.

---

Seth called Hurley and Hurley said he wouldn't be needed for a few days. So Seth got drunk at a bar up the road from his hotel, listening to a software salesman from Boston go on about how Washington should give California and Montana to the pot-smoking, gun-toting libertarian savages out there. "They'll run it into the ground, come crawling back when the first big earthquake hits." Seth drank and nodded. The thing inside of him gently nagged him to go retrieve Sarah Loire's body while it was still cold, while he could still forget his sedition against the unborn nation and to take his place in history.

Early the next morning, Seth sweated the booze out on the treadmill in the hotel gym. But that only made the waiting more pronounced. With Sarah gone, Washington was painfully hollow, its monuments like the ceramic fixtures in a gaudy, nouveau riche bathroom. So he drove up to New York. He called his lawyer, who called his ex, who said he could see his daughter after school. Embarrassed, Seth called his lawyer to ask his ex where the school was. The whole exchange cost him a few hundred dollars.

On the way up, Seth took the 895 tunnel around Baltimore—a long stretch without on-ramps or off-ramps. That's where he first noticed the forest-green Ford sedan. He punched it up past ninety, and the Ford kept pace, but didn't catch up. And it didn't catch up when he slowed back down to seventy. He dialed Hurley when he emerged from the harbor tunnel.

"What is it?" Hurley said, his syllables clipped.

"Nothing much. I just wanted to let you know I'm running up to New York for a day or two. I'm doing a few family things out on the island. But I should be free the day after next. And I think someone's trailing me. I wanted to give you a heads-up."

"Thanks for the heads-up," Hurley said. "Let me know if they're still behind you when you get to New York."

When the 895 rejoined I-95, Seth slowed down, joined the sixty-mile-per-hour dawdle in the right lane. The green Ford sedan pulled up within about twenty yards of him, and Seth tried to memorize its Virginia plate number from the rearview mirror. It slowed quickly, ducked a few cars back in the right lane and vanished.

Seth was no pro at spotting a tail. So he tried switching it up, running at sixty for a stretch, then at ninety, watching his mirrors. He made it up to Garden City an hour before he was supposed to pick up his daughter from school. That gave him enough time to buy a car seat and strap it into place.

The school was an ordeal. The desiccated principal xeroxed his drivers' license and spent at least five minutes on the phone with his ex before she let him take Elizabeth with him. They only had a few hours. Dusk had started its dramatic suburban floundering by the time they finished their McDonald's. Elizabeth was talking about a vacation that she had gone on with his ex and new Daddy, whom she now called simply Daddy. Seth was still old Daddy, and he wondered how long that would last.

"And the fishes all swim in the buildings the corals made. But their buildings aren't like our buildings. They don't have any windows. And the corals make the buildings out of their grandmas and grandpas," Elizabeth said.

"No kidding. Bethie," Seth started.

"It's *Elizabeth*!"

"Okay, Elizabeth. How do you like your new Daddy?"

"I like him. He's funny."

The words made Seth sad but also relieved. He could die or otherwise vanish and his daughter would be fine. His ex had managed, after a disastrous miscalculation, to find an exceptionally good man, who had the humility to raise another man's child. Seth marveled at these decent men, these stepfathers, whose hearts seemed to grow as their horizons shrank.

"Do you want to go to the toy store?"

"No, that's okay. Mom said you got me too many toys last time. She said we had to give most of them to the church, so that poor kids would have toys on Christmas."

"Huh. That was nice of her."

"Daddy?"

"Yeah."

"Next time we go on vacation, you should come. Mommy says you can't because she's with Daddy now. But I think you and Daddy could be friends."

"Maybe. Or maybe the two of us will go on a vacation somewhere one of these days, anywhere you want," Seth said, befuddled and lost.

"I wish we could all go. Daddy?"

"Yeah."

"How come we don't see you anymore?"

"I moved. I live in Washington now."

"With the president?"

"Right down the street from the president."

"Are you friends?" she asked him.

"Not really."

"Do you like it there?"

"It's okay. I have to be there for work."

"You should get another job."

"Maybe I will," Seth said

Pulling out of the McDonald's parking lot, the cold and the dark ruled out so many options. If he'd gotten a hotel room, they could go there and watch TV. But he had no ideas about what to do with the kid. So they just drove around, talking about ponies, spelling tests and the things he should say to the president for her. After an hour and a half, he brought Elizabeth back to a warm, well-lit, and loving home. His ex was busy, so new Daddy took Seth's child from him with a brisk handshake.

As Seth walked back down the shoveled path to the driveway, he looked at the snow in the front yard, marked by the meandering tracks of his daughter at play. His gaze travelled to the path shoveled through the half foot of snow. The path was straight, its sides smooth and square to the surface of the snow. Looking closely, he could see where new Daddy had flattened the sides of the path with a shovel. Seth marveled at the care taken and wondered what the hell he was missing.

The thing inside of him had told that missing whatever he was missing is what had marked him out for a more-than-human destiny. But Seth could no longer fight the sense that it was just something missing.

———————

Long Island was lousy with recriminations against which Seth had no defense. The thing inside of him sat mute in the floor of his gut and let him squirm. Vulnerable with regret, it whispered to him. *If you abandon your chance for greatness, there will be nothing to justify your basic human failures. You will have squandered your chance for a fulfilling human life, and squandered it for nothing.*

The cold made the taillights and headlights on the highway brighter, more distinct. Seth felt like he was collapsing into himself as he forked from the Southern State onto the Cross Island Parkway. From there, the ride was quick, moving opposite rush hour, and he reached Manhattan in no time. The hotel he chose was a slick midtown operation, with its security and bellhops in matching black suits. The elevator was so fast that his ears popped. He called the front desk for a steak, and to have his clothes laundered. In the muted flashing hyperbole of the TV news, he thought of new Daddy, of Elizabeth's blithe acceptance of his absence, and of Brenda, his first murder for Hurley. That was when it all turned for him.

After the murder, Seth had gone back home to Garden City, to his wife and child. He paid off a few credit cards and acted as though nothing had happened. Elizabeth had taken her first steps a few weeks earlier, and was running around the house. He remembered thinking that it was a good house, a good home, especially with the foundation sealed and a new carpet in the basement. He and his wife were decent, educated people raising their daughter in the proper fashion. Seth fed that line to himself for weeks. He'd expunged his juvenile record, at some cost, so there was no one to say anything but that he was a good man. Good.

*Good like the bouquet atop a coffin*, the thing inside of him quipped to him. It had earned a new boldness.

The weekend after Brenda was a nice weekend for them. He took Elizabeth and his wife to a park by a lake. It was one of the last weekends before the cold closed in. They passed the afternoon with other good, suburban types among the hills and trees that had been spared or contrived to set the park apart from the town's thicket of homes. But in the daylight, among the jungle-gym cries and laughter, Seth felt like a cross between a robot and a ghost. And that's when the thing in him spoke, taking words from the underground river of unthinkable notions that had pulsed in him at even the best of times.

*Look at you, taxpayer. When you get home, she'll ask you to fix the blinds in the guest room. Then the kid will shit herself. Then, if there's anything you want to do, it'll be too late. The wife will be too tired, then you will be too. Forget that bitch in DC, you're the one who's already dead. It's one smooth, paved, and costly road from here to the grave. You're worse than dead, living this life, a life for anyone at all. Don't shrink from what you did. What you did was your only way out of this graveyard. Talk to Hurley.*

The memory was interrupted by a room-service waiter with his food, a bellhop there to take his clothes. He ate quickly and walked the long way to Times Square, lingering at shop windows and doubling back a few times, until he felt it unlikely that he was being followed. He popped into one of the shady electronics stores that catered to tourists and bought a disposable phone. He walked up Fifth Avenue, whose stores had downgraded their window displays from Christmas spectaculars to desperate sales.

In Central Park, Seth watched the die-hard joggers and looked up a number from his Blackberry. He dialed his old friend Anthony, a lawyer he'd worked with at Fastuch Ritaloo. Last time Seth saw Anthony, he'd left to join a start-up, which went belly-up in time to leave poor Anthony woefully overqualified in the depths of a recession. Last he heard, Anthony was taking odd jobs and trying to stay above water on a big house he'd bought in Westchester. In the background, Seth could hear children's voices and a TV turned up too loud. Anthony sounded glad to hear from him, and hurried the conversation to a quieter room.

"Hey, Seth, how are you man? Long time no speak."

"Yeah. You know how it is. I've been pretty busy."

"Lucky you. Are you still over at Fastuch?"

"Yep. Still grinding out the billable hours. How about you?"

"This and that. It's a real mix. Web security one day, and then the next day I'm drawing up a contract for a Chinese restaurant down the street."

"Listen, I can't talk long. But I think I have a job for you. Can you come meet me in the city tomorrow?"

"I have a few things tomorrow. Can you do the day after?" Anthony said, the stress clear in his voice.

"Shit. I'm actually back in DC after tomorrow. Listen, if you can you cancel a few things, this should definitely be worth your while. It's a client with money to spend."

"Ah, what the hell. I never see any of the old Fastuch gang any more. How about you? You must be close to making partner by now…"

"Listen, I have to go. But tomorrow…"

Seth named a noisy Irish bar between Grand Central Station and the United Nations and Anthony agreed. Seth rose from the bench and watched the joggers, emitting billows of steam as they labored through the bitter cold. He wondered what they had to tell themselves to keep running.

The night was long. The lovers on the other side of the hotel wall kept Seth from sleep. He got out of bed, roamed the fashionably gray room, showered, and wrote a list of names on hotel letterhead. There was Hurley, Mankins, Roberto, Frederica, the colonels he'd met, and Burleson, followed by the names from the *Declaration*. At three AM, Seth gave up on sleep and wandered to an internet café in a Korean pocket of town by the Empire State Building. There, Seth researched the names on the list and a back-of-the-envelope moral algebra for each name, breaking down the list by the motivations at play—ambition, greed, fear, and finally, spite.

Seth hunted the web until he found a dodgy-looking website that promised to give vehicle registration information for license plates from all fifty states. Seth used the credit card he should have chucked when he got rid of his phony California license to buy information on the car he'd seen following him up from DC. It came back to him as being registered to a rental car company. Using the disposable phone, Seth called the company and gave the customer service woman William's name, asking about his last rental, saying he'd gotten in a fender bender and couldn't read his own handwriting from when he jotted down the details. He asked for the license plate number of the car he was driving. And it matched what Seth had written down. Seth said good-bye and quietly struggled to breathe for what felt like five minutes.

Seth slumped in the internet café's wobbly desk chair. A cab sped him past the gated windows of stores and restaurants back to his hotel. He slept a few hours, awakened by the arrival of his laundry—a delivery over which his DO NOT DISTURB sign apparently had no jurisdiction. He drank coffee and watched the TV's tales of a military supply truck hijacked in the Oregon desert, and of a Super Bowl to be played in an empty stadium. That afternoon, Seth was early, but Anthony was already waiting for him at the clean and modern Irish pub. The collar of his white button-down shirt stuck out from his dark sweater, almost like a priest's collar. Anthony was nursing a Diet Coke in the impatient glare of the waitress. He stood up to shake Seth's hand. Seth also ordered a soda and waved her away.

"So what's going on?" Anthony said, leaning his tan and pudgy face forward.

"Not much, just a ton of work. I honestly don't think I've spent a whole week in one town since the summer."

"It sounds crazy, but I envy you. Taking the train down to the city has become my version of a big adventure. I do most of my work from home. And that gives me the chance to watch the kids. So I guess I can't complain. It saves us on daycare."

"How's Pam?"

"She's good, the kids are good. Her ex is still an asshole. He still wants custody, as long as it's not on the weekends. Constant bullshit there. So she tells him that she doesn't need the child support. It's a whole brinksmanship thing. And I tried to tell her we need all the income we can get right now. But she won't listen. Anyway, listen to me going on after I said I couldn't complain. So how're things at the firm?"

"They're good, I guess. I'm always out of the office. Clients have me running all over. I wanted to talk to you about something I'm working on for one of them."

The waitress returned with a list of specials that took forever to recite. They ordered and got back down to business.

"So what do you need? Contracts checked? Tell me," Anthony said, sounding excited.

"Here's the story. I have a client, a big contractor for the government. Thing is that the client has reason to believe that someone either in the government or connected with it is selling their trade secrets to a competitor. So what I want you to do is run financial background checks on a bunch of people that the client suspects. Do whatever you have to—turn over any rock you can think of. I want to see unreported income, unexplainable assets, oversized campaign donations, shell companies, unlikely windfalls, family trusts, anything and everything. Money is really no object to this client. He's a paranoid, spiteful bastard. Hire a forensic accountant if you need to, but otherwise keep the circle small."

"Sounds good. But why the small circle?" Anthony said, his eyes flashing with the fear that this job could be one of the many disappointments in his unemployed life.

"Some of the people we think may be leaking the information are also our clients. And some of them are very well connected. We don't want them knowing that anyone is poking into their business. That's why I thought you'd be perfect for this job. You know the how to make inquiries, buy documents, whatever you have to do, anonymously. You told me once, how you could mask your computer's address…"

"Mask the IP address. It actually goes deeper than that. I can create an overseas identity that it would take Interpol a month to find out wasn't real. Remember the D'Angelo case, what he did was…" Anthony said, beginning a long, lively discussion with himself about matters that almost entirely eluded Seth. The waitress came with their food. Seth ate and let Anthony go on—he was clearly excited and proud to speak like an adult for an afternoon. Finally Seth had to interrupt.

"So how much will this cost me?" Seth asked.

"How many people?"

"About two dozen."

Anthony began rattling off expenses, and finally arrived at a number, which Seth offered to double if he could get it done in three weeks.

"How do you want to pay?" Anthony asked. "It's a lot of money, and I know how the firm can be about processing new invoices. I could probably do with say twenty percent up front, but I don't think I could do too much less than…"

"I'll give it all to you right now. Our client is in a hurry. And I trust you."

Seth reached into his leather bag and pulled out a large envelope, from which he counted out bank-bound stacks of money. From his wallet, he gathered some more cash and laid it on the table for the lunch.

"What format do you want the reports in?" Anthony said, nearly slack-jawed with the money in his hands.

"I'll call you in a week or two with the specifics. But wherever you find anything fishy, I'll probably want you to send anonymous letters to any agencies that might be interested. IRS, FTC, DoJ, SEC, State Attorneys General. Prepare the information and documentation for each of them, and any others that make sense, depending on what you find. But like I said, keep invisible otherwise."

They stood up and shook hands. Awed by the money in his hands, Anthony thanked him and thanked him again. It made Seth nostalgic for the days when money was his biggest problem.

---

As Seth climbed into his car, the broken-toothed spirit cursed its predicament. It blamed Hurley, and his blatant exposure. It blamed Sarah Loire and her suicidal desire for liberation. They had led him to its weakness, its name. And if Seth persisted, the thing inside of him would have to tell. And if Seth knew the name, he could chase it out. And the broken-toothed spirit didn't think it could survive another exorcism.

The former god blamed himself. He'd overreached by choosing a man as smart as Seth. It had gotten too excited at being close to Petronius, to Hurley, to real power, to the promise of a civil war and the hope of overturning some aspect of reality. And it had acted too boldly, made its wishes too well known. Its real wish was never for blood and sex, but to exist.

Now Seth was in full revolt, and wanted to know its name.

Though enraged, the broken-toothed spirit still held out hope for its prospects in Seth. The man was mortal and would need its help sooner or later. That was why it hadn't mentioned Seth's betrayal to Petronius, when Seth met with Hurley.

But being no longer able to control Seth with a seizure, to bully him or even insinuate itself into his thoughts undetected, the broken-toothed spirit was growing desperate.

———————

Seth drove back to DC in the rain on I-95. He hoped Hurley had something for him to do when he got there. Anything short of another murder would be fine.

The waiting had gotten harder since Sarah Loire. She'd taken something noxious from him, but hadn't left anything in its place but remorse and a hunger for revenge. Even on the road, flying across the Delaware Memorial Bridge at eighty miles per hour, Seth could feel it collapsing in on him. He was on the wrong side of too many things—his family, the law, the scheme and the thing he'd broken the law for. Repentance was out of the question. The only escape was a forward escape.

He was relieved when Hurley called. Seth pressed the button and Hurley's staticky voice filled the leather-and-wood interior of his car.

"Hey, where are you?" Hurley asked.

"I'm going through Delaware now. What's up?"

"I have something for you. Can you come by tonight?"

"Big job or little job?"

"Little one. I think you'll like this one. We'll talk about it when you get here."

The DC rush hour started in Baltimore. Traffic on the 95 crawled past the grim glass-clad shoulders of suburban offices that poked above the brown denuded trees. Inching forward in one long train of taillights, Seth wondered how many would die in the civil war his bosses were cooking up. The thought stirred the thing inside of him. It conjured wild, primeval scenes of the world soaked in blood.

"Who are you?" Seth demanded of the quiet interior of the car, turning down the talk radio, as if that would help him hear better.

The broken-toothed spirit lurched in his gut, conjuring an image of a thousand rifle butts knocking the teeth out of a thousand innocent mouths.

"You're a bitter thing, aren't you," Seth said to the air.

But the only response was the sound of the windshield wipers. The thing inside of Seth froze like a squirrel who suspects it's been seen. Until that moment, Seth had never been far enough from the thing inside of him to make out even a vague outline. Traffic abruptly halted. Seth decided that if he was going to speak to something that was, by fairly iron-clad consensus, not there, the car was the place to do it.

"We have this whole ride. And I'm all ears. You don't have to answer all of my questions, but tell me something, anything."

A fat raindrop hit the windshield. Another followed it. The rain intensified. Traffic became a red spine of brake lights. The inside of the car was silent.

*I was here before you. I was here before nations, before architecture, before the law and before history. I've been worshipped by the flower of humanity and feared by nations. I can crack open the feeble compromise you call a world and chew it into so much pigshit with a chuckle. So don't you dare question me.*

"Crack open the world? Huh. Then how come you're stuck in traffic with me?"

*Do you know what a fleeting concatenation of jissom you are? I offered to make you something, and you threw it away, like the trash you will always be. It's in your blood. Your mother was a cocksucking rat who had to find the biggest shit heap she could and fuck some inbred Indian from the most defeated tribe on earth just to make you. I held out the brass ring and you pushed it away for a junkie whore. And why? Because that ditzy cooze taught you to touch your fucking toes! What a pathetic joke. You're pissing away a kingdom, a golden age, a New Atlantis for some calisthenics and a blowjob from a dead slut!*

"What is your name?" Seth said in the car.

*It's not too late. It hasn't broken forty degrees in Washington yet. I know you check the weather every day. You can still do something with the body. After that, all you have to do is to call off your nerd in Westchester and get the documents back from Dolores.*

"Who are you?"

*If you think you can keep me at bay twenty-four hours a day…*

"Who are you?"

254

*You can't...*

"Who are you?"

*I am the seducer of virgins, the traveler of great distances. I bring disorder to the armies, fear to the brave, courage to the weak, wisdom to idiots and destruction to the mighty, I...*

"What is your name?"

The voice went silent. Seth asked his question again. But there was no response. The thing in Seth had retreated utterly and coiled around the base of his spine. Traffic began to move.

---

Seth was late for the meeting with Hurley, who waited at his usual table in the steakhouse below his office. When Seth sat down, the waiter set down two porterhouses.

"I assumed you'd be hungry," Hurley said.

Seth nodded. Traffic had stretched the ride from New York to DC to six hours. But his stomach reared up, as he remembered that it was likely Hurley who'd probably had him tailed.

"You said it. I should have taken the train."

"How was your trip?" Hurley asked, the bloody meat poised by his lips.

"It was good. I haven't had a chance to see my daughter much since all this got underway."

"Enjoy it while you can. They grow up fast. I have two daughters and a son. My oldest won't talk to me. You start to lose them somewhere around the seventh grade."

"Huh. I think it's starting a little earlier with mine. Anyway, I didn't want to say anything more on the phone. But did you ever look into the thing I called you about—the tail?"

"I checked around, did another full sweep for bugs, everything. I didn't find anything. Are you sure someone was following you?"

"It seemed that way. But I'm not exactly an expert. Aside from watching *The French Connection* a couple of times, I really don't know anything about being tailed," Seth said.

"Well, there's a lot on the line. You're right to be cautious. It's funny. I hired someone to call in a bomb threat last week to justify all the security at the office."

Seth cracked a smile and took a bite. The steak was good, bloody and buttery all at once. The waitress brought him a glass of wine. The two men ate in silence for a few minutes.

"So what's this job?" Seth asked through a mouthful of steak, careful to use the prop he'd been given to cultivate his image as a greedy, complacent compatriot.

"It's a good one. You get to meet a movie star," Hurley said, taking a forkful of potatoes and creamed spinach.

"No kidding. Who?"

"Kurt Lignam."

"Whoa."

For three decades of moviegoers, Kurt Lignam was the face of steely masculinity. He was the half-outlaw cop and the laconic cowboy who punished the wicked. He was the toughest of the tough guys on the silver screen, the unapproachable father who generations of American men had paid good money to silently approach. Now, he owned a chunk of the Northern California coast and directed movies.

"Told you it was a good one. Kurt's an investor in a few of Roberto's funds. And they went hunting together a few weeks back. They got to talking, and now it looks like Kurt's on board. He wants to see some figures, to get a few reassurances that the revolution will be solvent," Hurley said. "So I need you to show him a few documents, mostly about the shale deposits and the cost of extracting the oil. The job is to give him a few hours with the documents, but make sure he doesn't copy them or take down any notes, and to bring the documents back to me."

"What's Kurt Lignam doing on board? I mean, why do we need him?"

"Hearts and minds, hearts and minds. He's a steady, trustworthy face. He'll be important during the transition."

"How did we talk him into it?"

"Lignam's a patriot. And he hasn't liked what's been going on in Washington for a long time. And he's had a lot of trouble with the state about the water rights for his ranch, which has left him with a bit of a revolutionary fervor. We promised him that he would never have any government interference with his ranch ever again."

"When should I go out there?"

"The meeting is at his place the day after tomorrow."

"Really? Don't you have someone out there who could do this?"

"Lignam knew Bergman. But I don't think Bergman is the right man for this," Hurley said, smirking. "Besides, I want to keep the report in hands that I can trust. Right now, I have the only copy of it, and I'm not about to let it out of my sight. You're the next best thing to that."

"I wonder if my frequent flier miles will still count, after all of this," Seth said, shoving an oversized bite of meat into his mouth. Hurley laughed.

"You'll be flying private—at taxpayer expense—after all this. And that is the only way to fly."

The two of them toasted and laughed, ate and made small talk. Seth coughed up some sourly humorous anecdotes about his ex. Hurley countered back with a few from his first two marriages. When the steak was gone and only drinks remained, Hurley grew serious.

"Listen, I've been thinking about you lately. When we left it last, I mentioned a law-enforcement job in the, uh, new administration. And you said you wanted a judicial position. Well, something else occurred to me—we're going to need embassies. How would you feel about running one of those?"

"An ambassador?"

"Yeah, you know how to be careful, subtle, how to keep secrets. But you also know, well, how people, *are*—for lack of a better word," Hurley said.

Ambassador had a nice ring to it. But ambassador was also essentially an out-of-doors position. Hurley wouldn't give the keys to the inner sanctum to killers or whores. Seth took a second to consider it.

"I could see that working. But no third-world shitholes, right? We're talking Europe, or one of the Asian countries with proper toilets," Seth said, leaning back in his leather chair and gesturing to the waiter for another drink.

"If you insist."

"I do. And I don't think it's too much to ask."

Hurley smiled and leaned back in his chair.

"You're right. A few weeks from now," Hurley said slowly, "there's not much that will be too much to ask."

The waiter brought Seth's drink. He smiled wide and raised it to Hurley.

"Here's to that," Seth said.

They toasted like old friends on a great adventure. Hurley handed Seth the usual—an envelope full of documents and another one full of cash.

---

Over the next night, Seth read through the oil shale report, which was an exhaustive seventy pages, attested to by geologists, engineers, surveyors, miners, ecologists, and even a physicist. If you were inclined to believe the report, you'd put it down astonished to learn that there were oceans of cheaply extractable oil in the shale of the American West. You'd also be astonished to know that three quarters of that oil would, if the secession went as planned, belong to a government overseeing a mere sixty million souls.

Seth slept badly in the hotel, but well on the airplane to San Francisco airport. From there, he drove down the California coast. After the slushy gloom of the East, the sunlight and the mountains diving steeply down from above the highway and down into the sea were a happily preposterous apparition. On the little, two-lane road, no one followed him.

He found a shopping plaza in a sleepy coastal town. From there, he called Dolores on the disposable phone and explained that there would be another envelope coming for her to hold, along with more money. She gave him her home address. In the strip mall's post-office-box storefront, Seth got change and made a few copies of the shale report. He put the copies, along with bundles of cash into a FedEx mailer, which he sent to Dolores in Bullhead City. The thing in him protested weakly— a sensation not much stronger than gas.

As the sun sank into the ocean, Seth found his hotel, a big Spanish-style manse whose stucco walls glowed with the day's dying light. The desk clerk apologized for the lack of a bellhop, saying that the hotel was hosting a large wedding that same evening. Seth nodded dumbly, happy to be in such a beautiful place, where it seemed like he could become someone else. In the room, his dizzy eagerness to go out on the town, out to the beach, or up into the mountains was trumped by his exhaustion. He slept in his clothes until the awkward hour right before dawn.

That morning, with a few hours to kill, Seth drove to the beach in the early morning chill. The beach rested in a bowl formed by mountains covered in stunted, twisting trees. Seth felt at ease in the foreign environment, calm for the first time since he'd wept and coughed up black slime on the floor of Sarah's apartment. The voice returned.

*It will never work. Know that. I don't need you. And it won't take very much to get you killed. It's Sunday. You won't see next Sunday. Know that. Killing you wouldn't be much more than an inconvenience to me. But nothing you've done isn't reversible. You can still...*

Seth interrupted the broken-toothed spirit, again demanding its name. And it shut up. Back at the hotel, he showered, put on a suit and waited in front of the TV for an hour. Mankins' campaign was in the news after he called the current governor a federal Quisling. The Super Bowl was set for later that day. It was a sad affair in an empty stadium—a spartan three-quarters of a football game that started with one team already holding a 14-point lead. On the news, a talking head rattled off every pollable figure from consumer confidence to the president's approval rating. They'd all taken steep drops over the last week, with the Super Bowl being the cherry on top of a shit sundae of steady increases in all the classic misery indices.

Kurt Lignam lived on a road without a road sign. After missing the entrance twice, Seth drove up the winding dirt road, past cows, trees, and over a small ravine. The house was big, but hardly ostentatious. It looked like any other prosperous rancher's house. Seth knocked, and Kurt Lignam answered, an inch shorter than Seth, in a tucked-in polo shirt and jeans.

"You Seth?"

"Yes. It's an honor to meet you," Seth said, surprised to find himself so starstruck.

"You had better be Seth. Dressed like that, I figured you're either him or the FBI," Lignam joked, so at ease that it was intimidating.

"Excuse me?"

"The suit, I mean. Roberto says I can talk freely around you, that you know all of this," Lignam said in a disarmingly warm voice.

"I know some of it. I can speak to what's in the documents."

"You were up at the site?"

"A few months back. They did a demo with outside engineers, geologists. It all checked out, at least from what I could see. Everyone there seemed satisfied."

"You know I was a Marine before I went out to Hollywood. So I don't take any of this lightly. If I'm going to be a part of this, there had better be a plan."

You're already part of this, Seth thought. But you know that already, and it scares you. That's why I'm here.

"From everything I've seen, there is a comprehensive plan in place," Seth said, almost ending the sentence with a *sir*.

"Well, let me take a look at this report."

Seth handed it over and Kurt walked into the next room. Seth followed.

"It's going to take me a while to read all of this. Would you like to come back later?" Lignam said, some of his cop-who-is-himself-outside-the-law steeliness showing.

"I'm really sorry. But I can't let the report out of my sight. It's one of those things. You can take all the time you want with it. But you can't photograph, photocopy, or take notes directly from it. You can understand the need for precautions at this stage, I'm sure."

"I guess so. Does the living room work for you?"

"Sure."

"So, before I start, can I ask you something?"

"Shoot."

Lignam smiled.

"What did they offer you?" he asked Seth. "What position?"

"Ambassador. You?"

"Secretary of the Interior. Not that title exactly, but the same job, the national parks and the like. I always admired Teddy Roosevelt."

Seth could see the brochures already, the old cowboy returns to the Painted Desert, the Grand Canyon, Yellowstone, Monument Valley.

"That makes sense."

"Thanks. So I'm going to put on a little music and read this with you here in the living room. Just make yourself at home. There's a bookshelf and TV in the next room, and you can help yourself to the fridge in the kitchen."

Kurt flopped on one of the big leather couches in the living room. The room's rear windows flooded it with light. A cool breeze blew through the windows as the day heated up outside. Kurt read earnestly, flipping back and forth as he read, bookmarking pages with his fingers. Bored, Seth went into the other room and browsed the bookshelves. He came back with a hardcover of William Peter Blatty's *The Exorcist*. Five hours passed in the quiet jazz and sinking sunlight, then lamplight in the Lignam living room. Kurt finished the report and he seemed somehow more at ease than he'd been when Seth arrived. At the other end of the couch, Seth was deeply spooked by the old best seller he was halfway through, when Kurt spoke up.

"Ah dammit, I almost forgot. That cowardly excuse for a Super Bowl is on. Can I invite you to stay for a beer or two and watch it with me?"

Having a few beers and watching the Super Bowl with Kurt Lignam was like some mystical epitome of father-son bonding, and so Seth said that sounded good to him. The game was in the third quarter when they got to it. With the stadium empty, the game was eerily quiet, with the quarterback and the middle linebacker barking their pre-snap orders into the cavernous space. The impacts, the snapping of the pads, the grunting and the referees' whistles were all exaggerated by the church-like quiet of the dome. Between snaps, the players jogged back to the huddle in an ominous near silence.

"It looks like it's a practice," Seth said.

"I really don't like that they did it this way. Something's definitely missing. It's like the daily rushes of a movie, before they sync the sound," Lignam said.

"It's sad."

"I think that our friend Roberto is right. It's time for a change."

The Steelers scored to tie the game a few minutes into the fourth quarter. But they'd come in at too much of a disadvantage. The Packers took their time driving down the field for a go-ahead touchdown, leaving Pittsburgh with less than two minutes and no timeouts. They couldn't make it. The Packers looked awkward and self-conscious celebrating in front of no one but TV crews, which crowded them halfheartedly. The game left Seth and Kurt quiet and a little sad. Neither of them said anything as announcers faked a breathless excitement for the game. Kurt rose and nodded at him. Seth double-checked the shale report, gave a deep nod and a hard handshake, and left.

Driving back up the coast that night to the San Francisco airport, Seth couldn't help but think it was the best day he'd had in a long time. And he couldn't help but wonder when he would ever have a day that good again.

# PART FOUR

*A murderer... may well be fixated in the exhilaration stage of killing. But once there is a lull, and the murderer has a chance to dwell on what he's done, the revulsion stage sets in with such intensity that suicide is a very common response.*

        -Lt. Col. Dave Grossman
        **On Killing**

*"The gods have become diseases."*

        -Carl Jung

        **Commentary on "The Secret of the Golden Flower"**

The broken-toothed spirit knew better than to try it. Taking over completely was a bad idea with the busty freckled girl hundreds of years ago. And nothing had happened in the intervening centuries to make it a better idea. Like then, it was an act of wild lust and sick frustration.

To have nothing, no real hold on the world, was something it could almost get used to. But to have a grip and lose it to some seven-decades-and-out bag of weakness named Seth Tatton was too agonizing. It had hidden in a secular culture for a century, and couldn't fathom how Seth had ever learned to demand its name. The demand sickened it and began its excision. The demand renewed its primordial shame, reminded it all too well of its centuries-long failure.

In the time since that initial exorcism, the broken-toothed former god had lived, like a criminal, in aliases. But its true name was still there, pressing upward and throbbing like a compound fracture right under the skin. And now Seth could turn up that pressure whenever he chose.

What happened in the airport was a crime of desperation. The broken-toothed spirit should have seen the flaw right away. But like most crimes, it was an eruption of the will over fear and habit. And that left little consideration for what might happen after.

In the rental car shuttle bus of the San Francisco International Airport, Seth was exhausted. His mind wandered from daydreams of revenge to idle calculations about what a ranch costs to run. As he did, the broken-toothed spirit crept silently up from his stomach. It said nothing. Rather, it simply took control, quietly and completely, like a snake abruptly squeezing a prey it had already gently coiled around. There was no convulsion, no bugging of the eyes or anything an outsider might notice.

The thing in Seth froze him in his seat, seeing the world through human eyes for the first time since that spring afternoon on the warm fringes of the empire. Having not taken full control of someone since that disastrous mistake with the girl centuries ago, it was surprised at how complicated the world was and how utterly immediate. It had left so many details to Seth, ignored so much of life as the dreary make-work of small minds.

It rose from its seat on the shuttle bus, leaving Seth's bag behind. It walked into the terminal. It pondered the procedure of how to get on a plane for a full minute, trying to make sense of the signs and to recall how Seth did it.

*Gate.* The word *Gate* made sense to the broken-toothed spirit and so it walked where the arrow pointed. It encountered a bored and obese TSA agent. She asked to see his ID and boarding pass.

The broken-toothed spirit fumbled through Seth's pockets and handed her the ID and the ticket stub from his flight out to San Francisco. She clucked, and spoke very slowly, as if he was extremely stupid. She said he needed to go get a *new* boarding pass for his *return* flight. But first he would have to take the tram two stops, she said, because he was at the wrong *terminal.*

The thing in Seth wasn't ready for the immediacy of human life, with every moment so tangible, so inherently bereft of perspective. And it certainly wasn't prepared to sit back and take the condescension of the dull-eyed TSA worker. Teeth clenched, it quietly informed the TSA woman that he would feed her a pile of her own half-digested shit using her fingerless hand as a spoon. Before she could respond, he pushed the podium out of the way and ripped open the front of her shirt.

Someone yelled at him to stop. Wild with rage and drunk on the actual *effect* he was having on the world around him, it turned to face whoever spoke, its teeth bared and hands curled into claws. The yeller was a tall, middle-aged hippie woman in a cotton dress. It howled at her in Attic Greek that he would piss on her gaping remains and force her children to devour each other. She backed away and it pursued, cursing. By the time it found its English and began explaining the sort of rape it had planned, security was there.

The broken-toothed spirit, in command of Seth, threw the hippie woman at one of the security men with astonishing force. The first taser was a surprise. It crouched, to locate and to pounce on the man who'd fired it. The second a nuisance. It leapt, but fell well short of the security man. The third taser a concern. The fourth taser was a genuine problem. By the sixth, the airport cops were just pulling the strings of a broken puppet.

The former deity returned to Seth's senses in the back of a police car. It began to tell the cops what it thought of them. And they didn't appreciate his cursing all that much. So, between the airport and the police station, they pulled over the car to hit him with the taser again. But when they saw the bloody mess he'd made of his wrists with the handcuffs, they called the station to say that they were taking him to the hospital instead.

———————

What happened on the airport rental car shuttle wasn't like the seizures, for which Seth always had at least some small warning. It was like a crashing wave. One minute he had control over himself, the next he had none. After that moment, Seth saw bits and pieces of his own life as a horrified spectator. The TSA woman, the hippie, the security, the police, the orderlies with their restraints, the doctors and nurses and their sedatives: They saved him.

The thing inside of him had lacked the patience and circumspection to lead his life the way that it wanted to. It even lacked the foresight to kill Seth. And now it was restrained in a hospital bed, ranting and thrashing, slurring its curses and blasphemies through a fog of sedatives and antipsychotics.

At the hospital, no one knew Seth's name, though they asked periodically, which further enraged the broken-toothed spirit. Seth's bags, phone and wallet had been lost in one of the struggles, carried off by an opportunistic thief, or to a lost-and-found oblivion.

If the broken-toothed spirit had a moment to think at the airport, it could have called Hurley and snitched Seth out. If that woman hadn't confronted him about his lack of a boarding pass, humiliated him about being at the wrong terminal, perhaps it could have adjusted to life as another faceless man long enough for it to gain proper control and do what it needed to do. It could have done any of a dozen things. But it hadn't. And now it was tied to a hospital bed with fluffy but snug and seemingly unbreakable ankle-and-wrist restraints, a victim of its own rage. It refused food and raved about the sexual iniquities and undignified demise of whomever came to change Seth's IV and bedpan.

Death seemed the only way out of the corner it had painted itself into. And the staff sensed as much. Throughout the early nights, an orderly came up to the small rectangular window every fifteen minutes to make sure Seth hadn't slipped his restraints or brought himself to harm in some way.

———————

Words fail most of what happened to Seth in the days after losing possession of himself at the airport. If pressed to describe it, he would describe the place he went to as a high cavern at the bottom of a towering, luminescent tree, whose upper branches were occupied by a massive serpent. It was a massive, dim place, more familiar than majestic, suffused with the distinct feeling of the space behind a supermarket or a movie theater, a place no one really had any business being. It filled him with the *you-must-be-lost* feeling of an industrial park after dark.

Seth had some idea of the world beyond that place, and what was happening there. But it didn't come to him as pictures or sounds or smells, because his senses weren't his own anymore. But to experience the world without senses wasn't as jarring as it sounds. It was, rather, like knowing something without having been told.

His helplessness in the cavern was extreme. It was as if he was a speck of dust, frightened and hypersensitive, a floating mote of victimhood. But from that speck, Seth began to gather himself. The trees, the ground, the undulating luminous cavern walls—he slowly appropriated something from them, forming himself into a circle, then an oval, and then a soft, blurry human form.

From the walls, he carved sheets of skin, which he hung on his approximate form. But the process wasn't entirely that concrete. As he took on skin and bone, he took up his entire life—school and work, mother, father, sister and brother, ex-wife, daughter, friends, enemies, and lastly, victims. The victims were the hardest. They wanted explanations of why he'd killed them, which he couldn't provide. They wanted to live again, which he couldn't grant them. They wanted their last moments told and, some, their burial grounds identified, which Seth couldn't promise. They were long negotiations in which neither side could budge nor be satisfied. Seth willingly clothed himself in that hair shirt of unresolved grievances, and regained some license to his life. He wasn't forgiven for his sins, but given the strength to engage them, and to try to act as their living answer. In doing so, he reclaimed permission to live, reclaimed his life as an extension of his own soul. All he had to do was reclaim his body.

This reassembling took a while. Time was hard to judge in there. But by the time he was ready to confront the serpent, he was already at an advantage. He was the law and it was again the fugitive. That was clear to both of them. Seth made the first move, taking control of his eyes. He searched the bare hospital room for something, some symbol upon which he could fix his efforts. There wasn't much—no picture on the wall, no crossed windowpanes, no moving mandala of a clock, no talisman or beachhead in the outside world. Desperately searching for a focal point, Seth finally found what he needed. In the corner where the bare plaster wall met the soundproofed ceiling, their intersection formed an uppercase

*T*, its arms slightly upraised. The morning light illuminated the corner. He stared at it and did not blink.

The serpent stirred. The corner, encompassing the three dimensions unambiguously, spoke of the hardened law that had given this world to limited creatures like Seth and stripped it from the broken-toothed spirit. It was a source of profound embarrassment to the spirit. From embarrassment came a kind of sickened weakness. The broken-toothed spirit tried to move Seth's eyes, but he wouldn't let it. It reached his hands up to scratch out his eyes, but the fuzzy cuffs made that impossible. It arched his back and flailed his legs as much as the restraints would allow. But Seth kept his eyes on that corner.

"Now tell me your name," he demanded of the thing inside him.

The serpent coiled in its luminous branches. Focusing hard on the far corner of the hospital room, Seth asked again and it hissed. In its tail, the serpent brandished the large, plastic-handled kitchen knife Seth had used to stab the boy in Rhode Island, mocking him with it.

"This is your only authority," it said. "Who will stand with a murderer like you?"

That's when Sarah Loire appeared, as if real. Her sex appeal was muted, her eyes glistening with tears and yet placid. She radiated a peculiar peace. Her murder and strange disposal made perfect sense, her face seemed to say. As troubled, desperate and dead as she was, she nodded, and in doing so said that she would stand with Seth.

Bolstered by a strength not his own, Seth took the knife from the serpent. And it waved the blade he'd used on the woman in Washington, followed by a revolver he'd used outside of Boston, the knife he'd used on Eggleston, and the pistol he'd used in LA. One by one, Seth took the weapons, demanding the serpent's name. Sarah Loire looked on and quietly reminded him of how he'd strained in humiliating positions, under the command of a strange woman, all because he had wanted to be free.

"Tell me your name," he said, with a newfound confidence.

The broken-toothed spirit cursed him, cursed Sarah Loire, cursed Seth's daughter and mother, cursed everyone and everything Seth had ever held dear, mixing enough truth with its vivid maledictions to make them sting. But that distress only served to let Seth know he was still alive and still distinct.

He demanded the spirit's name, and it handed out aliases, from Poopy McFuckface to Soupy Sales to Mickey Mouse to Thoth, squirming in the high branches. But Seth kept demanding, calling upon Sarah Loire who watched over him, calling upon the unnamable thing that had remained of him to challenge the spirit, calling upon the unnamable thing that had remained of him even when he was a speck of dust trapped inside his own body, calling upon his own strength, even his own sins as proof of his ability and his will. As he spoke, it was as if he could feel Sarah's hands on his body, as they had been in her lessons, a gentle pressure reclaiming his body as he calmly demanded the name of the broken-toothed serpent.

It squirmed and froze under the assault. Exhausted, exasperated, and in tremendous agony, the broken-toothed spirit gave its name, its real name, not Broken Tooth, but the name his mother called him when was a young man who'd wandered from the tents of his people, in pain and despair, following a strange, fat old man, thousands of years ago.

With the cavern aflame all around him, and all the authority of the world coursing through him, Seth addressed the serpent by its true name and demanded that it leave. The flames seized the broken-toothed serpent. Its skin swelled and deflated with a terrible hissing screech. It stared down at Seth as it burned. Its eyes were calm and forlorn, human eyes, bloodshot and resigned as its body screamed.

Its shriek rose and ended abruptly. And it was gone. And Seth was back. But something was missing, something so large and hard to define that he hesitated to ask his fingers to wriggle for fear that they wouldn't obey. When they did, he breathed deeply and blinked tears from his eyes.

Seth smiled and began to sigh happily, but something caught in his throat. He began to cough and each cough called up a larger obstruction, making the next breath harder to gather and the next cough more desperate. As he hacked, his coughs seemed to bring up a metallic-tasting, bitter mucous. Seth struggled to breathe. Tied down on his back, his body wracked itself with spasmodic coughing and wheezing. He coughed until his vision was clouded to nothing. And with drool and thick, dark mucous running down his hospital shirt, something in his chest became dislodged. His throat stung and ached as he turned his head and retched up more mucous. But something was giving way, moving up and out of him. At the back of his throat, he gagged violently, half vomiting and half coughing as the object came to his mouth.

Feeling it in his mouth, the obstruction was a small, heavy object, and hard, though coated in bloody sputum. He violently turned his head and expectorated it onto his pillow, followed by yet more trailing strings of dark-colored muck from his body.

Once the last of the dry heaves passed, it took a few minutes for Seth to see clearly. He blinked the tears out of his eyes and caught his breath. The room was lit dimly—the idea being that it was dark enough so he could sleep, but bright enough so they could check on him regularly. Turning his head, Seth looked at the object he had expectorated. The dark sputum was draining off its dark form.

It took Seth a minute to recognize it and few more minutes to believe his eyes. The bloody mucous had left a dark stain below the object on his pillow. In the middle of the stain was a Matchbox car, like Seth had when he was a kid. He stared at it for a long time, incredulous, before he realized that it was a one-seventy-fifth scale model of the Mercedes sedan in which he'd murdered Jaime Bergman.

Without being able to understand why, Seth couldn't resist a strange conclusion: He'd been forgiven, without asking or deserving it. Tied down, his face covered in tears, blood and black sputum, Seth finally laughed.

Now all he had to do was get out of the mental hospital to which he'd been committed, and survive outside of it long enough to put a stop to a nearly completed conspiracy operated by some of the wealthiest and most powerful people in America. He laughed again, laughed awhile.

———————

Seth woke with the dark spittle wiped from his face and neck. He strung together a day and a night of polite small talk with the staff before they removed the restraints and put him in with the rest of the patients. They assigned him a normal room, with a roommate. The roommate was a wiry guy, with a face full of scabs, and bad yellow-brown teeth that made his age hard to determine. The guy introduced himself as Rory, and started talking almost immediately about what Seth could only assume was a powerful drug.

"It's like you get the stuff, you get on a run and you can really get to it, you know? Like you can talk to the boss, like finally confront him and say 'What's up? You have something you want to say to me? What's so fucking funny?' You just need to confront them, you know? Clear the air."

"Confront who?" Seth asked, because to ignore his roommate would be rude, even crazy.

"Man, who do you think? The bosses who run things. The real slippery bastards. The devils, the angels, the weird, fence-sitting ghosts and has-been gods, rogue CIA programs, all of them whispering, out on the edge of earshot. I mean, when you're in the everyday, their talk seeps through, like people talking shit about you behind your back. And it's fucking aggravating, but it's more than that, too. Well, I don't have to tell you about it," Rory said, lying in his bed across from Seth, his hands on his chest. Seth sat on his bed, shifting atop the rubberized sheet.

"What are you talking about?"

"You don't have to bullshit me, man. I see that hole in your aura—it's like a fucking crater. No bandaging that. No toupee or fake tits to cover that one with. You've been at it for real with one of these guys."

"I don't know what you're talking about."

"Am I not being clear enough? I'm talking about demons, astral beings, man, the illegal smuggling between the worlds, the savage conspiracies of disgraced gods—all that hardcore mental-illness shit. One way or the other, I see all of it. And it could all be the worst sort of bullshit. But from the look of your wrists, you've been up against something more than the nightly news and the pursuit of fucking happiness."

Seth looked down at his wrists. Even in the distance between beds, they were a giveaway. The broad, shallow cuts from the broken-toothed spirit's reckless battle with steel handcuffs had scabbed unevenly. And the bruising radiated yellow and maroon well into his hands and forearms. He shrugged at Rory.

"Hey man, I get what you're doing. And that's good. It's smart. You shouldn't tell that kind of shit to anyone, even if they ask. That's the way to do it, if you want to get out of here. I've been in and out of these places since I was twenty. One time, after I was discharged I asked my dad about this stuff, the shifts in color, the voices, the half-invisible snake people. And you know what he said? He said that he saw all of that shit too, but he never, *ever* talked about it. My dad, he was a sharp guy. He said the devil was like a homeless guy—you just had to walk by. Don't look down, don't give him the time of day, and never give him a dollar. That's what he said. So whenever I want to get out of one of these places, that's what I do."

"You talk a lot," Seth said, wondering if he should follow Rory's advice when it came to acting sane.

"The last guy, hell, my last two roommates, man, they were muttering zombies. You'll see them in the activity room. Don't get me wrong, you're a fucking mess, but at least I can tell you hear what I'm saying. Between the doctors who think I'm crazy and the other patients, who *I* think are crazy, man, it can get lonely in the loony bin."

"I'll bet. You seem like an authority on these places. So tell me. How do I get out of here?"

"Why should I tell you?"

"Because it'll give you an excuse to talk and me a reason to listen."

"True. True," Rory said, nodding. "First thing is: Are you sure you even want to get out? I mean, the food's not so bad here. I'm going to do a full ninety days, put some meat on my bones," Rory said, smacking his flat stomach inside the hospital t-shirt.

"Yeah. I want to get out. I have people counting on me outside of here."

"See, I'm the opposite. I have people looking for me outside of here. That's another reason I like this place. Did you know they're not even allowed to tell the cops you're in here? Cops need to come to the hospital with a fucking affidavit. Doctor-patient confidentiality or something."

"No shit. So, tell me more about how I get out."

"You? Brought in like you were—involuntarily, I mean— you won't get out tomorrow. Know that for starters. This is California, and you're most likely a fifty-one-fifty."

"What does that mean?"

"It means you came in on a suicide attempt, assault, or almost anything where they have to bring you in restrained. And that's a mandatory hold, probably fourteen days at least. You know how long you were tied down for?"

"Not really. I think it was three, four days?" Seth said. He looked at the floor, ashamed at not being able to account for himself.

"That's not great. But it could be worse. It gives you at least a week to convince these guys that the worst is over. The thing you have to remember is that you're not in a movie here. It's not *One Flew over the Cuckoo's Nest*. The staff isn't trying to oppress you, or to steal your humanity, not on purpose anyway. It's never on purpose. But at the same time, it's also not *Good Will Hunting*, you know. They're also not hell-bent on learning what makes you tick or on making you a healthy, whole human being, either. Know that. It's not either of those. Keeping that in mind will save you a lot of time."

"So what's the angle to play?"

"Remember that at a hospital like this, the doctors and social workers and so on are really just risk managers for the state. Trust me. I've had the other ideas. The people who run these places have been everything from Gnostic archons to manifestations of my own Buddha nature, to a karmic playback loop of atrocities from my past lives. But really, their job is to make sure that no one can sue the hospital if you go and commit some heinous act after they let you out. As long as you don't get anyone's attention, it's not much more than cost management. And it's hard to get anyone's attention in a nuthouse."

The lights in their shared room went out. Seth stretched out on the rubberized sheet and closed his eyes. And Rory kept talking, pouring forth a whole life of mania and disappointment in his small, hoarse voice. Rory was young enough and smart enough that he carried with him the peculiar excitement of a tragedy still in progress. Seth grumbled to let Rory know that he was drifting.

"Man, you're falling asleep? That's right—you're still on all those drugs. Listen, if you don't want to wind up crazy for the rest of your life, don't take any more of the drugs they give you. Whatever's going on, you should let it burn itself out. I doubt I'd still be bouncing in and out of these places if not for the drugs, the ones they gave me even more than the ones I gave myself to get even. It's like I'm spending my whole life trying to get back to even, like one of those bungee-cord rides at…"

The next morning, an orderly woke them, and they joined the shambling parade to breakfast. The orderly locked the door to their bedroom behind them. Seth turned and Rory grabbed at his elbow.

"Come on," Rory said. "They don't want us going back to our rooms to sleep all day. It screws up their schedule."

"Sleep?" Seth said.

"Right. Once you take your meds, if you take the meds, you'll see what I'm talking about. By the way, are you still serious about getting out of here?"

"Yeah."

"Then, seriously, palm the pills they give you. They'll calm you down at first. But they come with their own cost."

They shuffled down halls of buffed linoleum and pale aqua cinderblock. Breakfast was scrambled eggs and pancakes, bland and filling. The food alone made Seth want to go back to sleep. Rory ate his breakfast and the one belonging to the guy next to him, who was preoccupied with maintaining a complex facial tic. Seth leaned across the decades-old formica slab to Rory and whispered to him.

"So what else do I do?"

"No need to whisper. No one cares if crazy people pass notes. If you learn that, then you're practically sane."

"Okay. So what do I do?"

"To get out? Really? Even after that breakfast, you still want to get out?"

Seth nodded. And Rory told him what he needed to do. He followed Rory from breakfast to the medication line, where he followed Rory's lead in palming the medication. It didn't require much sleight of hand to avoid the inattentive eyes of the skeletal Spanish nurse. Later, in the bathroom, Rory sorted out their pills, taking a double dose of one, putting two in his sock and throwing two away.

"So you keep mine too?" Seth protested.

"Man, when you get out, you should look some of this stuff up on the Internet. You'll see I'm doing you a favor."

"Really? So why are you keeping them all?"

"These drugs really are bad news. But man, you seem smart enough to know that I'm not the type of guy who's going to do himself too many favors," Rory said, smiling and grinding his teeth.

The rest of the morning passed in the recreation room, over a Parcheesi board. Seth and Rory rolled the dice and went around and around without keeping proper score. Of the other two dozen or so patients, the most far-gone of them hung back toward the walls or windows, staring or rocking. The more with-it patients sat in chairs and plastic couches by a TV that stared down at them from about ten feet up, blaring soap operas.

"What's the story with the TV here? Can we change the channel?" Seth asked.

"Nurse has the remote. She'll change it if it's not too much trouble for her. What do you want to watch?"

"The news."

"Not gonna happen. The news is, you know, upsetting, probably by design. Plus, the last thing you want to give to a cluster of seething psychotics is hard evidence."

"Shit. How about the weather channel?"

"Weather channel, huh? I didn't peg you for a weather channel guy."

Seth thought of Sarah Loire in a vacuum-sealed laundry bag, on an inflatable bed in the middle of her makeshift mausoleum in DC. The candles would have burned down to a horseshoe of waxy smears around the inflated mattress. Recalling the scene, Seth wondered if he didn't belong in a psychiatric ward after all.

"Yeah, well I like to know the weather. Could we get her to change it to that?"

"Probably. Clouds moving over maps sounds soothing enough. Let me see if they'll do it."

After a period of hectic gesticulation by the nurses' station, Rory got the skeletal Spanish nurse to retrieve the remote and point it at the TV. After much flipping on the screen and some muted groaning and agitation from the couch, she found the place where multi-colored clouds moved over maps. Seth stared at the screen intently.

He felt his pulse race when the yellow number over Washington, DC, came up as 48. It was mid-February, sooner than he'd planned on for that kind of warmth. As fresh panic began to seize him, Seth was called in to see the doctor.

The orderly didn't speak except to mumble the turns in the hallway necessary to guide Seth to the doctor. After the series of whitewashed, fluorescent-lit corridors, the doctor's office was a humane aberration, its windows dimmed by thick curtains, full of oriental knickknacks, driftwood, blown glass baubles and framed psychedelic posters from old rock shows.

Doctor Paul Wetzelian was a bearded, middle-aged white guy in a white cable-knit sweater who greeted Seth with a soft handshake. His thin face was calm and his eyes flashed a wary sort of intelligence. He introduced himself and gestured for Seth to sit. From behind his desk, he paused, squinted and cocked his head.

"So, John Doe, I have to say that you look different today," the doctor began.

Seth didn't remember meeting the doctor and didn't want to guess how their first meeting had gone.

"I guess the best place to start is my name. It's Seth Tatton. I apologize for not giving it before."

"Why didn't you?"

"To be honest, I don't know. I've been under a lot of stress lately," Seth said, remembering Rory's advice.

"What kind of stress?"

"Well, my father died last month, and that was hard. We were never as close as I would have liked. He was sick a long time, but it still hit me harder than I thought it would," Seth paused and stared at the faux Persian rug. He took a deep breath to organize his lies.

"So… at the airport… the woman there…" the doctor began.

"It wasn't her. It wasn't my dad or the woman at the airport. Things kind of snowballed after my dad died. About a week ago, my wife left me. I guess I could see that coming. But two days later, at work, I was passed over for partner. I'm a lawyer. And there I am, thirty-eight with nothing to show for it."

281

The doctor watched Seth closely. Seth couldn't tell if it was out of sympathy or to find out how far his new patient would take this line of bullshit.

"And, uh, that was when I hit my head at the airport, on the luggage rack of the shuttle bus. I hit it hard. And I remember being so angry, so angry that I literally saw red. After that, well, I remember a few things, but nothing really."

He was conducting the session according to Rory's playbook. Give them a worldly, succinct explanation for why you lost your shit, something that says: Wouldn't any sane person, in a similar situation, react badly? Put a nice little head-injury bow on it for them, and give them a few simple reasons why it won't happen again.

"So you're a lawyer. Tell me about that," Wetzelian said.

"Mostly corporate law. A lot of arcane documents and government filings for hedge funds, IPOs, things like that."

"Does it pay well?"

"It does, or it used to. And I'll be happy to fill out the intake forms correctly. I should have insurance for all of this."

Wetzelian nodded and smiled. Seth got the feeling that he was playing his game against a more gifted opponent than his last interrogator in Washington.

"I'm sure someone will get around to that. But for now, I want to talk about the episode in the airport, and later, how you behaved when you arrived here."

"I honestly don't remember too much. What part are you referring to?"

"We see a lot here—strange voices, feats of strength, and abuse. But you made quite an impression."

"I'm afraid to ask. It's not the kind of impression I want to make. I honestly don't remember much of the last few days. And let me say that I'm deeply embarrassed by all of this. But in the last few days, I've started to look at my life a lot more clearly, and I think…"

"Fourteen days. I know. You want out after fourteen days. And we'll see about that. First, I'd like to know a few things. How many languages do you speak?"

"Enough French to order dinner. A little Spanish. That's about it. Why do you ask?"

"Because you spoke to me in Armenian a few nights ago. Do you remember that?"

"I don't. Are you sure it was Armenian?" Seth said, squinting and raising the pitch of his voice to underline his disbelief.

"You said you'd take my two sons, whose names you either knew or guessed correctly, and make them castrate each other with their fingernails. You said it in Armenian."

"Ahh… I don't know what to say, except that I guess I'm very sorry."

"What about Latin? Do you speak Latin?" the doctor asked.

"No. No one does, do they? It's a dead language."

"It is. But some people can speak it. Clergy, academics, and the like. I made out some Latin from you the night you came in."

"We had to learn a little Latin in law school. I probably picked it up there. The brain's a mystery. Isn't that what they say?"

The doctor laughed at that and stared past his tented fingers for a long moment at Seth's lying face. Seth had to struggle not to smile along.

"Yeah. It's mysterious all right. Some brains more than others."

The doctor pulled the folder off his desk and started checking boxes on the form, asking Seth if he'd been experiencing headaches, hearing voices, suffering hallucinations, taking any prescription drugs, taking any illegal drugs and so on.

At the end, he offered Seth use of his office phone.

"It's been almost a week now. Someone must be worried about you. I'll give you fifteen minutes."

---

Seth picked up the phone and started to dial. But a simple fact finally wormed its way through the fog of spiritual triumph and psychotropic cocktails. He was most likely in deep trouble. He'd lost the oil-shale document. He'd dropped off the radar for at least four or five days. If he called Hurley for help, odds are that he'd assume that Seth had been caught and flipped, by the FBI, the Secret Service, or someone worse. And that suspicion was enough to get him killed.

His original plan for revenge—to find and cultivate a few high-level contacts in the government but outside Hurley's cabal to feed his information to—wasn't one he could pursue from hiding. And Plan B, to go public with his information, would never work, not fresh from a stint in a mental hospital. He'd have to change his plan, and fast. Maybe the hospital was legally required to conceal his presence. Still, that didn't mean much to the people looking for him.

Seth decided to call Dolores. But after months of effortless flight across the country, cars rented with a nod and the flash of a plastic card, warm greetings and express checkouts at luxury hotels, the simplest of things had become very difficult. Getting to the answering machine on Dolores' home phone had taken almost ten minutes, with repeated calls to information, which had six Dolores Navarros in Bullhead City. He recognized her voice on the voice mail message of the fourth one. Seth circled that number just as the doctor returned, and crumpled the paper into his hand.

"Could you find anyone?" he asked.

"No. Do you guys have my cell phone, or my wallet? Anything?"

"No. Sorry."

Back in the recreation room, Seth found Rory, who was entertaining himself by playing three-card monte for checkers with a few other patients.

"Listen, Rory, I have another question," Seth said quietly.

"Again with the whispering. Come out with it. Come on. Speak."

"But what if I wanted to go the other way? What if I wanted to stay in this place?"

"I knew you'd come around. There's no living like institutionalized living," Rory said, raking in a handful of plastic checkers, backed by the full faith and credit of the moment and redeemable for nothing, ever.

While Rory knew of only one view to espouse and one mode of cant to get out of the hospital, he knew several ways of staying in. His meandering discourse on the subject took them through dinner and to bedtime. To hear Rory describe it, the challenge was to avoid being restrained and over-medicated, and at the same time to avoid being judged sufficiently sane for release. He said the best way to walk that tightrope varied from hospital to hospital.

"You got your doctors who are pure risk managers. Even if they think you're running a game to stay in, the doctors will sort of respect that, because they're also running a game to stay in their jobs. But after too long, they'll usually take a harder line and say you're 'not responding to treatment,' which means that you're costing them more than they think you're worth. It's also their way of warning you to settle down or they'll ratchet up the drugs and the discipline."

"It didn't seem like the doctor was too eager to buy my act, the whole thing you told me to say about having problems at work, but now seeing things more clearly," Seth said, lying on his bed on the other side of their cinderblock room. Talking so late at night in bed reminded Seth of a sleepover.

"Yeah, that's partly your fault. You caused a stir when you showed up. Even us patients knew something was up."

"Shit."

"Well, it's also Wetzelian. I heard he was a prison shrink before this. So he's probably used to hearing a lot of tall tales. He's a hard one to read in general. The guy's got a sense of humor, so he could be that other kind of doctor."

"What kind is that?"

"The kind who believes they can cure people, that there is such a thing as mainland sanity, and that it has real shipping

285

channels going to it from every darkened corner of the globe. He'll check the boxes when he has to, but he's not interested in hearing your bullshit. He wants to actually *do* the impossible job he has."

"Mainland sanity, huh?"

"That's the golden dream, I mean, if you play the psychiatric game for higher stakes than risk management. Mainland sanity, the true and inescapable prison, the all-towering-reality, the greatest lie ever told. Mainland sanity. But the truth is that we're all each alone on our own goddamn islands," Rory said.

In the silence that followed, Seth could sense that Rory was veering toward an angry place.

"So why do you want to stay here?" Seth asked.

"Probably the same reason as you. You tell me."

"I've been thinking about it. And I don't think there's much for me out there right now. I could be in some trouble when I get out. I need some time to figure out my next move."

"Me too. The law?"

"Could be. So tell me. What's the best way to play this here, to stay in?"

"When I want to stay in, I'll usually just speak my mind, let rip about the savage conspiracies of the gods. I bet you have some far out shit going on in your head about now. Lead with that. I doubt they'll give you a full ninety days right off the bat, but they should definitely extend you another week or two."

Rory sat up and tossed down two pills he'd saved in the waistband of his sweatpants, and dropped off to sleep. Seth stayed up late, calculating. When he got out, he could empty his bank account and start running. From there, he could get the documents and try to get them to the right people before mid-April, when Mankins would likely take over as governor of California. But he'd have to do his work from hiding, which was impossible. And the mental-hospital stint would be a nearly impossible barrier to credibility.

Option two was to go back to Hurley and explain his breakdown. Hurley knew about the thing inside of Seth, but that wasn't enough to guarantee mercy, especially because he was, in fact, plotting against Hurley.

As much as he hated it, medical incarceration made the most sense. With the broken-toothed spirit gone, he was alone, and a low growl of remorse chewed at his quiet moments. Seth was truly afraid for his life for the first time he could remember.

Counting his options, the revenge he'd begun to undertake for Sarah Loire was now his only route to survival. He tossed and turned until the blue glow of dawn warmed the chicken-wire honeycomb of the room's one reinforced window. Drifting closer to sleep, Seth's mind drifted over the years, back to September 11th and the often tense months in New York that followed. He remembered the day they evacuated his midtown office building, the cordon and the police in hazmat suits, the secretaries fleeing and men trying to look calm while they asked distracted EMTs what drugs they should take if it was really Anthrax that they found inside. And Seth remembered the punch line—the powder in the envelope wasn't Anthrax at all. It was a piece of chalk a kid sent as a gift to his aunt. It had been crushed to dust in the mail.

---

The next day, the weather channel said it was fifty-five in DC. Seth climbed up on a chair and proclaimed himself to be the god Apollo from a chair in the rec room, to general indifference. He climbed back down, embarrassed. Acting crazy wasn't as easy as he'd thought. That afternoon, when Doctor Wetzelian brought him a fresh set of intake forms, Seth put his name down as Tamerlane B. Screwtooth and his address as The Fallen City of Byzantium. Wetzelian laughed when he read the names.

"You must like the food here. Well, Mr. Screwtooth, I'll take this down to the admin office. We're done for today. Feel free to use the phone."

Seth dialed Dolores' number in Bullhead City. No answer. He dialed it again. This time, she picked up, sounding aggravated.

"Dolores, it's Seth. How are you?"

Her voice was sleepy. She said things were good. She told him about the casino, which was jerking her around about her weekend sets, and her kid, who her mother said was getting into trouble at school. With a calm familiarity, she relayed her normal, everyday life. It was a signal to Seth that she didn't always plan on being so fun or so available, that she trailed a whole world full of dreary odds and ends behind her shiny dress and her full, red lips. Seth understood the play. But it calmed him to hear that such lives were still taking place, and that he might somehow one day have a place in one of them.

"So everything's good? Nothing out of the ordinary?"

"Not really. I got a second job as a magician's assistant one day a week, back over at the Aquarius."

"Oh, no kidding. That sounds like fun. Hey, remember when I gave you those envelopes? You still have them?" Seth asked, working to keep an even pitch to his voice, struggling not to rush to the point.

"Of course. For what you paid me, I should remember."

"Well, Dolores, this is where I need you to earn that money. I want you to put the papers I gave you in the mail, but I need you to do it in a very specific way. If you do this right, I'll double what I paid before. And I'll be eternally grateful," Seth said. He forced a grin onto his face, hoping it would shape the sound of the words that came out her end of the phone into something charming.

He gave her a shopping list: Self-adhesive envelopes, self-adhesive postage stamps, rubber gloves and baking soda. He told her to mail the oil shale report first.

"Use a computer at the hotel's business center. Take your time and look at some other stuff on the internet, look at dresses, read the news, but get the names and mailing addresses of the Secretary of the Interior, the Secretary of Department of Energy and the Head of Security for the

Chinese Embassy in Los Angeles. Mail one envelope to each of them. Put Robert Hurley as the return address on each one, courtesy of The American Institute for the Preservation of Leisure. That address will also be online."

Then he gave her instructions on where to mail the still-unborn western country's *Constitution* and *Declaration*. He gave her the addresses to look up and send the envelopes to—the Secret Service, FBI, Attorney General, and a few others—all with the same return address: The Committee to Elect Chet Mankins.

"Now, in each envelope, I need you to put two tablespoons of baking soda. You're writing all of this down, right?"

"I'm writing it all down. Baking soda, right?"

"Two tablespoons of baking soda in each envelope, along with a printed note that reads: REBELLION IMPOVERISHES THE NATION."

"Give me a second to write that down. Just baking soda?"

"Yeah. Just pour it in loose, with the papers."

"Okay, but why the baking soda?" Dolores asked.

"These guys we're sending the documents to, they get a lot of mail. The baking soda is there to give the envelopes the right weight. It's a signal to them that the documents are actually from me. The baking soda, and the note, they're like a code, a security measure. Don't worry. You're not doing anything illegal."

"They weigh the envelopes?"

"These guys get so much mail every day, with so many markings, that it's the only way they know which ones to open first. That and the postmark."

"What's up with the postmark?"

"I need you to send all of these from Venice, in Los Angeles. Use one of those blue boxes on the street. But pick one far from the main strip. Take a few sick days if you have to. And if they give you a hard time at the casino, I can pay you more. But I need this done soon."

"So I have to drive to LA?"

"Sorry. But that's the job," Seth said, carefully gliding past it, knowing he had very little leverage.

"Okay."

"So can you do this? Tonight?"

"I guess so."

"Guess so?" Seth said, proud to hear the old menace in his voice.

"Yeah. I'll do it tonight. When are you coming back through Laughlin?"

"Soon. As soon as I take care of this."

"Where are you now?" she asked.

"I'm in California, I'm stuck, doing some delicate negotiations."

"What kind? You never talk about your work."

"It's complicated. I'm buying a hospital from the state. A hotel chain wants it," Seth said, glad that his talent for lying hadn't fled with the thing that had once been in him.

Wetzelian entered, hearing at least that last snatch of conversation. Of course, he could have heard all of it on an attached line. But Wetzelian's sweater, a tan cardigan with suede elbow patches, discouraged paranoia. Seth wondered if that was by design, as he flashed his index finger at the man.

"Listen, I have to go. If you do what I said, everything will be fine. I miss you."

"I miss you too," Dolores replied, in a hurried, awkward way that let Seth know his flash of affection had thrown her off balance.

"I'll call you soon."

"What if I have to call you?"

"You can't right now. Someone stole my phone at the airport. But I should have a new one soon. I'll call you as soon as I get a new phone. Bye."

Seth hung up and looked up at the doctor with uncertainty. Even practiced liars can never tell how undone their deception is in any given moment, but they know better than ever to ask.

"Well, Tamerlane, I'm sorry to say that your insurance didn't check out. Probably problem with Byzantium having fallen. So listen, I don't enjoy wasting my time. And I can see that you'd rather play crazy or play sane than talk about your actual problems. So what do I do here? There's a pharmaceutical solution."

Wetzelian folded his arms over his chest to underline his threat. Seth realized he would have to work with the man.

"Okay, doctor, that's fair enough. I'll make you a deal. If you give me one more full session with the phone tomorrow, and one more at some point in the next few days, then I'll give you a week of honesty, the straight-up truth about why I'm here, and why I have to play at being crazy. After that, you can decide what you want to do with me."

"Oh, so we're making deals now?"

"You think you can help me. And I'm not against that. I want to give you the chance. But I need to get a few situations in the outside world straightened out. I'll explain that part to you, as well."

"Fine. Longer lunch for me. But I have means at my disposal if you're jerking me around."

"And one more thing. I need a newspaper. The *LA Times*, preferably. I can't breathe being so cut off from the world."

"How about the *Chronicle*?" Wetzelian offered.

"Sure, that'll do."

"You better have a good story there, Seth."

"It's Reuben," Seth said, grinning.

"Really? Not Screwtooth?"

"Don't worry about it for now. The story I'll tell you is a good one."

---

The next day was dreary and full of Rory. Seth's thin and scabby guide began repeating his best material all too soon. Rory was a bore. Indulgent doctors, indifferent nurses and Rory's solipsistically lost colleagues were the only ones who wouldn't say so. Seth palmed his drugs and ate the cafeteria food. That afternoon, Wetzelian turned the phone around to Seth's seat and left his office. Seth called information twice and grappled verbally with unforgiving computers before he remembered the town in Westchester where his friend Anthony lived. Seth told him to get a pad and pen, reciting the same shopping list he gave Dolores, along with the same baking-soda instructions for mailing out the results of all the financial digging he'd done.

"I guess the security makes sense," Anthony said. "From what I found, it looks like we're going to fuck over some powerful people, and in a bad way."

"That's right. Take all possible precautions. Wear the gloves, and use the self-adhesive envelopes and the plain-jane fonts on the documents. Only the right people should know who this is from. No one else will have any way of finding out."

Then Seth gave more specifics, telling Anthony to send copies of everything he had found to the IRS, the Secretary of Defense, and the Secret Service. For some documents, he also included the House or Senate Ethics Committee and the Joint Chiefs of Staff.

"Okay. I guess that all makes sense. But what I don't get is why the baking soda?"

"It's a code. There are people at these institutions I know. And it's what we worked out. They weigh the envelopes."

"But how do they know how much the documents weigh? Some of these are fifty, sixty pages. Some are two pages."

"They expect that. The baking soda is to put the envelopes in the weight range that they're looking for. It's a code without names. That's why it has to be two tablespoons. That weight and the zip code is how they'll know. That's the other part of the job. I need you to mail them from one of the blue mailboxes outside of Penn Station. And don't drive. Take the train in and walk from Grand Central."

"This wasn't part of what we discussed."

"Are you paying your mortgage this month? And how about the two months after that?" Seth asked, a hard edge in his voice.

"Yes. I was only, only asking."

"Do this tomorrow and I'll pay a fifty percent bonus when I know it's done."

"Fifty percent?" Anthony said, surprised and frightened by the offer.

"You're as surprised by the money as I was. That's another reason I wanted to bring you in on this. This is the big time. It's worth it to the people paying us," Seth said, giving his voice some of the smooth baritone of success.

"I know. Thanks. I'll do it tomorrow."

"Anthony, thanks. This is a huge help to me. I'm glad I have a friend as reliable as you."

Seth's warmth surprised Anthony.

"Thanks. And for what it's worth, you really pulled my bacon out of the fire with this job. I was about to file for…"

"That's what you get for marrying a woman like that. She's a stone fox and you're…"

Wetzelian came in to grab a file and stayed for the show.

"A stone schlub," Anthony said, finishing the sentence. "Still, thanks. By the way, where are you calling me from?"

"It's a hospital in California. I'm trying to convince this crazy heiress to testify in a case that I'm working on."

"That sounds about right. No rest for the wicked."

"Tell me about it. Well, listen, someone stole my phone the other day. But I'll call you from the road later this week to make sure everything worked out. Get these things in the mail as soon as possible. But only send out one batch. Then you're done. No going back and sending more."

"Okay, boss. Take care."

"You too. Bye."

Seth put the phone down with authority. Wetzelian smiled.

"Well, Screwtooth, you're either the craziest or the sanest person I've ever had in this office. Either way, I expect a show tomorrow, and no more bullshit. Here's your paper."

He threw a limp *San Francisco Chronicle* onto Seth's lap. The front page screamed in big black letters that Jefferson had been shot dead on the border of Idaho and Oregon. There was a photo, taken from some distance, of his body on the side of a rural highway, next to a still of the big bearded man when he was alive, sitting in front of an old Betsy Ross flag. The related article below the fold said the governor of Montana was calling for a national day of mourning for Jefferson. The president condemned Jefferson as a domestic terrorist and the governor as a political opportunist.

Later, in the rec room, the *Chronicle* told Seth that the LAPD had recovered Bergman's body from the LAX lot. The heat in that trunk must have been intense. The body had decomposed and the gasses burst the laundry bag. The smell was un-ignorable, even by the hurried denizens of the long-term-parking lot. Police were pursuing multiple leads, was all that the paper said.

From there, Seth flipped through the paper. It was 45 degrees in DC, according to the nationwide weather that perched above the TV schedule. Seth shuddered at all the work he still had to do.

---

He passed the next morning arguing the rules of Monopoly with Rory, who called Seth's recourse to the rulebook fascistic. Seth gave up arguing and let his mind wander while he rolled the dice and his companion cheated. Rory had said that no one could find him in the hospital. But Rory didn't know the people who were looking for Seth. At lunch, he barely touched his sloppy joe. Then it was time to see Wetzelian. The doctor gestured him into his seat and sat to face him across the cluttered desk.

"So," Wetzelian said, and let the silence eat at Seth.

"Okay. Is there anywhere you'd like me to start?"

"You can start anywhere you want."

"Okay. You get a lot of crazies in here. You ever get anyone who was possessed?"

"Possessed—like by the devil?"

"Sure. The devil, demons, spirits—any of them?"

"We've had a lot of people who thought they were possessed, or said they were. Schizophrenia often shows up as voices, visions, instructions."

"What if I said that I have been possessed for years, but that I'm not anymore? What if I said I exorcised the thing that was in me?"

"What is that like, no longer being possessed?"

"It's not what you would expect. It's like being free. But it's also like something is missing. It's like being alone for the first time in ages, solely responsible and utterly unprotected."

Wetzelian cocked his head at an angle, to gauge if Seth was bullshitting him. He rubbed his beard and took a deep breath. For the first time, he gave a sign of believing that his patient was at least trying to tell some sort of truth.

"So how do you think that you came to be possessed?"

Seth took a deep breath. After decades of saying nothing, he was about to tell his story.

"I don't know. Actually, I think I might. Let me try to describe it to you. I was a kid in a small town in New England, in high school…"

Seth went on to tell the story of the aborted ride home in Rhode Island, the brawl, the knife, the police station, the interrogation, and the voice that saved him. Their session ran late that day. Wetzelian gave him another newspaper and said he'd see him on Monday.

In the hall, Seth felt relieved, less certain of the forces closing in on him. The paper said it had reached fifty degrees in DC. Seth imagined the bag with Sarah Loire's body in it slowly inflating. The paper said nothing more about Bergman, but a lot about Mankins, who seemed to be running against the federal government rather than the aged, half-slick party hack who currently held the office in Sacramento. One editorial praised Mankins' "sexy new take on anti-federalism." It made Seth feel sick. It made him root for a heat wave and an honest homicide detective in DC.

He read the paper over and over again that weekend. The hospital, never pleasant, was particularly grim on weekends. The bland food was worse and the staff less patient. Without afternoon therapy, the place showed its true colors as a prison. Seth started saving one of the pills from his daily dose so he could sleep at night. And Rory began ranting on about how people he didn't like were all versions of a freckled guy he met when he was a kid.

Sunday, Seth was able to take a proper shower. Under supervision, he could even shave. When he'd excavated his face from thick stubble, he gave the mirror the old predator's grin. Clean after a week in his own stale sweat, with the steam cutting through the mucous in his nose, Seth could smell the place properly. Acrid disinfectant waged a high-stakes war against the urine-and-feet reek of the patients.

Back in his room, Rory said that he knew who Seth really was. And it wasn't a good thing, from how he hissed it. He had skipped the shower, and his sour reek was especially pronounced. Rory didn't sleep, but he didn't talk that night either. His lips moved and a whispered word occasionally rose above the silence. Seth skipped his sleeping pill that night, stashing it between the rubberized sheet and the mattress. But he slipped off to sleep nonetheless.

He woke with hands on his neck, and Rory's maddened, sore-spotted face above him. It wasn't exactly frightening. Rory was already crying as he throttled Seth with his light hands. It didn't take much for Seth to throw his much smaller roommate to the hard linoleum tile floor. He leapt on Rory's back and bent the man's skinny arm behind his back. Rory howled and kicked. With a quick, merciless motion, Seth bent Rory's wrist up toward the back of his neck, twisting it until something gave way. Rory went limp and started to sob into the waterproof tiles.

Seth took two steps outside his door and called for a guard. The cleanup didn't take long. They sedated Rory and took him to get his arm splinted. The head nurse on duty asked Seth what happened, but lost interest before he could finish the story. She believed that it was Rory's fault. Seth's shave spoke for itself.

The next day, the nurses who handed out the pills made sure Seth put his dose in his mouth. They'd half dissolved by the time he could spit them into the styrofoam around a plastic tree. Nonetheless, he was tired and hazy the rest of the day. Wetzelian noticed the difference.

"Sorry to hear about what happened with your roommate."

Seth shrugged.

"How do you feel about what happened to Rory?" the doctor continued.

"I don't know. I guess I should have seen it coming."

"The report says that he started the fight. That's surprising. You're a big guy."

"Well, it could be that he really is crazy."

"And what about you? Did you have to break his arm?"

"It was a fight. Things happen fast in a fight. You don't know if what you're doing will work, or what will actually stop someone. If you hold back, if you don't take someone seriously enough, that's when you can get really hurt. And when a guy's crazy like that—there's no telling what he'll do."

"Regardless, he's in isolation for now. And he says someone, or something, made a deal with him. I only bring it up because we were talking about possession, and about making deals last week."

"I thought you would discourage this, um, line of inquiry," Seth said.

Wetzelian smiled, as if laughing to himself.

"If I'm going to help you, I have to know what you're thinking."

"Even if you don't believe it?"

297

"Belief isn't what this is about. At bottom, Freud's id and superego, the inner child, behavioral reconceptualization, and even possession are all metaphors, languages for understanding what has happened to us and why we do what we do. And if I'm going to understand your experience, it helps if I can use the same language."

"Okay, that's all well and good. But before we go back to all that, I need to know a few things. For one, who knows I'm here?"

"Right now, the State of California knows that Tamerlane Screwtooth is here. But it can't give out that information to anyone, not without a subpoena. Why do you ask?"

"Here's the thing, Doctor. I want to tell you the whole story. And I really don't want you to think I'm crazy. Because if I tell you all of this, I'm going to need you to help me in some way down the line. And I don't mean newspapers and phone calls. There's a chance that you'll be at some risk. And I understand if you don't want that. So we can shoot the shit, pass the hour, and then go our separate ways. We don't have to get into it."

"I think you know my answer," Wetzelian said, with a half smile.

"Right. But we need to start at the beginning, so you don't think I'm crazy. Who knows? Maybe I am crazy. And if that's the case, maybe you can point out where I ran off the rails."

"Fair enough. So we left off after the police in Rhode Island dropped the charges against you."

Seth told the story, about knowing things he shouldn't know, doing things he shouldn't do. And he told the doctor about the normal period in his life when his wife was pregnant and after, when Elizabeth was born premature and sick, when the thing in him was so quiet as to almost have never existed at all. Then they ran out of time.

---

With no one left to talk with in the rec room, Seth spent the afternoon focused on the weekend's papers, which Wetzelian had given him. He spent a long time on the front page. **Bio-Terror Scare Closes Federal Agencies** the headline read. The photo showed men in bulky yellow hazmat suits coming out of the Pentagon. The story also headed up the B section of the paper. The Pentagon, IRS, FBI, Department of the Interior and the SEC all got their letters, along with a "white powdery substance that tests later revealed to be harmless." The article had the authorities pursuing multiple leads, but didn't mention Hurley or Mankins. From there, the story petered out into speculation about domestic militia groups avenging Jefferson on the one hand and international terrorists with their usual gripes on the other.

If his letters garnered that much attention, Seth hoped the authorities at least read their contents and approached Hurley. The return addresses might be too blatant of a setup to throw lasting suspicion on him, but they drew attention and connected him with the shale documents. They also revealed a lot of his hidden assets. Seth wished he could be a fly on the wall for whatever interrogation Hurley was being subjected to.

That night, Seth got a new roommate, an old, bearded black man who didn't speak, and who smelled worse than Rory. The old guy stared, eerily sleepless, at nothing all night and compliantly shuffled to breakfast in the morning. The nurses ignored Seth enough so that he could again palm his pills. He spent the morning rereading the newspapers until he could go see Wetzelian.

"Hey, Tamerlane, we've gotten a few calls for a Seth Tatton. I think you know him," Wetzelian said, smirking, handing him a small pile of pink notes. They were all from Anthony. They all said URGENT.

"Thanks. Can I use the phone?"

"If you give me a good forty minutes you can have the phone for the last twenty. How about that?"

"Okay. So I was telling you about Elizabeth being sick. Around one and a half, one and nine months, she was better, eating well, sleeping through the night most nights. It was around this time that I started doing some work for this old client of the firm in Washington, a guy named Robert Hurley, a former senator…"

Seth told Wetzelian the truth, mostly. He told about the return of the seizures, his adultery, his unreasoning hatred of the happy home his wife and he had built, and his complicity in Hurley's illegal financial schemes. He lied, though, about the first murder for Hurley—Brenda the banker. In the story he told the doctor, he simply intimidated her. Wetzelian listened, his face growing sadder and sadder as Seth went on.

"So what happened with the banker?"

"She called Hurley and apologized. That was it. He never heard from her after that, as far as I know."

"You must have really scared her."

"That's forty minutes."

"Okay. But how do you feel about that woman? How do you feel about threatening her?"

"I feel like crap. I have a fucking law degree. I had enough money to get by, whatever that means. Anyway, there was no need for me to do something like that. No excuse and almost no explanation."

"So how would you explain it?"

"Now it's forty-two minutes. Forty-two minutes that I'm not particularly proud of, and a deal's a deal," Seth said, the hair on his head bristling in anger.

"Okay. But we'll pick it up here tomorrow. Until then, think about her, about how what you did makes you feel."

Seth nodded and glared. Wetzelian placed the phone on Seth's side of the desk and gathered his papers. And in the kind of move that only a psychiatrist could fully appreciate, left the door ajar when he left. Seth took out one of the slips of paper and dialed Anthony's number.

"Oh my God, Seth. What the hell? What were you thinking? What was I thinking? A code? Powder? What the hell are you doing? What was I thinking? Why would you do this to me?" was Anthony's hello.

"Hey, Anthony, I got your message," Seth said breezily. "What are you talking about—the thing on the news?"

"What the hell do you think I'm talking about? Powder in freaking envelopes? How could I be so stupid? How could you do this to me?"

"Oh that. That's not us. I talked to the guys, and they got the documents you sent. The thing on the news—that's another thing altogether. Why, has anyone gotten in touch with you?"

"What do you mean, *gotten in touch*? Like the FBI?" Anthony said.

"Yeah, the FBI, or anyone else, anyone out of the ordinary."

"No. Seth, I really don't have the stomach for this cloak-and-dagger shit. And why would the FBI even contact me if I didn't do anything wrong?"

"Exactly my point," Seth said. Sensing that he didn't have his bullshit in order, he raised and deepened his voice to a more bullying tone. "The point is that you prepared the documents with gloves on, and you mailed them from a public mailbox on a busy city street. Right?"

"Yes. Of course. You said…"

"I know what I said. I'm asking if you *did* what I said, if you took the precautions I *told* you to take."

"Yes."

"All of them."

"Yes, all of them."

"Good. Then you're fine. And you'll be fine as long as you don't start calling all over the place in a panic trying to reach me. If you can keep your cool, that's the end of the cloak-and-dagger shit for you. But don't call me, not on my cell phone and not here. I'll be in New York in a few weeks. Until I call you, don't call me again. I've got to go."

"But what if…"

"If nothing. There is no if. The only way *if* happens is *if* you try to contact me. Okay?"

"Okay."

"Everything will be fine. But I've got to go. I'll see you in a few weeks."

Wetzelian came in as Seth hung up the phone. It was suspicious timing.

"I don't know if I should let you use the phone anymore," Wetzelian said.

"I was getting to that part. It's a long story, and you'd never believe it if I jumped in right in the middle. But hell, I'll tell you the whole thing now, if you want to free up your afternoon."

"That's not fair to my other patients," Wetzelian said.

"They're institutionalized. I think they're used to a certain amount of unfairness."

Wetzelian shrugged and started to say something.

"How's Rory?" Seth asked.

"Not good," Wetzelian said, pausing to look at Seth. "All right, let me go clear my schedule. You've got me until dinner. No more using the phone though."

---

Seth told his story to the doctor for the next few hours, staying mostly honest, but replacing the murders with intimidations. He told the story without pause up through Eggleston, whose name he changed and who he told as a mild beating.

"So you did this to protect Mankins? Why would Hurley go to such lengths to silence someone who knew so little about Mankins?" Wetzelian asked, sounding disappointed that the story stopped making sense at the moment a public figure became involved.

"Well, they need him to be governor of California. That's a lynchpin of the plan. A girl dies or vanishes, and even if there's no evidence and no body, just saying that a senator's mistress came to a mysterious end is enough. Hurley was already pretty far down the road with Mankins, so that a cover-up made more sense than finding and cultivating someone else to run for governor."

"So, I still don't see why they needed Mankins. What was their plan?" the doctor said, with a stiffness in his voice, as if preparing to humor Seth.

"Do you remember in the Cold War, how we would destabilize a tin-pot government we didn't approve of? I'm sure we still do it. We would fund an opposition party, pay the bills for a revolutionary newspaper, and arm an unhappy minority or a student group. And even if the guys we paid didn't win, it would be a drain on the intelligence and military resources of the country we were messing with. And all it would cost us was money. Now imagine another country doing the same thing to us."

From there, Seth told the story of Hurley's vast graft from China, going back to when he was still a senator. He told how Hurley washed the money, kept some, spread some around Washington to raise his profile and gave the rest to militia groups like Jefferson's, who would beat their chests over a fire at a rural post office like it was the Battles of Lexington and Concord combined. And that was the state of affairs until a lobbyist, over dinner, began inquiring about the Strategic Oil Reserve, out west. Hurley threatened the lobbyist until he let slip about the new oil shale extraction method that could turn desolate stretches of the American West into the richest oil fields on the planet. That's when Hurley went from being another greedy party hack to hearing the trumpet blasts of History. Seth told the whole tale of the planned secession, of Hurley, Mankins and of his own role in the conspiracy. As he spoke, Seth hoped his story was steeped in enough money, oil, and tawdry ambition that it wouldn't sound utterly unhinged. At the end of it, Wetzelian stroked his beard and looked off. Night had fallen and it was raining outside.

"I think we missed dinner time. I'll make sure they get you something to eat," was all the doctor said.

"Okay."

"I have to think all of this over. Here's the newspaper. I'll see you tomorrow."

Wetzelian took Seth to the nurses' station, where an orderly took him the rest of the way to his room. His roommate was staring and stinking, lying on his back with one hand on his neck and the other on his crotch. A nurse came by with a ham and cheese sandwich wrapped in wax paper for Seth. Enough orange streetlight shone through the wired windows that Seth could read the headlines of the newspaper. The powder-envelope story had shrunk to a paragraph in the *National* section. The temperature in DC reached fifty-five degrees, unseasonably warm.

The next day, Rory was back in the rec room, in a cast, drugged silent. Seth tried to start a conversation. Rory mumbled sorry and walked away. Seth watched him pace by the windows. He thought of what Wetzelian had said about Rory making a deal with something. It made Seth deeply uneasy.

The next day, back in Wetzelian's office, Seth asked to use the phone right away. Wetzelian cocked his head, about to say no. But he could see Seth was upset. He told Seth he had ten minutes. Seth picked up the phone and dialed the one working phone number that he still knew by heart, his own.

"Hello," the voice said, friendly and deep.

"Who is this?" Seth asked.

"Seth Tatton, who's this?" the voice said. In the background, Seth heard a PA system holler a dull, impersonal phrase.

"Hey there, William."

"Seth. I was about to head back east to meet your friend Anthony, in Westchester. He sounded pretty worried when he called."

"Where are you?"

"Judging from the area code, not too far from you," William said.

"I know what you're thinking, William. But I'm going to do you a favor anyway. I'm in protective custody right now.

The FBI. So Hurley's done. Mankins is done. They'll shoot you on sight over here. But if you go to the San Francisco FBI headquarters and give yourself up to an agent there, these guys are still cutting deals."

There was silence on the other end of the line, but no click, so that Seth couldn't tell when William had hung up. But he did hang up. Seth's mind ran in molasses. He looked at his legs, clad in blue hospital sweatpants. No money, no weapon, no way out. The sweatpants didn't even have pockets. Wetzelian came back into the room.

"Are you all right?" the doctor asked.

"I don't think so."

"What is it?"

"Do you think I'm crazy?"

"I don't think that anyone is either completely…"

"Listen, I need you to be straight with me. Do you believe what I told you yesterday?" Seth asked, staring hard into the doctor's eyes.

"I believe that you believe it."

"Jesus. Come on. That's not what I asked. Do you believe what I said?"

"I think that, in anyone's account of what…"

"No. This isn't an academic situation. I have good reason to think that someone is coming here to kill me. You either believe that or not. And I fucked up. I have no more time to earn your trust. If I'm right and you're wrong, then I'm dead," Seth said, careful to keep the panic from his voice and to keep his hands in his lap.

"So, if we keep talking about the demon, about the conspiracy, about envelopes with baking soda in them, then someone will come here and kill you?" the doctor asked.

"No. They are on their way here, in a car, no matter what we say to each other."

"And if I do believe you, and I believe what you're saying, how can I possibly help you?"

"Jesus Christ, I know the guy who's coming. His name is William. He's careful. And even if he believed what I told him, it won't take him long to find out that it's bullshit. It probably won't take him more than two days to figure out a clean way in and out of here."

"This is a pretty secure hospital. And with 150 patients, I doubt he could find you even if he got in."

"Can I get a transfer?"

"By the time I could get it approved, your fourteen days would be up."

Seth looked at his sweatpants and hoped the man was right about the security and the bureaucratic complexity of the place.

Wetzelian insisted, so Seth continued his story, telling the doctor about the seizures. Seth described the meeting with Hurley, when he said he *understood*, and it seemed as if the two of them were acting as telephones for other voices. And he told Wetzelian about how Sarah Loire, confused and despairing, had helped him.

That night, Seth needed two days' worth of pale blue pills to get to sleep.

The next day, Wetzelian wanted to talk about the thing that had resided in him. But Seth's thoughts were elsewhere. He told the doctor that William would probably come to the hospital, probably disguised as a cop, possibly even with a fake subpoena.

He asked if Wetzelian could warn the front desk that an ex-patient with a grudge and an impersonating-an-officer MO had recently gotten out of jail, and that they should triple-check the credentials of any cop who came in looking for a patient.

Wetzelian talked through the details of the plan with him, but Seth couldn't gauge how serious the doctor was about it.

---

The rest of the week was tense, but uneventful. At his last session with Wetzelian, the two men talked mostly about what Seth would do when he was released the next day.

"So, do you think you'll be able to go back to your job?"

"I don't think the people who are after me are the type to complain to my boss. Hell, they're probably paying my hourly rate while they hunt me down."

The fact was that Seth didn't have a plan. He wasn't sure he would make it a block from the hospital.

"I wasn't sure whether or not to tell you this," Wetzelian said, sitting up and folding his hands in front of him on the desk. "But someone did come looking for a Seth Tatton a few nights ago. He had what looked like a real badge and subpoena. But I'd given them your story. So the front desk called in his badge number. They say the guy's info didn't check out, and that he left before the real police could get here."

"Did they get a description of him?"

"They said he was an Asian guy, big. They said he looked like a weight lifter."

"Thanks for that. I'm sure you don't often act so concretely on your patients' fears. You probably saved my life."

The next and last day was all filling out forms. The hospital gave Tamerlane Screwtooth a bill for more than any derelict could ever hope to earn. The restraints alone cost as much as a used car. They gave Seth back his suit, which had been folded but not cleaned. It felt good to be dressed like a person rather than a patient. Wetzelian met him by the exit, which wasn't part of the process.

"You look good."

"Well, the suit's a wrinkled mess. But it's better than sweatpants."

"I forgot to give this to you earlier. The orderly found it on your pillow the other night. He said it looked like you spat it up. Once you started telling me your story, I did some checking. And there's no toy version of this Mercedes, not Matchbox, not Hot Wheels. I thought I'd give it back to you."

The doctor held out the black Mercedes Matchbox car. The car rolled from Seth's fingers to his wrist.

"Thanks."

"Who did you get to pick you up, by the way?"

"No one. I figured I'd catch a bus back downtown."

"I doubt you'll have to. There's a limo driver out there waiting for you."

"A limo driver?"

"He's been standing out there the last few afternoons. And he's out there today, holding a placard with your name on it, like the drivers at the airport do."

Seth froze, considered throwing a fit or speaking in tongues, wondered if that would work. Wetzelian saw the change and gestured toward a vacant office off the last locked-down hallway. It was empty but for old cardboard boxes, a desk shoved against a wall, a mop bucket missing a wheel and a stack of folding chairs. The doctor walked Seth over to the wire-honeycombed window.

"There. That's him."

The man stood completely still. He was young, fit, well kept. He wore his brown hair short, a dark suit and sunglasses. He held a cardboard sign with SETH TATTON written on it.

"Hey, listen," Seth said. "Do I have to leave through the front door?"

"You're serious?"

"Unfortunately."

Wetzelian paused for a second, tilted his head in contemplation and shrugged.

"I'll tell you what, I have to go to lunch. I can give you a ride down the street. We'll go out the back. The staff parking lot is there."

Passing back through the hallways, Seth could sense the eyes of the few still cognizant patients on him. It wasn't normal—a patient in street clothes, walking through the ward unescorted. After a few hallways Seth had never seen, he and Wetzelian emerged in the sunlight. Seth blinked at the brightness. Tie gone, suit and shirt a mess, Seth looked like a man in the middle of a long slide down the class system. But aside from some scars on his wrists, he wasn't much the worse for wear as he walked out to the staff parking lot.

Despite his expectations, no hail of bullets met them.

---

Their good-bye was a short handshake in Wetzelian's Volvo a few miles from the hospital. With no name, no money and only a vague notion of what to do next, Seth walked downtown. After two weeks in a bland and soothing environment, the streets of San Francisco were disconcerting. Occasionally, a vagrant seemed to bark his name. Shoving his hands in his pants pockets, he found a twenty-dollar bill. He walked until he came to a BART station, rode a robot train to a commuter train, which took him to a tram, which took him around the airport.

Seth waded into the profound and sluggish indifference of the airport lost-and-found. It took an hour, and a great deal of supervised sorting and deliberately vague excuses before the gaunt old woman with a gold badge would let him have his wallet and phone. The wallet had no cash in it, but the cards were there. And his phone was there, which surprised him. William must have cloned it.

He took the rental car shuttle and dealt with the rental car company's own lost-and-found, retrieving his bag. After a ride back on the shuttle to the airport, he booked a flight to DC, passed through security, all too conscious of how his wrinkled suit set him apart from the casual fastidiousness of the other business travelers. He changed into equally wrinkled but cleaner clothes in the bathroom. Seth found an ATM and hit it up for all the cash it would allow him to remove in a day.

If it was Hurley looking for him, and not the cops, he figured he had a safe few hours in the airport. The credit card purchase made a blip, and the ATM had to make the blip that much harder to ignore. Seth decided to go all out and turn on his cell phone. And at an empty gate between a bathroom and a Cinnabon, in a cloud of frosting stench, he dialed his own cell phone number.

"Hello?"

"William."

"Seth, I didn't expect another call from you."

"Well, I felt bad that we couldn't have the visit that you tried to arrange. Stopping in on an old pal in the hospital—and they say common courtesy is dead. That must have been a disappointment. No one looks twice at a suicide in a mental hospital. It would have been a layup."

"Nice bit about the protective custody, by the way."

"I was surprised you weren't there to pick me up when I got out."

"Don't feel so disappointed. I'll get around to you," William said.

"I doubt it. I know a few things that you don't. The first is that Hurley's over and done with. He's going down and he's going down hard."

"I talked to him and he says it's just a tax hassle. They don't have anything on anybody."

"William, where are you now?"

"Depends. Where are you?"

"I'd like to talk to you. When can you get to San Francisco?"

"Tomorrow at the earliest."

"That's bullshit and we both know it."

"I can be there in a few hours," William said. Seth could hear the gears turning.

"I'm at the airport. You're here in two hours. After that, I'm gone and you never get another sniff of me—not until you see me at your trial or from a pool of blood. Am I clear?"

"Okay, where in the airport?"

Seth gave William the information.

———————

An hour and twenty-five minutes later, William showed up, wearing a polo shirt and a brown blazer, looking right for the airport. Seth waited at the bar, on the airplane side of the metal-detectors and security pat downs.

"You're a real pain in the ass, you know that?" William said, pulling up a chair across from Seth at the bar's wobbly metal café table.

"Well, I thought of cutting my own throat, to save you the trouble. But I went with something else instead."

"I had to buy a fucking plane ticket to get past security."

"Whatever. Expense it."

"Guess I will. So where are you going?"

"Maybe DC. Maybe Jakarta. I'm not sure yet," Seth said.

"So no protective custody, no witness protection?"

Seth pulled back his jacket and shirt cuffs from one wrist so William could see the scars, the swelling and bruises that lingered.

"I've had a few things happen that weren't part of the plan. But there are no authorities involved, no real ones yet. I asked you here because we've all worked well together, this latest indiscretion notwithstanding. And I want to do you a favor."

"A favor? This I'd like to hear."

"This thing that we're involved in, it's about to come crashing down. And when it does, Hurley and Mankins, if I know them, will throw everyone they can to the wolves, especially you and me. We need to do something about them before something is done about us."

"Crashing down, huh? Mankins is up *fifteen* points in the polls, with four weeks until the election. Hurley's as good as ever. He paid the IRS, and they're done hassling him."

"Yeah? Lot of tax hassles with that bunch lately. You notice that? And I bet they're having trouble keeping their generals and colonels in line. That must be keeping you busy. Is that why you couldn't pick up your old pal from the hospital? And when Hurley told you it was only a tax hassle, did he also ask you for a passport? Did he ask you for more than one?"

"You're fishing."

"Maybe. But what you need to know is that Hurley's going to fold, or he's going to run, or he's going to do something rash. If he folds, he'll give us up. That's obvious. We're the ones with blood on our hands. If he runs, we'll be left holding the bag for the Mankins girls and more. Are you still listening?"

Up to that point, William had vacillated between looking intently into Seth's eyes to see if he could believe him, and looking intently away, as if Seth's words bored him.

"Yeah. Say what you have to say," William said, leaning back in his chair.

"So say Hurley doesn't fold. That probably means he does something rash, which means he'll get you to do something rash. And that leaves you out there, taking risks you know better than to take."

"So why call me at all? Why the bluff? Why not go to the authorities, sell your weak bullshit to them and get on the winning team, Mr. protective custody?"

"You and I have been on the wrong side of the law too long to develop a sudden faith in it this late in life. I'll go over when I have to, if I have to. For now, I like my freedom. I can do more where I am. I know a few things you don't."

Seth finished the last of his beer as he spoke. William noticed that Seth's fingernails were untrimmed and dirty.

"Like what?"

"I know that if Hurley has you hunting me and herding his generals at the same time that he doesn't have a very deep bench of hitters. So if I take care of you, I'm either home free or at least up against a lesser opponent. I know that the cops are about to find Sarah Loire's body, along with a healthy dose of incriminating evidence. And that's if they haven't found it already. So you have to make a decision."

"What's that?"

"Are you with me or against me?"

"Really? Just like that?"

"Think of all the things you've done, in the last twenty-four hours alone, just like that. And if you bring this back to Hurley, you may find yourself with a bull's-eye on your back."

"So I side with you now, or you come after me?"

"I always liked you better as a friend."

William looked Seth in the eyes, gave a long look over his shoulder and exhaled, as though relieved.

"Okay, so what do we do?"

"What's next is you tell Hurley that you saw me here, in the airport. Tell him I was in a mental hospital. Tell him I had a breakdown, and that it was a horse-versus-rider problem. He'll understand what that means. Tell him I'm sorry, but I need some time off. And give him this."

Seth pulled the shale report out of his bag and handed it to William.

"Is that what I think it is? The shale report? I've been tearing all over California looking for it. You'll never guess who I met."

"Kurt Lignam."

"I guess you will guess who I met. That was not a pleasant meeting. So, if I give Hurley your apologies and your peace offering, then what?"

"We take the next step when I know you're serious, when I know I can trust you. That's going to require a gesture. I need you to go out to Oak Pines in Frederick. Find the house, on Bluejay Lane where first Mankins girl, Sandra, is buried, and burn that house down. Do it this week and we'll meet right after."

Seth said good-bye to William and boarded a flight to DC. Before it taxied, he got off the plane, apologetically feigning a panic attack. William was gone when he returned to the terminal. Seth did some shopping in the airport, buying newspapers, toiletries, a pay-as-you-go cell phone, and other sundries. He ditched his Blackberry and took a cab back into San Francisco. In the Tenderloin, he found a hotel that took cash and paid the uninquisitive Greek a week up front. The ashtray by the window had been dusted, but not washed. The room smelled like an old person.

He spent a few days walking, sweating up and down the hills. Every other day, he checked the internet at a pay computer in a sandwich shop in the financial district. He spent his nights in his room watching the news on the old, bubble-screen TV and drinking. The TV said Mankins was a lock for governor. It said the governor of Idaho was refusing to allow the National Guard to aid the FBI in an operation against the militia groups up there. The internet said that a warm spring was elating the East Coast.

On Sunday night, it all broke. The hotel room's little TV with a black line across the top of the picture said that the governor of California had fired his attorney general. On Monday, the new attorney general granted the DC police a writ of extradition against Chet Mankins. Seth went to the sandwich shop downtown and started to read the details as they came out. The cops had found Sarah Loire's body. And there was more. Looking through the local Maryland newspapers online, Seth smiled to see that a fire had destroyed half a block in a Frederick subdivision called Oak Pines. Seth called William, who sounded relieved to hear him.

"Nice job in Frederick. I take it you heard about Mankins?"

"Yeah. Hurley says the cops will screw up the case—chain of evidence, some shit like that."

"He might still be able to pull that off. But Mankins won't be governor. Not with two dead ex-girlfriends in the news and their mothers crying on television."

"What is this about, Seth?"

"I'm trying to get things right. You still want to meet?"

"Yeah."

"This time next week. Come with two sets of ID for me, and two credit cards for each ID. We'll meet in LA or Las Vegas. I'll let you know the day before."

Though frightened and alone, Seth felt better than he had in a very long time. But he also sensed that if his plans came to fruition, with the deaths of Hurley and Mankins, he would be truly homeless. He'd have to do the thing he'd avoided for so long and try to piece together an ordinary life.

Boarding the commuter train to San Jose, Seth wondered uneasily if he had truly rid himself of the poison that had chased him from his family and made him exult in killing, hiding and lying. In the San Jose bus station, Seth pondered the ways he could get close to Mankins.

———————

After being expelled in the mental hospital, the thing that had lived in Seth was reduced to a shade of a shade.

Toes and fingers were a problem. It kept losing them. Only its painful jaw and broken teeth persisted, like a staple holding together gossamer rags.

If the broken-toothed spirit raised his voice to a scream, it took so much out of him that he'd lose half of his body. Only the most sensitive and damaged people could hear him. The broken-toothed spirit nearly disappeared altogether trying to talk Rory into his doomed attack on Seth. Simply existing in its deeply diminished state took so much effort that it was painful. It was difficult to move, to remember where its legs went, how its arms connected to its hands.

It managed to have a vagrant mutter the word *assassin* at Seth in the Tenderloin. But that was all it could do to the man it had saved from jail and worse so many times. The only satisfaction it knew was in watching Seth, once so upwardly mobile and hopeful, now lost in revenge, like it was. Seth had become a shade of sorts, seeking proof of his own now-lost love of Sarah Loire, and looking for evidence of his own existence and decency as a human being through the destruction of others. That made the broken-toothed spirit grin. Little else did.

The former god still had something to hold it together: It had an appointment. It travelled east. The going was slow, and it couldn't grasp onto a living person to travel with. More naked than the living could ever be, the winds ripped at it, time itself seemed to erode and chafe its dim flicker. After living centuries in spite of everything, spite was its last remaining strength. And even that was beginning to fade.

It would find a way back to Washington, DC, and to Petronius. It would reveal Seth's plans, his friends, and what he intended to do. Petronius and Hurley would take care of the rest.

It followed the highway from San Francisco over the Sierras. It was trying to strike up a rapport with a low-rolling loser on Virginia Street in Reno. The town was cold and sad, with half of the casinos on the main strip boarded up. The flashing lights of the surviving gambling halls and souvenir shops seemed to be sucked up all too quickly and completely by the surrounding shadows.

The ex-deity waited in the vestibule of one souvenir shop, running a tongue over its broken teeth to remind itself of its own existence. The panhandler it had been trying to seduce with visions of wealth and power back east had been given a dollar from a saucer-eyed tourist and had wandered off distractedly to buy a fresh can of malt liquor.

That's when the broken-toothed spirit heard someone say his name, his real name. The sound of it made him jump. But it was The Sigh, his old mentor, there in the electric squalor of Virginia Street, seeming fainter and yet somehow luminescent. Unlike Petronius and the other spirits left in the world, though, The Sigh's features weren't distorted into a rictus or a snarl. He seemed calm, still entirely like himself.

"You? How did you find me?" the broken-toothed spirit asked.

"I could always find you," The Sigh said, standing very still before it.

"But how could you let this happen to me?"

"You are thousands of years old. You said you knew what you were doing. I couldn't have stopped you if I wanted to."

"But how could you let me *do* all that I've done? Why didn't you say anything?"

316

"I would have. But you were too healthy to hear me."

The Sigh began to speak in the language they used when they were both living men. It was a rough tongue, not spoken in millennia and never written down. But it was the only language the broken-toothed spirit could understand without irony or rancor.

In that mix of sounds and gestures, The Sigh explained to the broken-toothed spirit how he could untangle the remaining threads, and finally die.

———————

At the San Jose bus station, Seth paid a vagrant to buy him a bus ticket to Las Vegas. Even with William burning down the house in Maryland, there were too many places trouble could still come from. Seth wandered around the shabby neighborhood abutting the bus station and bought a bag of chips, a pocket knife and a crucifix. Between the ATM withdrawal at the airport and the cash in his carry-on bag, Seth was set for money for the moment.

The bus ride was what Seth remembered long bus rides to be—squalid tedium broken by moments of awe, as the landscape revealed itself. On the first leg of the trip, Seth sat next a young Spanish kid named Jorge who was on his way to an internship at the capitol in Sacramento. He and Seth talked politics for a while.

"I think what happened was that the attorney general read the polls and decided he had a better chance to keep his job if he stalled on Mankins' extradition. But, from what I heard, the governor caught wind of it, and he didn't even call the AG. He just fired him. A friend of mine used to work in the AG's office and said that the governor left it to the new AG to tell the old AG that she and her entire staff were all fired," the kid said. "The new AG was some guy who was working in consumer affairs or something before."

"So the governor had to reach pretty far down the ladder to get the extradition executed?" Seth said, chip crumbs in his stubble.

"Yeah. Everyone was getting ready for Chet Mankins to be the next governor. My friend said that nothing was getting done in his office—all this work piled up while everyone was looking for a way to keep their jobs or move up when Mankins came in. Until all this happened, I was going to vote for Mankins."

"No kidding. You won't now?"

"The whole thing seems fishy, if you ask me. But why risk it? They could be right."

"What seems fishy about it?"

"I mean, not one, but two murder indictments, only a few weeks before the election? The guy has enemies and the timing of it seems weird," Jorge said.

"I guess you could say it was suspicious if it was the FBI that brought the indictments. I mean, Mankins has gone out of his way to piss off the feds. But I don't think the DC police would go out on a limb to stand up for the honor of some insulted bureaucrats. And I heard that the town in Maryland is also filing murder charges. And I can't even guess what their angle would be."

"You know a lot about this. Do you work in Sacramento?"

"I almost did. But I'm between things right now," Seth said and looked down at the crumpled foil bag of chips in his lap. Jorge said nothing. If you were almost forty on a Greyhound, the unspoken subtext was something hadn't worked out for you.

"I hear you," Jorge finally said, to break the silence.

"But it sounds like exciting times for you."

"Yeah. We'll see. I'm in the lieutenant governor's office. He's close with Chet Mankins. I even saw Mankins in the office a few times. Now they're saying that the governor might be looking for a new lieutenant governor, too. So I don't know how long I'll even be there."

"Still, it's good for you to see how things work, to learn it while you're young, before it's your own career on the line."

At Sacramento, Jorge got off and Seth ran to a gas station mini-mart and bought a new disposable phone to replace the one he'd left in San Francisco. After Sacramento, the bus picked up a half dozen men from Folsom prison, with their possessions in numbered cardboard boxes. The two black ones sat together up by the driver. The white and Spanish ones spread out around the bus. As the bus rose from the farmland into the foothills of the Sierras, it began to snow, first gently, enchantingly at first, but then threateningly. In Colfax, they all learned that the 80 was closed. Riders could stay the night in Colfax or take the bus back to Sacramento.

Seth was one of the few who went back, along with one of the white convicts and pair of old ladies travelling together. In Sacramento, Seth changed his ticket and hopped on a crowded, all-night bus to Los Angeles. He slept tangled in the power cord of an obese teenage girl's handheld video game, and woke at his destination. He ate a bus-station burrito among the ragged dawn-hour scavengers and weary travelers, keeping a hand on his pocket knife. As the sun rose, the bus departed for Las Vegas, full of poor Mormons and poor gamblers.

Somewhere around San Bernardino, Seth gave up trying to sleep. He smelled of stale sweat and corn chips. It was one hundred three degrees when the bus passed the world's tallest thermometer. In Las Vegas, Seth followed a ragged pair of white drunks from the bus station to an old motel that didn't ask for anything but money. He showered and turned on the TV news and fell asleep to news that a pair of generals and three colonels from all four branches of the military faced court-martials for taking bribes from military contractors. Fieldspurhoff led the story. They'd found the disgraced test-pilot and one-time astronaut dead from a self-inflicted gunshot in the parking lot of a state park.

Strangely, Seth caught a tear welling in his eye as he fell into a shallow sleep. The motel TV was bolted to the dresser and its air conditioner loud. Among the gamblers and prostitutes, there were a few families living there, some fallen and some working. Around three, Seth was woken by the sound of kids playing in the pool. At dusk, he took a cab to Fremont Street and got lost among the tourists gawking in the tunnel of electric lights. He turned on his disposable phone and dialed William.

"Hey, what are you doing in Sacramento?" William asked.

"This and that," Seth said, glad to have the phone's area code as some cover. "So it'll be Las Vegas, tomorrow night. Do you have everything?"

"I'll have it. But hey, I'm in Sacramento now. Why don't we meet here?"

"No. It has to be Las Vegas. I'll call you at this time tomorrow."

Seth pulled the battery out of the cheap phone. He walked until the night got cold and he ran out of sidewalk by a construction site whose signs promised the biggest casino ever—Galactos—a casino based on the entire universe. He hailed a cab and went back to the motel.

On the TV, the governors of Idaho, Montana and Wyoming were standing with the US Attorney General, as well as the regional heads of the FBI and ATF in front of a massive pile of assault rifles. The talking heads speculated that the joint press conference marked a détente between the governors and federal law enforcement. But Seth knew why the governors had made friends with the FBI, ATF and DEA. Their names were on the *Constitution* and *Declaration* that had come to the attention of every major law enforcement agency in Washington, just a few weeks too soon.

Seth turned up the air conditioner so that its growl and clatter challenged the TV, climbed under the blankets in a storm of static sparks and went to sleep, properly.

---

Seth set the meeting with William in a casino modeled on the splendor of old Babylon and named for a New Jersey real-estate mogul. He scouted the place, playing slots. Finally, he settled on a second-floor lounge with a hanging gardens theme. He called William and set the time, played fifty-cent hands of bar-top video poker and nursed a Coke and a plate of Nebuchadnezzar nachos for a few hours until William arrived.

He had looked better. A shave and a shower at the motel only did so much. He was still pale from the hospital and he needed a haircut. His suit needed pressing. Scanning the lounge, William missed him at first. Seth waved and they went to one of the one of the many empty tables. William sat down and ordered them a pair of beers. Before either of them said anything, William poked Seth's knee with a stiff envelope under the table. It was small—two IDs and four credit cards. Seth slid it into his pocket.

"Well, partner, I guess we're really in the shit now," William said.

"It looks that way. I'm a little surprised you decided to see things my way."

"Well, I wasn't sure how to play it at first. But you're right. Our boy Hurley is righteously fucked."

"He's still free, isn't he?" Seth asked.

"Yeah, and he seems calm enough, on the surface. But about a week after you disappeared, he calls me and says he wants you reeled in, one way or the other—doesn't matter which, he says. But as soon as I get started on that, he has me get him a half dozen passports—all different names, different countries. So fine, I get started on that. Then he wants me back working on you. And while I'm working on a way into your hospital, he calls me to go meet with this colonel out of Andrews Air Force Base."

"He's trying to keep the whole scheme from unraveling."

"And it gets worse. Before I can even get the guy to agree to a meeting, he calls and tells me to get back to Washington. He wants me to talk to a buddy of mine in the DC police to have him grab some items from the evidence control unit there. It turns out the stuff is related to the first Mankins girl, so I back off, and tell Hurley he doesn't want me going back on that. Police make connections, and in my case they'd be dead right. That's what I was trying to explain to him when you called from the airport."

"Well, I'll give you that much. You know a good deal when you see one," Seth said.

"I know enough to get out of the rain, anyway. But Hurley was still paying—is still paying. Thanks for the report by the way. He's not on my ass to find you like he was before he got it."

"Did he put someone else on it?" Seth asked.

"On you? I don't think so. I think that you giving back the shale document, and being in the funny farm, was enough for him to de-prioritize you. But he wanted the name of the hospital. I think he's wants to feed your records from the hospital to the police in DC, try to get them to them connect those dots."

"We'll have to see about that. I was there under a false name. And I have a friend in there."

"Hurley's still pissed, but he seems distracted."

"What about the guy he sent to pick me up from the hospital?"

"That was my idea. While Hurley had me in DC trying to bribe a police lieutenant, he also wanted a progress report on you. So I came up with the idea of hiring a car service to wait outside the hospital for you. I figured there was some chance you'd go along with the guy."

"And then?"

"It wasn't the strongest plan. The guy would take you a hotel, and call me. That was before I looked at the facts, and bought a gallon of gas in a can at the Sunoco in Frederick."

"Big fire, by the way."

"Yeah. I wanted to make sure you heard about it. And I forgot which house it was. They all look the same."

"That's when you made up your mind?"

"Not totally. I was keeping my options open. I figured I could still shine you on a bit, light a fire to get you out in the open, maybe get one more big pay day from Hurley," William said, raising his drink for a toast. Squinting, Seth raised his.

"So?"

"So Mankins gets shipped back to DC in cuffs, and they find the girl under the house in Frederick. I try calling Hurley, but he's cloistered with his lawyers twelve hours a day. And when he calls me back, he says he wants to meet me in the trees out by the Tidal Basin, near the Mall. So I go there, and he offers me more money than I planned on making in this lifetime. And all I have to have to do is assassinate the governor, in Sacramento."

"The governor, huh?"

"I mean, in this business especially, you have to know your limits. And that kind of thing is way beyond me. But I also keep getting the sense that Hurley's on his way out. So I say I need the money up front, to get a team together. He finally gives me half, and offers me a bonus if I can get it done by the end of the week."

"So why not skip the country, sit the rest of this out? It sounds like retirement money to me," Seth said.

"That's the thing. A beach on a remote island sounds pretty good to me. But I know I'm not seeing something here. Some angle. I feel like Hurley's ready for me to take the money and run. You were always the clever one."

"Let's look at it for a second: Mankins has a long trial ahead of him. But he's still got money and can still call in favors. By the time the trial starts, who knows what shape the evidence is in, or if they'll be able to dig up any real witnesses. So he's down, but not out. And he's seen us. But it's Hurley. He's the one to watch for. He's pinned down for the moment. But no one's filed any charges against him, and he has the resources to come after us."

"So we go after Hurley?"

"I think we have to go after both of them."

"Why?"

"Because of what Mankins did to those girls. Because he knows us and may be able to pin this on us, especially if we vanish to a beach or to the morgue. And also for the same reason that I don't take all this to the police. There's too much money on his side. At the same time, both Hurley and Mankins have good reasons to want us gone. Killing both of them is the only way to be safe."

"Okay. I also don't like the idea of Mankins spilling his guts and implicating us when his case falls apart," William said. "Oh, before I forget. This is, well, it's where your calls have been going."

William dug into his pocket and pulled out a cell phone. He handed it over and they shook hands. Seth pulled the battery out and put it in his pocket.

"You should check it. You have a bunch of messages from some cop in DC."

––––––––––––

After William left, Seth listened to the clone of his old Blackberry that William had given him. Detective Rudy Carlson even sounded fat on the phone, with the plosive *b*'s and *p*'s popping softly throughout his five messages. Each was calm, each reminding Seth of his previous messages, and each patiently repeating his phone numbers. Seth closed the phone and removed its battery again, then moved his real driver's license and credit cards to the pocket in the spine of his billfold.

He used his new credit cards to buy some fresh clothes in the hotel's *Store of Babylon* and caught a cab back to his crummy hotel off the strip, where he fell into a deep sleep. In his dreams, he was in a suburban kitchen in a house by the ocean. Eggleston, Bergman, the two victims before them and the poor kid he knifed in high school were all giving lumpy manila envelopes to each other. His daughter came up from the basement and told him he was running out of time. So he climbed the branches of a huge tree and scratched a hole in the blue sky, and saw the kitchen of his old house in Long Island on the other side of it. Seth woke breathless and relieved to be in a crummy Las Vegas motel room with an air conditioner that sounded like it ran on scrap metal.

He sat up and shuffled the cards in his wallet to put one of William's fake IDs at the front. As always, the resemblance on the IDs was close enough to get him through most situations. He caught a cab to the airport, where he bought a ticket to DC and boarded his flight under the name on the fake California ID. Jammed into a middle seat on a packed flight, Seth tried some of the breathing techniques Sarah had shown him—long inhale, hold the breath, long exhale. Either the techniques or thinking about Sarah kept him calm through the flight.

In the airport, Seth felt his confidence returning. He was wearing one of his favorite suits, wheeling his bag behind him. His purpose was clear and he felt like he was a step ahead of the forces aligned against him. That's when he saw the limo driver. It wasn't the same one from outside the mental hospital. He was tall, as tall as Seth, with a chiseled jaw and a professional aloofness. Even in the fluorescent light of the baggage claim, he kept his sunglasses on. He held a cardboard sign reading *TATTON.*

Seth kept walking, too confused and afraid to do anything else. Was Hurley ready for him? Had William betrayed him? Was there another group of people tracking him? Walking closer to the limo driver, Seth stared into the man's sunglasses. And the man raised his chin, as if preparing to nod in recognition. Seth looked down at the gray high-traffic carpet and walked past, flexing his arms and preparing to strike out if anyone grabbed him from behind.

But no one did. Outside, he waited for the rental car shuttle bus, afraid to look back at the terminal. In the bus, he slumped in his seat, full of a silent panic. Though he kept his own car in the long-term parking lot of the airport, Seth rented a car with the California ID. He used the same one at the Hyatt by the Capitol, where the front-desk clerk said he was lucky to get a room. Cherry blossom season, she said.

The room was small, done up in brown and tan, soothing adult colors. It occurred to Seth that it might be his last hotel room.

———————

With a disposable phone he bought in Las Vegas, Seth dialed the number William had given him for Chet Mankins.

"Hello?" the senator answered.

"Hello, Senator. How's DC treating you?"

"Who is this?"

"This is the guy you can't get rid of, and the guy who can get rid of you," Seth said.

"How did you get this number?"

"I'm not without means. I can reach almost anyone."

"You're... Steve, Seth, Steve. You put that girl up in an apartment for the winter," Mankins said.

"That's right. I handled that situation, and the one before her. Her I picked up from you directly. You remember that. You were still bloody when I got there."

"So what? You're going to the cops? Now? It's a little late."

"Not too late. But that's up to you. I'm still a lawyer, and I clean up good for court."

"What do you want?"

"I want out. I want to be done with all of this."

"Fine, you're out."

"We both know it's not so simple. I'll be in DC tomorrow. I want you to keep your schedule open and get some liquid assets together, quick. You're going to want the star witness for the prosecution as far out of the country as possible."

Mankins responded with a long, audible exhale.

Seth told him to be in Georgetown tomorrow afternoon, alone, with the money. He gave out a figure and Mankins didn't reply or negotiate. He closed the call with the boilerplate bluster about what would happen should Mankins fail to have the money, should he tell anyone or bring anyone. He hung up and called William, who was in his room an hour later with his own rolling suitcase, checking over both shoulders as Seth opened the door.

"Good flight?" William asked.

"It *was* good. There was even a limo waiting for me when I landed."

"I saw that too. You didn't talk to the guy, did you?"

"No. But he definitely saw me."

"Not to worry. The limo driver was a limo driver. Hurley's got them all over the place, New York, DC, Las Vegas, San Francisco, all the major airports, all the terminals."

"That's got to be expensive."

"Money's never an object for that guy. It makes me nervous about running off with so much of it."

"Well, let's get to work on putting your mind to rest. How'd you do?"

William smiled and opened the suitcase, proud to reveal a series of bulging gym socks. Each sock contained a handgun. Seth picked out a snub-nosed revolver. From the little he knew about guns, it seemed to be in good shape, and simple to operate. William pulled out the ammunition for it.

"This should do. You have any idea about how to go after Hurley?" Seth asked.

"Yeah. Lately, he's been wanting to meet in these out-of-the-way places. He's worried, but not about me, I don't think. More about being seen. I figure I'll play on that to lure him someplace quiet, maybe a park down by the Potomac, and hit him there. What do you think?"

"It's as good a plan as any. You call him yet?"

"No. I wanted to get your go-ahead on it first."

"Okay. Call him now."

"Now?"

"We have to move fast. Hurley's going to find out that I'm in town before long. Call him now and tell him you have a bead on the governor, but the plan to hit him is a little out-there, and you want to run it by him first. And tell him to make sure he's not followed."

On the phone with Hurley, William raised his voice, repeating that it was *his ass on the line*, that he wouldn't give broad strokes, *not on the phone*. From William's voice, Seth could tell Hurley had him on the defensive at one point, with William complaining limply *no one knows where he is*.

The only way that assassinating the governor of California would make sense was if Hurley had a deal with the lieutenant governor. It was a desperate last grasp to make his revolution happen.

On the phone, William had recovered, booming that he was *careful not paranoid*, and suggesting to Hurley that *maybe you should be more paranoid yourself*. By the time William hung up, Seth knew William had gotten what he wanted, a time and remote place to meet Hurley.

"We are all systems go," William said, bouncing on the balls of his feet.

"Great."

"How about you? You got any ideas for Mankins?"

"I'll figure it out. I can't risk trying to meet Mankins in a dark alley. And I doubt he'd show if I tried to meet in one anyway. My best bet is to meet him someplace he's comfortable, someplace near where he lives in Georgetown. From there, hopefully I can get him somewhere quiet, like the canal paths, or if I have to, a quiet side street. When are you meeting Hurley?"

"Tomorrow, five."

William left. Seth stowed the gun in his suitcase. On TV, the newscasters were subdued. One stood before the empty steps of a courthouse in Montana. Looking deflated, she reported that the birthday of newly martyred militia leader Jefferson had passed without incident. The TV didn't help Seth's nerves. It spoke too much to what was on his mind—Mankins. It isn't often that the firebrand candidate for governor of one of America's most populous states gets indicted for the murder of two young women and vows to fight it in court. Maybe they didn't have a war, but the networks did have that.

---

The next afternoon, Seth bought a new suit, dark blue, but light fabric, a spring and summer suit. It didn't fit perfectly, but close enough. In San Francisco, the old tried to dress like the young. But in Georgetown, the young tried to dress like the old. He wandered the neighborhood, passing the stairs from the movie *The Exorcist*, and wondered if he'd get the chance to throw Mankins down them. They were long and steep enough to kill the older man, Seth figured. He wandered the streets for a few hours before settling on a defiantly old Irish pub whose warped-wood walls were covered with black-and-white pictures. He circled the block for a half hour until he got a parking spot with easy egress—down the block from the pub, in the direction of traffic, right behind a bus stop where no parking was permitted.

It was a warm spring day. At three thirty, the streets were full of teenagers fresh from school. He called Mankins and told him the name of the bar and gave him ten minutes to get there, or else, alone, or else, and tell no one, or else, etcetera or else. Seth watched the bar from a frozen yogurt place across the street, dipping his plastic spoon into a slowly melting dish of lactose, petroleum, cellulose, and strawberry. At first blush, the senator arrived alone. Even with the wig, baseball hat, and sunglasses, Mankins was hard to miss, tall, with a lantern jaw.

A few minutes later, a bull of a man, with a keen sense of his peripheral vision, climbed out of a nearby sedan, and after a half-block of too-casual window-shopping on Wisconsin Avenue, entered the bar. Seth crossed the street from the frozen yogurt shop, full of the irrational confidence of a man who had a revolver in his belt.

The bull from the sedan sat at the bar with a pint of beer holding its own on the dark wood before him, pointedly not watching Seth as he entered. Mankins had taken a table at the back of the restaurant, studiously avoiding attention. A week in the TV's disfavor had taken a toll on the senator. He looked as though he'd aged a decade and had begun collapsing into his oversized athlete's frame. The wig was a good one, but still a wig. Nonetheless, Mankins was dressed well, a nice gray suit with no tie. Arriving at Mankins' position in the gunfighter's seat, Seth leaned over him.

"Tell that linebacker at the bar to clear out of here. If I see him again tonight, or ever, you will go to prison for the rest of your life," Seth said, slowly and deliberately.

Mankins started to talk, and Seth leaned in and grabbed the lapel of his suit jacket.

"Shut up. Don't make the mistake of trying to bullshit the last man on earth who will ever do you a favor. If you think there isn't a pile of money to be made selling you out then you're crazy. Now go."

Seth released his grip, and the senator nodded and walked, stooped, over to the linebacker, and said a few words. The linebacker sprinkled a few singles on the bar and left. Seth took the senator's seat, and his drink.

"Chet, what did I tell you? I told you to tell no one and bring no one."

"I know, and I'm sorry about that. I want to do this like you said. I have the money. And I have every intention of carrying out our arrangement honorably. But I was worried, well… since I was arrested, people have been saying things, and there have been a lot of threats. I mean, you can indict a ham sandwich, you know? Fucking blogs and message boards, all these anonymous idiots sounding off, but you never know who's serious, you know? It doesn't mean…" the senator said.

"Scotch this early?" Seth said, taking a sip of the senator's drink.

"Why the heck not?"

"Exactly. Have one yourself. I insist."

With Mankins' linebacker gone, the bar was mostly empty. Seth ordered two fresh sets of drinks from a waitress who actively resented the early shift and the fact that her only customers had selected so distant a table. Seth finished the rest of Mankins' drink and Mankins kept talking.

"It's tough. People see the TV. They make assumptions. And maybe, now that I think about it, I'd always benefitted from that. But now, Jesus, it's swung the other way and then some. It would be funny if it wasn't so scary. This morning, I was actually looking forward to seeing you. What you said, about being my last friend, you were more right than you know, crazy as it sounds. You're one of the only people who knows what all of this was about. You saw where it was headed—The Ascent of the West, my and Hurley's dreams of being Founding Fathers, Roberto's messianic bullshit. But you also saw... You also saw those girls," William said, taking a drink and shaking his head.

"What about Hurley and Roberto? I thought they were your friends."

"You kidding me? They won't talk to me. Not now."

"Hurley cut you off?"

"Not exactly. He found a way to pay my legal bills, for now. But he said he'd have me killed if I ever called him directly again. And I heard Roberto's gone off to build some utopian city out in China. He may never come back. I know Frederica never liked me. Aside from that, everyone wants to know what happened. But they want to know about all the wrong things, about the girls, women, whatever. And they would string me up from the highest tree if I said a true word. So there's you. And here's that."

Mankins gestured with his chin downward to the spot under the table. Seth reached down and pulled the leather satchel onto his lap. Unbuckling the bag, Seth eyed the stacks and saw it was just about all the money he'd asked for.

"You probably want to go," Mankins said, sadly.

"You held up your end. You got rid of your linebacker. If you want, I'll go a drink or two. There are things I don't know, about the girls, how that happened."

"Hurley said you got to know Sarah," Mankins said, beginning a grin and sheepishly withdrawing it.

"A little bit," Seth said, taking a belt of scotch.

"Sandra and Sarah. They're the same now, to everyone. But they were really very different kinds of women. I mean, Sandra," Mankins said, losing the thread for a moment. "Sandra was the typical overachiever that we get at the office: Summa Cum Laude or some damn thing, more eager than smart, very much captive to a narrow idea of success, not a creative type. Sandra was younger than Sarah, still in that giddy bloom of youth. But she was also so isolated, lonely. She called me Senator even though I saw her every day. I've known so many girls like that. Their drive isolates them. They work too hard, too long for this idea, this *career*. And you're the *Senator*— a million miles above them, a father in a family of three hundred million. Of course they fall in love. And I guess I'm a type too, or at least I was: The older man who sees a reprieve from decrepitude and death between a younger woman's legs. So I fell in love too, at least with some idea of her. She sees me, sees the buildings named for the other senators, and this idea of history and of accomplishment takes root in her. Those ideas swept us up until neither of us was quite real to each other," Mankins said, took a drink, and waved for another round.

There was a commotion at the front of the bar. The kind of homeless man who seems to have been hard at work on perfecting the type, had wandered in. He was yelling something about an assassin. But no one seemed bothered, and Seth kept his face still. The bartender came around from behind the bar to chase the man out.

"A poor crazy," Mankins said.

"Well, who isn't, right about now? But go on."

"Yeah, Sandra. Anyway, those ideas, they aren't real. But they're why you work, why she works. And then, they're why you're naked with this woman. And you're both already naked, so why not go try to get at something that *is* real? So you try to upset her, to crack her ivy-league equanimity. You slap her

332

around a little during sex. She's inexperienced, and you can tell it rattles her. But she's also young, playing an adult's game, and she doesn't want to admit to what she doesn't know. And maybe you take that false bravery the wrong way, take it as evidence of her unreality. So you up the ante. You get rougher, do things that you think no woman could ever want done to her. But because she's played along this far, she plays along some more. And you're strange and distant, and she imagines that this is what it's like to be with a powerful man. And what's more, she's become bound to you by simple shame, because of the things she's let you do to her. And one night, you're alone together, and you look for her. But she's just a rubber Halloween mask of these ideas you have about her. And she took the train and a bus to see you, like some unrelenting robot. So you test her until she breaks. And, I guess that was Sandra."

"And so you call Hurley."

"He'd helped me out of jams before. Nothing on that level, but women have a way of bringing out the worst sometimes."

Mankins rolled his pale blue eyes and then watched for Seth's response. Seth settled on a forlorn smirk.

"So how does Hurley fit in with this?"

"Hurley. Where to start with Hurley? You probably know that it was Hurley who arranged the money and planted the seeds for the recall election, and the campaign. I mean, you know about the revolution and the new shale technique. And why lie? I wanted to be president, to be the founder of a new country. I guess I thought once I was in the big chair, I could make some amends for what I'd done. That's what I told myself. But that's bullshit. Hurley owned me. He knew if he helped me get out of that one with Sandra, he'd be able to pull my strings for life, come presidency or high water. "

"So what about the other one?" Seth said, fighting to maintain his calm.

"Sarah?"

"Yeah. Her."

"Well, at that point, there was a lot of pressure from Hurley, from the campaign. And I guess I was more upset about Sandra than I wanted to admit," Mankins said, and paused. The senator's attempt at an excuse made the hair on Seth's head bristle and his hand slide down his tie toward the snub-nosed at his belt. He stilled his hand. The bar was filling up with an after-work crowd. Mankins shook his head, smiling to himself.

"What's so funny?" Seth asked as mildly as he could manage.

"Listening to myself. *Upset. Under a lot of pressure.* I guess all monsters have their reasons. I don't know—what's the difference between a reason and an excuse?"

"My experience is that the difference is usually based on how angry the person is who you're explaining it to."

Seth grinned at his own little joke. Mankins raised an eyebrow, laughed and raised his glass.

"That's my life now," Mankins said. "Anyway, Sarah, she was a different story. It was after Sandra. By then, I was starting to feel like I was a kind of monster. I'd killed. I was already in business with Jefferson and his militia out there. But I don't think I was a monster yet when I met Sandra. I was a prick, a little bit of an asshole, but what man worth his salt isn't? It was after Sandra that I'd gone over, become something else. And I was a monster with a license to kill, thanks to our friend. Maybe at the time I didn't know I was a monster. But that girl, Sarah, she knew it. That was the draw with her, I think. It's complicated. Listen, I want to talk to you about this. And this may sound insensitive, but I really have to use the restroom, I was tense and nervous all day, and a few scotches just…"

"Go ahead."

"Steve, it's Steve, right?"

Seth nodded.

"You're all right, Steve. I meet a guy like you, and I wish that Hurley's scheme had worked out. We could have done some great things," he said, smiling his best politician smile.

Mankins squeezed out of his seat and down the crowded aisle. From his disposable phone, Seth called William. After a few rings, someone picked up who wasn't William and demanded to know who was calling. Seth ended the call and threw the satchel of cash over his shoulder. He tossed a few bills from his wallet onto the table and walked toward the bathroom. At the waiter's station, he pretended to drop something and pulled a wood-handled steak knife from the plastic bin and secreted it in his jacket sleeve, the serrated blade pressing into his wrist.

The bathroom was small, a urinal and a stall. An empty yellow mop bucket sat in the corner. The stall door was closed. A ruddy guy in a blue shirt and yellow tie was finishing a very thorough hand-washing routine when Seth entered and began a pantomime of urination. Seth buttoned his suit jacket and popped the lapels up. The blonde guy left and Seth pulled the stinking, piss-soaked urinal cake from the bottom of the urinal. The toilet next to him flushed.

With the steak knife, Seth cut the urinal cake into a rough wedge, turned and jammed it under the door with his wet fingers. He gently tapped it into place with the tip of his shoe as he heard the man in the stall flush again and begin to buckle his pants. He turned in time to step out of the way of the stall door as it opened. For some reason, he said *Hey* as he shoved Mankins back onto the toilet bowl. Mankins tripped backwards, and smacked his head on the tile wall, his wig slipping over his eyes. Seth pulled the gun from his belt and beat Mankins with it in the face and head fast and hard until blood poured down the older man's face and peeked through his wig, and the senator no longer raised his hands to protect himself. Seth pocketed the gun and took the knife out of his jacket pocket. He jabbed the tan neck of the fit, middle-aged man with the serrated blade and sawed until he hit the vein. Blood poured over the lapels of the senator's jacket, down his lap and into the toilet, soaking the gray fabric of his impeccable suit. Seth sawed until the man's throat seemed a useless wreck.

He pulled the stall door closed with his unbloodied hand at the moment the door to the bathroom began rattling in its frame. He hurriedly turned the stall door's flat-head exterior lock with the bloody steak knife and dropped the knife back into his suit-jacket pocket. He turned and kicked the urinal cake out from under the door.

"I know, the door is *all* fucked up," Seth said, avoiding eye-contact and affecting a slur to the would-be pisser at the door.

In the bar, the waitresses had changed shifts and the new one only knew he'd left a good tip. Seth staggered through the bar, and walked hard down the block to the rental car and drove off across the Key Bridge, into Virginia. He knew Mankins was dead, that William's attempt on Hurley hadn't entirely succeeded. And absent any divine or demoniacal guidance, all he knew for certain was that he hadn't thought quite far enough ahead.

But he could still think like a killer. And after a killing, he knew that the points of view he must fastidiously ignore were his victim's and his own. Both engulfed, smothered, stunted, and would only serve to make him stupid and sloppy. He abandoned the car in Arlington, and disposed of his bloody jacket, dress shirt, tie, knife and gun, as well as his disposable phone down a series of storm drains. He gave a saucer-eyed beggar a big bill for a ratty Baltimore Orioles hat. He took the Metro to BWI in time to catch the last flight to Las Vegas.

At the airport, they asked Seth about the enormous amount of cash he was carrying. Between what he already he had in his luggage and what he had from Mankins, it was a lot.

Seth told a story about how he'd caught his bitch wife in bed with his two-faced best friend, and now he'd emptied their bank account and was starting a new life in Las Vegas. The booze on his breath made his story plausible enough.

On the plane, the adrenaline failed, the scotch took its toll and Seth slept until the plane landed and emptied entirely, except for him.

In Las Vegas, Seth took a cab to the Babylonian casino-hotel. At the bar, Seth took the cloned phone William had given him out of his bag. He turned it on, listened to detective Carlson's last message, and dialed the number the man had slowly repeated so many times.

"Detective, it's Seth Tatton. I'm sorry it took me so long to get back to you. I wanted to wait until I checked with my lawyer before I called you. How can I help?"

"I take it you've seen the news."

"About Sarah?"

"About her, and about Chet Mankins."

"Yeah. Geez. It's an ugly story."

"The story just got uglier. Mankins was just murdered."

"Really? I can't say I'm sorry to hear it."

"When can you come in? I'd like to ask you some questions."

"Well, my business has taken me away from Washington for the foreseeable future. But I'll definitely drop you a line the next time I'm in town."

"Actually, if you could…"

Seth hung up his phone and wandered down the garishly carpeted stairs from the bar to the roulette wheel. There, he lost five grand so fast that someone from the casino offered him a suite. Seth took the suite under his own name, checked in and went back to the gaming floor to make as many withdrawals as he could at the casino ATM, before catching a cab to the airport. Outside the airport rental car office, he threw all of his Seth Tatton IDs and credit cards into a garbage can, along with the cloned cell phone. He rented a car with the Florida ID William had given him, his last safe identity. Sam Tethurst, a resident of Tangerine Sands, Florida.

The rented Cadillac's dashboard display told Seth the name of the song on the radio, the tire pressure, the gas mileage at the rate he was driving, the odds of him hitting a deer, the legal costs if he hit a man, how long it would be until he'd need a new Cadillac, how dark the night is compared to other nights, the money he'd need to keep this up, everything.

Through the desert's midnight of mind-boggling blackness and futuristic gas stations, Seth tore back to Laughlin. He found the casino where Dolores had climbed the marquee to the spot above $7.99 PRIME RIB SUN–THURS.

---

Seth woke to the TV speaking the names that echoed in his dreams. Mankins's murder dominated the coverage. Seth watched like a child opening presents on Christmas Day. Hurley, who'd been shot and was critical, didn't rate half as much coverage. A shootout on the edge of the National Mall made a stir, but not enough of one for the TV to bother with the faces and names of the other men in the gunfight. After all, the Oscars were three days away.

The newscasters didn't give out much news about William. But reading between the sound bites, it seemed like Hurley had been ready for something. One security guy Hurley had with him took a bullet in the leg, and it sounded like the other ran when the shooting started. Later in the day, it came out that Hurley was alive, but unresponsive. Doctors were tinkering, but not optimistic. The TV described William as a "former Tampa Police Officer" on the news. It said he was in stable condition.

Seth went back to sleep and woke in the afternoon, but couldn't find a reason to get out of bed. His future, previously an intricate network of intersecting shortcuts, hallways and necessary deceptions, had opened onto a prairie-wide blankness. The next day and the day after stretched into a forever as blank as the sky. The only thing he couldn't shake was the image of Mankins with the wig over his eyes, after he could no longer protect himself, the blood coming up through a small tear in the fabric under the blonde hair. The image put Seth off his room service. It was a killing he had to carry completely alone.

That night, Seth found an outlet store and bought some fresh clothes, along with a platinum-and-diamond bracelet. He found Dolores singing to a half-empty room of gamblers taking a break and desert dwellers who'd followed the promise of family entertainment to Laughlin. Seth set up at the bar and ordered a soda. Dolores was in a ruffled blue dress. She was singing "I'll Be Seeing You" in a voice so sweet and steady that Seth said a silent prayer. She came over to him during her break.

"Hello, mister baking soda. I never thought I'd see you again."

"I wasn't so sure myself."

"You know I could have gotten into a lot of trouble for that."

"I know. I did all I could to keep it from coming to that. But I had to do it. And I'm sorry. I owe you," Seth said, opening the jewelry box. Against her will, her eyes widened when she saw the bracelet.

"It's nice, I guess."

"I know that I owe you more than that. And I can get it to you tonight, or tomorrow, or the next day."

"Are you okay? You seem different."

"Yeah. I, uh, I guess I just retired."

"No more real estate, huh?"

"Yeah. I think I'm done with it," Seth said.

Dolores smiled back. So did Seth, and not because he felt he should.

"So what are you going to do?"

"I was going to pay you back."

"Yeah. You can afford that?"

"I thought I'd stick around, maybe pay you back over time."

Bullhead City was quiet at night. Dolores left around five to sing at the casino across the river and was usually home by twelve. She showered off the makeup, sweat, and cigarette smoke and then they'd eat a late dinner. That was their routine. On nights when she had her son over, they'd still have the late dinner. They'd just be quiet about it.

The sum Seth got from Mankins in that Irish pub in Georgetown was gone in the first six months. He paid off his friend Anthony and helped buy William back the use of his legs, after the bullet from Hurley's security guy nicked his spine. It also bought William the kind of lawyers who could sell the District of Columbia on the theory that William, Hurley, and the security guards were all shot by a third party. That was almost as expensive as the legs.

It also bought Dolores a house in Bullhead City.

She won a big singing contest in Laughlin not long after Seth returned. But aside from the prize money, nothing much came of it. The big red plastic marquee letters would always be for out-of-town talent, the known faces that had glowed, however briefly, on the television before fate rightly or wrongly deposited them on the southernmost Nevada shore of the Colorado River.

That September, Dolores started teaching music part-time at a middle school in town, only singing in the casinos on weekends. She started talking with her mother about having her son Keith move back in. The old woman wasn't so sure. Dolores started taking Seth along with her for dinners with Keith and her mother. Her mother wasn't so sure about Seth either, not at first. Seth didn't call or write anyone from his old life for that first year. He kept his lawn watered and mowed.

340

He lived as his last good identity, Sam Tethurst from Florida. Dolores was fine calling him Sam, and never asked about it.

Months passed and Hurley still breathed, even if he did nothing else. Everything waited on Hurley. When William was well enough, he bought Hurley's chart from a nurse at the hospital. After six months, he was still comatose, his brain activity sporadic, though his heart and lungs were strong. He could die at any moment, or he could last another thirty years in the coma, or he could wake up tomorrow. Until Hurley died or woke, Seth couldn't do much.

Elizabeth was Seth's last big risk. After the first year, he flew back to New York to see her, and to see his mother in Connecticut. After being gone so long, his daughter knew him like she might know an uncle. New Daddy had become Daddy and stayed Daddy. Seth had gone from being Old Daddy to being Seth.

Once William was out of the hospital, Seth spoke to him every few months. After a long rehab, William started a security and investigation outfit in the Maryland suburbs. And even if he used a cane to get around some days, he ran a profitable operation. He kept Seth up to date on the investigation into the Mankins killing. The police had a sketch artist get what he could out of the waitress. But she had a pill problem and couldn't give them very much. And the cops never made the connection to the rental Seth left in Virginia. What they had was fingerprints on a stall door. But there were a lot of prints on the door. And Mankins had a world full of enemies on that given night. The case slipped from the papers after a few weeks, and went genuinely cold not long after that.

Around Christmas, Dolores and her mother had a long talk. And Dolores' son, Keith, came to live with her and Seth full time. Keith was hostile at first, then just suspicious. But the kid was eight, and crazy for baseball. Seth started playing catch with him after school. For hours, they'd say nothing, except when the kid was throwing the ball wrong. Weekends, they'd go to the park and Seth would throw him batting practice until the sun went down. Seth realized one day, with some astonishment, that he had become a stepfather.

About eighteen months after the Mankins killing, William started paying Sam Tethurst a small income as a consultant. It was part-time, chewing the fat on the phone, giving advice here and there. But the house was paid for and the cost of living was low in the desert.

Some nights, when Keith was asleep and Dolores was at the casino, Seth would go sit out on the back porch and drink a few beers, two or three. He'd listen to the hush of the trucks on the distant I-40, and the wind would kick up, and he'd hear a familiar voice.

It told him that his latest disguise wouldn't last. It said that his hands would always be stained with blood. It said his enemies would never stop looking for him. The voice said that even if he could hide, hiding was all he would ever do, and that he would die a small, frightened nobody, a nothing who may as well have never been born.

But Seth didn't have to listen.

# THE END

# ABOUT THE AUTHOR

Colin Dodds grew up in Massachusetts and completed his education in New York City. He's the author of several novels, including *The Last Bad Job*, which the late Norman Mailer touted as showing "something that very few writers have; a species of inner talent that owes very little to other people." Dodds' screenplay, *Refreshment – A Tragedy*, was named a semi-finalist in 2010 American Zoetrope Contest. His poetry has appeared in more than a hundred publications, and has been nominated for the Pushcart Prize. He lives in Brooklyn, New York, with his wife Samantha.